Time After Time

Also published by Poolbeg

Love Hurts
Love Child
Hush Hush

LINDA KAVANAGH

Time After Time

POOLBEG

This novel is entirely a work of fiction. The names,
characters and incidents portrayed in it are the work of the
author's imagination. Any resemblance to actual persons,
living or dead, events or localities is entirely coincidental.

Published 2008
by Poolbeg Press Ltd
123 Grange Hill, Baldoyle
Dublin 13, Ireland
E-mail: poolbeg@poolbeg.com
www.poolbeg.com

13 5 7 9 10 8 6 4 2

A catalogue record for this book is available from the British Library.

ISBN 978-1-84223-309-2

Typeset by Patricia Hope in Bembo 10.5/13.5
Printed by
Litographia Rosés, S.A., Spain

About the author

Linda Kavanagh has worked as a journalist for several Irish newspapers and magazines, and was a staff writer on the *RTÉ Guide* for fifteen years. She lives with her partner in Dun Laoghaire, Co Dublin.

Her previous novels, *Love Hurts, Love Child* and *Hush Hush*, were also published by Poolbeg.

Author email: lindakavanagh@eircom.net

Acknowledgements

Sincere thanks to Paula Campbell and all the Poolbeg team, and to editor Gaye Shortland for her amazing attention to detail. To Mike Gold for all his love and support, suggestions, and endless cups of tea.

Finally, thanks to all the readers who have bought my previous novels – I hope you'll enjoy this one!

To Susan, Elaine and Robert
with Love

Part 1

CHAPTER 1

"I like that design best, Caro," said Caroline's cousin Liz, pointing to a long satin gown in the book of wedding-dress patterns that she was holding. "Those long tapering sleeves would suit you perfectly – and the matching train – you'd look so elegant in it."

Liz, who'd got married the year before, considered herself an authority on all things matrimonial.

Caroline Leyden leaned over her cousin's shoulder and took a closer look. "Hmm, you could be right, but I also like the one two pages back – yes, that one there – with the lace trimming around the neckline."

"Too fussy," Liz pronounced, turning to the elderly woman sitting in the armchair beside her. "What do you think, Aunt Dolly? I think Caro should choose a simple, elegant dress – she's got the height and the figure to carry it off. All that fussy detail will only detract from the bride herself. And besides, it won't show up in any of the photos, so why bother?"

Caroline's eyes lit up. "Speaking of photos, I've just

discovered an old family album! When I was up in the attic, looking for Mum's sewing box, I found it among the Christmas decorations. It must have been up there for years!"

"Where is it?" said Liz.

"Hang on a tick and I'll get it." Caroline looked across at her aunt. "Aunt Dolly, there are even photos of your wedding in it. That was quite a hairstyle you had!"

Annoyed, her aunt pursed her lips together. "Well, in another twenty years, we'll be able to have a good laugh at *your* wedding photos!"

Liz raised her eyes to heaven behind Aunt Dolly's back, and Caroline took the album out of a drawer in the sideboard. Just then, Caroline's mother Stella arrived from the kitchen with a tray of mugs and biscuits, and the four women moved to the dining-room table, where Caroline had already opened the old photograph album.

"Oh my God!" squealed Liz, leaning across to look. "That's not you is it, Aunt Stella? That fuzzy hairstyle – and those shoes!"

"I was the height of sophistication at the time," said Caroline's mother, smiling. "Anyway, you needn't bother laughing – I've heard that those platform shoes and fuzzy perms are coming back into fashion again!"

"What's a perm?" asked Caroline.

Her mother ignored her, gazing sadly at a picture of herself and her late husband. "Oh lord, didn't my Paddy look handsome back then?" She sighed. "Before the cancer took him – "

Caroline gazed at the picture of her father. She'd been eight when he died, and although she hardly remembered

4

him now, she wished he could be there to walk down the aisle with her on her big day, the day when she would marry Ken Barnes. Big, gorgeous, happy-go-lucky Ken, the man she loved dearly.

"My God, I can't believe those gaudy patterns were so fashionable!" said Liz, giggling as she pointed to a group of women that included her Aunt Dolly and Aunt Eliza. "All the women in that photo look as though they're wearing tablecloths!"

Caroline had to stifle a grin, because what Liz said was very true – the individual patterns the women wore clashed horribly with each other. And the hats they wore were hideous! But no doubt at the time they'd all considered themselves to be the height of fashion. Which was another good reason for picking a relatively plain wedding dress, Caroline conceded. She didn't want to give her children and grandchildren a cause for mirth at her expense!

"Aren't they your old school friends, Rosemary and Eileen, standing beside you, Mum?" she asked, pointing to two young women, one in a particularly startling pattern of orange and brown, the other in vivid pink.

Her mother nodded.

"And there's Liz's mum, Aunt Teresa, on the other side," Caroline added, pointing to a small woman dressed in startling shades of blue.

Aunt Dolly moved uncomfortably in her chair and Liz, as if on cue, began to turn over to the next page of the album.

"Hold on –" said Caroline, turning the page back, "I don't recognise that other woman – the one on the left-hand side of the photo."

5

Suddenly, there was silence in the room, and Caroline noticed that Liz was glaring at her. Looking at the others, she saw that Stella had suddenly turned quite pale, and Aunt Dolly wore a thunderous expression. Liz moved quickly to turn the page of the album again, while Stella and Aunt Dolly glanced at each other surreptitiously.

Caroline looked in amazement from one to the other. They had all suddenly started behaving oddly – what was going on?

"So who is she?" she asked again.

There was a palpable silence, as though each woman was suddenly frozen in situ. Glancing around at them all, Caroline was instantly reminded of a Dutch painting, in which a moment in time had been suspended by the artist for all eternity.

"I – well, I don't know," said Stella at last, flustered. "She must have been somebody's friend that was just included in the photo. You know how photographers put groups of people together – "

Caroline might have believed her mother if it hadn't been for her initial hesitation, and the change in atmosphere. The air had become distinctively chilly, and Caroline felt that as though she'd stepped into a minefield and just trodden on an unexploded grenade. So she quickly did her best to take remedial action.

"So who's for a cup of tea?" she asked brightly. "Aunt Dolly – two sugars in yours? And how about some biscuits? And I'll refill the kettle, in case we need a second cuppa."

Without waiting for an answer, Caroline rushed out to the kitchen and switched on the kettle. What exactly had she done in there? It was as though she'd somehow thrown a switch and plunged everyone in the room into an icy abyss. The temperature had instantly dropped by several degrees when she asked about the woman in the photograph, and she felt that she had somehow fractured the happiness of the afternoon.

Nor did anything change when she went back into the dining room. Every face looked set in stone, and no amount of bright comments or attempts at humour could dispel the hostile atmosphere.

Caroline began to wonder if her wedding day could end up like this. What on earth would she do if a chance remark or throwaway comment resulted in her entire family going into a collective huff? What on earth was going on?

At the first available opportunity, she sidelined Liz in the kitchen. Liz, who was a little older than Caroline, was the daughter of Caroline's Aunt Teresa, her late father's sister.

"What the hell is going on in there?" Caroline whispered fiercely. "It's as though an Ice Age has suddenly descended on this house, and somehow I seem to be responsible for causing it."

"Shhh! You're not supposed to know what's wrong, and neither am I," whispered Liz. "You've just touched a raw family nerve. Forget about it."

"How can I? You could cut the atmosphere in there with a knife! Please – what did I do to upset them all? I just asked who the woman in the photo was. If I don't understand what I've done wrong, I might accidentally do the same thing again. C'mon, Liz – you've got to help me out here!"

"Nobody talks about Gina," said Liz, shaking her head. "Her name is taboo in the family, and if you're wise you'll never mention her either."

"Who's Gina? And what did she do? Go on – tell me who on earth she is!"

Her cousin pursed her lips. "I'd rather not. What's past is past, so let it go, Caro."

Just then, Aunt Dolly came into the kitchen, and Liz slid seamlessly into a totally unintelligible conversation about the weather. Caroline sighed, knowing that there was no hope of getting any more information out of her cousin. For the present anyway. But she didn't intend to give up. Oh no. She intended finding out all about this disgraced Gina.

It quickly became clear that Caroline's *faux pas* had brought the pleasant afternoon to a close. With indecent haste, the mugs and tea things were washed up, Aunt Dolly clearly in a huff and anxious to leave.

"I'll give you a lift home, Dolly," said Stella, and Caroline was annoyed at how Aunt Dolly, as imperious as ever, could command her underlings to do her will without even as much as a word. Aunt Dolly was a wealthy widow and well able to afford a taxi – it annoyed Caroline that her own impecunious mother was always expected to do her older sister's bidding.

"I'll drop Aunt Dolly home," Caroline volunteered, but her offer was quickly and frostily turned down by her aunt.

As soon as her mother and Aunt Dolly had left, Caroline followed Liz into the kitchen.

"Now," said Caroline determinedly, "you're going to tell me all about this Gina."

Liz sighed, as though accepting the inevitable. She made two cups of tea and brought them to the kitchen table.

"All right, but you're to keep this to yourself. I'm not even supposed to know about it but Mum let it slip."

"Know about what?"

"I'll be shot for telling you this." She leaned forward conspiratorially. "Promise me you'll never repeat a word of it?"

Caroline nodded earnestly. "Who on earth was Gina? Was she a cousin? Or a family friend?"

Liz shook her head. "She was your mother's and Dolly's sister."

"W-what?" Caroline was shocked. That couldn't be true – she had only one aunt on her mother's side – Aunt Dolly – that was all. Altogether, she had two aunts, including Liz's mother.

"How could – I mean –"

"It's true, Caro – but nobody ever talks about her. And you won't either, if you know what's good for you."

"But –" Caroline's mind was reeling. She had an aunt – her mother had another sister – whom she herself knew nothing about! "Where is this Gina? Why doesn't anyone want to talk about her?"

Liz sipped her tea with maddening slowness, and Caroline longed to give her a good kick to get her moving. "Please, Liz –"

"Look, it's not my business to tell you. I'm not even supposed to know. Go and talk to your mother."

"But –"

Despite Caroline's entreaties, Liz refused to say any more.

CHAPTER 2

"Come on, Mum – you've got to tell me what you know!"

Caroline stood in her mother's kitchen, her arms folded across her chest. She looked ready for combat, and Stella realised that she wasn't going to be able to fob off her daughter any longer. She sighed.

"Look, love – why don't you just leave well enough alone? There's nothing to be gained from dragging up the past. You've just got a bee in your bonnet because of what Liz's been telling you. Besides, it's none of her business anyway. She's only a cousin on your father's side – it's not *her* family history!"

"Well, I want to know, anyway," said Caroline stubbornly. "I can't believe that I have another aunt that everyone's deliberately kept quiet about!"

"It was all so long ago," said her mother defensively. "There's hardly any point in bringing it up now."

"Mum, it was only thirty years ago!"

"Look," said her mother, making a last-ditch attempt to avoid the subject, "you and Ken are about to start a new life together – you don't want to start digging up sordid family history. Look to the future – not the past."

"Nice try, Mum – but if you won't tell me, I'm going to ask Aunt Dolly."

Her mother's face suddenly paled, and Caroline felt a momentary stab of guilt. Maybe she was being unfair to her mother.

"Oh, don't ask Dolly, for goodness sake!" said her mother, clearly shocked at the prospect. "Unless, that is, you want to start World War Three!" She looked exasperated, took her glasses off, then put them on again. "Oh dear, I suppose I'd better tell you, although why you want to wallow in the past, I just don't know."

Caroline grinned. "Thanks, Mum."

Her mother sighed, unsure of where to start. "Well, you probably know most of it already, since that busybody Liz has been filling you in. Although what business it is of hers, I'll never know!"

"Mum, Liz's told me very little. All I know is that Gina was – is – your sister. What on earth happened to her?"

"Oh dear," said her mother, fiddling with the edge of the tablecloth as she sat down at the kitchen table. "I wasn't there myself – I was at the pictures with your father that afternoon –"

"You weren't there when?"

Stella sighed, as though gathering her strength to tell the unpalatable tale. "It was a Saturday, and Mother and Dolly had gone into town to do some shopping. At that time, Dolly and Owen had been married for about two years . . ." She sighed again.

"And?" Caroline gently prompted.

11

"If I remember correctly, Dolly was looking for some heavy velour material, to make cushion covers for her new three-piece suite. And since she found exactly what she wanted in the first shop they visited, she and Mother hadn't needed to traipse all over town. So after a cuppa in Bewley's café in Grafton Street, they got the bus back to Mother's house a lot earlier than expected." Stella took a deep breath. "Dolly and Mother came into the drawing room – and found Owen and Gina –" she hesitated, "– on the sofa together."

"You mean they were having sex?" asked Caroline, an amused grin on her face.

"Yes, and it's no laughing matter!" said her mother crossly. "Needless to say, Dolly was devastated. Of course, Gina swore that it was all an accident, but neither Mother nor Dolly believed a word of it. I mean, Gina was always flirting with Owen, and giving him the glad eye . . ." Stella's eyes narrowed. "I often wondered why Dolly never took her aside, and marked her card for her – I mean, it's not right to be flirting with your sister's husband, is it?"

Caroline got the distinct impression that her mother was trying to find justification for her sister's ostracisation. "Well, why didn't *you* say anything to her, Mum, if you felt her behaviour was inappropriate?"

"For heaven's sake, I wasn't even living in the house any more! Your father and I had just got married and were renting our own flat so I didn't realise what was going on. Besides, Gina wouldn't have paid any attention to me anyway."

"So how old was Gina when all this happened?"

Her mother began tidying the dishes on the draining-

12

board. "Well, as you know, Dolly was a bit older than either Gina or me – Dolly was thirty-five when this terrible incident happened. I was twenty-eight and Gina had just turned twenty-two."

"So Gina was thrown out there and then?"

Stella nodded. "Not surprisingly, Dolly went into hysterics when she saw the two of them half-naked on the sofa. Mother had to send for the doctor to sedate the poor thing. When Paddy and I dropped by later that evening, Dolly was upstairs in bed, Owen was in the doghouse, and Gina had already left."

"Why was Owen in your mother's house that day, anyway?" Caroline asked. "Presumably he and Dolly had their own home?"

Stella nodded. "Oh yes – they'd just bought that big house in Ballsbridge that Dolly still lives in. But that day Owen had offered to fix a leaky pipe under Mother's kitchen sink while Dolly and she were out shopping."

Caroline grinned. "But he opted to do a bit of freelance plumbing with Gina instead!"

"Caroline, there's no need to be so crude!" said Stella angrily. "What might seem amusing to you was the most devastating thing that ever happened to our family."

"But Owen got off lightly, didn't he?" said Caroline. "Why was he let off the hook, while Gina was kicked out?"

Her mother shrugged. "I suppose it had something to do with the fact that Owen and Dolly were married. I mean, the sanctity of marriage was seen as such a big thing back then. And even if Dolly had wanted to leave him, there was no divorce anyway. Besides, being a wife was always a better option than being a spinster, and Owen, being a

13

research chemist, was considered a good catch – especially for someone who'd reached thirty, like Dolly had, before she snared him."

Caroline had to suppress the urge to laugh, as she visualised Aunt Dolly hiding in the bushes, with a lasso to catch the unsuspecting Owen as he loped by like a rabbit.

"Is that why Aunt Dolly has always been a snooty cow?" she asked, and was amused that her mother didn't rebuke her. "Presumably she thinks she's a cut above the rest of us?"

Reluctantly, Stella nodded. "Yes, Dolly's always had notions about herself. You see, she was secretary to the managing director of BWF Pharmaceuticals where she and Owen worked. That was regarded as a very good job for a woman back then, and her boss Charles Keane valued her very highly. Also, being married to the Medical Director was another feather in her cap. When Owen died, Dolly was well looked after by the company."

"Owen died in a car accident, didn't he, Mum?"

Stella nodded. "He was driving home late one night, and he took a bend in the road too quickly and ended up in the river. It was a tragic end to a brilliant man, and of course Dolly was distraught. I mean, she still cared about him despite the business with Gina." Stella sighed, remembering. "But the pharmaceutical company was very good to Dolly. Her boss, Charles Keane, did everything he could to make things easy for her, even to the point of paying for the funeral and awarding her a lump sum. In fact, she never went back to work again, but the company paid her full salary for the first few years, and a pension after that. Even today, Charles Keane takes her to lunch once a month, and drops by to see her every now and then."

"Dolly certainly seems to have worked for a very caring company," said Caroline. "There aren't many of those around!"

Stella nodded. "Although Dolly doesn't think it — she always sees herself as the victim — she's led a charmed life. Many women are widowed, but not all of them are lucky enough to be left financially secure."

Caroline nodded. She knew that her mother was indirectly referring to herself. Stella had been widowed when Caroline was eight, but their lives had been very different from Dolly's. They'd had to struggle to survive, whereas Dolly had lived her life in comfort. Yet her aunt had never offered any help or support, and Stella was too proud to even think of asking.

"And Aunt Gina, Mum? Has anyone heard of her since that day?"

Caroline's mother shook her head. "We never talk about her. When my own mother was dying, she asked us to find Gina, so that she could make her peace with her." She shook her head sadly. "But we never managed to locate her. Then, after Mum died, we didn't bother any more. I mean, Dolly wouldn't have wanted to find her anyway . . ." Her voice trailed off.

Caroline was appalled. "But Owen's long dead, and Gina is Dolly's own flesh and blood! Surely now, after all this time, she should be prepared to forgive? And surely you would want to see your own sister?"

Her mother shrugged her shoulders. "Sometimes, Caro, things are best left alone."

Caroline shook her head in disbelief. "So nobody knows where Gina is today?"

Stella shook her head sadly. "No, we have no idea. But I

don't think Gina had any intention of ever coming back, anyway. That was the way families dealt with awkward situations back then."

"So the bad apple in the barrel conveniently disappears, and everyone else gets on with their lives, and pretends that nothing has happened," said Caroline angrily. "What hypocrisy!"

Her mother nodded sheepishly. "I suppose today people handle things a bit more openly and humanely." Then she smiled sadly. "I couldn't imagine never seeing you again, Caro, no matter what you might have done!"

Caroline suddenly grinned. "Well, there's one thing I can assure you of, Mum. There'll be no family scandal caused by me – since Liz's husband Ronnie is all that's on offer and he's perfectly safe from me!"

CHAPTER 3

Caroline was determined to have the wedding of her dreams. Although she and Ken didn't intend spending a huge amount of money on their big day, it would nevertheless be the most important day of her life.

She and Ken had been together since their schooldays, and had more or less grown up together. All her adult life, it had been Ken she'd envisaged waiting for her as she reached the altar, and now, at last, that happy dream would soon come true.

As a couple, they were happy and content together, in a settled, no surprises kind of way. In fact, they were like a settled married couple already, Caroline realised with a feeling of surprise. The actual wedding day would merely put the legal stamp on their union. Then they'd continue more or less as they had been doing. She and Ken already lived together, and they owned a small three-bedroomed semi-detached house in Monkstown, an upmarket suburb in County Dublin.

Caroline loved Ken's easy-going, lackadaisical attitude

to life. Nothing ever got him worried or upset. While Caroline experienced highs and lows, Ken seemed to jog along at a calm, even pace. For this reason, he was her rock, her support in a crisis, the cheery smiling face waiting for her at the end of a difficult day. In a fanciful way, she often likened him to a safe harbour, into which she steered her little boat after it had been bobbing up and down on the relentless sea of life. Once in safe harbour, Ken would enfold her in his big hairy arms, and all would be well with the world.

Caroline had never really considered being with any other man. Ken had always been there, and he'd shared all the milestones of her life to date. Of course, she'd flirted at parties, and had been asked out by more than a few men. But always, she'd returned to the safe haven of Ken's arms, content after the brief heady jolt of confirming that she was still attractive to other men. And now, at last, they were getting married! Finally, the day she'd dreamed of since childhood was about to arrive.

* * *

Caroline stood alone in her room, staring out the window. When she'd told Ken about her mysterious aunt, he'd smiled indulgently. But he hadn't been quite so keen when she'd told him that she intended finding her aunt and inviting her to their wedding.

"Jesus, Caro – do you think that's wise?" he'd said. "It'll drive your mother and Dolly wild! Look, think about it for a while before you do anything. Sometimes it's better to leave well enough alone. I mean, your mother and your aunt might refuse to come to the wedding if Gina was there – have you thought about that possibility?"

Caroline hadn't, but that made her even more determined. Surely, if she could locate her aunt before the wedding, they could all settle their differences, and attend her wedding as a family? Maybe Aunt Gina even had a family of her own by now, so there could be a wonderful family reunion!

Caroline had felt angered by Ken's lack of encouragement, since she'd been so fired up with enthusiasm for her search. She and Ken were planning to spend the evening drawing up a list of possible wedding gifts – for all the work colleagues and friends who begged her to let them know exactly what they wanted – but she'd been so cheesed off by Ken's lack of support that she'd decided to go to bed early and forget about the list. When Ken expressed surprise, Caroline had given him a monosyllabic answer, and headed straight for the bedroom.

In the privacy of the bedroom, Caroline had dialled Hazel, her best friend. Surely *she* would support her in her planned search! But Hazel had been equally unresponsive.

"Caro, I think you're being a bit naïve," she'd said. "If your mother and aunt haven't tried to contact this Gina in all this time, they obviously haven't wanted to. You could be opening up a whole can of worms."

Off the phone, Caroline silently fumed. Why did no one want her to find her poor aunt? In Caroline's fertile brain, Gina had assumed heroic proportions, and she was determined to have her at the wedding. It would bring a whole new dimension to her marriage. She sniffed. Assuming she and Ken made it up again. He hadn't been too happy when she'd walked out of the living room and slammed the door behind her!

But where would she start her search for Gina? No one seemed to know anything about her from the moment she'd been evicted from the family home, thirty years earlier at the age of twenty-two. Caroline sighed. It probably was an impossible task. Gina would now be fifty-two herself and much changed, assuming she was still alive.

It was clear to Caroline that she wouldn't find out anything else from her mother, even if she knew anything. And Dolly was a definite no-no! So that only left her cousin Liz and her mother Teresa. Maybe Liz knew a bit more about what had happened, or perhaps Aunt Teresa could be prevailed upon to reveal whatever she knew.

Caroline picked up the phone again and dialled Liz's number. Her cousin's husband Ronnie answered, but quickly put Liz on the line.

"Mum's told me everything about Gina," Caroline told her cousin, extending the truth slightly, "but there are a few missing links that I thought either you or your mum might know."

"Like what?" Liz asked cautiously.

"Oh, I don't know – anything that might give me an indication of where Gina went after she was kicked out."

"Listen, Caro, are you sure you should be doing this? I mean –"

"If I wanted a lecture, Liz, I'd have gone to the one that's on in the RDS tonight. Tell me anything you know. Like, had Gina any particular school friends – a boyfriend maybe?"

"I honestly don't know myself," Liz told her, "but I'll ask Mum, if you like. I know she got her information from your dad, who presumably would have known all about it."

Caroline smiled. At last she was making some progress. No doubt her parents had discussed the subject of Gina's departure many times, and her father, in turn, would have kept his sister informed.

"Thanks, Liz. Give me a ring as soon as you find out anything."

In a more mellow mood, Caroline put down the phone and looked out the window once again. As she gazed out into the distance, she wasn't looking at anything in particular. Instead, she was thinking that her Aunt Gina was out there somewhere – and soon, with a bit of luck, she was going to find her.

Feeling conciliatory, she left the bedroom and padded down to the living room again.

"Hi, chicken – look, I'm sorry for biting your head off earlier –"

"That's okay, Caro – I know you were upset about your aunt. The one you didn't know you had."

He hugged her silently, and Caroline knew that Ken would always be there for her, no matter how badly she treated him. It was comforting and irritating at the same time. Her fiancé was very easy-going, and put up with her mood swings with equanimity. Once again, she'd been testy and irritable, and it hadn't been Ken's fault.

As she climbed into bed, Caroline vowed that the following evening after work, they would resume drawing up a list of all the things they needed for the house. So far, they only had a few basics, and most of those had been donated either by her mother or various friends. Caroline was looking forward to having their own, personally chosen, household items, and to developing their own individual style.

And on her way home from the accountancy practice where she worked, she'd pick up a take-away at the local Chinese restaurant. She didn't even need to ask Ken what meal he wanted. It was always the same – sweet and sour chicken with egg-fried rice. For some reason this suddenly annoyed her. Why didn't he eat something different for a change? Had he no sense of adventure where food was concerned?

She also felt unaccountably annoyed that Ken always gave in so easily every time they had a row – no, if she was honest, it was every time *she* picked a row – he was so forgiving! Sometimes, she wished he'd be a little less accommodating when she took out her annoyance on him, or was in one of her irritable moods. But he always made excuses for her.

Reluctantly, Caroline admitted to herself that what she longed for in her relationship was a bit of excitement, a bit of uncertainty that would set her pulse racing. But Ken was always there, faithful and dependable. In some perverse part of her nature, she craved the delicious fear of uncertainty. Maybe she'd respect him more if he was less forgiving. If he stood up for himself and told her where to get off. And then, of course, there'd be the joy of making up . . .

Caroline sighed. She really was being unkind. She had a great guy, who loved her to bits, and whom she loved dearly too. They had a lovely house, and were about to start their married life together. Hopefully, it would be a long and happy one. It was just all so predictable . . .

CHAPTER 4

"Kelly – when is bloody Fitzsimons back from holidays?"

"Haven't a clue – anyway, you're the boss, so you should know."

"I might be the boss, but no one ever tells me anything."

Dan Daly, the disgruntled editor of the *Daily News*, scratched his head. His scalp felt quite tender, and there seemed to be less and less hair on it each time he scratched it. Jesus, he thought, I'm nearly bald and I'm not yet forty-five! What a way to go! It must be all the worry over getting this bloody rag out on time each day. It was driving him into an early grave.

He headed back into his office, which consisted of a small area off the newsroom, partitioned off by glass windows. It conferred spurious seniority on its incumbent, and enabled him to keep an eye on who was working on a story and who wasn't, but it provided no insulation from the outside clatter and clack of computer keyboards, the wire service machines and assorted office gadgetry. However, after ten years in the job, Daly no longer heard them.

His head was hurting him badly, but Daly knew that he'd get no sympathy from any of his staff. He'd gone on the piss the night before, mainly because Brenda, his soon-to-be-ex-wife, had taken up with an old boyfriend of hers again.

He scratched his head again and yelped. Not only was his head hurting, but his brains were also falling out. And all because that bitch was trying her best to take revenge on him. Just because he'd made one mistake. One lousy mistake. Well, two really, if he was to be honest about it.

Daly felt like venting his anger on the whole world. Just wait till that other bitch Alice Fitzsimons gets back, he thought savagely. He knew perfectly well when bloody Fitzsimons would be back in the office – Dan had been counting the days. Then he'd make her life hell. In the meantime, crime reporter Brian Kelly would do.

"Kelly – are you nearly finished that goddamned story?"

"Yeah, Dan – I'm just on the last few lines."

"Well, get a move on! The bloody paper's going to bed in exactly –" he took an exaggerated look at his watch, "– thirty minutes."

He didn't really give a shit if Kelly got the story done in time for this issue – it was a topic that would keep, certainly until the following day's issue. In fact, he had more than enough copy already subbed, set and ready for printing. But he liked to keep the troops on their toes – let them know who was boss. On the other hand, Daly knew well that there was a fine line between how far you could push people and the necessity of having their full cooperation if he was to do *his* job. So he blustered and bluffed a lot, the reporters paid homage to his title, then ignored him in every other respect. But they got the work done on time because they were professionals, and some of them actually liked Dan Daly in a peculiar sort of way.

Staff photographer Isobel Dunne sat in her cubicle at the far end of the newsroom, filling out her worksheet and wondering how soon she could escape. She'd just spent the afternoon scanning in a series of archive photos from old negatives for a new series that Dan had decided on. It was boring work, and she was longing for a decent news assignment, which she hadn't had for at least a week. Currently she was out of favour with Dan Daly, so the other photographers were getting to cover the best stories. Isobel shrugged. She had no idea why this was so, but then Dan didn't need a reason. He was a difficult man to work with at the best of times. The important thing was never to let him know he was getting to you. So she'd embraced the archive job with enthusiasm, and watched Dan's displeasure as she thanked him for the chance to work on these rare old photographs.

Isobel sighed. There was nothing quite like a good murder or scandal for creating great pictures. But, for now, she'd just have to wait until Dan's mood changed and she returned to favour once more.

She peered around the door. Hopefully she could sneak out while Dan was upbraiding some other unfortunate soul. Theoretically, her work was independent of Dan Daly, and when her daily workload was finished, she was entitled to go home if she wished. But Dan had the knack of always spotting anyone trying to make a quick getaway, and he would then find some ruse to detain them. It could be a discussion on a previous assignment, a future assignment, or a discussion about nothing at all.

But she, in turn, had become equally adept at thwarting Dan's efforts to keep her in the office. She would take her cosmetic bag and exaggeratedly walk to the staff toilets. He could hardly stop her from going to the bathroom, could he? Fortunately, the toilets were out of view of Dan's office, and close to the exit, so she could then slip out without being noticed.

She looked up just in time to see Daly return to his office. Poor old Dan, she thought pityingly, he hasn't a clue how to handle people, or that bloody wife of his. Come to think of it, she had to admit that she wasn't exactly a hot shot in that area herself. But now that she'd been on a diet for the last month and had lost nearly a stone, maybe the guys in the office would be impressed when they noticed the new, whittled-down version. She currently had the hots for crime reporter Brian Kelly, but so far she hadn't got any return vibes from him. Her friend, investigative reporter Alice Fitzsimons, was always saying that she was too obvious in her approach to men, and maybe Alice was right. After all, Alice had managed to bag herself a good-looking wealthy guy, so she clearly knew what she was talking about!

Isobel took an emery board from the drawer in her desk and began filing one of her nails. Damn – it had split, after months of hard work. Just as she'd got all her nails to a perfect length. Now the dilemma was – should she cut them all down and begin again, or wait for the broken one to grow? Would she look ridiculous with nine beautifully long nails and one stubby one?

She sighed, and kicked the desk. At least Alice would be back soon. She was bored to death without her friend in the office. When the two of them were together, they had a great laugh. They particularly enjoyed working on assignments together, but since Dan couldn't stand seeing anyone else happy, he invariably tried to split them up and send them on separate assignments whenever he could.

Isobel hoped Alice was having a great time in Cyprus. Her friend deserved the break and Isobel was delighted for her, although she herself had spent the entire fortnight counting the days until Alice would be back! Alice's husband Bill worked so hard that he and Alice didn't get away too often. Still, that was the price you had to pay for such a comfortable lifestyle. Alice had the house of her dreams in Killiney, and undoubtedly that required some sacrifices.

Getting out her office diary, Isobel opened it and turned the page to the following Monday, when her friend was due back in the office. In bold writing, she scrawled '*Alice back!*' across the page. Then she grinned. Suddenly, she felt a lot better.

Grabbing her cosmetic bag, she headed for the staff toilets and home.

CHAPTER 5

"Well, Liz – what did you find out?"

"You're not going to believe this – Mum went to St Rita's Senior School, the same one that Stella and Gina went to! She was several years ahead of them, so back then she wasn't particularly friendly with either of them. She'd left school and got a job by the time all this business with Gina happened."

Caroline sighed. "Is that all she was able to tell you?"

"God, you're a slave-driver!" said Liz. "Gina had a best friend called Maeve Harding, but Mum has no idea what her name is now, assuming she got married."

"Maybe she didn't take her husband's name. Some women don't – I'm not going to take Ken's name when we get married."

Liz sniggered. "Knowing you, you probably intend making poor Ken take *your* name!"

"That's not a bad idea – seriously though, did your mum ever find out where Gina went?"

"No, she didn't. But she remembers that Gina had a boyfriend called Larry, although she doesn't remember his surname. A spotty young lad with bright red hair, who went to St Peter's School – just round the corner from St Rita's."

Caroline sighed. Probably both dead ends. But she'd have a shot at contacting this Maeve Harding and Larry What's-his-name. At least she had a few names to begin with.

"Thanks, Liz. And thank your mum for her help. I'll let you know how I get on."

"Make sure you do. And –" Liz hesitated, "– be careful, Caro. You could find yourself holding a hot potato."

Putting down the phone, Caroline inwardly fumed. Hot potato indeed! And Hazel had called it a can of worms. Why was everyone so opposed to her finding Aunt Gina? They all seemed to feel that her family, friends and Ken should be enough for her. But all she wanted to do was put right a wrong that had been done three decades earlier, and bring her family back together, with a happy-ever-after ending to the story.

Caroline sighed. Maybe she was also hoping that her missing aunt would add a new dimension to her own life. After all, Dolly hadn't exactly been an exemplary aunt – she didn't like children, had no sense of humour, and never brought presents like Aunt Teresa did. Caroline had always envied her friends, who all seemed to have lots of warm, cheerful aunts and uncles, who regularly showered their nieces and nephews with sweets and presents. Gina might have been the kind of aunt who would have made all the difference to her life when she was growing up . . .

Caroline imagined Gina as a slightly frivolous, fun-loving creature, who would have been immense fun to be with. Even now, Caroline imagined them shopping together, laden down with bags and laughing and giggling like two schoolgirls instead of grown women. And Gina would be equally thrilled to find Caroline, who would fill a huge gap in her otherwise empty life.

Caroline had also invented another fantasy whereby she discovered that her aunt had a large and wonderful family of her own, who took Caroline to their hearts, providing her with a new and wonderful extended family of cousins.

Who am I kidding? Caroline asked herself. Gina is probably nothing like I imagine. I'm bound to be disappointed, and no doubt she'll be disappointed in me. Nevertheless, I really would like to find her!

Suddenly, she remembered her mum's old school friend Rosemary. She'd have known Gina – hadn't she been in that fateful photograph too? Maybe she'd remember Larry's surname, or Maeve Harding's married name.

Quickly, Caroline looked at her watch. It wasn't too late to give Rosemary a call.

"Hi, Rosemary – it's Caroline."

"Hello, Caroline! How are you?"

"Oh, I'm fine, thanks. Rosemary, Mum and I have just been looking at old family photographs, and talking about Gina's friends –" Caroline tried to sound as though she and her mother had been cheerfully and companionably chatting about the past, "– and we were wondering if, by any chance, you could remember Gina's boyfriend's second name. Mum remembers that his first name was Larry . . ."

Much to Caroline's relief, Rosemary didn't seem to find anything amiss in her queries. Perhaps she'd forgotten the trauma of Gina's departure, or assumed that with the passing of the years the trauma had abated sufficiently for the topic to be considered a safe one again.

"Hmm . . . let me think . . . Wasn't he that red-haired

young lad? Sorry, Caroline, I don't remember his other name, or what became of him. Nice lad, though – always polite, unlike some of those other gurriers, who used to pull our hair and take our sweets. Then there was –"

"Thanks, Rosemary, you're a star," said Caroline, cutting her mother's friend short before she began to waffle. Rosemary was noted for her ability to drone on and on about nothing in particular. "Do you by any chance remember Maeve Harding?"

"Indeed I do – she married a fellow called Kevin O'Donoghue – he runs some sort of business on the north side."

There was a slight air of disapproval in Rosemary's voice. Clearly, the fact that Maeve was now living on the north side was displeasing to Rosemary. Obviously the older woman felt that Maeve had committed treason by moving to the other side of the city!

"Of course, I don't ever see her any more – it's difficult when someone lives so far away . . ."

Caroline smiled to herself. The other side of the city was less than fifteen miles away! But Rosemary, like many others, saw the city's geographical divide as a social one as well!

Thanking Rosemary, Caroline quickly rang off before her mother's friend could begin querying her sudden interest in Gina's past.

Now, at last, she had a name! She'd look up Maeve and Kevin O'Donoghue in the phone book, or check out the Golden Pages for an entry for Kevin O'Donoghue's business, whatever it was. Who knows, she thought, maybe Maeve O'Donoghue is still in contact with Gina! Wouldn't that be wonderful?

CHAPTER 6

"No, dear – I'm afraid not. I wish I *did* know where she was."

Caroline was seated in a large comfortable chair in Maeve O'Donoghue's drawing room in Clontarf. Having rung several possible numbers listed in the phone directory, Caroline had finally located Maeve, and had virtually invited herself around for a chat.

Nevertheless, Maeve was delighted to see her.

"I still miss her, you know," she told Caroline, a sad look in her eyes. "Gina was such good fun, and we always had such a laugh together. We'd been friends since we were in junior school, and I'd assumed we always would be."

There was a few moments' silence as Maeve poured out two cups of tea, and gestured towards the plate of biscuits on the coffee table.

"But fate intervenes, doesn't it?" she added rhetorically. "What happened was terrible, but I wish Gina had kept in touch when she left. She didn't need to do to *me* what was done to her by her family."

Since she arrived, Caroline had said very little, merely

smiling encouragingly, and hoping that Maeve would continue with her colourful reminiscences. Caroline longed to know as much as possible about her aunt, and so far, her own vision of her aunt seemed very similar to Maeve's recollections.

"Did she disappear immediately after the – after, eh, what happened?"

Caroline was unsure of how much Maeve actually knew about the events surrounding Gina's departure from the family home. If Gina had disappeared immediately after the incident with Owen, then Maeve mightn't even be aware of it. But Maeve's next words left Caroline in no doubt that she was fully aware of everything that had happened.

"Oh no, she didn't go immediately. After your grand-mother threw Gina out, she came to stay with me for a while. I was sharing a flat in town with several other girls, and it was great having Gina with us. It was like old times – me and Gina having a laugh together and going to pubs and discos – but one day, exactly two months after she'd moved in, she moved out again. Cleared out all her stuff and disappeared."

"My God! Did she leave you a note?"

Maeve nodded. "Yes, she said she'd be in touch when she got sorted out."

"And you never heard from her again?"

"Oh, no – she sent me an invitation to the wedding in London."

Caroline's mouth dropped open. "The wedding?"

Maeve nodded. "Yes, she and Larry Macken got married exactly a month to the day after she left the flat. I was stunned, needless to say. She'd been going out with Larry off-and-on since she was at school, but I knew she didn't really fancy him, so I never thought it was all that serious."

"And did you go?"

Maeve nodded. "It was only in a registry office," she confided, as though that was a less valid form of marriage than one in a church. "But she seemed happy enough. Of course, Gina told me never to let any of her family know about the wedding, and I never have – until now. I suppose there's no harm in telling you after all this time."

"What took them to London?"

"Larry got a great job there – an apprenticeship with a big architectural practice. It was too good an opportunity to turn down, so Gina went with him."

"Do you think they might still live there?"

"I suppose Larry might, but I'm afraid Gina disappeared again, two months after the wedding."

Caroline gasped. "Disappeared? What do you mean?"

"Exactly that," Maeve told her, smiling sadly. "Neither she nor the baby were ever heard of again."

"The baby?" Caroline felt like a parrot that couldn't stop repeating.

"Well, I suppose it wasn't technically a baby then – I mean, she was only three months pregnant when she got married, and – oh-oh!" Maeve's hand shot to her mouth and she covered it, as though to prevent any more words from spilling out.

Caroline's mouth fell open, as her brain did some quick calculations. Gina had stayed for two months with Maeve and her flatmates, then she'd disappeared to England and got married a month later. Two months later, she disappeared again. That added up to five months. So Gina was five months pregnant when she left Larry.

"So it wasn't Larry's baby," she said.

Maeve nodded, almost in tears, feeling that she'd inadvertently betrayed a longstanding trust.

"Presumably it was Owen's baby?"

Again, Maeve nodded, this time bursting into tears, and then jumping up from her chair in agitation

"Don't worry, Maeve – I won't be telling anyone else," Caroline assured her, still in a state of shock herself. She rose from her chair and put her arms around the older woman.

"Larry never knew – he thought she was pregnant by him," Maeve added, brushing away her tears with the back of her hand. "He was devastated when she disappeared. I felt awful that I couldn't tell him that the child wasn't his –"

"But she never turned up again."

Maeve looked defeated. "No, neither of us ever saw her again. She left Larry a note, saying she'd be in touch later, but he never heard from her again."

They sat again and Maeve topped up both tea cups with fresh tea.

"Owen once contacted me, you know," she went on. "He was looking for Gina, and I told him that she'd moved to London and married Larry. He was very upset about it, so I gave him the phone number and address I had for them in London. He said he was going to contact her, to wish her well in her new life." She grimaced. "But I don't know if he ever did. Poor Owen died in a car accident a few weeks later, and I phoned Gina to let her know. She was devastated. At first, she wouldn't believe me, then she hung up on me. Shortly after that, she walked out on Larry. He rang me in desperation, hoping that maybe I'd heard from her, but she

35

never got in touch with me again." She sighed. "I just wish she'd kept in contact. I would have helped her, if she'd let me. I've often wondered if she ever had the baby, and if so, what became of them both? Larry and I kept in touch for some time, ringing each other regularly to see if there was any news of Gina. But we eventually lost touch, you know how it is . . . Larry moved house and didn't send me his new address –"

Suddenly, they both heard the turn of a key in the front door.

"That'll be Kevin," Maeve said

"Well, I'll be off then," said Caroline, standing up to leave. "Just one more thing – whereabouts in London did Larry and Gina live?"

"North London – I think it was Haringey, or was it Hackney? I can't remember now . . . it was so long ago –"

Just then, a tall pleasant-faced man entered the room, smiling in surprise at finding Caroline there.

"Hello," he said, stretching out his hand, "I'm Kevin O'Donoghue."

He and Caroline shook hands.

"Will you stay and have something to eat with us?" Maeve asked.

But Caroline shook her head. "I've taken up enough of your time. Thanks for the information, Maeve. I'll let you know if I have any luck in finding her."

On the doorstep, Maeve gave Caroline a quick hug. "If you find her, please give her my love," she whispered, "and tell her to get in touch immediately. We've so much to catch up on!"

"I will," Caroline promised. But in her heart she felt that

the chances of finding her aunt had just lessened considerably. After all, Gina had walked out on her husband four months before giving birth to another man's child!

Caroline sighed. Somehow, she would have to find Larry Macken.

* * *

"I'm going to take a few days off work and spend a long weekend in London," said Caroline. "A very long weekend! Want to come with me?"

"Love to, but I can't possibly take time off right now," Ken said, looking at her over a pile of documents on the dining-room table. "Big meetings all next week, so I've loads of paperwork to get finished. Anyway, why London? Can't you shop for the wedding here?"

"Eh, yes – I suppose I can, but there's a much bigger selection in London. I might even find a wedding dress while I'm over there. I haven't found anything I really like up to now."

Which was perfectly true, Caroline conceded. She would definitely do a bit of shopping while she was there. But the real reason she was going there was to track down Gina's husband. And since Ken wasn't coming with her, there was no need to tell him of her plans. The topic of Gina hadn't been mentioned since Ken had expressed his disapproval and they'd had a minor row over it. Obviously, he assumed she'd forgotten about Gina, as did her mother. And that was the way Caroline wanted them to think. It's best to let sleeping dogs lie, she thought. Why aggravate them when there was only a slim chance of finding Gina anyway?

"Since you can't come, my love, I think I'll ask Hazel and Liz if they're free," she told Ken now.

"Hmm, good idea," Ken answered absentmindedly, continuing to read one of the reports in front of him, and not really paying attention.

"I'll go and ring them straight away," said Caroline, jumping up from the sofa and heading for the phone.

Caroline's suggestion of a shopping trip to London was enthusiastically received by both Hazel and Liz.

"Brilliant! I've got a few days annual leave left over from last year," said Hazel happily. "Woo-hoo, I can't wait to get shopping!"

And Liz, when Caroline rang her, was equally delighted at the prospect. "Fantastic!" she said. "I need a break from Ronnie – he's driving me mental with his preparations from some charity hill walk he's taking part in. You'd think he was going to climb Mount Everest, instead of rambling up and down a few hills in Kerry!"

Caroline laughed. "I think, Liz, rambling in Kerry involves a bit more than going up and down the odd hill. Besides, they don't have hills there – they have mountains, and big ones at that."

"Oh well – whatever," said Liz dismissively. "I'll still be glad to get away from him for a few days! Husbands can be a pain sometimes – you'll find that out soon yourself, Caro!"

The three women agreed that travelling to London by boat and train was the best option. Not only was it a pleasant and relaxing way to get there, but it also meant that there were no luggage restrictions. Since all three planned to shop till they dropped, they wanted to ensure that they could get all their purchases safely back home!

Caroline hadn't mentioned to either of them that she intended trying to trace Larry Macken when she got there. There would be time enough to tell them of her plans when they set out on their trip, and she would swear both of them to secrecy. Caroline wasn't keen to hear any further disapproval from either Ken or her mother. But she fully intended to find her Aunt Gina, no matter what either of them thought. No doubt Liz and Hazel would also try to discourage her when she told them what she was intending to do, but she knew they'd support her nonetheless.

CHAPTER 7

As they sat in comfortable window seats on the boat from Dun Laoghaire to Holyhead, watching the Dublin coastline recede into the distance, Caroline finally broached the subject of Gina with her cousin and best friend.

"When I'm in London, I intend to try and contact Gina's husband Larry," she told them, unsure of how they'd react.

A slow grin spread across Liz's face. "You sly old devil – I might have known you hadn't forgotten about it! Well, good luck to you – just make sure that I'm not present when you mention this to Aunt Stella!"

"I have no intention of letting my mother know what I'm doing – and neither will either of you!" said Caroline darkly. "What she doesn't know won't bother her. And I'm not telling Ken either."

"Ooh! Keeping secrets from the man in her life already!" said Hazel in mock horror. "Not a good sign, is it?"

Liz stared back at her cousin. "So you're really serious about finding your aunt? Rather you than me, Caro –

what'll you do if she turns out to be some awful old crone who's high on drugs or drink? Or maybe she's a prostitute in the back streets of London – or married to a gangland criminal, who'll come after you and your family, and rob you of everything you've got!"

Caroline shuddered. She'd never given a thought to such a possibility. In her mind, Gina was a wonderful person who'd been wronged thirty years ago, and whose case she was championing. But suddenly, the idea of searching for her aunt didn't seem quite so appealing. Maybe Liz was right. In fact, maybe her own family knew all about Gina already, and were simply trying to save her the heartache of discovering what her aunt had become . . .

"I'm only joking," said Liz hurriedly, seeing Caroline's worried face. "I'm sure Gina will be lovely, assuming you ever find her."

"Yes," said Hazel, winking at Liz. "Don't worry, Caro – even if things turn out for the worst, Liz and I will come with you for support when you visit your aunt in prison . . ."

"Stop it, the pair of you!" said Caroline, laughing. "You're just trying to wind me up!"

By early evening, after a restful boat journey and a connecting high-speed train into Euston Station, the trio found themselves in London. Immediately, they headed for the underground station that would take them close to the hotel near Charing Cross that they'd booked over the Internet.

"What a wonderful city!" said Liz enthusiastically, as they boarded the train. "So many shops, so little time!"

"Well, I intend to fit in as many shops as I possibly can," vowed Hazel. "Oxford Street should be possible to do in one morning. Then, Piccadilly in the afternoon, Kensington High Street at some point, then the market in Petticoat Lane on Sunday morning, and —"

Liz grinned. "Dear God, Hazel — the weight of your shopping bags will sink the boat on the way back!"

"Don't worry," said Caroline, getting into the spirit of things. "We can sit at opposite ends of the boat, to balance out the weight!"

Caroline was genuinely looking forward to doing some shopping herself. Apart from a wedding dress, there were lots of things she might pick up more cheaply in London, such as invitation cards, wedding-cake boxes, gifts for the bridesmaids . . . not to mention some pretty clothes for her honeymoon. She and Ken were heading to Sicily for some sea, sand and —

"I presume we'll try to take in a show as well?" asked Liz, interrupting her thoughts.

"Why not?" said Caroline happily. "Sounds like fun."

As they emerged from the underground train that had deposited them near to their hotel, Caroline stopped to survey the unfamiliar and magnificent buildings all around her. Somewhere in this city, she thought, my Aunt Gina could be living. I might even pass her in the street, yet neither of us would know each other.

"Come on, lazy boots!" Liz called to Caroline, who was lagging behind. "Hazel and I are knackered, and want to get a shower as soon as possible. Last into the hotel pays for the drinks!"

Caroline grinned, hurrying after them.

Having showered and changed, the trio of friends met in the hotel foyer and headed towards the bar.

"Let's eat in the hotel tonight," suggested Hazel. "I'm exhausted. Is that okay with you two?"

The others nodded back, and Caroline yawned as if to prove the point.

"And tomorrow, we hit the shops!" said Liz, grinning happily.

"Well, you two can head off," said Caroline, as they took their places at the bar counter, "but I've already checked the phone book for the Haringey area, and believe it or not, I've found a Larry Macken listed there. So I'm going to head out there tomorrow morning. Since it's a Saturday, I'm hoping that he'll be at home."

Hazel made a face. "We'll miss you, Caro, and you'll miss all the bargains!"

"All the more for us!" said Liz cheerfully.

Caroline smiled at her two friends. She was so looking forward to these few days in London. And with a bit of luck, she might be going home with more than a few bags of shopping.

CHAPTER 8

"Another glass of wine, Dolly?"

Charles Keane waited, the wine bottle poised over Dolly's glass.

"Why not, Charles? That's a particularly nice wine."

Charles nodded approvingly. "It ought to be, my dear – it's a premier cru Chateauneuf du Pape. Expensive, but well worth it."

Dolly sipped her wine appreciatively, as Charles studied the menu. The two were meeting for their monthly lunch at the Shelbourne Hotel, where they'd been dining, off-and-on, for the previous thirty years. Both elderly now, they felt comfortable in each other's company. While they shared many interests, what linked them more closely than anything else was BWF Pharmaceuticals. It had been many years since Dolly worked as Charles Keane's secretary, but their friendship had remained strong. At Charles's instigation, Dolly had bought shares in the company, and she continued to take a lively interest in BWF Pharmaceuticals and its progress. Both Charles and Dolly were conservative and strait-laced in their attitudes, and they found solace in each other's company from the tiresome modernity that impinged on their sedate little world.

The waiter appeared at their table, and Charles and Dolly ordered from the menu, Charles opting for the seafood with fennel and lime as his starter, and seared beef with cucumber and seaweed for the main course. Dolly decided on the gazpacho soup, followed by the marinated chicken with sautéed potatoes.

"An excellent choice," said the waiter, inclining his head in their direction.

Dolly gave him a gracious smile in return. It was always a good idea to treat staff as though they actually mattered. Years ago, Charles had taught her that you got better service that way. No doubt the waiter was only being nice in the hopes of getting a large tip. If she'd been paying, he'd get nothing, but Dolly knew that Charles always tipped well. He maintained that it ensured you were well looked after on return visits.

As Charles topped up her wine glass, Dolly allowed herself a surreptitious glance at her generous benefactor. He was still a fine-looking man, even though his white hair had thinned somewhat, and his jaw had slackened a little. But to her, he was still the wonderful man he'd always been.

She sighed contentedly as she sipped her wine. With Owen long dead, and Charles Keane's wife recently deceased, people were wondering if she and Charles might now tie the knot themselves, given their years of devotion to each other. She was wondering the same thing herself, but she would never dream of raising the matter unless Charles did. To a woman of her years, decorum dictated that any suggestion of marriage would have to come from the male of the species. She found it difficult to embrace such new-fangled ideas as a woman proposing marriage to a man, or even instigating a date. She shuddered as she thought of how dreadfully the world had changed in the space of a few decades. It was all the fault of those radical feminists with their hairy armpits, who didn't care how they looked, and who regarded men and women as equal. Covertly, she glanced at Charles Keane again. How on earth could any woman be as clever and as intelligent as dear Charles?

She grimaced. And now that niece of hers, a young woman with notions above her station, was gallivanting all over the place in search of Gina, whose existence she hadn't even known about until recently! Inwardly Dolly fumed, and an angry puce colour suffused her cheeks. How dare her niece interfere in matters that were none of her business!

"There's something bothering you, Dolly – isn't there?" asked Charles gently. "C'mon – tell this old friend of yours. A trouble shared is a trouble halved, so they say."

Dolly pursed her lips together even tighter. She had no wish to discuss the recent events with Charles. It would be embarrassing to have to bring up a topic that she preferred to forget about. After all, she and Charles were out for a pleasant lunch, and she didn't want anything to put a damper on the pleasant atmosphere.

But Charles continued to look questioningly at her, tilting his head to one side, and Dolly knew with certainty that he wouldn't let up until she told him what was on her mind.

At last, she gave an exasperated sigh. "It's my niece, Charles. I thought we'd put that unsavoury episode with my sister Gina behind us years ago – but oh no, Caroline has found out about her, and has to start asking questions! Now the silly child has got the notion into her head that she'll track Gina down, get everyone to sort out their differences, and invite her to the wedding!"

Charles laughed ruefully. "Oh dear!" he said, reaching across to squeeze Dolly's hand. "I'm sure it will all come to nothing. Wherever your sister is, it's obvious that she doesn't want to be found. She's probably in Australia, or perhaps America. I'm sure your niece will never manage to find her – she'll eventually forget about this foolhardy escapade when she gets embroiled in her wedding plans. When exactly is the wedding?"

"October," Dolly informed him. "Of course, you'll receive an invitation, Charles, and I hope you'll be able to attend." She shuddered. "There's bound to be lots of ghastly young people running amok at this wedding, so I'll be glad to be able to sit beside someone of my own vintage."

"Of course, Dolly," said Charles, smiling. But his mind was elsewhere. Privately, he was deeply disturbed.

Just then, their starters arrived, and the conversation was temporarily halted. But as soon as the waiter departed, Charles made it his business to continue the conversation in the same vein.

"And young Caroline – what exactly has she been doing to track down your sister?" he asked, wearing his most avuncular expression.

Dolly raised her eyes to heaven. "Apparently she's been talking to anyone and everyone who might have known Gina here in Dublin, and now she's off to London, supposedly on a shopping trip for her wedding. But it wouldn't surprise me if she has plans to look for Gina while she's over there."

"Good lord!" said Charles, topping up their glasses of wine. "What would make her think that Gina is living there now?"

"I've no idea," the aggrieved Dolly replied. "Maybe someone's told her that Gina went to London all those years ago. Anyway, Caroline is unlikely to tell me anything. She's well aware of how I feel about my younger sister."

"Yes. I know how hurt you were at the time," Charles said gently. "I was so glad that you felt able to confide in me."

Of course he'd also used the situation to his advantage at the time.

"It's all water under the bridge now," said Dolly stiffly. "I'd really rather not talk about it."

Charles sighed. Water under the bridge indeed. Hopefully, Gina's story would stay there, lost in the murky waters of the past. It would be unfortunate if young Caroline discovered more than it was safe for her to know . . .

CHAPTER 9

Alice Fitzsimons lay happily on her sun lounger, feeling the glorious rays of the sun on her skin. Only one more day of their holiday in Cyprus left, but she intended making the most of it. She stretched and wriggled her bare toes, luxuriating in the sensuousness of wearing hardly any clothes. In her opinion, the sun really did make you feel sexier! No wonder Irish holidaymakers overdid it when they hit the beach – they were trying to squeeze a whole year's sunshine into a fortnight, with little hope of any sun for the rest of the year!

She sighed drowsily. If only she and Bill could stay here forever! On the other hand, if life was all holidays, it would get very boring and routine before long. Besides, she absolutely loved her job as a journalist with the *Daily News* – it was just Dan Daly, the chief sub-editor, that she wasn't so keen on! On the other hand, she was dying to see her best friend, photographer Isobel Dunne, and catch up with all the gossip from the world of journalism. Nothing escaped Isobel's beady eye, and Alice knew that her friend would have her in stitches as she related everything that happened since she'd left the office two weeks earlier.

Foraging for her watch among the items in her beach bag, Alice was surprised to discover that it was six o'clock already. She must have dozed off! Bill would probably be back from his visit to the ruins of some amphitheatre nearby, so it was time she packed up and made her way back to the hotel. After a shower to wash off all the sun cream, she intended wearing the gorgeous wispy little sundress she'd bought at a nearby boutique, when they went out to dinner. She might as well wear it on holiday, since it was unlikely she'd get a chance to wear it in the Irish climate!

Since it was their last night in Cyprus, she intended making a special effort to look nice. Bill hadn't been in great form throughout the holiday, and Alice suspected that something was wrong at work. Her husband's financial wheelings and dealings were largely a mystery to Alice, although they afforded the couple a very comfortable lifestyle. Alice suspected that, in some of Bill's business transactions, he sailed rather close to the wind, but he always assured her that he knew what he was doing. Anyway, since she knew little about the world of finance, she was happy to let him get on with it, while enjoying the money his job provided.

On a few occasions during the holiday, there had been calls to his mobile phone. Each time it had happened, he'd taken the call in private, either walking away from her if they were sightseeing, or going into the bathroom if they were at the hotel. Obviously he didn't want to bother her with office business, but nevertheless Alice felt uneasy despite his reassurance that all was well, and that it was simply some "inefficient moron" from the office who couldn't follow the instructions he'd left for them.

Well, tonight she'd made a special effort to cheer Bill up. Whatever was eating at him, she'd try to make him forget it, at least for a few hours. She'd ply him with plenty of wine over dinner and get him to loosen up a bit, then she'd take him dancing at the nearby nightclub, and by the time she was finished with him, the only thing on his mind would be taking her back to the hotel and making love to her all night . . .

Back in the hotel, Bill greeted her absentmindedly and Alice grinned to herself, thinking of the night of passion she was planning! He wouldn't be quite so vague when she was finished with him . . .

"Had a good day, love?" she asked him.

"Hmm . . . oh, yes, fine thanks."

"Was the amphitheatre impressive?"

"What? Oh yes, very."

"I hope you didn't mind me not going with you – I was dying to catch the last bit of sun before we head home."

"No, not at all – as long as you enjoyed yourself."

Bill seemed preoccupied, and Alice left him sitting on the bed as she headed into the shower.

As she lathered on the shower gel, Alice hummed happily to herself, revelling in the warm water cascading over her body. She inspected her newly acquired golden tan, and was pleased at how much better her skin looked now than when she'd arrived two weeks earlier, pasty-faced and in need of some natural vitamin D. She sighed. From tomorrow on, it would be back to jumpers and woolly socks and the unpredictable Irish weather!

On the other hand, she didn't really mind going home all that much. She loved her garden, and was looking forward to seeing so many of her flowers and shrubs in bloom. She and Bill owned a magnificent old house on half an acre of gardens close to the sea in Killiney, and Alice relished every moment that she could spend in her beloved garden. She loved tending to her plants, and talking to them as she trimmed, mulched, re-potted and cultivated them. And they repaid her devotion by producing an extravagant display of blossoms and berries throughout the year. She was especially looking forward to seeing the crinodendron she'd planted three years earlier. Its red lantern-shaped flowers had been forming just before they'd left on holiday, and should be in full bloom by the time they got back.

"You should get a gardener in," Bill had said. "It's not as though we can't afford one. It would save you all that back-breaking work and you wouldn't have to spend all your free time mucking about in the dirt."

"But I love it, Bill!" Alice had told him, citing the mantra of all true gardeners. "I get immense satisfaction out of seeing new seedlings and cuttings coming up, and watching all my plants developing."

She'd wiped a smudge of earth from her nose. "There's nothing as enjoyable as feeling the earth run through your hands, Bill – honestly. There's something almost primeval about it – you feel the link between yourself and nature."

Bill had given her a sceptical look as he'd gone back inside. But Alice didn't mind. Like all gardeners, she'd become quickly absorbed once again, and hours went by while she happily pottered.

She and Bill had been lucky to find such a beautiful

house. It was hidden up a side road, completely off the beaten track, and it was only by chance that Alice discovered it. But she instantly fell in love with its dilapidated charm, and while Bill was not quite so swayed by his emotions, he immediately saw the house's potential.

They'd had to out-bid several developers at the auction, who wanted to knock down the house and build apartments, but Alice was determined that the garden would be one in which nature would continue to reign supreme. It had been the most nerve-wracking afternoon of her life, but when the hammer finally went down, she and Bill were the proud owners of Ivy Lodge. Alice knew how lucky she was. How many young women of her age owned a home in one of the most prestigious suburbs in the country?

Once out of the shower, Alice towel-dried her hair and put on her new pretty dress. She was looking forward to this evening. She loved the atmosphere here in Cyprus. No one ever seemed to be in a hurry, and you could sit all evening in one of the many restaurants, drinking wine and talking to the locals, who'd invariably engage you in conversation. For their last evening, she intended taking Bill to a gorgeous little taverna she'd spotted while strolling back from the beach. She'd had the presence of mind to call in and book a table, and she'd even selected the table of her choice – one situated in a cosy corner, offering intimacy while giving them an overview of the other diners, and the bay beyond. Alice smiled. Hopefully, the evening would be just perfect.

Bill had been happy to let Alice organise their evening's dining experience. He was still quite edgy, and still taking mysterious calls on his mobile phone, but Alice felt he'd relax once she got him settled in the restaurant, and that all-important first glass of wine into him. She felt sorry for Bill, since he seemed to take work with him even on holiday, whereas once she'd left the newspaper offices, she didn't need to think about work again until she was back at her desk in the newsroom.

In the restaurant, Bill fiddled with his napkin, until Alice felt she'd go mad if he twisted it one more time.

"Bill, can't you forget about work for just one evening?" she said, annoyed. "You'll be back in your office in a few days' time – surely we can enjoy ourselves between now and then? You could make a bit of an effort for our last night here, you know. I'm beginning to wonder why you bothered coming on holiday at all."

Bill put down his napkin and turned to face her, looking almost surprised to see her there. It was obvious that his thoughts had been miles away.

Just then, their starter arrived, and any further discussion was temporarily suspended, as they both began eating their mixed salads.

Alice took a sip of her wine, noticing that Bill was already pouring himself a second glass. He was clearly worrying about something, and she wished that he would tell her what was bothering him. A trouble shared was a trouble halved, so maybe she'd just ask him outright.

"Bill – I know you're worrying about something," she said finally. "Why don't you tell me what it is?"

For the next few seconds, Bill looked as though he was trying to come to a decision. Then he sighed, putting down his fork and turning to stare at her.

"Ahem." He cleared his throat. "Yes, Alice, there's

something I need to discuss with you. I've been having a few money problems."

Alice leaned across the table and squeezed his hand supportively. "Don't worry, love, I'm sure it'll sort itself out soon. Hopefully it's just a temporary problem."

Bill looked at her warily. "I'm afraid it's not that simple. I've rather over-stretched myself this time."

"Oh?"

"Yes. The bank intends to call in the loans."

"What loans, love? I didn't even know you'd borrowed any money."

"I needed it for the business. Things haven't been going too well for a while now."

"But you never said – I wish I'd known, love. God, I feel so –"

Alice was overcome with guilt. Poor Bill had been struggling all this time, and she hadn't even noticed. Throughout the holiday she'd been aware that he wasn't in the best of humour, but she'd been having such a good time herself that she hadn't bothered to ask him what was wrong.

"I'm sorry, love, for being so unsupportive," she said. "I didn't realise what you were going through. But it can't be too bad, can it? I mean, we're still living comfortably, aren't we?"

"That's just it – we're not. I've been borrowing to fund our lifestyle as well."

Alice was momentarily shocked. "Well, hopefully the worst is over now," she said encouragingly, as the waiter took away their salad bowls. "If that apartment complex in Portugal sells well, you'll be on the pig's back again soon, won't you? I know my salary can't match yours, but it's good by most people's standards. And it can tide us over while you get back on your feet."

Bill clenched his teeth. Alice hadn't a clue how serious things were. He would just have to spell it out to her.

"Alice, I had to offer some security against the loans."

Alice looked at him quizzically. "I don't understand. Surely the projects themselves –"

"Alice," said Bill, exasperated, "banks aren't charities. They don't lend against possibilities – they want security, realisable assets."

"Well, the company is an asset, isn't it?"

"It's been losing money for the last two years – that's not the kind of asset the banks want."

"Then what – ?"

Bill sighed. "The house, Alice."

Alice looked puzzled. "*Our* house?"

Bill nodded, biting his lower lip.

"But you couldn't have! I mean, I'd have to sign too –" Her words froze in mid-sentence. "Oh, no! You didn't forge my signature . . ."

Bill said nothing, but his guilt was evident by his posture.

"I don't believe this!" Alice screamed, the other diners in the restaurant turning to see what was happening. "How could you? Oh, Bill – how much did you borrow?"

When Bill told her, Alice thought that she was having a heart attack.

"You won't tell the bank about the signature on the loans, will you?" he begged. "I could be in big trouble if they found out –"

Alice could hardly contain her anger. "That's all you're worried about – your own bloody skin!"

As the realisation began to sink in, Alice reached for the wine bottle. She would get drunk – it was the only way she could cope right now. If she started thinking about losing her beloved home and garden, she'd start howling and never be able to stop. How could she survive without the views of the sea that she loved so much? And the stained-glass window in the hallway that spread coloured light across the walls in the evening . . . she could hardly bear to think of losing it all.

Just then, their main course arrived. Alice looked at it with indifference, then finally pushed her plate away. She'd totally lost her appetite.

CHAPTER 10

The following morning, Hazel and Liz headed off for Oxford Street as soon as they'd eaten breakfast. They were determined not to lose any time in getting to the shops!

"See you later, Caro – and good luck," said Hazel, giving her a hug.

"Hope you find what you're looking for," Liz whispered, giving her a pat on the back as they left.

After they'd gone, Caroline went back to her room and checked the L to R phone book for a second time, almost unable to believe that finding Larry Macken could be so easy. Yet there was only one Larry Macken among the listings, and the entry she'd checked the previous evening was still there in black and white. Caroline felt a tingle of excitement run through her. Hopefully, Larry would be in when she called, and hopefully he'd be able to tell her Gina's whereabouts.

Caroline had decided that she'd call unannounced, since she was afraid that he might otherwise refuse to see her. After all, it was nearly thirty years ago since Gina had walked out on him. Undoubtedly he'd moved on with his life since then, and probably didn't want to be reminded of the woman who'd left him after only two months of marriage.

It only took one change on the underground, and a five-minute walk when she left the station, before Caroline found herself outside the address listed in the phone book. Walking up the path to the newly painted shiny front door, Caroline realised that she was actually shaking with fear and excitement. Pressing the bell, she hovered anxiously on the doorstep. Hopefully, within the next few minutes, she'd learn something more about her long-lost aunt.

Suddenly, the door was opened by a middle-aged man. His hair was red, turning grey at the sides, and momentarily, Caroline found herself unable to speak.

"I – eh, hello," she said at last, extending her hand. "My name is Caroline Leyden, and I'm your wife's – I mean Gina's niece. I wonder if you'd mind telling me anything you know about her?"

Then she realised that this man mightn't even be Larry Macken, so she apologised and mumbled who she was looking for.

The man smiled, and suddenly he looked years younger, although the many lines in his ruddy freckled skin showed that the passage of time hadn't been kind to him.

"Yes, I'm Larry Macken," he said, in a soft Irish accent that was so at odds with the sharp London accent that Caroline had been hearing since she'd arrived in the city. "Come on inside."

Caroline was led into a cosy room where the television was blaring. Switching it off, Larry gestured to an armchair, and sat down in an adjacent one himself.

"Okay," he said, staring at her, "we've got an hour before my wife Clare arrives home from shopping. Maybe you'd like to tell me why this sudden interest in Gina? She disappeared almost thirty years ago, and no one's ever bothered to make contact with me before now."

Caroline had registered surprise when he'd mentioned a wife, yet why wouldn't he have remarried? No doubt Gina was just a distant memory to him now.

Quickly, she explained how she had found out about her long-lost aunt, and her desire to have her present at her wedding.

"Well, I doubt if I can help you," said Larry. "After Gina disappeared, I never saw or heard from her again. To this day, I've no idea what happened to her."

Caroline noticed that he was clasping and unclasping his hands in agitation.

"Back then, I loved her very much," he said at last. "She was expecting our baby when she disappeared – she was three months pregnant and already starting to show. I was worried sick that something had happened to her that day – I was afraid she might have had a miscarriage, or an accident."

Caroline noted that he'd said *three* months pregnant. Clearly Gina had lied to him in order to make him think she'd only got pregnant shortly before their wedding.

"Gina left a note saying she was leaving me, but that she'd contact me soon and explain her reasons for going – but I never heard from her again. I knew she didn't get on with her family since they never turned up for our wedding, so I didn't like to contact them after she left. I knew *she'd* never contact them, and I felt duty-bound to honour what I believed would be Gina's wishes."

"Even though she'd left you."

Larry smiled. "Maybe even more so, because of that. She must have had her reasons."

He shifted in his chair. "Do you know her friend Maeve?"

Caroline nodded.

"For a while, I used to check back with Maeve, to see if Gina had gone back to Dublin, but the answer was always no. Eventually, Maeve and I lost touch."

Caroline smiled sadly, thinking what a lovely and decent man Larry Macken was.

He stood up and began to pace the floor. "I met my partner Clare shortly afterwards. She was unbelievably supportive – there were other people who thought I might have been responsible for Gina's disappearance, but Clare was beside me through it all."

Caroline nodded. "It must have been difficult for both of you."

Larry gave a bitter smile. "It was hell for a while. Even today, I still can't help wondering if I've got a son, or a daughter, out there somewhere."

Caroline felt deeply sorry for Larry, and longed to put his mind at rest regarding any possible offspring of his. But it wasn't for her to tell him.

Any fears she might have had about his culpability in Gina's disappearance were also dispelled by his naïve belief that Gina had been only three months pregnant instead of five. Unless he was a brilliant actor, he seemed like a genuinely decent man, who had been put through hell at an earlier stage of his life.

Caroline leaned forward. "Larry, do *you* think that Gina is still alive?"

Larry grimaced, shaking his head. "I really don't know. I'm still not sure why she left. We were happy together – well, I thought so, anyway – and looking forward to the birth of our child. She promised in her note that she'd get in touch later, and explain why she left, but maybe she just said that to take the sting out of what she was doing. Anyway, I never heard from her again."

For a short while they sat in silence, Caroline unsure of what to say next.

"Sorry I can't help you," said Larry at last, "but there's nothing else I can tell you. Being married to Gina for such a short time meant that we never had time to build up many memories together."

By mutual assent, their conversation had come to an end, and Caroline stood up to leave. She was deeply disappointed. Her chances of finding her aunt seemed to be fading fast. If the man who'd loved her had nothing to tell, it seemed as though she'd reached a dead end.

As she reached the front door, Caroline turned back to Larry, who was following behind her.

"I don't suppose you'd have a photograph of her, would you?" she asked. "I've only ever seen one – a group photograph at my Aunt Dolly's wedding – but it's hard to make out her features clearly."

Larry thought for a moment. "Eh, yes, I have. In fact –" he hesitated, "– there's an old suitcase in the garage – the one Gina brought with her from Ireland. It still has some of her things in it, and I put our wedding photos and any remaining personal stuff into it when I met Clare. Out of consideration to her, when she moved in." He gave a sad smile. "I've always been meaning to get rid of the old case, but I never had the heart to do it. But if you'd like it —"

"Oh yes, thank you very much!" said Caroline fervently, her eyes shining.

Excusing himself, Larry went out through a side door in the hall that obviously led to the garage. In the hallway, Caroline stood anxiously waiting, suddenly afraid that he wouldn't be able to find it, or might change his mind when he did. But he returned a few minutes later, carrying an old-fashioned cardboard moulded suitcase that sported elaborate protectors on each corner. It was covered in dust, and Larry looked sheepish as he handed it over.

"Are you sure you really want it? There's nothing of any value in it — maybe a few clothes and bits and pieces — and our wedding photos."

"Yes, I want it," said Caroline firmly.

"It was all so long ago," said Larry sadly. "Meeting you has brought back memories I thought I'd forgotten."

"I'm sorry," said Caroline contritely. "I shouldn't have barged in on you like this, but I didn't know what else to do."

"No problem," said Larry, smiling at her. "It's just a shock to be reminded again after all this time. After the hell I experienced back then, maybe I actually *chose* to shut Gina out of my mind."

Caroline leaned up and kissed him on his ruddy cheek. "Thanks for the suitcase. I'll treasure it, and the photos too."

"You'll let me know if you ever find her, won't you?"

"Of course."

"And the baby. Although it wouldn't be a baby now, would it? It'd be an adult."

"Goodbye, Larry," said Caroline, avoiding any promise to tell him about the child Gina might have had. Because that child would have been Owen's.

Walking down the road towards the underground station with the suitcase, Caroline could feel the excitement building inside her. At last she had something with a tangible connection to her aunt! Now she might learn something about this mysterious woman, even if it was only to hold the clothes her aunt had once worn, and look at the pictures of her wedding, taken all those years ago.

At this point, Caroline reluctantly accepted that she'd probably never find Gina, but she was looking forward to examining Gina's old suitcase. Even though her search had reached a dead end, she at least had some things by which to remember her aunt. Maybe something from Gina's suitcase could be the 'something old' that she'd wear on her wedding day.

CHAPTER 11

Back in her hotel room, Caroline was relieved that neither Hazel nor Liz were back from their shopping expedition in Oxford Street. Although she felt tired and sticky and longed to leap straight into the shower, she was anxious to look inside Gina's suitcase before the others returned. She wanted to do it in private, since she didn't immediately want to share her findings with anyone else. Besides, she knew that once they arrived, she'd have no more free time that evening since they'd want to show her all their purchases, then drag her off to some restaurant or cocktail bar for a night on the town. Quickly, she opened the suitcase, knowing that she didn't have long before they got back.

At first glance, the contents of the suitcase were disappointing: nightdresses, slips and other underwear, dresses, blouses, cardigans, skirts, a few pieces of cheap jewellery, and a large envelope with what looked like a bulky document in it – she glanced at it and noted that it seemed to be an article of some sort, nothing useful like birth or marriage certificates. The most interesting thing, as far as Caroline was concerned, was the small photo album that Larry had put there in deference to his new wife.

Looking at the photos inside, Caroline studied the smiling faces. Gina looked radiant in a smock-style maxi dress covered in geometrical patterns of green and purple. Her dark hair escaped in tendrils from under a ridiculous green floppy hat, and in several of the photos she was smiling as she straightened her new husband's huge boldly-patterned tie, while he gazed down at her adoringly. Larry looked uncomfortable in his wide-lapelled suit with its hideous bell-bottom trousers covering his feet. He looked so different back then, Caroline thought, his hair a luminous halo of bright red, and a big red moustache drooping down each side of his mouth. The guests were people Caroline didn't know – except for one woman whom Caroline thought might be Maeve O'Donoghue née Harding. Now she'd be able to contact Maeve again, show her the photographs, and hope that she could identify some of the other guests in attendance. Maybe there were other guests at the wedding who could throw light on Gina's disappearance, or who might know something that would enable Caroline to take another step in the right direction. Looking through the photos, Caroline decided that she wasn't ready to give up her search just yet.

Looking at the radiant Gina, Caroline found it hard to accept that she hadn't been happy that day. But based on what she now knew about her aunt, it seemed likely that she'd only married poor Larry to cover up her pregnancy by Owen. So Gina's overall feeling that day would have been one of relief. Caroline longed to believe that Gina really had loved Larry – after all, they'd been going out together since their schooldays, and her tryst with Owen was probably a tragic mistake that she instantly regretted.

Caroline sighed. On the other hand, this probably meant that her aunt hadn't been the wonderful person she'd envisioned. She'd deceived poor Larry, marrying him only because she was pregnant by another man. But what choice did Gina have? She'd been evicted from her home, and later found herself pregnant by her sister's husband. She mightn't have known how to get an abortion, or else she hadn't wanted to.

Puzzled, Caroline scratched her nose. But why had Gina disappeared before she was due to give birth? She'd had a husband who clearly loved her, and who assumed that her child was his. Even if the child was born two months early, it was unlikely that Larry would have queried its paternity. Its early arrival could have been explained away by a variety of reasons, such as early labour brought on by exertion, stress or high blood pressure. Larry wasn't a medical man, so Gina could have made up a perfectly believable story. Even today, Larry still believed that Gina's child had been his.

Caroline sighed. So she must have had an accident – there could be no other explanation.

Just then, Caroline heard the sound of voices outside in the corridor. There was a lot of giggling and muffled conversation, then she heard keys turning in locks. Hazel and Liz had arrived back. Soon they'd be banging on her door to tell her all about their day, and show her their purchases.

Caroline closed the suitcase and slipped it into the bottom of the hotel wardrobe. Any further exploration of Gina's life would have to wait until later.

* * *

"Caro, what do you think of this?" said Liz, twirling around in a short satin dress with shoestring straps. "And this jacket – wasn't it a steal at thirty quid?"

"Lovely, Liz – you did very well," said Caroline, doing her best to look interested.

"And your trousers, Hazel – they're exquisite. Looks like you both had a good day!"

"Oh, it was brilliant, Caro! You should have come with us!" said Hazel, almost breathless with delight. "We had lunch in the Post Office Tower, then we went down Regent Street, although that was too pricey by far, so we went up Tottenham Court Road – that's where I got these trousers!"

"We saw lots of bridal shops too, Caro," added Liz, "I'm sure you could pick up your wedding dress while you're over here. There are some beauties – and they're very reasonably priced. Probably far cheaper than getting it made."

"I'll take a look on Monday," Caroline promised. "Right now, I'm dying to have a shower – because I'm sure you pair have already made plans for this evening!"

"Yes – wear your Sunday best tonight, Caro, because we're hitting the town!" said Liz. "We found a cute little bistro with a side garden decorated in twinkly lights. We knew you'd love it, so we've booked a table there for eight o'clock. Yippee – tonight, we're dining *al fresco*!"

"What's the food like?"

"Who cares about the food – the waiters are gorgeous!"

"By the way – how was *your* day, Caro?" Hazel suddenly asked. "Did you have any luck with that Larry fellow?"

"Yes and no," Caroline replied, trying to underplay the excitement she still felt from looking at the photographs. She wanted it to be her secret for a little longer. "I'll tell you all about it later, over dinner. But this very minute I'm hopping into the shower!"

* * *

Later that evening, the three women enjoyed a delightful meal in the bistro garden, and were fussed over by several very handsome young waiters.

"This is the life, isn't it?" said Hazel contentedly, as she sipped a sambucca at the end of the meal.

All three of them were very mellow, having consumed several bottles of wine.

Caroline told them all about her meeting with Larry Macken, and they were pleased for her that it had gone reasonably well.

"And what about the suitcase?" asked Liz then. "Was there anything useful in it?"

"I've only really looked at the wedding photos," Caroline explained. "There are a few bits of clothing also, and a big envelope with some business papers in it, but I haven't looked at them yet." She yawned. "I'll look at them tomorrow." She smiled at the others. "But right now I'm knackered and ready for bed! Unless, of course, you two think we should be heading off to some nightclub?"

With sheepish grins, both Liz and Hazel confessed to being exhausted too, so reluctantly the trio began making their way out through the bistro garden to the restaurant exit, amid entreaties from the young waiters to return at the earliest opportunity.

"God, if I wasn't so old – and married – I'd love to have a roll in the hay with that young lad!" said Liz, gesturing towards one of the waiters.

"Keep your voice down!" hissed Hazel. "I think he heard you!"

"So what?" said Liz in an even louder voice. "Why shouldn't I let him know that I fancy him?"

"C'mon, cradle-snatcher, we'd better get you back to the hotel!" said Caroline, grinning, as she and Hazel steered Liz out of the restaurant before she could cause any more havoc.

Grinning at each other over Liz's bent head, Caroline and Hazel were both well aware that Liz would be suffering a hangover the following morning!

After a taxi had delivered them back to the hotel, they quickly got Liz into bed, insisting that she drink several glasses of water before they'd allow her to lie down. Finally, when she was sleeping like a baby, they left her and headed back to their own rooms, agreeing that they both needed to consume plenty of water themselves!

CHAPTER 12

"Oh God, I'm never going to drink again!" Liz sat nursing her head in the hotel restaurant the following morning, while Caroline and Hazel both tucked into big breakfasts of bacon, eggs and sausages.

"Surely you're going to eat something?" asked Caroline solicitously, stuffing thickly buttered toast into her mouth. "Eating greasy food is the best way to deal with a hangover, Liz – honestly!"

Hazel waved her fork in Liz's direction. "Think of how much worse you'd be, if Caro and I hadn't force-fed you with water last night!"

Liz shuddered as she watched Caroline dip her toast into the egg yolk on her plate. "Did I do anything – well, embarrassing last night?"

"Not really," said Caroline, trying to keep a straight face. "Other than bringing that young waiter back to your room . . ."

All the colour drained from Liz's face. "I didn't! Did I? Oh my God!"

"Relax – Caro's only teasing you," Hazel assured her. "But you might have – if we'd let you have any more sambuccas!"

Getting up from the table, Caroline headed to the breakfast buffet, and brought Liz back a plate of bacon, sausages, eggs and mushrooms.

"Go on – give it a try," she coaxed. "Otherwise, you won't be fit to come to Petticoat Lane with us later."

Remembering that her purpose for being in London was to shop, Liz focussed her attention of the plate in front of her, and made a valiant attempt at getting most of it down her throat. After washing it down with several cups of tea, she gradually began to feel human again, and before long she was able to hold her head up without the room spinning around.

Later, as they sat in the underground train that was taking them to Aldgate East, Caroline was looking forward to what would be her first day of shopping. She loved street markets, and there was nowhere better to find them than London.

After spending the morning at Petticoat Lane, the trio, laden down with shopping bags, took the Circle Line to King's Cross, and the Northern Line to Camden Town, where they walked to Camden Lock market, and Caroline bought a white headband sewn with tiny pearls, white satin shoes, several gorgeous dresses for her honeymoon, and an antique lamp that would look wonderful on top of the bookcase in the drawing room of her house.

It was a weary threesome that trudged back to the hotel later that evening. Having truly shopped till they dropped, they were all far too exhausted to contemplate another night on the town. So they simply stopped at a fast-food burger restaurant en route to the hotel.

"I know this food is crap, and is full of trans-fatty acids and all sorts of other undesirable stuff, but it's just perfect at the moment," said Liz, sighing with pleasure as she attacked a large burger with all the trimmings. She hadn't fully recovered from her hangover yet – although she hadn't allowed it to interfere with her ability to shop – and she was now longing to crawl into her bed.

"Thank goodness you both feel as knackered as I do," said Hazel, helping herself to another mouthful of fries, "because there's no way I could go out again tonight!"

"Well, an early night now means that we can get an early start in the morning," Caroline reasoned.

The others nodded, relieved that by general consensus, they were all heading back to the hotel and straight to their beds!

"God, I can't believe how tired I am!" Caroline yawned as they took the lift up to their rooms. "An early night in bed, with the TV on, sounds just perfect!"

* * *

The following morning, the three women were up early. This time, they all tucked into a hearty breakfast in the hotel, since they didn't intend breaking for lunch. That would mean losing valuable shopping time!

"Everyone looks bright-eyed and bushy-tailed this morning," Caroline commented, pouring herself another cup of tea.

"I'm reporting for duty," said Liz, giving a mock salute. "Credit cards to the ready – for plenty of action!"

"Are we still planning on going to the theatre tonight?"

Hazel asked. "I've been checking in the *Evening Standard*, and there are several shows I wouldn't mind seeing. It also says that you can get cheap tickets for most of the shows if you book them at the ticket kiosk in Leicester Square."

The others nodded. They were all happy to leave the choice of performance to Hazel.

"So where are those bridal shops that you spotted the other day?" Caroline asked Hazel and Liz. "If you two don't mind booking for the theatre, I think I'll head off and take a look at some wedding dresses myself, then meet up with you two later."

"Sure you don't need our help?"

Caroline shook her head. She preferred to shop alone, or at least to check out what was available before making decisions. If she found any dresses she liked, she'd then bring her friends back for a second opinion.

Having been given shop names and their locations, and graphic descriptions of dresses she wasn't to miss, Caroline parted from her two friends outside the hotel, and headed towards Oxford Street. It was a pleasant dry day, and she enjoyed the sensation of wandering along on her own. People-watching was a favourite hobby of hers, and as she window-shopped, Caroline also observed the stylish people who hurried past, and wondered where they were all rushing to in such a hurry. She supposed that many of them were tourists, others shoppers like herself or workers going to or coming from their offices. At the thought of work, she grinned to herself, luxuriating in the joy of being free of job constraints for at least the next few days!

Caroline easily found the shops her friends had been

referring to, and spent several hours wandering through the displays of exquisite gowns. She felt as though she'd walked into an enchanted world, where each dress was more gorgeous than the one before. Each time she thought she'd finally made a decision, she spotted another gown that she liked even better. Eventually, she felt that her brain was going into overload. Who could possibly choose just one dress from so many amazing ones?

Accepting defeat, she decided that she couldn't possibly make a decision until she'd taken a break. Maybe a cup of coffee would help to clarify her thoughts. Besides, she conceded, there was no rush – she could think about the dresses she'd liked, and come back the following day. Maybe she'd ask Liz and Hazel to come with her, and help her to narrow down the final selection of dresses that she'd then ask to try on.

Leaving the mystical world of wedding gowns behind, Caroline stepped out into the street, momentarily blinking in the natural daylight outside. Which reminded her – she'd need to check her final choice of dress in the daylight before she paid for it. She didn't want to discover that it was a different shade of white from the shoes and headdress she'd bought the day before. Clearly, she needed to bring the new accessories with her when she selected one of the dresses. *If* she selected one of these dresses. There was still the option of getting her dress made. She particularly liked one of the designs in the pattern book she had at home – the one Liz hadn't liked. Caroline grimaced as she remembered. That had been the fateful day when she'd brought out the old photo album, and learned about her Aunt Gina . . .

Suddenly, Caroline felt herself fall forward, and she cried out in shock as her knees and hands grazed the pavement. Someone had pushed her from behind! She felt pressure on her arm and suddenly realised, to her horror, that someone was trying to steal her handbag!

Instantly, she thought of all the cash and credit cards she had in it, and she was filled with terror at the prospect of losing it. But her terror was immediately replaced by anger, and she continued to grip her handbag tightly, refusing to let go of it as her assailant tried to pull it from her.

"Help!" she cried, to anyone who would listen. "Someone's trying to steal my bag!"

Quickly, the thief let go of the bag and melted away into the crowd, and Caroline felt strong arms help her up from the pavement.

"Are you okay?" a concerned voice asked, and Caroline looked up to find a pair of dark brown eyes looking into hers.

Dazed, she nodded her thanks. Ruefully, she surveyed her jeans – both knees were torn, and flecked with blood from her scraped skin underneath.

"Let's get you a cup of tea or coffee," said the kind man. "You've had quite a shock. You need to sit down and take it easy for a few minutes."

Gently he guided her into a nearby café, settled her in a seat near the door, asked what she wanted to drink, then went to order two coffees.

Suddenly, Caroline found that she was shaking, and as the man returned with the coffees, she burst into tears.

"Don't worry, everything's all right," he told her, giving her hand a reassuring pat. "You've had a terrible fright, but thankfully no harm's been done. You've still got your handbag, haven't you?"

Caroline nodded, wiping her nose on the napkin he passed her.

Surveying her rescuer properly for the first time, Caroline noted that he was probably in his early thirties and had gorgeous wavy brown hair that flopped down over one eye. Suddenly, she was overcome by an impulse to push it back off his forehead. Instantly she blushed, astounded by her desire to touch this stranger, whose name she didn't even know!

"I'm Simon, by the way," he said, smiling and extending his hand.

"I'm Caroline. Thank you so much for your help!" She felt weak at the touch of his hand.

"I'm sure someone else would have helped you," Simon replied self-effacingly. "It's been *my* good fortune to be on the spot when it happened. It's not every day that a gorgeous woman falls at my feet!"

Caroline smiled. He was flirting with her. And even more to the point, she was enjoying it! Then she realised that she must look a mess, with her torn jeans and her blotchy tear-stained face. Quickly, she considered going to the bathroom to repair her make-up, but feared that he might slip away before she had a chance to get to know him better.

Then she came to her senses. There would be no 'getting to know him better'. She was about to get married to Ken, the man she loved, and besides, this handsome stranger was probably married anyway. Just because he'd been chivalrous to her in her hour of need didn't mean that there was any more to it than that. No doubt he lived in some gorgeous leafy suburb of London, or maybe even somewhere out of town, like Sussex or Kent. And there would be a beautiful wife, and probably a perfect baby, waiting for him when he got home each evening. And this particular evening, he'd mention to his beautiful wife that he'd met a daft Irish woman in Oxford Street, who'd been so brain-dead from shopping that she hadn't noticed the mugger until he'd actually grabbed her bag.

"Are you feeling a bit better now?" Simon asked, looking concerned. "You might have a delayed reaction, you know. I'll stay with you until you feel fully recovered."

"No, please – I don't want to delay you," Caroline said, her heart plummeting. It was obvious that he was only hanging around to make sure she was okay. No doubt he wanted to rush home to the beautiful wife and perfect baby.

"I don't *want* to go – unless you want to get rid of me," Simon replied, an earnest look on his face. "I'd really like to see you again."

Caroline felt her hormone levels surge. She could hardly believe it – this gorgeous man wanted to see her again!

"Unless, of course, you're married, or about to be," Simon added hastily. "I wouldn't want to offend you in any way."

"Oh. No, I'm not married," Caroline told him, hiding her left hand which sported Ken's engagement ring.

Simon looked pleased. "That's a relief. It's just that I saw you coming out of the bridal shop just before that guy attacked you. So I was afraid you might have been shopping for wedding stuff."

"One of my friends is getting married," said Caroline hastily. "Three of us are over here on a shopping trip."

"Well, thank goodness you haven't lost your money or credit cards," said Simon, smiling. "Being mugged is bad enough, but losing your cash would really put a damper on your trip." He surveyed her carefully, and Caroline felt herself turning pink again. "I think you're getting your colour back. You were as white as a sheet when I helped you up off the street. Are your knees still hurting?"

Caroline had become so enamoured of Simon that she'd completely forgotten about her knees. Now she checked them, and noted that the blood had dried up, although her jeans were a write-off, and her palms were still sore.

"I'm fine thanks," she told him, smiling. Even if her knees had been killing her, she wouldn't have wanted to draw attention to them, or to the torn jeans. Simon was immaculately dressed, whereas she now felt like a tramp. She had no idea how he could possibly be attracted to her.

"Would you like another cup of coffee?"

Caroline shook her head, then regretted refusing. She was all mixed up, but she was becoming deeply conscious of how awful she looked, and how desperately she wanted to get back to the hotel and get changed. She felt that the longer Simon saw her like this, the more likely he was to regret asking to see her again. At least refusing the coffee would bring things to a head.

"Okay then, if you feel well enough to leave, I'll walk you to the nearest underground station," said Simon cheerfully. "Are you staying with family or friends?"

"No, we're staying at a small hotel near Charing Cross. We found it on the Internet."

"Great! I live in Belsize Park, so we're both on the

Northern Line. Can I take you out for dinner this evening?"

Caroline's heart soared, then she remembered with annoyance that she and the others were going to the theatre that evening.

"Sorry, Simon, but my friends and I are going to the West End this evening to see a show – but I'm free tomorrow night, if that would suit?"

"Fine," Simon replied. "I'll pick you up at your hotel tomorrow evening at seven. Is that okay?"

Caroline nodded.

"And let's exchange mobile numbers as well, so that there's no chance of me losing you," Simon added.

Caroline's heart was beating wildly. He really wanted to see her again!

Later, as she sat in the tube taking her back to the hotel, Caroline marvelled at what could happen in the space of a few hours. She was thrilled and excited to be meeting Simon again, but unsure of what she would say to the others. She'd tell them the truth, of course, but she knew they'd be astonished and perturbed that she'd arranged a date with a man other than Ken, and concerned that she might be jeopardising her future.

Caroline shrugged her shoulders. She felt reckless. She wasn't married yet, so she was going to have some fun with Simon. It wasn't as though she was going to sleep with him, was it? Yet even as she thought the words, she realised that more than anything, she wanted to feel his lips on hers and hold his naked body close to hers. A thrill ran through her. Or was it a chill? Maybe she *was* jeopardising more than she had a right to.

Briefly, Caroline thought of Ken, but just as quickly she

dismissed him from her mind. She felt excited and giddy, as though Simon had hypnotised her and she was enjoying the sensation of having no control over the situation. Smiling to herself, Caroline sat back in her seat and watched the underground stations fly by. This time tomorrow, she'd be getting ready to meet Simon.

CHAPTER 13

The journey back to Dublin had been miserable, with neither Bill nor Alice saying a word to each other. Alice was angry, and ready to attack Bill if he dared to open his mouth. Bill was contrite, and uncertain what to say or do that wouldn't antagonise Alice further. In stony silence, they took a taxi back to Killiney, to the beloved house that would soon no longer be theirs.

When Alice saw the house from the taxi, she immediately burst into tears, and Bill had been left to pay the astonished taxi driver while Alice disappeared into her beloved garden to seek sanctuary among her plants. An hour later, she let herself into the kitchen, and Bill heard her making a cup of tea before taking it into the spare bedroom.

The next two days were spent in mutual misery, with both Bill and Alice fielding calls as much as possible. Other than confirming their safe return and great holiday to family and friends, neither left the house. Alice rang the newspaper office and told Dan Daly's secretary that she'd picked up some sort of bug in Cyprus, and wouldn't be in for a few days. She felt that this brief respite would enable her to get her act together.

Alice could hear that Bill was still engaged in huddled phone calls behind closed doors. No doubt, she thought savagely, he was trying desperately to delay the inevitable, or to cover his tracks. Well, let him work his way out of this dilemma without dragging her into it! Then again, she was already in it, wasn't she? She was losing her beloved home because of Bill's carry-on. But perhaps worst of all was the fact that the man she'd married wasn't the man she'd thought he was after all.

Alice busied herself in the garden, weeping intermittently in the garden shed when it all got too much for her. She felt that her beloved plants were facing the death penalty, since undoubtedly a developer would get his hands on the property and build as many faceless apartments as the site would hold.

On the third day after their return home, Alice made a trip into the city centre, and returned home feeling even more depressed. She'd been to see an accountant, to get an unbiased view of their present financial situation, and the discussion had only confirmed her worst fears.

As for her marriage – well, Alice wasn't sure if it could survive. Her mind was in turmoil, and at times she felt that she was losing her sanity. Although she still loved Bill, she hadn't a shred of respect left for him. Could a marriage survive on that basis?

Did she love him enough to stay with him, even though she despised him? Her love had been shaken to its core, and all the dreams she'd had, of a long and happy life together, were suddenly meaningless.

For the first time in her marriage, Alice was glad that they didn't have any children. As a couple, they'd decided to establish themselves in their careers before starting a family. Now Alice was relieved, since she doubted if she could have coped with the demands of young children while feeling this way. The thought also sneaked into her mind that maybe it was better that way, just in case the marriage didn't survive. On the other hand, she'd never contemplated having anyone else's children but Bill's. Now, she wondered if she'd ever have his children, and the uncertainty left her feeling wretched.

Alice felt both tearful and disloyal at even having such thoughts, and angry with Bill for creating the situation whereby the future of her marriage was called into question. Sometimes she loved him, other times she hated him. When she loved him, she hated him for breaking her heart, and when she hated him, she felt the urge to throw her arms around him and tell him that they'd survive somehow. She was totally mixed up, and there was no one she felt able to talk to.

On the forth morning, Bill came into the kitchen just as Alice was about to put the kettle on.

"Look, Alice – this can't go on. We've got to talk."

Alice continued to ignore him, busying herself with filling the kettle, and pointedly making herself a solitary sandwich.

"Alice – if you'll just listen to me, there might be a way we could save the house –"

Alice stopped what she was doing, a wild look of hope in her eyes.

"You know that inheritance you've been left by your late father's sister –"

Alice raised her eyebrows. "It's not even through probate yet."

"No, but it will be in another month or two. If you let me use it to pay off some of my creditors, and re-schedule the debts, then we might be able to save the house."

Alice looked at him with contempt in her eyes. "Bill, yesterday I went to see an accountant, and he says that in order to properly assess the situation, he'd need you to list all the company's assets and liabilities, as well as our own personal financial situation. Are you prepared to do that?"

Bill gulped. "I can't. There's more to it than that, I'm afraid." Suddenly, he slumped down into a kitchen chair, and Alice was overcome by a further sense of foreboding.

"Like what?" she whispered. Could things get any worse?

"Oh God, I'm sorry about all this." Bill looked up at her, his face bleak. "Deposits that people have been paying me for those apartments in Portugal – well, I've been using them to prop up the company, and now all that money is gone too." He refused to look her in the eye. "There are other things too, things I can't tell an accountant about . . ."

Alice could barely speak. "What sort of things?"

Bill fell silent. Finally he looked up at Alice, as though deciding how much he should tell her. "There's quite a bit of tax owing as well. And an associate of mine asked me to wash some money for him –"

Alice could hardly believe what she was hearing. "Wash some money – as in money-laundering? Oh Bill, how could you?"

"Look, I had no choice! Besides, it was just a once-off thing –"

Alice felt as though she was crying inside. This man

she'd married – this man to whom she'd committed herself for life, was suddenly a stranger to her. How could he have done such underhand things? He was no better than a common thief, and their home – the house she loved so much – had been bought using other people's money. She felt sick.

"So there's really no guarantee that the house can be kept out of the bank's clutches, is there?" she said coldly. "You'll promise me anything to get yourself out of a difficult situation! If I let you use my inheritance, I could simply be throwing good money after bad. And if you fail –" she gave him a contemptuous look, "– then I've lost my inheritance as well as my home. I don't think so, Bill."

Bill slumped across the table, his head now in his hands. "I thought you'd understand, Alice – you of all people. You're my wife, godammit, you're not supposed to turn your back on me . . ."

Alice turned and walked out of the kitchen. She could no longer bear to look at Bill. The last few days had led to a quantum shift in her respect for her husband. Yet in all honesty, wasn't she herself partly to blame? She'd willingly availed of all the good things that Bill's career had provided, without ever questioning the ease with which so much money came their way. She'd made too many assumptions, and those assumptions had now been proved totally wrong.

Then again, should she throw away her marriage just because they'd have to get a smaller house, and live a bit more frugally? She earned a good salary herself, so they wouldn't exactly starve. Assuming that Bill loved her too, maybe they could still make a go of it. Alice knew that the one thing she could never forgive was infidelity, but Bill's stupidity and venality was hardly grounds to give up on a relationship. Women stood by their husbands even when they went to jail, didn't they? Alice shivered. Jail was also a distinct possibility for Bill if he couldn't resolve his present financial problems. She couldn't let him go to jail, could she? Not while she had the means to prevent it. Maybe she *would* give him the inheritance money. Whether or not their marriage survived, perhaps she owed him that much anyway. But she needed time to make her mind up about that, and about her own future.

And suddenly, she knew what she was going to do.

Turning on her heel, she returned to the kitchen, where Bill was still sitting, gazing miserably into space.

"Bill, I'm going to take a break – go away for a while." She couldn't help but feel satisfaction at the incredulous look on his face. "Yes, I know – we're only just back from holidays. But I need time to figure out a lot of things. I've been appalled at what you've told me about our finances, and I'm devastated at losing the house. And besides, I don't think we're the best of company for each other at the moment. A bit a space might be a good thing for both of us."

"Where are you thinking of going?"

"South America," said Alice firmly. "Argentina, to be exact. I've always wanted to go there, and I think that this is the ideal time. I'll travel around on my own, and it'll give me time to think about the future."

Bill wore a stunned expression on his face. "But what about work? You've already used up half of your annual leave going to Cyprus."

"I actually don't care," said Alice firmly. "I intend leaving for Argentina next week, or certainly by the week after, and if Dan Daly doesn't like it, too bad. I can always get another job when I come back."

Bill looked at her incredulously. Alice had always taken her career so seriously! She was well known and highly regarded as an investigative journalist, and her name was on most people's lips when they wanted to learn the truth behind some public or private scam.

"Bill, I need some space. I can't go on like this – I need to get away. Your financial wheelings and dealings have made a mockery of my job anyway. How can I write about exposing corruption, when my own husband is up to the same thing? Maybe I'm fooling myself, but I feel that I can sort things out more easily when I'm at a distance from here."

"You mean from me," said Bill sullenly.

Alice didn't reply. He was right – the person from whom she wanted to distance herself most was him.

Bill looked up at her, his eyes tired and despairing. "But your mother and your friends – and my family too – what are we going to tell them?"

"You can tell your own family whatever you like," Alice said curtly. "I intend telling my mother, and Isobel, the truth. As for anyone else, it's none of their business. I'll tell other friends and people I know that I'm simply taking a sabbatical while I work out what I'm going to do with my future."

Bill looked at the ground as he spoke. "Am I part of that future, Alice?"

"I don't know, Bill," she said sadly. "Right now, I just don't know.

CHAPTER 14

"I don't believe it! You met a man in the street, and you're going to go out with him?" Liz looked horrified as she stared at her cousin.

The three women were in Caroline's hotel bedroom, where she was gingerly removing her torn jeans and examining her bloodstained kneecaps.

"So?" said Caroline, shrugging her shoulders. "I'm not married yet, and besides, I'm only meeting him for dinner. There's no harm in that, is there?"

"It's what happens later that I'd be worried about," said Hazel darkly. "Assuming he pays for dinner, he's going to want a *quid pro quo,* isn't he?"

"God, you're such cynics!" said Caroline in disgust. "You haven't even met the man, yet you're both ready to condemn him. He's really very nice, you know." She stared indignantly at them both. "Besides, I haven't heard either of you expressing much sympathy for my ordeal at the hands of the mugger!"

"It's the mugger I feel sorry for," Liz riposted.

"What about Ken?" asked Hazel pointedly. "Have you forgotten that you're on a shopping trip to buy your wedding dress – for your forthcoming marriage to your fiancé?"

"Stop, both of you!" said Caroline, annoyed. "Maybe I just want a bit of excitement before I settle down."

"This guy could be a mass murderer," added Hazel ominously. "You don't need *that* kind of excitement. Remember Ted Bundy!"

"You're both determined that I won't have any fun, aren't you?" said Caroline indignantly. "I should never have bothered telling you!"

"Aw Caro, we're only concerned about you," said Liz, giving her cousin a hug.

"We told Ken we'd look after you – I don't think he'd be too impressed if he knew you were going out on a date with another man!"

"Well, he's not going to find out, is he?" Caroline retorted. "You both know the saying – 'What goes on tour stays on tour'!"

"Obviously, our lips are sealed," said Liz soothingly. "But why are you doing this, Caro? Is Ken so boring that you need something else in your life?"

"I don't know," Caroline replied sullenly, sitting down on her bed. "I'm probably scared of the inevitability of it all. Nice man, good job, nice house. Is that all the future holds?"

"That's good enough for most women," said Hazel.

At which point Caroline burst into tears.

"There, there," said Liz, putting her arms around her cousin. "You're obviously on edge because that nasty bastard tried to snatch your bag. You're probably having a delayed reaction."

Liz and Hazel nodded imperceptibly to each over Caroline's head, both of them now satisfied that Caroline's 'date' was no more than a bizarre reaction to the afternoon's earlier stressful events. By tomorrow, she'd probably be embarrassed, and begging them to get rid of this Simon fellow when he called.

"C'mon – it's time to get showered and changed," said Hazel, attempting to change the subject as she headed for the door. "Caro, do you feel well enough to go out? If not, we can forget about the theatre, and just go for a quiet meal instead."

"No, I'm fine," said Caroline, not wanting to ruin the others' evening. In truth, she'd have preferred to stay in her hotel room and avail of room service, but she knew the others were excited about seeing a show in London's West End.

"See you in half an hour," she told the others as they left and headed off to their own rooms.

But as soon as they'd gone, Caroline realised that she was definitely having a delayed reaction to the mugging. She felt herself shivering uncontrollably, and she hoped that a shower and a change of clothes would remedy the situation. Suddenly, she wished that Ken was with her. He'd put his big arms around her and assure her that everything was all right. He'd protect her, and make sure no one ever harmed her again. If he'd been with her, nothing like this would have happened anyway.

In the shower, she let the warm water soothe her as it cascaded over her body. But the warm water also made her knees sting, and ruefully she examined the scabs that were now forming on both cut knees. No short skirts for *her* for the next few weeks!

As she lathered her body with shower gel, Caroline wondered what she would wear the following evening for her date with Simon. The clothes she'd brought on the trip with her were mainly casual, designed for shopping rather than dating! Maybe she'd just have to buy something stunning for the occasion. As for her underwear – well, what she'd brought with her was serviceable, but certainly not sexy! Then again, London had lots of specialist lingerie shops, so maybe she'd treat herself to a pretty lace bra and panties, to wear under her new sexy outfit.

Suddenly, Caroline froze. What was she thinking of? She was getting married to Ken in a few months' time, yet here she was, planning to dress sexily for a date with another man! She ought to be ashamed of herself. Liz and Hazel were right – the mugging must have affected her brain.

Quickly, she stepped out of the shower, dried and dressed herself. She selected a T-shirt, jeans and a short cotton jacket, and smiled as she surveyed the finished effect in the bathroom mirror. She looked comfortable and casual, and perfectly dressed for an evening in which there was no pressure on her to perform. Tonight, the actors onstage would be the ones in the limelight.

In the hotel lobby, Liz and Hazel surveyed Caroline's relaxed demeanour with obvious approval as she stepped out of the lift to join them. Clearly they'd decided that her earlier outburst had merely been a temporary aberration, and that she'd now returned to normal.

"I hope you're both hungry," said Liz. "I'm starving!"

"Me too," said Hazel. "I could eat a farmer's arse through a chair, as the expression goes!"

"I'm hungry too," Caroline admitted, realising that she

hadn't eaten all day. She'd been about to break for a snack when the mugger had struck, and she'd only managed a coffee with Simon.

"Great!" said Hazel. "Liz and I have booked pre-theatre dinner for three at a restaurant near the theatre."

Caroline gave each of her friends a quick hug. "You're wonderful, the pair of you," she told them, checking her watch. "Now, let's go and eat or we'll be too late for the show."

CHAPTER 15

The following day, the trio went shopping again, but this time Caroline wasn't thinking about wedding dresses. Instead, she was looking for a tight, sexy dress that would show off all her curves – and drive Simon wild when she met him later that evening.

Both Liz and Hazel were careful not to mention Simon at all, each of them hoping that Caroline had decided against meeting him again. But they glanced worriedly at each other when Caroline declared that she intended going off shopping on her own for a while. They were both keen to keep as close tabs on Caroline as possible.

"Will you be all right?" Liz asked her anxiously, unsure of whether she was worried about Caroline meeting Simon, or meeting another mugger.

"Wouldn't it be better if we all stuck together?" Hazel added brightly.

"I'll be fine," said Caroline determinedly. "I want to do some shopping on my own, but I'll meet you later for something to eat, if you like."

Liz and Hazel looked at each other with resignation. When Caroline was in a determined mood, there was no way of stopping her from doing exactly what she wanted.

"She's up to something," Liz whispered to Hazel, as Caroline set off on her solo shopping expedition. "Do you think she could be meeting this Simon fellow for lunch?"

Hazel shook her head. "If she was, she'd have spent a lot longer in front of the mirror. She's dressed too casually, and she's wearing no make-up at all. After all we've heard about Simon, I suspect he'll be getting the full works if she decides to meet him."

An hour later, Caroline turned up at the restaurant where they'd arranged to meet, looking happy and excited. She was clutching several shopping bags, and surreptitiously Liz and Hazel tried to read the store names on them. Curiosity was killing them both, but assuming Caroline didn't intend telling them what she'd bought, they definitely weren't going to ask.

After a light lunch, Caroline announced that she was heading back to the hotel for a rest. Liz and Hazel looked at each other in alarm. This wasn't like Caroline at all! Then suddenly, it dawned on them simultaneously that she was going back to get ready for her date that evening! Action was definitely called for.

"So you're meeting this Simon fellow this evening," Liz said matter-of-factly, taking the bull by the horns.

"I am," said Caroline stonily, "and I don't want to hear any further comments from either of you. I'm a big girl now, and I can take care of myself."

"Of course you can," said Hazel supportively. "We only want you to be happy, Caro."

Caroline suddenly grinned. "Then you can blow-dry my hair for me this evening. No one can get it looking quite as good as you can, Hazel."

Hazel grimaced. "Well, since you put it so nicely, what else can I do?"

Then Caroline turned to her cousin. "As for you, Liz – you can make yourself useful by giving me a manicure."

Liz raised her eyes to heaven. "God, how I rue the day I ever let you know I could do nails! By the way, what are you going to wear this evening?"

Caroline grinned wickedly from one to the other. "You'll just have to wait and see," she told them.

Liz and Hazel caught each other's eye. Now they both knew what was in Caroline's shopping bags!

"Well, Liz and I will stay out shopping for a little longer," Hazel announced, "but I'll be back at the hotel by five to do your hair. What time are you meeting Simon?"

"Seven."

"I'll do your nails while Hazel's doing your hair," said Liz, "but I feel as though I'm committing a crime against poor Ken. Hazel and I told him we'd look after you – I don't think this is quite what he had in mind!"

Back in her hotel room, Caroline unwrapped the gorgeous dark green dress she'd bought earlier. It really was fantastic! It clung to her body in all the right places, yet it was elegant and didn't make her look cheap. Next she unwrapped the contents of the second shopping bag. Just as important as the dress were the sexy undies she'd be wearing underneath! Simon might never see them, but she'd feel good just knowing they were there. Suddenly, Caroline grimaced to herself. Who was she fooling? She had every intention of letting Simon see her new underwear – briefly, before it came off! She felt giddy and guilty at the same time, and she quickly dismissed the vision of Ken that crept unbidden into her mind. She knew that she was being unfair to her fiancé, but some inexplicable and reckless force was urging her on. She felt frightened and exhilarated at the same time, and she longed to experience another man's touch and love-making before she settled down with one man for the rest of her life.

Later that evening, as Liz and Hazel helped Caroline get ready for her date, neither could resist a last-minute attempt at pricking her conscience.

"Are you phoning Ken before you go?" Liz asked pointedly as she buffed Caroline's fingernails. "I mustn't forget to ring Ronnie before Hazel and I go out for something to eat."

Caroline said nothing, just gave her a daggers look as she slipped into her new dress. Her hair had been blow-dried by Hazel and was looking fantastic.

"I presume you've asked this Simon fellow if he's married?" Liz ventured.

"No," said Caroline, annoyed, "but he'd hardly ask me out if he was, would he?"

"I don't see why not!" Hazel retorted indignantly, forgetting that she was barred from making any such comments. "English guys have a reputation for being economical with the truth in that respect."

"That's an awful thing to say!" said Caroline indignantly. "I'm not sure if it's racist or sexist, but I doubt if it's any more true of them than of Irish guys!"

"Well, what about all these randy vicars that we keep reading about in the English tabloids?"

Caroline gave a wry laugh. "I'm sure their vicars are no worse than our randy priests! I'd certainly prefer that they were intimate with other consenting adults, instead of those poor children in orphanages and industrial schools!"

"Well, I have to say you look stunning, Caro," said Liz warmly, trying to defuse the situation, "and your dress is absolutely gorgeous."

"Good luck, Caro," said Hazel, giving her friend a quick hug, but taking care not to muss Caroline's hair or crumple her dress.

Simon was collecting Caroline at the hotel, so Liz and Hazel intended taking a peep over the banisters at this man who'd managed to make Caroline forget all about her fiancé back home.

"He'd better be worth it," muttered Liz to Hazel as the duo stood at the bend in the stairs leading down to the foyer where Caroline was now waiting.

"We should probably be hoping that he doesn't turn up," whispered Hazel, "but I couldn't bear to see poor Caro disappointed."

Suddenly she felt a dig in the ribs. "Oh my God, that must be him!" Liz hissed. "He's gorgeous!"

Looking down, Hazel had to concede that Simon was, indeed, gorgeous. And his happy grin, when he saw Caroline approaching him, was endearing and heart-lifting. As both women turned and looked at each other, they were both having exactly the same thought. Could Caroline's instincts actually be right, *was* Simon the man for her?

"Oh God, it's so romantic, isn't it?" Liz whispered.

Hazel nodded. She and Liz had been hoping that Simon would turn out to be smarmy and horrible, so that they'd have no hesitation in urging Caroline to drop him. But now, they both felt torn by what they'd witnessed. As Caroline and Simon left the hotel, he'd kissed her cheek affectionately, and he'd taken her hand in his – both women wholeheartedly approved of men who made romantic gestures, and this Simon fellow seemed to be treating Caroline with obvious tenderness and affection.

"Oh God," said Liz again, this time resignedly. "I know I should feel worried that she's jeopardising her future with Ken, but maybe Caroline's instincts are right."

"I know," said Hazel, grimacing at her. "I don't know what to make of it all, either. Let's just hope that Caroline knows what she's doing."

CHAPTER 16

At that very moment, Caroline was perfectly sure that she knew what she was doing. Any doubts she might have had about the wisdom of meeting Simon again had been blown away when she saw him standing in the hotel foyer. He was every bit as gorgeous as she'd remembered. She loved his quirky smile, and the way his left cheek dimpled when he laughed.

His eyes lit up as he saw her waiting there.

"Are you okay?" he asked gently, as he took her hand in his. "Hopefully, you're over the shock of yesterday afternoon."

"Yes, I'm fine, thanks," Caroline replied, thrilled that he was so concerned about her welfare.

"And the knees?"

"Already starting to heal," Caroline informed him. That very moment, she wanted to thank the mugger, for providing the opportunity of meeting Simon!

Initially, Simon took her to a bar for an early evening drink, then to a delightful French restaurant, where he'd already booked a table. Caroline was impressed by his easy and relaxed attitude. He wasn't trying to impress or embarrass her by selecting a very expensive dining experience. Instead, he'd chosen somewhere that was perfect for the occasion. The atmosphere was low-key and relaxing, and as the evening progressed, Caroline realised that she hadn't enjoyed herself this much in ages.

In fact, they both laughed a lot, and experienced none of the awkward silences that often occurred between people who hardly knew each other. They had no need to search for common ground, because they found so much to talk about.

As they ate, Simon explained that he worked as a probate researcher for a large London company, and that his work involved finding heirs to estates where people had died intestate. Although the food was delicious, Caroline hardly tasted the food at all. All her attention was focussed on Simon, as she listened to the interesting and amusing stories he had to tell about his job. Although he was based in London, his work took him all over the country, as he tried to put relatives and estates together.

"In this country, if someone doesn't leave a will, the money goes to the Crown if relatives can't be found," he informed her.

"It's the same in Ireland," she informed him. "It goes into the government's coffers. What a pity some people don't leave wills – do you think it's because they're afraid to face their own mortality?"

"Probably," said Simon, "but it's silly, since there's nothing more certain than that we're all going to die. So why not have a say in where your money's going to go?"

"I'd leave anything I had to one of the animal charities – they never seem to get proper funding," said Caroline.

"Good idea," said Simon, approvingly. "I got my two cats from one of those animal rescue charities – they do sterling work."

Caroline gazed adoringly at Simon, hoping that she wasn't appearing quite as transparent as she felt. He was absolutely gorgeous, he liked animals – what more could any woman want?

"What are your cats called?"

"Oh, er – Anne and Derek."

"That's unusual – why haven't you called them something like Blackie or Spot?" Caroline asked, chuckling.

Simon grinned, shrugging his shoulders. "I suppose they feel like people to me. Anyway, by the time you fall off your perch, you'll probably have a large family to leave your assets to," he added.

Hopefully with you, Caroline thought, clamping her lips tightly together for fear she might say it out loud. Where had those words come from? What on earth was she thinking of? She must have had far too much wine!

In turn, Caroline told him about her own job as an accountant, then about her search for Aunt Gina, and of her visit to Larry Macken.

"Wow! That sounds really interesting!" Simon told her. "Maybe I can help you. In my line of business, I have access to lots of data that might prove useful."

Caroline was thrilled. It sounded like Simon intended seeing her again!

"More wine?"

Caroline nodded, and Simon topped up her glass. Feeling content and relaxed, Caroline sat back and sipped her wine. It was great having London's wonderful transport system for getting about. It meant that you could have a few drinks without worrying about driving home, or about having to pay the astronomical cost of a taxi, like you did back home. Briefly, Caroline wondered what would happen when the meal was over. Would Simon say goodnight and leave her at the underground station, or would he come back to the hotel with her? Or would he invite her to his place?

She had decided right from the start that she wouldn't be jumping into bed with Simon straightaway, in case he thought she was easy. But as they left the restaurant and he slipped his arm around her, she felt an overwhelming desire to spend the night with him. She felt giddy and happy, and absolutely enthralled by this wonderful man.

"I'll take you back to your hotel," he told her, and Caroline nodded happily in assent. Simon obviously wasn't going to try it on, for which she was grateful. Or was she? Suddenly, she was worried. Maybe he didn't find her attractive enough? Then she remembered that she had a fiancé back home in Dublin, but she quickly dismissed any thoughts of Ken from her brain.

Holding hands, she and Simon made their way towards the underground station, chatting as they walked along. Caroline marvelled at how relaxed she felt in his company, and hoped he felt the same. Although she'd always felt relaxed with Ken, this was different. Between her and Simon, there was still an acute awareness of each other, and an underlying excitement of something yet to be fulfilled. With Ken, there wasn't any excitement any longer.

Back in the hotel foyer, Caroline was relieved that there was no sign of either Liz or Hazel. She'd been worried in case they'd be waiting for her, ready to pounce on her and wrest her from Simon's grasp, just in case she was thinking of being unfaithful to Ken. At the very least, she feared they'd be lurking in the foyer, waiting to hear every detail of her evening. She was relieved that they weren't in the hotel bar either when Simon suggested a drink there and Caroline happily accepted. At least he wasn't saying goodbye yet, she thought gratefully, which seemed to confirm that he might reciprocate her feelings.

In the bar, where numerous other guests were relaxing, she and Simon sat beside each other on a large comfortable sofa. This gave them the opportunity to continue holding hands, and Caroline could sense that his desire was as strong as her own.

For a while, they made small talk as they each drank another glass of wine, then Simon made a move to stand up.

"I'd better be going," he said ruefully. "Early start tomorrow, you know."

Caroline nodded, almost afraid to speak, willing him to ask her out again.

"Can I see you again?" he asked, as if on cue.

Caroline let out a sigh of relief. He *did* fancy her!

"I'd love to, Simon, but I've got to get back to Dublin now and I can't be back in London for at least another week," Caroline told him. She was now frantically planning to take time off work, and get back to London as soon as possible!

"I don't think I can wait that long," Simon said, smiling at her. "Can I come and see you in Dublin?"

"God, no! I mean, that's a lot of trouble for you," Caroline said hastily. "I'll try to get back to London a bit sooner, if you like."

Caroline had visions of Simon arriving at the house she shared with Ken. What a disaster *that* would be!

Still holding hands, Caroline and Simon walked out to the foyer, Caroline savouring every moment that they were together.

"Goodnight, Caroline," Simon whispered, taking her in his arms and kissing her gently.

As his lips touched hers, Caroline felt a fire rage through her body, and she crushed herself to him. All pretence was gone – she wanted Simon, and she had no hesitation in letting him know it.

"Oh Caroline – you're gorgeous!" he whispered, as she felt his manhood pressing against her in response.

Never had she desired a man so desperately. When she and Ken made love, it was always gentle and unhurried, and comforting rather than earth shattering. With Simon, she wanted him in her, on her, under her, surrounding her. She couldn't get enough of this man. His body excited her, his mind intrigued her, his smile made her weak at the knees.

"Simon – do you have to go?" she whispered, hardly believing her own brazenness.

In answer, Simon kissed her again, and silently they both walked to the lift, still holding hands.

Outside her hotel room, Simon hesitated. "Are you sure about this, Caroline?" he asked, his fingers gently tracing the contours of her face.

"Yes," said Caroline, opening the door.

CHAPTER 17

The following morning, Caroline was up early, and down to breakfast before either Liz or Hazel made an appearance. As she helped herself to a bowl of grapefruit, she couldn't stop grinning, and she felt certain that everyone else in the dining room must know what she'd been up to the night before!

For some reason, she'd developed an amazing appetite. After she'd finished the grapefruit, she helped herself to a large fry from the hot buffet, and two slices of toast. She was halfway through buttering the first slice when Hazel appeared at her table.

"Good morning, Caroline! How are you today?"

"Fine, thanks," Caroline replied enigmatically, popping a piece of toast into her mouth.

"How was your evening with the gorgeous Simon?"

"Lovely, thanks. He's really nice."

Hazel was clearly angling for information, but Caroline wasn't going to make it easy for her! Besides, she wasn't sure if she wanted to tell either Hazel or Liz about her evening – her time with Simon felt private and personal. She found herself grinning again. Certainly, the latter part of the evening had been *very* personal!

Just then, Liz arrived.

"That Simon of yours is gorgeous," she said without preamble, sitting down at the table and helping herself to a piece of Caroline's toast.

Caroline was pleased to hear Liz refer to him as 'her' Simon. She gave Liz a big beam, then focussed on buttering the rest of her toast.

"So come on — tell us what happened," Liz begged.

"Why don't you get yourself some breakfast first?" Caroline suggested, deliberately prolonging their agony, and enjoying every second of it. It wasn't often that she could hold either of them to ransom like this!

At last, all three were sitting around the table, food in front of them, and a large pot of tea in the middle. Caroline continued eating her breakfast with obvious gusto, munching a lot and making a point of enjoying her food, much to Liz's and Hazel's annoyance.

"Go on — put us out of our misery," Liz said at last, her exasperation clearly showing.

Caroline feigned surprise. "What do you mean?"

"You know exactly what we mean!" said Hazel. "What happened with Simon? Where did he take you?"

"Did you go back to his place, and did you go to bed with him?" Liz added.

Caroline looked slowly from one to the other, clearly enjoying winding them up.

"That's a lot of questions," she said slowly. "I wonder which question I should answer first? Will I take them in chronological order, or will I answer the last one first?"

"Yes, please – last one first!" squealed Liz, "That's the only really important one! Did you have sex with him?"

Caroline didn't need to answer. Colour rushed to her cheeks, and all she could do was grin as Liz and Hazel stared at her.

"I don't believe it!" Liz shrieked, looking at her in amazement. "And to think that all these years, I thought butter wouldn't melt in my little cousin's mouth!"

"Are you going to see him again?" Hazel asked loudly. "If so, are you coming back to London, or is he coming to Dublin?"

Both of them were talking so animatedly that other diners in the room turned to see what was happening at their table.

"Stop making a holy show of yourselves!" Caroline told them both, feigning annoyance. But she couldn't stop grinning as the duo continued to stare at her in astonishment. "Eat up your breakfast, both of you!" she ordered, "or it's going to go cold!"

"Yes, Mammy," said Liz sarcastically.

Both Liz and Hazel began tucking into their food, feeling that they might need to build up their strength, in preparation for any further shocks Caroline might deliver!

As Caroline finished eating her own breakfast, she found herself blushing again as she thought back to the night she'd just spent with Simon. She couldn't believe she could behave so rampantly and passionately with anyone! She'd assumed that once she'd agreed to marry Ken, he'd be the one who'd fill her dreams, and would continue to be the only man she'd ever make love to again. But Simon had awakened a need in her that she'd never realised was there.

What exactly that need was, she wasn't sure. Was it just a need for excitement and novelty, or was it real gut-wrenching desire to always be with this man? Whatever it was, right now she was loving every moment of it.

Had she ever felt this way about Ken? Caroline had to admit that no, she never had. For as long as she could remember, Ken had been there, ever since the day they'd met in a group of friends outside the school gate, and he'd offered to carry her satchel of books home for her. He'd been tall and gangly then, but he'd filled out into a fine handsome man as he'd matured. A man, Caroline conceded, that any woman would be proud to marry.

From that day onwards, she and Ken had fallen into a routine of being together, and they were accepted as a couple by all their friends. Theirs had always been a warm, comfortable relationship, with no great insecurities, but equally no surprises. There has always been a tacit assumption that they'd marry one day, and their relationship had been conducted on that basis. They'd grown up together, partnered each other to their respective debs and university balls, studied and revised together before exams, and were pictured hugging each other in their graduation photographs. In turn, they'd been with each other at their respective Christmas office parties, family birthdays and anniversaries. Many of their friends had been openly envious of their strong relationship, and there had been times when Caroline had felt particularly fortunate and secure, especially when friends were having their hearts broken by callous guys who loved them and then left them.

Maybe the overwhelming passion she felt for Simon was simply because they'd met as adults rather than as school friends. From the outset, they were a mystery to each other, whereas she and Ken knew everything about each other, including each other's families, and had shared with each other all the milestones of growing up. Her relationship with Ken had provided a security net that protected her against unwelcome surprises. Caroline sighed. Perhaps that was exactly the problem with Ken – there were no surprises any more.

Was her attraction to Simon just the novelty of being with a man from a different culture, with different schooling, and a different way of life? Caroline shook her head vehemently. After all, she herself had been born in England, and had spent the first few years of her life in London, when her father had worked there in the building trade. She'd recently had to send off for a copy of her birth certificate in preparation for her wedding, and it had reminded her of places she'd long forgotten. Issued by the London Borough of Wandsworth, she was listed as the daughter of Stella Leyden, formerly Kiernan, and Patrick Leyden, and born in July 1978. She'd only hazy memories of the city, but lots of memories of her parents' love.

Her parents had returned to Dublin when she was of school-starting age, and fortunately, they'd managed to buy a house before inflation led to rocketing property prices. Theirs was a modest redbrick in Blackrock, a pleasant Southside suburb, but it was worlds away from the home Aunt Dolly had in Ballsbridge, the city's most exclusive suburb. A few years later, her beloved father had died of cancer, and her life, and her mother's, had been turned upside down. Even today, she missed the kind loving man she still remembered.

As Caroline finished her breakfast and drained her teacup, she suddenly remembered that Simon had also offered to help in her search for her Aunt Gina! But due to the excitement of the evening, all thoughts about finding her aunt had been temporarily suspended! Well, now she had an excuse for coming back to London the following weekend – to continue her search for Gina. And see the delectable Simon of course!

Suddenly Liz spoke, breaking in on Caroline's thoughts. "Are you seeing him again, Caro?"

Caroline nodded, the thought of Simon making her smile again.

"But what about Ken?" Hazel added, looking worried.

Caroline sighed, her smile fading. "I don't know," she said, "I honestly don't know."

CHAPTER 18

After half an hour back in the newsroom of the *Daily News,* Alice felt as though she'd never been away. In one sense, its monotonous routine was comforting. While the gathering of news was, in itself, exciting, its dissemination and shaping into news features often involved hours of sitting at a computer screen, which bored her rigid. But it was a necessary part of the process, and at times, particularly after several busy assignments, it was a relief to merely sit and type. Right now, there was nothing she would welcome more than a few hours of routine research. But she knew it was not to be.

After lots of banter and queries about her holiday in Cyprus, her colleagues left her alone and returned to their workstations. Now, it was time to face the lion in his den.

Purposefully, Alice strode into Dan Daly's office.

"Good morning, Dan."

Dan Daly turned a sour face towards her. "What's good about it?"

"Well, I thought you might be pleased to have your ace reporter back."

Daly snorted. "If you ever manage to turn in some decent copy, sweetheart, I might consider you'd reached junior-cub level. What do you want anyway? Your assignments for today are up on the board. Or have you forgotten what a duty roster is?"

Alice had indeed noticed that Dan had rostered her on for the coming weekend – a nasty gesture that was typical of the man.

"Dan – I really need to take some time off. While I was away, something happened, and I need a break –"

Dan Daly looked at her in disbelief. "For fuck's sake, Fitzsimons, you're only back! Is this some kind of joke? Because if it is, I'm not exactly in the mood for jokes –"

"You never are, Dan, but believe me, I need this time off. I wouldn't ask you otherwise."

"Does it look like I was born yesterday?"

Alice gave him a brief grin. "A newborn baby is bald and toothless, Dan. You're much better looking than that!"

Then she had a sudden inspiration. If she pretended that she was following up a story, she might manage to get the time off!

She leaned forward conspiratorially. "Dan, the truth is, I want to go undercover on a story."

"Under the covers with who, I wonder? Go on the piss, more likely. What do you take me for? On second thoughts – don't answer that."

"Dan –"

"Jesus, Fitzsimons – call yourself a fucking journalist? What the hell could you have to say that would fill more than a postage stamp?"

Alice grinned. "Well, Dan – you'll just have to wait and

see. But it might be worth taking the risk – and you'll be the guy who'd get most of the credit."

"The sack, you mean. Are you out of your mind, Fitzsimons? You've just had two weeks' holiday, and four days sick leave. Go take a hike."

"I swear, Dan, I have to go. This story won't wait."

"And I love you too, sweetie. Fuck off, Fitzsimons – I've got more important things to do than give you another holiday."

Annoyed, Alice left Daly's small office, to find Isobel Dunne waiting to go in. It was obvious that she'd overheard the final exchange of words between the two.

"Thanks, Alice," Isobel said, grinning sarcastically, "you've put him in a great mood. Now I'm going to get it in the neck too."

"Dan's never in a good mood," Alice replied, thoroughly pissed off.

"Well, he's even worse today – it looks like he's finally decided to divorce Brenda."

"Really? Well then, I wish he'd get on with it. They've been on the verge of break-up for years."

"They got back together while you were away on holidays. Then Dan blew it by picking up some bimbo in a bar."

Alice laughed. "God, he's a right old drama queen! Can't stand the boredom of a happy marriage."

"One of them is as bad as the other. Brenda's now gone back to some former boyfriend of hers, and Dan's ready to blow his top."

"Just my luck to need a favour when he's in that kind of mood."

Dan suddenly banged on the window of his office. "Have you pair of witches got nothing better to do than gossip?"

Isobel's expression quickly became contrite. "Sorry, Dan – I'm just coming in to talk to you –" She winked back at Alice and did a quick twirl. "Notice anything?"

"Yeah – you've lost weight. You look great."

"Does that mean I didn't look great before?"

Alice grinned in exasperation. "That's the last compliment you'll ever get from me, Dunne! Who are you directing your feminine wiles at these days?"

"I was hoping that Brian Kelly might finally notice how gorgeous I am."

Alice nodded, although her thoughts were elsewhere. "Are you free for coffee later?" she asked "I need to talk to you before I leave."

Isobel raised her eyebrows. "Leave where?"

"The job, if necessary. I've got loads to tell you."

Isobel looked shocked. "My God, things must be bad – you love your job! Okay, I can be free at lunch time – I'll meet you in the bistro for a sandwich, at one."

Alice nodded, and Isobel squeezed her arm encouragingly before marching into Dan Daly's office.

Alice looked around the office, and was suddenly filled with a terrible sense of loss. She loved this office; she liked most of her colleagues and didn't want to leave. But she had to get away. If Dan Daly wouldn't allow her to take any leave of absence, she'd simply tell him where he could stick his job. She was a good enough journalist to get another position when she got back. In fact, she'd recently been approached by a rival newspaper whose editor liked her investigative style. She could always approach them if Dan got really nasty. She sighed. Right now, she was longing to get on that plane to Argentina.

In a few hours' time, she'd explain everything to Isobel. It would be good to talk to a trustworthy friend.

* * *

"You're not serious! Argentina? But why, Alice?"

Quickly, Alice filled in her friend on all that had happened since she'd left to go on holiday.

"Oh my God, you poor love!" Isobel said, her eyes wide with shock. "I could strangle Bill for putting you in this position. And the house – oh Alice, I know you love it so much! Is there any hope of saving it?"

Alice shook her head, tears beginning to fall into her coffee cup. It was so therapeutic to be able to talk to Isobel like this. She'd need to tell her mother in due course, but right now what she needed most was the non-judgemental support of a close friend.

"I just need to get away, Izzy – can you understand that? I just want to put distance between myself and Bill for a while – I need to sort out in my own head whether I'm going to stay with him or not."

Isobel nodded sympathetically. "And to think that I believed you two were the original lovebirds – together forever!"

Alice nodded, chewing her lip, her eyes filling with fresh tears.

"Well, maybe you will be," Isobel added hastily. "I presume Bill wants the marriage to continue?"

Alice nodded. "He's even making plans to use my inheritance to get him out of trouble."

"What? Well, I never!" Isobel looked outraged. "But that's your money, left to you by your father's sister. You're not going to give it to him, are you?"

Alice sighed. "I don't know, Isobel. I'm going to think about it while I'm away. Part of me thinks I should, then the other part thinks – to hell with him! If I knew for certain that it could be used to save the house, I'd definitely hand it over, but I don't think debtors can specify to their creditors what their cash injection is to be spent on!"

"Couldn't you take on the mortgage yourself?"

Alice shook her head. "It's far too large – no bank would lend to me anyway, since my salary wouldn't even make a dent in the repayments."

"So what are you going to do now? Are you coming back to the newsroom today?"

Alice nodded. "I've booked a flight to Buenos Aires for this day next week, so I'm going to finish out the week at work. I'm actually glad to be back – it's keeping me from thinking about how bad things are at home." She sighed. "And maybe I can work on Dan Daly, and get him to give me the time off." Suddenly, she grimaced. "Earlier this morning, I tried to convince him that I wanted to go undercover on a story, but he didn't fall for it!"

"Well, you'll probably find some interesting stories while you're on your travels anyway. You could certainly get Dan to take a travel piece for the weekend supplement."

"To be honest, I just want to forget about journalism while I'm away," Alice said. "Besides, if Dan wants to be awkward, I could be looking for another job when I come back. But I really don't care."

"You'll have no trouble getting another job – maybe

even a better one," said Isobel supportively. "But I'll miss you terribly if you leave! We'll only get to meet up in our spare time – I like having you around every day!"

The two friends hugged emotionally.

"We'd better stop this whinging," said Isobel at last, "in case some of the guys from the newsroom come in for lunch. We don't want them knowing any more than they have to."

"And you wouldn't want Brian Kelly to spot you in another woman's arms," said Alice, grinning. "He might get the wrong impression, and it might ruin your chances!"

Just then, their sandwiches arrived, and Isobel ordered fresh coffees.

"How long are you going to Argentina for?" she asked, as they munched in unison.

"A month. At least, that's the plan at the moment," Alice replied. "Luckily, I've an open ticket, so I can change the return date if I need to."

"It sounds fantastic!" said Isobel dreamily. "I wish I was going with you! If it wasn't for my own mortgage, I'd tell Dan Daly to stuff his job and come with you."

Alice grinned. "Surely you couldn't bear to be that far away from Brian Kelly?"

"Maybe he'd miss me so desperately, that he'd propose the minute I arrived back!"

"But you haven't even been on a date with him yet!"

"I know, but I'm certain that everything would work out perfectly!" said Isobel dramatically.

Alice grinned. Her friend's love life was erratic and confused, to say the least. Isobel was always on the lookout for Mr Right, but so far none of her relationships had worked out. Privately, Alice thought that Isobel tried too hard, but nothing could dissuade her friend from throwing herself at every reasonably good-looking man that crossed her path. Alice regularly urged caution, but Isobel's exuberance always won the day.

"So tell me," said Isobel, as she finished her sandwich, "what's Argentina like?"

"At the moment, I know very little about it," said Alice. "Anything I do know is gleaned from guide books. But I've always wanted to go there – I have this idea in my head that Argentina consists of vast open spaces, fields of crops and cattle stretching as far as the eye can see, hot and dusty streets in little towns and villages . . ."

"Sounds so romantic!"

"Maybe you and Brian Kelly can go there on your honeymoon," said Alice grinning mischievously.

"You may well laugh, you cruel woman," said Isobel disdainfully, "but by the time you get back, I'll definitely have Brian Kelly eating out of my hand."

CHAPTER 19

Ken was waiting at Dun Laoghaire port when they arrived back in Dublin, and Caroline had the decency to blush as Liz and Hazel both gave her knowing looks.

"Caro – it's great to have to back!" Ken whispered, gathering her into his big arms, and hugging her tightly. "I've missed you terribly!"

Then, much to Caroline's relief, he released her and hugged Liz and Hazel too.

"Did you all have a great time?" Ken asked them conversationally as they loaded their luggage and shopping bags into the boot of his car.

"Yes, brilliant!" said Hazel, giving Caroline a dig in the ribs. "Unfortunately, Caro didn't have any luck with finding a wedding dress, but she did manage to pick up some other interesting things on her travels!"

Caroline gave Hazel a daggers look. "Yes," she said hastily, "I got some very nice clothes, and an antique lamp for the house. The hotel was lovely, and we ate in a lot of nice restaurants too." She knew she was babbling, but she felt the need to fill the silence so that neither Hazel nor Liz got the chance to make any further innuendoes.

While they sat in the back seat behind Ken, Liz raised her eyebrows in Caroline's direction. At which point Caroline decided that she wasn't going to make eye contact with either her cousin or her friend until she had to say goodbye to them outside their own homes. She felt guilty enough about her liaison with Simon, and didn't want the two women making her feel worse by their nudges and innuendos behind Ken's back. She knew they were only teasing her but, beneath the camaraderie, she was aware that they were also worried in case she was risking her long-term relationship for the sake of a brief fling. Caroline was worried herself too, but she didn't feel that Simon was just a fling to her. She desperately wanted to see him again, yet she also desperately wanted to protect Ken from being hurt. Was she just being dishonest with herself, as well as with Ken?

Eventually, when Liz and Hazel had been dropped off at their respective homes with all their shopping bags, Ken headed back towards their own house in Monkstown. As Caroline sat beside him, her thoughts were still of London, and of the man she'd left behind. If Ken noticed her silence, he said nothing. Hopefully he assumes I'm tired, Caroline thought, glancing guiltily at her fiancé.

Arriving back at their semi-detached house in a small housing estate, Caroline studied the other houses dispassionately. Is this all I want for the rest of my life? she asked herself, then felt horribly guilty when Ken came around and opened her car door with a warm smile on his face.

"Poor old Caro, I know you're bound to be exhausted after your trip. You go inside and I'll bring in all your shopping, okay?"

"Thanks, Ken – I *am* knackered."

"And I thought we'd just get a take-away this evening. Is that all right with you?"

Caroline nodded. The very last thing on her mind was food.

Inside the house, she surveyed her surroundings. Everything was exactly the same as when she'd left – except for her. She wasn't the same person who'd once chosen the coffee-coloured paint for the walls or the cream three-piece suite. She felt different. She *was* different.

Cheerfully, Ken collected Caroline's luggage and new purchases from the boot of the car and brought them into the living room.

"I like the lamp, Caro, but what's this clapped-out old suitcase for?" Ken asked, carrying in the suitcase that Larry Macken had given her. "I thought it belonged to either Hazel or Liz, but they both assured me it was yours." He grinned as he placed it beside her on the sofa. "You didn't bring that old thing all the way from London, did you? I hope this isn't your idea of an antique!"

Amused at his own joke, Ken began whistling as he went out into the kitchen to put on the kettle.

Caroline pursed her lips. How dare he comment on her aunt's suitcase in that way! It might look rather quaint now, but she had no doubt that back in the 70s, it had been considered quite stylish. Antique indeed!

"Yes, I did bring it all the way from London, because it belonged to my Aunt Gina," she told him angrily as Ken returned with two mugs and placed one on the coffee table in front of her.

"You didn't tell me that you were going to look for your aunt," said Ken, looking injured.

"Oh, it was just a spur-of-the-moment decision," Caroline

lied. "Since I was over there and had some spare time, I thought it might be worth looking up Gina's husband."

Bewildered, Ken shook his head. "I thought we'd agreed you weren't going to upset your family by raking up the past?"

Caroline immediately bristled. "I never agreed any such thing, and besides, it's none of your business what I do about my family!"

"Well, if they're coming to my wedding, then it *is* my business!" Ken snapped back.

"Oh, so it's *your* wedding now?" said Caroline. "Next you'll be telling me I have no say in it at all! Well, if that's your attitude, you can take a hike!"

Gathering up the old suitcase and all her new possessions, Caroline marched into the spare bedroom cum office and slammed the door shut. She was relieved to see that the bed was already made up, so she wouldn't have the embarrassment of having to leave the room again to go and collect bed linen from the hot press.

Sitting on the spare bed, Caroline fumed. How dare Ken tell her not to search for her aunt! And Liz and Hazel seemed to think that they could tell her what to do about Simon. How dare they all sit in judgement on her! She was sick and tired of everyone interfering in her life. If she wanted to find her aunt, and if she wanted to see Simon again, she'd do exactly as she pleased! It was her life, and any mistakes she made were her responsibility. She wasn't asking anyone else to pick up the pieces if things went wrong, was she? In both instances, she felt that she had to see things through to the end. Whatever that might be.

If she could find her Aunt Gina, then she'd have solved a family mystery. And it might enable her to bring all three sisters together again. As an only child herself, she'd often longed for a sister of her own. Had she been lucky enough to have one, she'd never have let time and distance separate them, like her mother and her two siblings had.

And Simon. She'd never felt such excitement and passion as when he made love to her. Maybe he truly was the man for her. Surely it was only right that she should give herself the opportunity to find out?

Caroline sighed as she lay down on the bed. She knew in her heart that she'd engineered the fight with Ken so that she wouldn't have to sleep in the same bed as him, and therefore he wouldn't be able to make any sexual advances to her. Right now, she didn't want anyone making love to her except Simon.

Suddenly, she was conscious of knocking on the door.

"Caro, your tea's made. Will I bring it in?"

"I don't want any bloody tea!" Caroline shouted back. She knew she wasn't being fair to Ken, but somehow, she couldn't stop herself.

There was a few moments' silence.

"Well then, what about the take-away – do you want the same as usual?"

Caroline, feeling angry and confused, hurled the lamp she'd bought at the door which it hit with a thud, then crashed to the ground, its beautiful shade dented, the base in smithereens.

The same as usual, indeed. Caroline curled up in a ball and wept.

CHAPTER 20

Alone in the spare bedroom, Caroline dried her tears at last. She knew she was behaving ridiculously, but Simon seemed so far away, and she missed him desperately. She also felt guilty since poor Ken hadn't done anything to deserve her callous treatment of him. Jumping up off the bed, she opened Gina's suitcase. Even though things weren't going well with Ken, she might at least be able to advance her search for her aunt by going through the items in the suitcase again. She didn't care if he felt peeved about her search. Gina was *her* aunt, not his, and besides, the way she was feeling right now, there probably wouldn't be a wedding anyway.

Inside the suitcase were the photographs of Gina's wedding that she'd already looked at in London, and a selection of clothing that she now took out and examined in detail. She immediately recognised the long maxi-dress with geometric patterns on it – that had been Gina's wedding dress! It smelled musty after years of being locked in the suitcase, as did the flimsy chiffon top, the polo-necked jumpers, some blouses and long skirts. There was also a pretty half-slip at the bottom of the case, which Caroline thought might do as her 'something old' for her wedding day. *If* there was a wedding day. Right now, she didn't think she'd be marrying anyone. Maybe she'd become a nun, and lead a cloistered life of prayer and self-mortification. The peace and solitude would be preferable to the whirlwind of emotions she was currently experiencing!

Noting the size on the labels, Caroline realised that Gina and she were the same size. Quickly, Caroline took off her own clothes and slipped into Gina's wedding dress. Disappointingly, it only reached mid-way down her calves, so it was obvious that she was taller than Gina had been. Looking at the wedding photos again, Caroline could see that the dress had almost covered Gina's feet, and only the platform shoes had prevented her from tripping over it.

I wonder how she felt that day? Caroline wondered, as she gazed at the photos of the smiling Gina. Assuming she was pregnant with Owen's child, those smiles would have been hiding a lot of sorrow. And poor Larry, gazing rapturously into his bride's eyes, looked happy but self-conscious in his wide-lapelled suit with bell-bottomed trousers and wide kipper tie. Yet for him, that joyful day was just a precursor to the sorrow and loss that would soon come his way.

Will that happen to me, too? Caroline wondered. *Will I be standing at the altar, marrying a man I'm not sure I love any more, because I'm too scared to disappoint everyone? Or am I afraid to take a risk with Simon? After all, it may not work out, and then I've lost Ken anyway.*

Caroline was also aware that at almost thirty years of age, her options were narrowing. *Not that I need a man to* be happy, she conceded. I'm a liberated, intelligent woman with my own career. But she *did* want a man in her life, as well as a career. And she wanted to have children too, and to do the whole 'happy families' thing. But would it be Ken she'd do it with? Right now, she just didn't know. Meeting Simon had turned all her ideas and dreams on their heads.

Taking off Gina's wedding dress, Caroline put it back into the suitcase, and took out the large envelope that lay on the bottom. It didn't look particularly interesting, but Caroline lived in hope that somewhere in this suitcase she would find something – maybe part of a letter, or an old bill – that would lead her directly to Gina.

But when she emptied the envelope, she merely grimaced. Clearly, the answer to Gina's disappearance wasn't going to be found in here! The only thing the envelope contained was a document, maybe thirty pages long, that referred to a vaccine the author considered to be harmful. Glancing at the author's name, Caroline was surprised to discover that Owen Brady, her Aunt Dolly's late husband, was the author of the report. And her Aunt Gina received a smaller credit at the bottom.

Annoyed, Caroline tossed it aside. It wasn't likely to have any relevance today, was it? Since it was over thirty years old, whatever information it once held hardly mattered now. Maybe Gina had kept it for sentimental reasons, since she'd worked with Owen and had obviously contributed to the research data it contained.

There was nothing else in the envelope. Feeling disappointed, Caroline considered putting it back in the suitcase, closing the lid and forgetting all about it. She was exhausted from all the travel, and especially from her lengthy bout of crying. On the other hand, maybe she should give the research document to Aunt Dolly, since her late husband Owen was the principal author. Then she remembered how rude and offensive Dolly usually was to Caroline's own mother Stella, so she decided against it. Dolly could take a hike as far as she was concerned.

On the other hand, somewhere at the back of her mind, Caroline remembered that a journalist with the *Daily News*, someone called Alice something-or-other, had recently been writing a series on corporate accountability. And suddenly she remembered that the journalist had also had a go at BWF Pharmaceuticals quite recently, and as usual, Aunt Dolly had risen to Charles Keane's defence.

Aunt Dolly had been visiting Stella when Caroline had called to see her mother, and she'd wondered, with irritation, why her aunt was so often there. Probably lonely, Caroline conceded. But since she looks down on us so much, why is she always slumming it at Mum's house? And availing of my mother's hospitality?

Dolly, imperious as ever, had been ranting on about the journalist's latest attack on public liability companies. "Look at this!" she said, angrily prodding the newspaper she was holding. "That witch Alice Fitzsimons is forever causing trauma to poor Charles. She's been challenging the company's safety record for years, but of course, she hasn't been able to prove anything. As if Charles, the dear man, would put people's lives in danger. That woman is just trying to make a name for herself, and using Charles to do it."

Alice Fitzsimons – now Caroline remembered the journalist's name.

Suddenly, Caroline had an idea. Before she could forget

the name, she jumped up from the spare bed and went to the bureau in the corner of the room, where she found a pen, paper, stamps and a roll of sticky tape. Hastily, she scribbled and enclosed a brief hand-written note, taped up the old envelope containing the research document, stuck a stamp on it and re-addressed it.

Caroline grinned to herself. Tomorrow morning, on her way to work, she'd post it. Anything she could do to rattle Aunt Dolly would give her the greatest of pleasure!

CHAPTER 21

Dolly stood before the mirror in her bedroom, surveying her reflection in her new outfit. She was pleased with the dress's elegant lines, and she twirled around to check how it looked from the back. It was perfect. Then she slipped on the matching jacket, and smiled happily at the well-dressed woman in the mirror. Now her only problem was – would she save the outfit for Caroline's wedding, or would she wear it when she next met Charles?

She'd been pleased when Charles had phoned and asked her to meet him two weeks earlier than usual. She always looked forward to their monthly get-togethers, but this month Charles appeared much more attentive than usual. He'd already phoned her twice for a chat, and now he'd invited her to lunch at a new exclusive restaurant on Stephen's Green.

Dolly allowed herself to daydream a little. It was only three months since Mary, Charles's wife, had passed away, so maybe Charles was feeling lonely. Maybe he'd begun to realise what a wonderful companion his former secretary was, and perhaps a proposal would soon be in the offing . . .

Dolly had no problem in becoming Mrs Charles Keane. In fact, it would be a remarkable step up the social ladder for her. She could just imagine the shock and envy on her sister Stella's face if she told her that she was finally going to marry Charles.

Dolly decided that she would wear her new outfit to the restaurant. She could always buy another outfit for the wedding. After all, money was no problem for her. In fact, she could buy ten outfits a month if she felt like it.

She surveyed her reflection again. Yes, Charles would approve of her new outfit. He liked women to look elegant rather than brassy, and Dolly had always taken care to dress with decorum. When she'd worked for Charles, she'd taken her position as his secretary very seriously, and had always dressed with an elegance befitting her position as his right-hand woman and confidante. Dolly had never worn a mini-skirt, or any type of casualwear to the office. Even in her free time, she always dressed formally. Others might have considered her mode of dress to be old-fashioned, but to Dolly dressing with dignity meant always keeping her arms, knees and bosom covered.

Dolly checked her Cartier wristwatch. She'd be meeting Charles in an hour's time, so it was time to ring for a taxi. These days she never bothered to drive anywhere, although Owen's vintage Bentley still sat in the garage. Thank goodness he'd been driving his old Vauxhall the night he'd crashed! It would have been a tragedy to see such a beautiful car destroyed. Yet even after all these years, she'd never bothered to sell it, since she'd no need for the money. It was probably worth a fortune now anyway – at least three times what Owen had paid for it – and more than once, she'd seen her sister Stella gaze longingly at it when she'd driven Dolly back home after a family get-together. It always gave Dolly great satisfaction to watch Stella's envy, but combined with her sadistic delight at Stella's longing, she also felt affronted that Stella would even *think* she might let her drive such a valuable car! No, Dolly reasoned, Stella's Ford Fiesta was good enough for her – clearly Stella didn't look after it either, since it was always breaking down. Dolly sighed. There were some people who just didn't deserve to drive decent cars.

Having rung her usual taxi service, Dolly waited in the hallway for the taxi to come up the driveway to collect her. Impatiently, she checked her watch – the taxi was late, so she intended giving the driver a piece of her mind. And there would be no tip either! While most people gauged the tip at ten percent of the cost of the journey, Dolly always felt that this was far too much. She didn't care if the taxi drivers drew uncomplimentary comparisons between the mansion she lived in and the miserable few cents she gave them. Dolly was oblivious to anyone else's feelings.

Having chastised the taxi driver for his tardiness, Dolly sat back in the taxi and gazed out the window as it headed towards the city centre. She was looking forward to seeing Charles again, and to trying the new restaurant. Hopefully, as Charles's wife, there would be many occasions to visit exclusive new restaurants.

She smiled with pleasure as she recalled their years of friendship. She and Charles had been friends for more than thirty years now, united primarily by their mutual love of BWF Pharmaceuticals. But they also found common ground in their dislike of modern society with all its permissiveness, their annoyance at the behaviour of 'today's young people', and their disgust at the greed and corruption that permeated every strand of society today. Not surprisingly, the word 'hypocrite' never entered either of their minds.

* * *

"It's good to see you, Dolly – as always." Charles kissed her cheek, and Dolly turned pink with pleasure.

"You too, Charles – and how good of you to invite me to this beautiful restaurant."

Dolly gazed around her appreciatively. The restaurant was truly opulent, and she was glad that she'd worn her new outfit.

"Only the best is good enough for you, m'dear," Charles responded, pulling out her chair, and helping her into the depths of its luxurious velvet folds. "The owner is an old friend of mine, so when he suggested I come to lunch and bring a friend, you were the obvious choice. I know how much you enjoy fine dining, Dolly, so I thought we could sample Dublin's top fare together."

Dolly's cheeks dimpled with pleasure. Charles seemed to know all the right people! Not for the first time, Dolly thanked her lucky stars that her path had crossed Charles' early in life. Since she began working for him all those years ago, he'd been a tower of strength to her, even engineering a marriage for her with the company's newest and most senior scientist. Then, after Owen's death, he'd always been there when she'd needed advice or support.

As they sipped their complimentary premier cru St Emillion, Charles brought Dolly up to date on his latest golf score, his recent business trip to America, and the latest political scandal, which he learned about first-hand from a friend who was a top civil servant.

"Good lord!" said Dolly, shuddering. "What on earth is the world coming to, Charles? I can't believe that a government minister's been a director of a company directly benefiting from the legislation his department has passed! Presumably he'll be instantly dismissed. How corrupt, and how arrogant of him to assume nobody would find out!"

"I know – it's disgraceful, isn't it?" said Charles, "According to my friend, the press will have the story by tomorrow, so it'll be on every front page." He sighed. "Corruption seems to be everywhere these days, doesn't it, Dolly? What difficult times we live in, m'dear!"

Dolly nodded. She always agreed with Charles, since he seemed to have his finger on the pulse of society, and knew all the movers and shakers. What a wonderful, upright and decent man Charles was! And how lucky she was that he regarded her as a friend. Her cheeks coloured as the thought crossed her mind that one day soon she might even become more than a friend.

A waiter in full livery took their order and before long he'd returned with their starters. Dolly's warm orange, pomegranate and halva salad looked delightful and tasted superb. Charles' chicken breast with aioli and grilled spring onions brought a smile of anticipation to his lips. Tucking in, the two ate in silence, Dolly savouring the ambience and luxury of her surroundings.

"The food is delicious, and the restaurant is magnificent, Charles," she said at last, putting down her cutlery. "I know it's rude to clear one's plate, but I couldn't bear to leave anything!"

"Glad to see you enjoying yourself, m'dear!"

Throughout the rest of their lunch, Dolly listened enthralled as Charles regaled her with stories from the annals of BWF Pharmaceuticals. These included the secret romantic liaisons of employees that hadn't escaped Charles's beady eye, and the recent take-over bid that had been rejected by the board of directors.

"That means your company shares have increased in value again this week," Charles told her with a smile. Due to Charles's shrewd advice, she had more money than she knew what to do with.

Charles's main course of roast beef and Dolly's quail in garlic were equally as delicious as their starters. But when Charles's dessert of grilled nectarines with Amaretto and ice cream was before him, he tasted it and then laid down his spoon, glancing sheepishly at Dolly.

"Is something wrong with your pudding, Charles?" she asked. "You're not worried about your waistline, are you?" she added coquettishly. "You're still as trim as the day I met you!" She then blushed at having inadvertently drawn attention to part of Charles's anatomy – obviously the premier cru wine had gone to her head. At least she hadn't made any reference to a part of his body that had any sexual connotations.

"No, m'dear, it's not that – I've just realised that I've been hogging the entire conversation since we arrived!" he confessed. "I'm sorry, Dolly – you must consider me a terrible bore!"

"Not at all, Charles!" she gushed. "I find your insights from the world of business and politics terribly enlightening."

"You're very kind, m'dear – I know you're too polite to put me in my place, as I deserve. But come, tell me about what's been happening to you since we last met," he urged, at last moving the conversation in the direction he wanted.

Dolly took a spoonful of her mascarpone, cherry and

grappa trifle. "Truthfully, nothing much, Charles. *You're* the one leading the high-powered lifestyle!"

"Well then, tell me how young Caroline's plans for the wedding are coming along?"

"Oh Charles!" Dolly simpered. "After all your news from the cutting edge of society, *my* family's day-to-day lives can't be of any interest to you!"

Charles leaned forward and patted her hand. "On the contrary, dear Dolly, anything that concerns *you* is of concern to me. What sort of friend would I be if your happiness wasn't to the forefront of my mind?"

Dolly blushed with pleasure. Maybe this was the moment when Charles would tell her that there was no woman in the world whom he'd prefer to be his wife than her. But he said nothing, and she felt obliged to fill the void between them.

"Well, did I tell you that Caroline came back from London without finding a wedding dress?" She shuddered. "You know, Charles – it wouldn't surprise me if that young woman opted for a black or red gown instead of the traditional white. Young people today seem to have no regard for the traditions of old!"

Charles nodded sympathetically. "I remember you mentioned that she was trying to find your younger sister. Did she manage to contact her yet?"

Dolly's bosom heaved with rage. "I don't know what's got into that young woman – while she was in London, she visited Gina's *husband*! It came as quite a big shock – until Caroline told her mother, none of us knew that Gina had actually married Larry Macken all those years ago. You probably wouldn't remember him, Charles – he was Gina's boyfriend during her schooldays."

Charles's face registered surprise.

"Apparently she left Larry shortly after they got married, but Caroline is determined to keep searching. Since Larry Macken gave her an old suitcase belonging to Gina, with photographs and old clothes in it, she's been like the cat that got the cream!"

"Poor Dolly – all this must be very distressing for you," Charles said, squeezing her hand supportively. "Eh, was there anything else in the suitcase?"

Dolly smiled gratefully at Charles. The dear man was genuinely concerned about her happiness, and he was worried that her niece was causing her grief by her foolhardy pursuit of Gina. Dolly had no wish to ever see her sister again, and the thought of Caroline dragging home the errant Gina was more than she could bear.

"If there was, I'd be the last person on earth that Caroline would tell," said Dolly, a note of bitterness creeping into her voice. "Although I could ask Stella, if you like – I can usually get her to tell me what's going on."

She looked closely at Charles, suddenly aware that he was looking worried.

"My goodness, you don't think –"

"Don't worry, Dolly – it's not really important," Charles assured her, patting her hand.

"I hope not, Charles," Dolly said, looking concerned. "Even if it *was* there– surely it couldn't have any relevance after all this time?"

Charles smiled warmly at her. "You're right, Dolly – of course it doesn't matter any more."

He patted his lips with a napkin. Within the next year or two, he'd be retiring from BWF Pharmaceuticals, the company he'd devoted his life to building up. Under his guidance, it had gone from a small but pivotal company to being part of a multinational of global proportions. So he wasn't going to stand idly by and see all his hard work undone by a little flibbertigibbet who wanted to find her long-lost relative.

He bit his lip. It was obvious that he wouldn't be able to retire just yet . . .

CHAPTER 22

Alice began tackling her weekly assignments by making phone calls and setting up interviews for the next few days. Straight after her lunch with Isobel, she'd gone into Dan Daly's office and told him firmly that she'd be taking leave of absence from the following week, and that if he didn't like it, she'd get a job elsewhere on her return. Perhaps her determined manner had cowed him, but he'd said nothing, and Alice left feeling that she'd scored a minor victory. Dan Daly was a bully but when confronted he usually backed down. Only time would tell if she had a job to return to, and right now she didn't really care. She would finish her week's work with her usual professionalism, and after that, the ball was firmly in Dan Daly's court.

Having set up her interviews for the week, Alice looked lethargically at the piles of post on her desk. It had built up to such an extent in her absence that she could hardly see the desk. She sighed. This was the job she hated most. Occasionally, there might be something interesting among the pile of letters and packages she received daily, but usually they were just from PR agencies, product samples or begging letters of one sort or another. Most went straight into the bin. Would she tackle them now, or would she just go home? Better get them sorted, she decided reluctantly, since there would be another large pile arriving the following day. She'd be really snowed under if she left her post unattended for several more days. Unenthusiastically, she began the job of sorting the useful items from those going into the bin beside her desk.

Halfway through the post, Alice came across a large thick envelope. It didn't have the usual PR agency logo on the front, so there was no way of knowing what was inside until she opened it. Inside, she found that it contained what looked like a research document. The paper was old and partly faded, and looked as though it had been typed on a typewriter rather than a computer. She scanned it briefly, but it didn't make a lot of sense to her. The research report was dated thirty years ago, and Alice felt irritation. Who was sending her this old rubbish? Was this somebody's idea of a joke? Reaching into the envelope, Alice found an explanatory letter, dated earlier that week, and suddenly her interest was piqued. This might prove useful in connection with a feature she'd already been researching on the pharmaceutical industry.

Alice stuffed the report and the letter into her briefcase. It was unlikely that she'd get an opportunity to look at them before she went to Argentina, but she'd at least take them home with her in case she found the time. It would be just the thing to keep her mind occupied and away from thoughts of what might have been.

CHAPTER 23

Alice retrieved her Peugeot from the small car park behind the newspaper's city centre offices. She was sick of Daly's vindictiveness. He'd given her another late-evening assignment! Ever since she'd returned to work, Daly had made life as difficult as possible for her. She didn't care about the time off she'd get in lieu – she was already knackered after a long day, and just wanted to go home to bed. Bill was away in Portugal, much to Alice's relief, and just as soon as she'd wrapped up the interview, she intended stretching out on the sofa at home and watching mindless TV programmes until her brain was numb.

But now, she needed to concentrate on the matter in hand. She was about to interview an elderly historian – Dan's idea, she reflected sourly. She'd been given another boring assignment as punishment for requesting time off. Dan Daly had it in for her, and all Alice could do was pretend that she didn't care. Daly would love it even more if he thought his nastiness was having any effect.

As she drove along the docks on her way out of town,

Alice angrily pondered her situation. Thank goodness she wouldn't have to stomach Daly for much longer. The day after tomorrow, she'd be on her way to Buenos Aires! Dan had reluctantly conceded to her request for four weeks off, but he'd done it with such bad grace that Alice would have preferred an outright row. Then she could have told him what to do with his job and stormed out. On the other hand, maybe it was better to have a job to come back to!

Driving along, her thoughts miles away, Alice didn't realise how close the other car was behind her. Until it hit her. Reacting quickly, she swung the wheel of the Peugeot back, to prevent her vehicle from heading towards the sea. Then she looked behind, not sure what to expect, only to find that the car had now come alongside, and was ramming her from the side.

Shocked, Alice realised that someone was trying to run her off the road, and that there was nothing between her and the sea except a row of flimsy-looking bollards. Frantically, she looked around, but there was no other traffic or pedestrians around. Why had she chosen such a lonely route home? There were no witnesses to what was happening – the ideal setting for a road-rage driver, or teenage joy rider. As the other vehicle kept bumping her, Alice realised that if she continued driving straight ahead, she would eventually hit the solid concrete storage building looming up ahead. Clearly the driver intended that if he couldn't push Alice into the sea, smashing her into the up-coming wall would do just as well.

Frantically, Alice tried to think of what to do. There was no time to locate her phone and ring the emergency services. She racked her brains – what were you supposed to do in situations like this? Steer in the direction of the skid – but she wasn't in any skid. Keep driving – don't pull over. She remembered that bit from some training manual she'd read, but if she kept driving, she'd ram straight into the wall.

In her mind's eye, she saw herself drowning helplessly, locked in her car on the seabed. She saw the winch pulling her car out of the water, the emergency services standing by, in the vain hope that the occupant might still be alive. Then another image replaced it, of her car bursting into flames on impact with the concrete wall, with nothing left but a blackened corpse. She saw all these images within the space of a few seconds, a sure sign she felt, of her impending doom.

Suddenly, Alice caught a blurred glimpse of the driver, who was wearing a woollen cap pulled down over his head. Alice couldn't see his face, but she was suddenly filled with anger. She wasn't going to let some testosterone-overloaded teenage joy rider end her life! So she braked suddenly, then thrust the car into reverse, surprising herself as much as the occupant of the other car. Praying that her engine wouldn't stall, Alice quickly pulled out around the other car and streaked off down the deserted street. The other car quickly recovered and started off in pursuit, but Alice just managed to race through the next set of traffic lights before they changed to red. Looking in her rear-view mirror, she was relieved to see that the other car wasn't following. Clearly, the occupant wasn't prepared to risk his own life by running a red light.

Her chest heaving, Alice continued driving as fast as she could, while constantly checking in her rear-view mirror. Thankfully, there was no sign of the other car, but she kept up a steady speed until she felt certain that it was no longer following her. At last, she reached a better-lit and more populated area of the city, where she felt a lot safer. Now, what should she do? Her car was undoubtedly damaged, but she didn't exactly feel like getting out and inspecting it, just in case the other driver might still be following at a distance.

After checking her rear-view mirror yet again, Alice quickly turned into a small side road, locked her doors, turned off the engine and dowsed the car lights. She felt a lot safer now. Taking out her mobile phone, she tried to dial the historian's house, and realised that her hands were trembling uncontrollably. She would postpone the interview, since she knew that there was little hope of doing it competently now.

The old man was willing to put off the interview until the following day, so with relief Alice turned her Peugeot in the direction of home. Inspection of the damage could wait until she got there. She wouldn't risk exposing herself to another possible attack.

There was little point in phoning the police, she conceded. What on earth could she tell them? She hadn't got the registration number of the car, and she couldn't identify the driver. The car was probably stolen anyway. Little bastard, she thought. She'd never been the victim of joy riders before, but she was aware that it was a serious problem in and around the city. Two police officers had been killed by joy riders a few years before, when a stolen car was deliberately rammed into their patrol car.

There was little point in phoning Bill either, since he was in Portugal trying to sort out the calamitous situation regarding the apartment complex he was involved in. Besides, if he'd been at home, she'd dissolve into tears if he said a kind word to her and, given their strained relationship, she didn't want any reason to feel grateful to him.

Outside her house, Alice finally surveyed the damage. The side of the Peugeot was badly dented, and since the driver's door could no longer open, she had to climb out through the passenger door. At this stage, it was impossible to tell whether or not the suspension had been affected too. She surveyed the damage bitterly. Her insurance would cover it, but that would only hike up the price of her annual premium. Shit. She'd be wiser to pay for the repairs out of her own pocket.

Letting herself into the house, Alice headed for the kitchen, and turned on the kettle with shaking hands. On second thoughts, maybe a brandy would be better, she conceded. Turning off the kettle, she headed to the kitchen cupboard where the drinks were stored, and poured herself a large measure of brandy. It would help to steady her nerves.

CHAPTER 24

Three days later, Alice left for Buenos Aires. Bill wanted to see her off at the airport, but Alice flatly refused his offer, informing him that her mother was taking her instead. Their goodbyes on the doorstep were formal and brief, and Alice was relieved to step into her mother's car for the hour-long drive to the airport.

Alice's mother Joan was delighted to have some alone-time with her usually busy daughter, but she was also perturbed to learn that Alice was taking time off work, and also taking a break from her marriage. Alice gave her mother a severely edited version of the truth, since she knew Joan would only worry. She played down Bill's financial situation, saying that she needed some time to think about her future.

"Anyway, I've always wanted to see Buenos Aires, Mum," she told her mother, who tearfully clung to her only daughter before she went through to the departure area. Alice omitted to tell her mother that she'd be backpacking alone through much of Argentina, since she feared Joan might have a heart attack at the thought.

Isobel rushed up to the barrier just before Alice went through, and the two friends hugged each other tightly.

"Have a great time, Alice," said Isobel, wiping away a tear, "and make sure you come back to us! Don't go falling in love with some good-looking gaucho out there!"

"Keep an eye on Mum for me, will you?" Alice whispered, hugging her back, "and good luck with Brian Kelly – or whoever takes your fancy next! It wouldn't surprise me if Brian Kelly was history by the time I get back!"

Waving goodbye to Joan and Isobel, Alice headed through to the departure area, where her hand luggage was checked through the x-ray machine. Alice smiled to herself – usually, in this situation, she had trouble fitting everything into one small bag. But this time she was travelling light. Her rucksack had already been checked through to Buenos Aires, and all she needed for her two flights was some reading material.

As her first flight to London took off, Alice took a deep breath. It was too late to change her mind now. Several times earlier in the week, she'd questioned her own sanity. What on earth was she doing, travelling thousands of miles to South America, to a country she knew nothing about? Was she running away, or would this trip genuinely help? On more than one occasion, she'd seriously thought of calling the whole trip off, but her pride wouldn't let her, especially after all the fuss she'd made about getting time off work. Besides, she genuinely wanted time away from Bill. But a niggling little thought inside kept asking – did she really need to travel thousands of miles from home to do it?

When the flight to Buenos Aires took off from London, Alice finally began to relax. She was on her way, and she might as well make the most of it! She began to feel genuinely excited as she studied the tourist guides she'd brought with her. So many possibilities, so little time! She planned to stay a few days in Buenos Aires, where she'd already booked a city-centre hostel over the Internet. Then she'd take some form of transport into the countryside, booking ahead for the next hostel or hotel as she went. Maybe she'd travel by train, or by bus, or she'd hitch a ride on one of the big trucks that traversed the dry and dusty sun-drenched plains. The country was vast and there was so much to see, and she was well aware that she'd only be able to cover a small area of it.

As she ate the first of her in-flight meals with gusto, and consumed two small bottles of wine, Alice was feeling good. Here she was, travelling alone, to a different continent, on the biggest adventure of her life! Yet always lurking at the back of her mind was the awareness that she might never see her beloved house in Killiney again. It would probably have been repossessed and sold by the bank by the time she returned to Ireland. Perhaps subconsciously, she'd chosen to make the trip for that reason, so that when she returned, the sale of the house would be a done deal.

Resolutely, she banished any further maudlin thoughts, and asked one of the stewards for another bottle of wine. She was going to forget all about Bill, the house, and all the problems back home. She was going to Argentina, and she was going to have a wonderful time!

CHAPTER 25

As she lay beneath a tree in the Argentinean sunshine, a bottle of water to her lips, Alice Fitzsimons felt at peace with the world. After several days spent exploring Buenos Aires, she'd hitched a lift with a truck driver who'd been heading into the interior of the country. From there, she'd stayed at several hostels, meeting lovely people – and even another Irishwoman – on her travels. Now, already into her second week, she was in the outback, about two hundred miles from the city, and was feeling thoroughly relaxed. All around her, the gentle sounds of the countryside soothed her, and filled her soul with a sense of timelessness.

She was comfortably lazy, and the idea of dozing in the heat for the rest of the afternoon was a pleasing prospect. On the other hand, if she wanted to get to the next town by nightfall, she'd need to be on her way soon. The sleepy village of Villanova had little to recommend it, so she might as well move on.

The elderly female receptionist at the tiny hotel waved a lethargic hand in response to her apologies. Everyone who came to Villanova left earlier than planned, she seemed to imply. Why should Alice be any different?

"I'll settle my bill now –"

"*Si si, senora,* no problem."

Alice grinned to herself. All over the world, even in remote places like Villanova, everyone used the expression 'No problem'.

Looking around the dusty little hotel, and out into the dusty little street, she idly wondered what sort of a life people lived in a place like this. No doubt it was great for a holiday, or for passing through – but to live there? My God, the boredom! Yet people spent their entire lives in places like this. Her journalist's heart gave a shudder. What on earth was there to do here?

Having paid her bill in cash – obviously the taxman didn't benefit too often in rural Argentina – she collected her rucksack from her room, and headed out into the sunshine again. Maybe she'd been a little hasty in packing up so soon. It was now late afternoon, and she'd be relying on a passing goods truck to give her a lift to the next town. Well, if no one turned up, she could always go back to the hotel. It wasn't as though it was exactly full. In fact, as far as she knew, she was the only guest staying there.

Making her way up in the direction of the highway, Alice passed several small farms where cattle grazed lazily. It was an idyllic scene, and she felt a sudden rush of sentiment for the same rural scene back home in Ireland. The only difference would be that at home it would probably be pouring rain!

As she walked along, Alice began planning the next stage of her journey. Now she was in the heart of the

Argentine countryside, travelling to wherever the buses, trains and truck drivers would take her. She was comfortable with hitching, since she was experienced in karate and could look after herself should anyone try to attack her. But so far, she'd met with nothing but kindness wherever she went. People were friendly, proud of their country, and anxious to help her have a wonderful stay in South America. She stayed mainly in hostels or small hotels, and booked ahead to the next destination whenever possible. Eventually, she planned to head back towards Buenos Aires, where she hoped to spend her last few days before heading home. This trip was a watershed for her. She needed the time and space to make big decisions about what she wanted to do about her future.

Then, on the right-hand side of the road, Alice noticed open gates at the entrance to a winding driveway – obviously to a house a lot more prosperous than its neighbours. It was probably a house that had once been part of an *estancia*, one of the vast ranches found over much of Argentina. There were trees meandering up the driveway, and suddenly Alice felt the urge to discover where it led. It would only take a minute, she reasoned. Besides, she could discreetly relieve herself behind one of the large trees.

The driveway weaved to the left and then to the right, finally revealing a fine old house that had clearly seen better days. Once painted a warm terracotta, it now had paint peeling off its exterior walls, and an unlived-in look about it, as though its owners had one day walked out and never come back.

Rounding the corner to the back of the house, Alice found it equally deserted, except for a young goat that was tethered to a post near the back door. Hopefully it's not the owner's lunch for next week, she thought with compassion. Being city born and bred, she preferred her dinner to arrive in a neat plastic-wrapped pack from the supermarket.

Squatting down behind a bush, Alice quickly relieved herself, then realised that she was still carrying the empty water bottle from earlier that afternoon. She'd stuck it in the back pocket of her shorts intending to find a rubbish bin – now she espied a large household rubbish container just past the curious goat.

"Hello, young fellow," she said softly, edging her way around the goat, "you wouldn't butt me if I just dropped this bottle in the bin, would you?"

The goat looked at her territorially, undecided as to whether to charge at her or ignore her.

Suddenly, Alice heard a voice calling from inside the house. Shit, she thought. Surely someone isn't going to object to me discarding an empty water bottle?

The call came again – more urgently this time. It sounded like a woman's voice, but it was so faint that Alice wasn't quite sure.

"*Hola!*" she called back in Spanish. "I'm sorry if I disturbed you. I'm going away now!"

"No – please!" This time the cry came louder and more urgently. "Please come inside – you must help me!" the faint voice cried. "The key – it is hanging just inside the door . . ."

Slipping her hand through the broken windowpane, Alice found the key and let herself into the dim interior. There was dust everywhere, accompanied by a general odour of decay. Clearly, it was a house that hadn't had the benefit of a spring clean for a long time.

"Here – I am here!" called the disembodied voice, which Alice followed until she reached a tiny attic room up a few stairs at the end of a short corridor.

Inside lay a frail old woman, her white hair fanned out across the pillow. The room smelled of decay and stale perfume, and Alice felt herself wanting to gag.

As she approached the bed, the old woman stared at her, suddenly shrinking back into her pillow.

"Mother of God – you've come back from the dead!" she whispered, making the sign of the cross. "I had nothing to do with what happened!"

Alice smiled reassuringly. "It's okay, I'm very much alive. Please don't upset yourself."

"If you're not dead, then you must be the other . . . oh, please be careful! They will kill you too, because they got the picture from your husband – I heard them talking . . ." Her rheumy old eyes closed, and she fell silent. Alice thought she'd fallen asleep, but then she suddenly opened her eyes again. "Please," she whispered, "find Father Ricardo in the village – I need to receive the last rites before I die."

"Of course I'll get the priest for you," said Alice, patting the old woman's arm to reassure her. "But shouldn't I send for a doctor first?"

"No, no – it is too late for that," the old woman whispered. "I need sustenance for my soul, not my body, young woman. Please, can you get Father Ricardo quickly? Please!"

Galvanised into action, Alice rushed out of the house, past the goat and down the driveway. Presumably Father Ricardo was to be found somewhere in the village or, if not, in or near the tiny church on the opposite hill.

Racing into the small hotel, Alice confronted the receptionist, who didn't look as though she'd moved a muscle since she left.

"Father Ricardo – where can I find him?"

"Try the church, senora. Why do you need him?"

"An old lady – up in the big house with the driveway – she wants him to visit."

"Aah – Senora Delgado. She lives all alone in that grand house." The receptionist shrugged her shoulders. "She is an independent old lady, who always does her own shopping and cleaning. She has never wanted anyone's help."

"Well, she needs it now – she's ill, perhaps dying," said Alice. "So excuse me, I've got to go. If you see Father Ricardo before I do, please send him up to the poor woman."

"Si, senora. By the way, two men have just been here enquiring about you –" The receptionist shrugged her shoulders. "I thought you had left town, so I told them you had moved on – I'm sorry, senora. I hope it was not important."

Alice looked surprised. Who on earth would know where she was? She hadn't told anyone where she was staying. "Did they ask for me by name?"

"No, senora – they asked about the dark-haired Irishwoman."

Alice had no idea who they were, so she simply smiled and thanked the receptionist. She had a more urgent matter to deal with right now – finding the priest for the old woman.

Racing up the hill to the church, Alice was grateful that she was in good physical condition. The road was steep and dusty, and she was exhausted by the time the reached the summit.

The tiny church was deserted, its interior a cool and pleasant respite from the heat outside. But there was no sign of Father Ricardo. The only movement was from the motes that danced in the sunlight as it streamed in through the tiny arched windows.

Damn. Alice took several deep breaths. The old dear seemed in a bad way. And while she wasn't qualified to pass judgement on the woman's state of health, it was evident that she was desperately in need of this Father Ricardo. Where the hell could a priest get to in a small village like this?

Alice set off down the hill again, this time stopping a group of villagers who were on their way up. None of them had seen Father Ricardo, although there were lots of "*Si, si's*" and promises to send the priest immediately to the old woman's house if and when he could be found.

Back in the village, there were still no sightings of the elusive priest. With further promises from the receptionist at the hotel to send Father Ricardo to the old woman's house when he could be found, Alice decided that she'd better return to the house herself, and assure the woman that every effort was being made to find the priest. Whether or not the poor woman was dying, it would be churlish to leave her alone.

The goat now greeted Alice like a long-lost friend, and seemed disposed to giving her a friendly nip. Gingerly, she sidled around it and into the house.

"It's me again!" she called out in Spanish, so as not to frighten the old woman.

As Alice entered the old woman's room again, she was shocked at the changes that had overcome her during the brief absence. Her pallor had turned to grey, and her skin had taken on a waxy sheen. Her breathing was laboured, and her eyes were no longer focusing – perhaps she was no longer able.

All Alice could do was sit silently beside the dying woman. She wondered where the damned priest had got to. Surely he should be around when his parishioners needed him?

For a while there was no sound, and Alice began to wonder if the old woman had already died. Then suddenly she spoke again, her voice weak, but urgent.

"I was so frightened of them – I had to hide in here, because they would have killed me too."

"There, there!" Alice soothed. "You're safe now. I'll stay with you until the priest comes."

Alice squeezed the old woman's hand gently to let her know that she understood. Which, of course, she didn't. She had no idea what the woman was rambling on about. Where on earth was the priest? She felt awkward listening to someone else's private business, especially since it was obvious that the woman thought she was someone else. Clearly, the old girl was hallucinating.

At that moment, there was a rustle in the corridor outside, and a dark-haired young man in priest's garb appeared at the door of the room. Alice began to stand up, but he gestured for her to stay where she was.

The old woman gave a deep sigh of relief at the arrival of the priest, and when he took her hand in his she gripped it briefly. Then he slipped on his stole, and began to softly intone the last rites.

A little while later her frail body arched, and was still. A tiny gurgle sounded in her throat.

Alice looked up at the priest. "She's gone."

The priest nodded, then made the sign of the cross on the old woman's forehead and murmured another prayer. Together, they left the room and walked out into the corridor, where the last rays of evening sunshine were filtering through the west-facing windows.

"I must now send for Doctor Sanchez to certify Senora Delgado's death," the young priest told Alice. "Then I will ask some of the good ladies of the town to lay her out."

"She said some very strange things to me before she died – I think she thought I was someone else," Alice told him.

The priest inclined his head. "Sometimes people become confused when they are dying. They remember earlier times, maybe even their childhood. Please do not worry about it – she is at peace now." He looked pointedly at Alice's rucksack. "Are you arriving in Villanova?"

Alice shook her head, explaining that she was from Ireland, was touring around Argentina, and was actually on her way out of town. They formally shook hands, and the priest informed her that his name was Father Ricardo Alvarez.

"Please," he said, "it will be dark soon. It is too late for a young woman to be hitch-hiking." He smiled gently. "Come and stay tonight at the presbytery. Tomorrow will be a better day for travelling. I can provide you with a room, a bed with clean sheets and something to eat. What do you say, eh?"

Alice smiled. "That's the best offer I've had all day."

Father Ricardo closed the front door of the old woman's house, and they had begun walking down the driveway when Alice suddenly remembered the goat.

"That young goat – we'd better find it a new owner. Maybe you could keep it at the presbytery for milk?"

The young priest smiled. "I think, my friend, you will need a miracle if we are to get milk from a male goat."

Alice laughed. "Uh-oh! Just shows you how little I know about country life."

"But Ireland – is it not full of sheep, goats and cows?"

Alice grinned. "In the country, yes. But I'm a city woman through and through. Can't sleep without concrete under my feet."

The priest turned towards her. "Then why did you choose to come to South America?"

Alice grimaced. "I had a big decision to make."

"And have you made it?"

"No, not yet."

"Come," said Father Ricardo, "let us go back to the presbytery and open a bottle of wine. Then you can tell me all about it." He inclined his head. "If you wish to, that is."

Alice nodded. It would be a relief to tell someone all that had happened before she'd escaped to Argentina.

CHAPTER 26

In the cool, dim interior of the small presbytery, Alice felt able to relax at last. Yet the old woman's strange words kept repeating in her mind. What on earth had she meant, and why was she so agitated?

In the small tiled shower room, Alice stretched herself as she revelled in the luxury of the cascading hot water. She wondered how Bill was. Was he missing her? She sighed. In another few weeks she'd see him again. And by then, she'd have decided what she was going to do.

As she stepped out of the shower, she could smell something good cooking. Was Father Ricardo doing the cooking himself? Or did he have the ubiquitous housekeeper lurking somewhere around the presbytery?

As if to answer her question, she heard him calling her to the table. Quickly, she dried herself off, threw on a clean T-shirt and a wrap-around skirt, and headed for the dining room. When she stepped into the small room, feeling refreshed and clean, Father Ricardo was dishing out some fish and rice.

"I hope my cooking is up to your standards."

"Smells great, Father," said Alice, helping herself to some thickly sliced bread that was in a basket on the table. She was starving, and the modest, tasty spread was just what she needed.

The priest smiled. "Please stop calling me 'Father'. I am uncomfortable when it is used by someone my own age."

"Okay, Fa – I mean, Ricardo."

The priest poured himself and Alice a glass of wine from a large carafe on the table. Simultaneously, they raised their glasses in a silent toast.

Alice took a big gulp of wine. It was quite a rough, obviously local wine, which must be, she decided, an acquired taste. But it was just what she needed, and she had every intention of quickly getting used to it!

For a little while, they talked of pleasantries – Alice learnt that Father Ricardo was exactly the same age as her, and that he had studied at the University of Buenos Aires before joining the priesthood directly from college. Alice shared similar personal information, telling him about her job back in Ireland, the beauty of the Irish countryside, and how she was enjoying her trip to Argentina.

"But travelling alone – surely it is dangerous for a woman?"

Alice smiled, touched by his concern. "I'm very good at karate! Besides, everyone I've met has been more than helpful. And most of the time I'm not hitching anyway – I'm using local buses and trains wherever I can, and booking ahead to the next hostel or hotel, so that I won't be stranded when I arrive." She took a mouthful of fish and rice. "Besides, I haven't been alone all the time – in fact, I met another

Irish woman during my first week here, and we travelled through part of the countryside together. Amazing, isn't it? That we should both be travelling independently, and literally bumped into each other thousands of miles from home!"

The young priest nodded approvingly. "I am relieved to hear that you had company for part of your journey. But –" he hesitated. "– you gave me the impression that this trip of yours involves a journey of another kind, yes?"

Alice coloured. Originally, she'd been determined not to discuss her private life with anyone, but there was something about this young priest that seemed to invite confidences. Maybe a different perspective would help her make decisions. Naturally, she'd talked to Patricia, the Irishwoman she'd met, but that had been different. Two women – far from home and each with personal problems to sort out – would inevitably confide in each other.

"I – well, actually, I'm married, Ricardo. But I've discovered that my husband hasn't been telling me the truth about something."

The young priest looked sad. "I'm sorry to hear that. Has he been having an affair?"

"No – well, I don't think so," Alice replied, furrowing her brow, "but he's been lying to me about our financial situation. Recently he confessed to me that he's been getting deeper and deeper into debt, and that several months ago he re-mortgaged our house by forging my signature. Now the bank want their money, and we're going to lose our home."

Ricardo grimaced. "That is indeed a distressing situation. But am I right in thinking it is not just the money that matters to you – you have also lost respect for your husband, right?"

"Exactly!" Alice banged her glass on the table, spilling a little wine, which Ricardo quickly mopped up.

"And you are very angry, because you do not know if you can love him, or trust him, any more," he added.

Suddenly, Alice began to weep. It was as though the floodgates she'd kept tightly sealed had finally opened. The priest let her cry without interruption, eventually passing her his handkerchief to mop her tear-stained face.

"I'm sorry, Ricardo – I don't know what came over me," said Alice finally.

"There is no need to apologise – the decisions you have to make are momentous ones."

Alice nodded. She'd been disgusted by her husband's duplicity. How could he forge her signature and re-mortgage the house – of which she owned half – without telling her? What had happened to the trust between them? Part of her felt sorry for Bill – it wasn't until after their marriage that she'd come to realise that despite all his posturing, he was really quite insecure. Perhaps all the 'big deals' he got involved in were a form of ego-boost for his lack of confidence.

Alice spoke at last. "But there's something else, Ricardo. I've just been left a substantial inheritance by my late father's sister, and Bill wants me to let him use it to clear his debts." She sighed. "It's not just the house that's been lost, Ricardo – Bill owes money to lots of people."

"And you feel that he will squander your money, too."

Alice nodded. "Bill's always getting himself involved in money-making schemes – some of them do actually produce good returns, but I suspect–" she coloured, "no, let's be honest, I now *know* – that some of them are downright immoral. I suppose I was so in love with him when we got married that I didn't question how he made his money. Now I know he'd do anything to make a quick buck."

Father Ricardo nodded. "And you do not want your inheritance being used to support further immoral ventures."

Alice nodded, then began to cry again. It was a relief to tell the young priest all about it, and also to face her own culpability in never bothering to find out how her husband made his money.

Eventually, when she had no more tears left, Alice wiped her face again with the handkerchief. "I'm sorry, Ricardo – I've made quite a mess of your handkerchief. I'll wash it for you in the morning."

The priest waved his hand dismissively. "It is of no consequence. But you must make me a promise –"

Alice nodded.

"You are in no condition to travel on tomorrow. Promise me you will stay a little longer in Villanova."

Alice nodded again, this time in agreement. She felt overwrought and exhausted from all the crying, and she realised that a day or two of relaxing in the tiny village of Villanova was exactly what she needed. Earlier, she'd dismissed the village as having little to recommend it, but now she was beginning to appreciate its merits as a place in which to recharge her batteries.

"Okay, Ricardo – I'd be happy to stick around here for another day or two. I'm sure I can move back into the hotel. It's not exactly full."

"No, no!" Father Ricardo protested. "I will not hear of that. You will stay here at the presbytery."

"Well, if you're absolutely sure –"

The priest dismissed the subject with another wave of his hand. Then he picked up the carafe from the table and began pouring the contents into Alice's glass. "Now – let us have another glass of wine."

CHAPTER 27

"Caroline – is that you?"

"Hi, Simon, yes – it's me. How are you?"

Caroline's heart filled with joy. Simon had phoned her! While she'd felt quite sure he would, somewhere in the back of her mind was the fear that maybe he wouldn't. Men often said they'd phone and didn't bother.

"I'm fine, thanks – especially now that I've heard your lovely Irish accent again!"

"What's the weather like in London?"

"Oh, much the same as usual. Dull, with regular showers. I forgot my umbrella yesterday, and got soaked."

Caroline giggled. "I'd forgotten how important an Englishman's umbrella is! Do you, by any chance, wear a bowler hat as well?"

Simon laughed. "God, no! That's only for City types. Personally, I think they're ridiculous, but if you wanted me to wear one, I'd do it for you."

Caroline had visions of a naked Simon wearing only a bowler hat . . .

"Well, maybe in the bedroom . . ." she teased.

His voice softened. "I'm counting the days till you get back to London, Caroline."

"I'm looking forward to it too."

"I've looked up your aunt's name in the current Register of Electors, under both her single and married name, but I didn't find her listed anywhere."

Caroline was surprised and pleased he had tried. She was aware that it was a mammoth task to check all the different boroughs. "Thanks, Simon, that's very good of you."

"No problem – in my job, I have access to a lot of information and computer programmes that could be of use. When you get back to London, we can check out some other options."

Caroline was overjoyed. Not only was Simon prepared to help her find Gina, it sounded as though he intended seeing her many more times! How lucky she was – she'd found a gorgeous man, and he was willing to help her in her search for her missing aunt!

It was arranged that Caroline would come to London the following weekend, and that she would stay at the same hotel as before.

"Sorry I can't offer to put you up," said Simon apologetically, "but I'm having my flat painted this weekend. You don't mind, do you?"

"No, of course not," Caroline assured him. But in truth, she *was* disappointed. She'd been looking forward to learning more about Simon, and she'd felt that visiting the place where he lived would reveal more about his personality and tastes.

"I can't wait to hold you again," Simon told her before he rang off.

Caroline felt a thrill run through her at his words, and she cradled her mobile phone long after the connection between them had been broken. Was this love? Or was it just lust? Whatever it was, she had never experienced anything like it before.

There was just one problem on Caroline's horizon. Ken. They were still living together, and she found it awkward having to connect with him on a daily basis. She was still sleeping in the spare bedroom-cum-office, so there was no question of Ken invading her private space, but they still had to talk to each other whenever their paths crossed. Which was quite regularly in a small semi-detached house!

She also felt bad about treating him so unfairly. Ken hadn't done anything, other than not be Simon. Sometimes, Caroline asked herself what exactly she was doing. Presumably, she was trying to have her cake and eat it. She was deeply attracted to Simon, and wanted to give the relationship time to develop before she made any life-changing decisions about Ken. Fortunately, Ken assumed that her new-found happiness was due to her preoccupation with searching for her aunt, and Caroline was happy to leave him thinking that way, for the present at least. At some point, she would have to make a decision, and choose between Simon and Ken. But not yet, she hoped. Just not yet.

Caroline decided that it might be best if she gave herself and Ken some space. Time away from Ken would help her to clear her mind, and maybe enable her to figure out what she wanted from life. Her mother's easy company and home cooking was just what she needed.

That evening, when Ken arrived home from work, Caroline was waiting for him in the kitchen.

"I'm thinking of moving back to Mum's place for a while," she said evenly. "I just think we're getting on each other's nerves at the moment."

But Ken didn't behave acquiescently, as Caroline had expected.

"I think finding this bloody aunt of yours has become more important to you than the wedding itself!" he roared. "Are you sure you want to get married at all? Why don't you find this aunt of yours, and go and live with her instead? She seems to matter a lot more to you than I do!"

Caroline was momentarily shocked. She'd never seen Ken react like this. He normally let her have her way in everything. Yet in a way she was pleased at his outburst, since it allowed her to dislike him, and justify what she was doing.

Having rung Stella and asked if she could stay for a few days, Caroline packed a bag, then put it and Gina's old suitcase into the boot of her car. In the relative peace of her mother's house, she'd be able to relax. And hopefully sort out the dilemma that had turned her life on its head.

When she arrived at her mother's neat little house in Blackrock, Stella expressed concern at her daughter's move back to the family home.

"Why, Caroline?" she asked plaintively. "I thought everything was fine between you and Ken."

"Don't worry, Mum," Caroline told her, smiling. "It's just a little tiff. But I need a break. And I also miss your wonderful cooking!"

Stella sighed. It was only a few months to the wedding, so maybe it was pre-wedding jitters that had caused the rift between Caroline and Ken.

"Well, I won't bake any of my fruit cakes or apple pies,"

Stella told her sternly. "You don't want to put on any weight between now and the wedding."

The thought of the wedding brought a frown to Caroline's face. It seemed to be drawing oppressively near, and at times she felt as though the Sword of Damocles was hanging over her head. Surely she shouldn't be feeling that way, if her marriage to Ken was meant to be? Was her heart telling her something that her brain didn't want to acknowledge?

"Let's have a cup of tea, Mum, and I'll show you Gina's wedding photos," Caroline said. "I'll dig out her wedding dress too –"

"Oh dear!" said Stella, visibly upset. "Poor Gina! You're not persisting in this search of yours, are you, Caroline?"

"But Mum, I'm doing so well!" Caroline replied, her eyes dancing with enthusiasm. "Who'd ever have thought I'd find Larry Macken so easily!"

"I wish you'd leave well enough alone," said her mother, polishing her spectacles in preparation for viewing the photographs. "There's too much at stake."

"What do you mean, Mum?"

"Nothing," said Stella, suddenly looking guilty. "I've already said too much."

CHAPTER 28

The following morning, after a pleasant breakfast together, consisting of eggs, honey and bread – all local produce – Father Ricardo left Alice to her own devices and headed off to the church to say Mass, to make arrangements for Senora Delgado's funeral, then to visit the sick of the parish.

"I am glad you are staying for a few days," he told her before he left. "It will suit us both – I am pleased to have company, and you need a few days of rest." Then he grinned at her. "But if you feel the need to make yourself useful, you can prepare something for us to eat tonight."

During Father Ricardo's absence, Alice washed out her soiled socks, panties, shorts and T-shirts, and hung them on the small clothesline at the back of the presbytery. The intense heat of the day would ensure that everything would be well and truly dry in no time. She didn't mind looking crumpled as long as she felt clean, and it was a luxury to be able to hang the stuff out, rather than trying to dry it over the sink in some hotel or hostel.

Later, she set off to the local stores, where she bought

fresh bread, a few bottles of wine, and the ingredients to make a stew for that evening. Realising that she was enjoying herself immensely, Alice felt guilty for her earlier denunciation of the little village. The people were friendly and helpful, and seemed amused to find a young woman staying at the local presbytery. They were reluctant to take money from her for her purchases, and on several occasions Alice had to insist that she be allowed pay for the items she was buying! It was clear that the young priest was held in high esteem, and it appeared that any friend of his was a friend of the locals too!

As Alice made her way back to the presbytery, she felt glad that she'd spent all those boring hours in Spanish class at school and university – finally it was paying off!

Later that evening, as they were enjoying the stew Alice had cooked, Father Ricardo announced that as soon as Senora Delgado's funeral was over the following morning, he had to go to the nearby town for a meeting with the bishop.

"I would be grateful if you would attend her funeral –"

"Of course," Alice said immediately. "I fully intended to be there. Do you know yet what she died of?" She immediately regretted asking, since she probably had no right to know.

"It was a heart attack," Ricardo told her sadly. "Doctor Sanchez was surprised, since the Senora had always been in robust good health. He wondered if anything had happened to distress her during her last few days."

"She was certainly distressed when I found her," Alice confirmed. "She'd never met me before, but she was rambling on about people trying to kill me, and about her having to hide from some people. It didn't make any sense."

"Poor woman – hopefully she is at peace now," Ricardo said. "Sometimes people become confused just before death, and hark back to earlier times. I have seen this happen myself many times. I'm just sad that her last moments on earth were such stressful ones." He suddenly smiled. "That is enough sad talk for one evening – now we must make plans for the living! After the funeral tomorrow, you will stay here and rest while I visit the Bishop, yes?"

Alice nodded, happy to have someone else make decisions for her. Before long, she would have to make a monumental decision herself, and the longer she could put it off the better.

They ate their meal in companionable silence, the only sound being the grunts of approval from the young priest.

When his plate was empty, Father Ricardo sat back contentedly. "Now – there is another little matter that we must attend to."

Alice raised her eyebrows.

"Our friend the goat – we cannot leave him tied up behind Senora Delgado's house. He will be hungry – and lonely. So I think he must come to the presbytery for the present, do you agree?"

Alice laughed, pleased that the goat's future was secure, at least for the present. "Ricardo, you seem intent on filling up the presbytery with all sorts of waifs and strays! First me, now the goat – where will it all end?"

The young priest smiled. "But first, I must go to the church and pray for Senora Delgado. Will you come with me?"

Alice nodded. "Of course I will."

In companionable silence, they walked up the hill to the church together. Dusk was falling, and when they arrived the inside of the church was illuminated with hundreds of candles lit by the local faithful. It looked beautiful, and Alice remembered the days of her childhood, when she'd been mesmerised by similar sights in the school chapel.

"These kind local woman have prepared the body," Father Ricardo said softly, gesturing towards the coffin in front of the altar. "They lay out the dead as a means of gaining extra graces in the next life."

Alice nodded. It was still the same in parts of rural Ireland.

Following the priest's example, she knelt down in the old, silent church. It was so long since she had prayed, or even been in a church, that she was unsure of what to do. But she instinctively joined her hands in the universal symbol of prayer, and silently waited as Father Ricardo communed with his God.

Alice liked this young man kneeling beside her. Father Ricardo Alvarez was one of those religious who was truly a man of the people. A simple but open-minded man, who accepted human nature with all its frailties and imperfections. She felt a great comfort to have him kneeling by her side. Because when she thought of where destiny was currently leading her, she felt sick with apprehension.

Father Ricardo suddenly spoke, and Alice, deep in her own thoughts, almost jumped with fright.

"My friend," he whispered softly, "I am asking God to watch over you, because the road ahead will be difficult."

The priest's face glowed, lit only by the candlelight, and Alice thought, as she looked at his profile, that he was one of the kindest men she'd ever met. She felt humbled to have a comparative stranger more worried about her welfare than her own husband.

After they left the church, the duo walked down the hill and though the darkness until they reached the winding driveway leading up to Senora Delgado's house. In the moonlight, the house looked eerie and even more forlorn than before. Alice gave a shiver, even though it wasn't cold.

She was relieved when the priest quickly released the goat from its tether at the back of the house, tied a piece of rope around its neck and led it firmly back down the driveway. The goat was delighted to see them, and was keen to play, which to his way of thinking meant nipping them both as they walked along.

Once Alice was away from the old woman's house, her sense of humour returned.

"Thank goodness my clothes are dry, and already put away," she said, grinning at Ricardo. "I may be a city woman, but I'm well aware that a goat will eat almost anything – including the contents of the clothesline!"

As Father Ricardo released the goat into his back yard, and was opening the door of the presbytery, Alice turned back to take in a last glimpse of the area by night. She watched a bat fly by, squeaking as it dipped and dived. Suddenly, she thought she saw a light in the distance.

"Ricardo – look! Is that a light on in Senora Delgado's house?"

"Where?" The priest re-adjusted his eyes from the lights of the presbytery to the darkness outside. "I do not see anything."

He was right. There was nothing visible any more.

I probably imagined it, Alice thought. It was probably just a trick of the light.

CHAPTER 29

The next morning, Alice accompanied Father Ricardo to the church, where he said Requiem Mass for the repose of Senora Delgado's soul. After the church service, her remains were interred in the tiny cemetery beside the church. The funeral was a low-key affair, with just the local community turning out to pay their respects.

"I do not think she had any family," Father Ricardo said afterwards. "It is sad, is it not, to end your life with no one to care for you?"

Alice nodded. "And you, Ricardo – what family do you have?"

Father Ricardo's face lit up. "My parents live a long way from here, so I only see them once or twice a year, but I have a brother nearby in the city. We are very different, but I love him dearly. And he loves me."

The priest's mention of the mutual love between him and his brother brought a lump to Alice's throat. She had no siblings to love her, although she knew her mother loved her unconditionally. And Bill – could she honestly say that her husband loved her? With hindsight, Alice realised that Bill only seemed to care about her when she was massaging his ego and telling him how wonderful he was. And she realised suddenly that this was not a role she was prepared to play any longer.

"Now," said the priest as they walked back to the presbytery together, "I must leave for my meeting with the bishop. Hopefully, you and the goat will have a restful day while I'm away." Then he grinned mischievously at Alice. "Of course, should I return to find a nice meal on the table, well –"

"Don't worry," said Alice, smiling. "I'm happy to make dinner. Will your meeting with the bishop be difficult?"

The young priest grinned, shaking his head. "I will flatter him, and all will be well."

"Maybe you'll be a bishop one day, Ricardo."

The young priest shuddered. "I would hate it, more than anything in the world! For me, being a priest means ministering to people's needs, not getting caught up in church politics."

Alice smiled, once again aware of the contrast between the gentle priest and the husband she'd left behind in Ireland. And she knew which one she would prefer to depend on in a crisis.

After Father Ricardo left, Alice busied herself with tidying up the kitchen, washing the dishes and wiping down the work surfaces until everything gleamed. Then she tackled the bathroom, scrubbing the tiles until every trace of soap residue had been cleaned off. Then she dusted the furniture and polished the old linoleum underfoot until she could almost see her reflection in it. It was the least she could do, she felt, in return for Ricardo's generosity, and it gave her a great sense of achievement when she surveyed her handiwork.

As she tidied and polished, Alice's thoughts flitted from one problem to another. She had a huge decision to make about her marriage. Could she honestly stay with Bill now that she despised him? On the other hand, was it cowardly to leave him now that he was in serious financial difficulties? She remembered those words from the marriage ceremony: 'For better for worse, in sickness and in health'. Up until now, she'd been happy to live off the spoils of Bill's dodgy dealings. No, she corrected herself, she hadn't exactly been happy about it, but she'd nevertheless taken what was on offer. And now, when he was in financial difficulties, she was proposing to dump him. Oh God, what was she going to do?

To stop herself from becoming too maudlin, Alice switched her thoughts to her stay in Argentina. She'd come to love this country, with its beautiful landscapes and its warm friendly people. In fact, being far away from home had made the loss of her house seem less important, and Ricardo's simple lifestyle had forced her to confront her own previously privileged, yet empty, way of life.

Taking her lunch into the back garden, Alice sat alongside the young goat who now had the freedom of the yard, and together they shared her bread and cheese. Nuzzling the young animal's head, Alice wished that he could speak.

"I wish you could tell me about your late owner," Alice said. "Why on earth did she think she knew me? Was she just confused because she was dying?"

The goat decided that since Alice was directing her

conversation towards him, it must mean that he had permission to chew the hem of her skirt, so a mini-battle ensued as Alice laughingly tried to extricate the material from the animal's mouth, while dodging a series of friendly nips.

"Okay," said Alice at last, "you win. Just give me back my skirt and I'll get you some more bread. Have we a deal?"

As though he understood, the goat immediately let go the hem of the skirt, and followed her meekly to the back door, where she got some bread for him. She wasn't sure if bread was suitable for a goat's diet, but the goat certainly wasn't saying no.

As she made herself a cup of tea in the cool kitchen, Alice wondered how her new friend, Patricia Martin, was getting on in Santa Katerina. Patricia, who she'd first met at one of the backpackers' hostels, had been heading for the relatively unknown caves there, and had been excited at the prospect of exploring them. She'd told Alice that she was adept at hiking and climbing, and was looking forward to the chance of getting close to such a mystic location.

Each woman had been astonished to find another Irish woman travelling alone in Argentina, and they were even more amazed to discover that each was using the time abroad to make major decisions about their future. Patricia had career decisions to make, which would mean moving abroad if her career was to advance, but she dreaded leaving her parents and siblings behind.

They'd laughed when they discovered that they'd each brought Barry's tea bags and Tayto crisps in their luggage! And they'd been astonished to discover that they lived less than fifteen miles from each other back home in Dublin!

The two women had quickly become friends, travelling together for several days, staying in the same hostels – often in the same dormitory, when the hostels were short of private rooms. However, since they had different itineraries, they'd eventually parted company. Patricia had headed north for Santa Katerina, and Alice had opted to head south through the countryside that led to Villanova. But the women had assured each other that they'd meet up again, just as soon as they were both back in Dublin.

Taking her tea out into the garden, Alice sat down on the old rusty garden bench. She was relieved to see that the goat was happily munching the scrub grass at the bottom of the hedge, so there was no immediate need to protect herself from his little love bites!

Thinking of home once more, Alice wondered what she would do when her time in Argentina ran out. She loved her job, and certainly didn't intend leaving journalism. On the other hand, would she return to Bill? He'd sorely tested her feelings for him. Idly, she wondered if Patricia had reached any decision on her career yet. One thing was certain – she herself was as indecisive as ever.

CHAPTER 30

That evening, as Alice checked the casserole in the oven, she heard the front door open as the young priest arrived back. She was pleased to see him, and was looking forward to another of their relaxing chats over dinner. She'd grown to value his perspective on so many things, and she particularly loved to hear his stories about life in rural Argentina.

"Hi, Ricardo – I hope you're hungry, because I've made a big feed for us!" she called to him.

The priest nodded as he entered the kitchen, a strained expression on his face.

"You look tired," said Alice, immediately concerned. "Was your meeting with the bishop difficult?"

Slumping into a chair at the table, Ricardo shook his head. "No – the bishop, as always, is easy to flatter. All I had to do was to sound enthusiastic about his plans for a new cathedral in his diocese."

"Then what's the matter?" asked Alice gently. "I think I know you by now, Ricardo – there's something on your mind, isn't there? Well, you can tell Auntie Alice – you've listened to *my* woes for long enough. Now it's my turn to help *you*, if I can."

Reaching into his briefcase, the young priest extracted a newspaper. "While I was in the town, I picked up the latest copy of *La Nacion*," he told her, "and I regret to tell you –" He hesitated. "I'm afraid, Alice, the news is not good."

"W-what do you mean?"

"You mentioned, did you not, that you became friends with another Irish woman on your travels?'

Alice nodded.

"Well, I have sad news – in the newspaper, it says that a young Irish woman died accidentally a few days ago, in Santa Katerina."

Alice was shocked. "Oh God, no – that's where Patricia was heading!" Reaching for the newspaper, she quickly scanned the story, tears filling her eyes as she realised that there could be little doubt about the woman's identity. "Oh, poor Patricia – she was so excited about going to explore the caves there. What a tragedy – to fall down into one of them!" She looked incredulously at Father Ricardo. "How on earth did it happen? I mean, she was so adamant about the importance of wearing her safety harnesses. She showed me all her gear, and told me she was an experienced member of a climbing club back home." Alice's hands shook as she poured wine for herself and Ricardo. "And now this happens to her! How terrible!"

According to the newspaper, the woman's identity was not being released until her family had been informed, but there was little doubt that it was Alice's friend.

Dinner proved to be a sombre affair, as neither Alice nor

Ricardo had much appetite for the delicious meal that Alice had prepared.

"Well, our goat friend will eat well this evening," said Alice, pushing her plate aside.

"He can have mine too," added the priest. "That is not to say your cooking isn't excellent, Alice. But, like you, I no longer feel like eating. Although I did not know this Patricia – from listening to the stories of your travels together, I feel that I have lost a friend too."

Alice was unable to reply because of the large lump that was blocking her throat.

Ricardo smiled gently. "I know you were planning to leave Villanova tomorrow, but in view of what has happened, I would urge you to stay a little longer."

Alice nodded, grateful not to have to leave while she was feeling so wretched. Right now, Ricardo's gentle companion-ship was exactly what she needed.

"Thanks, Ricardo – I really appreciate your offer. I'm feeling a bit fragile right now – I just can't believe that this has happened to poor Patricia." She took a gulp of wine. "When I get back to Ireland, I'll go straight to visit her family in Castleknock. They must be devastated, but at least I'll be able to tell them about her last days – I was probably the last person from home to spend time with her, so I can tell them how much she was enjoying her trip –" Unable to hold back any longer, Alice burst into tears.

CHAPTER 31

The following morning, Alice slept late, and when she finally awoke, she had a thumping headache. She was emotionally exhausted from the news of Patricia's tragic death, and physically ill from the amount of rough wine she'd consumed the night before.

When she finally roused herself from bed and went into the kitchen, she discovered that Ricardo had already left to say Mass and hear confessions, but he had left her a note explaining where he was. So she made herself a cup of tea and some toast, and brought the previous day's surplus vegetables out to the young goat, who devoured them ravenously.

As she washed up her breakfast dishes, Alice decided that it was finally time to move on. Although she'd agreed the previous night to stay on a bit longer, she felt that she couldn't impose on Ricardo's generosity any more. And besides, now that she'd learnt about Patricia's death, she felt a responsibility to the dead woman's family. Now they'd be arranging a funeral instead of welcoming her home. When she returned to Ireland, she'd convey to them the memories of Patricia's last days in Argentina, while they were still fresh in her mind.

Alice decided that Villanova would be the turning point in her travels – from there she would turn back and head towards Buenos Aires. Somehow, she didn't have the heart for travelling on any further. Instead, she would meander slowly back to the city, stopping off at towns and villages that took her fancy, since she still had more than two weeks left before her return flight. And during that time, she would reach a decision on her own marriage.

When Father Ricardo returned, Alice informed him of her plans.

"Whatever you wish, my friend," he told her. "I will be sorry to see you go, since I have enjoyed your company so much. But I realise that you must get back to your own life in Ireland." His eyes twinkled. "I suspect the goat will miss you too, since I feel he has a special place in your heart."

"I'll miss you both," said Alice, her voice suddenly choking with emotion. She rushed to the young priest and hugged him fiercely. "Thank you for everything, Ricardo – you've been a great friend. I hope we can stay in touch – I promise I'll write when I get back to Dublin."

"Indeed," said Father Ricardo, who had turned pink with both pleasure and embarrassment, "I shall look forward to your letters, Alice. I will be waiting to hear what you decide to do about your marriage. I will pray that you make the decision that's right for you."

Alice nodded, tears in her eyes. How like Ricardo to be non-judgemental! He hadn't banged on about the sanctity of marriage or the importance of her marriage vows, merely expressed concern that she would make the right decision for *her*.

That evening, Father Ricardo announced that he would cook the meal for their last evening together. "And I will prepare something special for our friend the goat as well," he announced.

Alice nodded, unable to speak. Now that she'd made her decision to leave, she wasn't sure if she really wanted to go at all. On the other hand, it would be unfair to Ricardo to keep changing her mind. She sighed. Besides, she'd have to go eventually, so it was probably easier to go sooner rather than later.

Excusing herself in order to pack her rucksack once again, Alice climbed the rickety stairs to her tiny bedroom upstairs. As she looked around it, she knew she would never forget her time in Villanova. The simplicity of Ricardo's life, coupled with his humility and kindness, had awoken something inside her that had long been dormant. She realised that whatever choice she ultimately made about her marriage, she would never give over control of her life to another person again. Even if she and Bill stayed together, she would make a point of knowing exactly what business dealings he was involved in. She would never again turn a blind eye to his moneymaking schemes, or accept a comfortable lifestyle that might be gained at someone else's expense.

As she watched the setting sun from her tiny bedroom window, Alice could hear the sounds of Ricardo moving around in the kitchen downstairs. He'd turned his ancient radio on, and she could hear the low drone of what sounded like a news bulletin. Then she heard the clatter of dishes, and something being washed in the sink. After that, she heard him talking to the goat, who was obviously lurking outside the back door, and Alice was overwhelmed by a sense of loss at the thought of leaving Villanova. And to think, she chided herself, less than a week ago, I thought this town was an awful kip. Now, I'd gladly spend my entire life here.

"Alice – can you please come down here?"

Alice suddenly awoke, and realised that she must have lain down on her bed and dozed off.

"Alice – please!"

Jumping up, Alice hurried out of her room and descended the stairs. Ricardo had sounded worried. Maybe he'd burnt the dinner, Alice thought, although she didn't really care. Nothing was going to spoil their last evening together. She would happily eat dry bread, and she knew that they still had several bottles of the local wine in the pantry.

But the table was laid out with two plates of piping hot food, and Alice felt momentarily puzzled. Ricardo looked distressed without any obvious reason.

"Please, Alice – I am afraid that there is more bad news about your friend."

"Patricia?"

The young priest nodded.

Alice continued to look puzzled. What could be worse than being dead?

"I just heard on the radio – your friend's death was not an accident. It is now being regarded by the police as murder."

Alice gasped. "What? Oh, poor Patricia! What happened, Ricardo?"

"According to the pathologist's report, there were certain

injuries that were not consistent with a fall – it didn't specify what they were – but it did mention that her face and skull were badly crushed."

"Oh my God!" Alice shook her head in disbelief. "Why would anyone want to kill her?"

Ricardo shrugged his shoulders. "I do not know, Alice. But I can tell you one thing – you are not leaving here tomorrow. It is obviously dangerous at present for young women to travel alone."

Alice's shock was punctuated with relief. Now she wouldn't have to leave Villanova just yet.

Ricardo gestured to Alice to sit down at the table, as he poured glasses of wine for them both. "Let us at least eat our dinner, Alice – we cannot help your friend by starving." He smiled. "And our friend the goat has already been well fed – not only has he had our generous donations from last evening, but I have also given him all the leftover vegetables from the meal I have just prepared."

Alice nodded and began to eat the meat, sweet potatoes and vegetables that Ricardo had prepared, but it tasted like sawdust in her mouth.

"But now," said Ricardo, "I think it is time we paid a visit to my brother in the city."

Alice looked up from her food at Ricardo's serious tone. "Your brother? Why?"

"My brother is a Police Inspector – I am sure you will want information on your friend's murder, and he is the man who can tell us. Then, when you visit your friend's family back in Ireland, you will be able to tell them the full story, and explain what is being done here to bring the perpetrator to justice."

Alice nodded. She was surprised to learn that Ricardo's brother was in the Argentine police force – for some reason she'd assumed he'd be a teacher, a social worker or a local magistrate. Then she felt guilty. She'd been so wrapped up in her own problems that she'd never even asked about him.

"Let us go to the city tomorrow," said Ricardo, "after I have said Mass."

Alice nodded in agreement. As she sipped her wine, she glanced gratefully at the young priest. How thoughtful of him to think of the needs of Patricia's family. And he was right. It would be better to get the details of what had happened directly from the Argentine police. Otherwise, information might get lost in translation, and poor Patricia's murder would eventually be reduced to a pile of documents ferried from one police force to another. She herself could add the personal dimension to the last days of Patricia's life.

CHAPTER 32

The following morning, Alice was up bright and early. She stretched, then grabbed a towel and headed downstairs to the shower room. She was looking forward to her trip to the city, and relieved that it was no longer the day of her departure from Villanova. She'd realised that she wasn't quite ready for that yet.

Ricardo had said Mass earlier than usual – much to the consternation of the local faithful – and after changing out of his vestments, he donned sombre yet casual clothes for the journey. After a hearty breakfast, and a nip from the goat when Alice gave him the leftovers, the two prepared for departure.

Having checked the local train timetable, Ricardo was aware that there was a train within the next half-hour that would take them reasonably close to his brother's office in downtown Buenos Aires.

Before they left, Ricardo rang his brother. "I have a house guest at the moment," he said, "and I will bring her with me when I come to your office. She hopes that you may be able to help her with some information she seeks."

His brother said something at the other end, and Ricardo hung up, smiling.

"My brother – he works so hard. Always working, no time for anything else."

Alice smiled. She wasn't sure if a reply was needed. But she sensed that there was something else that Ricardo wasn't saying.

As they began their leisurely walk downhill in the direction of the station, Alice tried to keep thoughts of Patricia at bay. She knew that if she started remembering the good times they'd spent together, she was bound to become maudlin and spoil the day for both herself and Ricardo.

The rickety old train was dusty outside, but in its dark interior the seats were surprisingly comfortable. The ancient carriages were clearly from a bygone age, and Alice was fascinated by the array of people who climbed aboard. Before long, their carriage had standing room only, and Alice found that she and Ricardo were sharing the bench seat with a cage of chickens, a large woman and several young children. She strained to understand them as they spoke in rapid-fire Spanish, but she had to confess herself lost before long.

The journey was several hours long, but Alice found the children and her surroundings highly entertaining. She and Ricardo had brought home-made sandwiches, which they shared with the woman and children who, in turn, insisted that Alice try some home-made brew called *maté* which tasted like a bitter version of tea. Gingerly, Alice swallowed it, trying not to offend anyone, watched by a highly amused Ricardo.

It was just noon when the train finally pulled into Buenos

Aires' main station. As it reached the outskirts of the city, Alice had spent her time gazing eagerly out of the window as the dry plains gave way to shantytowns, then city streets. She sighed with pleasure. She was looking forward to being back in Buenos Aires. It was a vibrant, colourful city, teeming with people, and although she'd only stayed there briefly on arrival, she'd originally planned to spend several extra days there before returning to Dublin. As thoughts of returning home filled her mind, her mood darkened. And thoughts of Patricia almost reduced her to tears.

After demonstrative goodbyes from their fellow travellers, it took another fifteen minutes of walking through the city streets before Alice and Ricardo arrived at the downtown office of the south city police precinct.

On the outside, it was a dull, dingy building, similar to police stations the world over. But once inside, Alice and Ricardo were confronted with a hive of activity. Telephones were ringing, people were calling to each other, others were typing up reports and drinking either coffee or *maté*.

Following Ricardo, Alice made her way up a narrow staircase to the next floor, which housed a series of individual offices. Ricardo knocked perfunctorily on an already open door, then ushered Alice inside. His brother was seated at his desk, a phone in one hand, a report in the other. He waved his hand and gestured to the two vacant chairs, while he continued talking rapidly into the phone.

Alice stared across the desk at him. The brothers shared the same gleaming black hair and dark brown eyes, but there the resemblance ended. In contrast to his leaner, gentler brother, Enrique was stocky, with hairy arms and strong square hands. He seemed to exude a raw vitality, and

191

his eyes had a penetrating quality that Alice found somewhat unsettling, maybe even a little frightening.

Suddenly, Enrique put down the phone, and caught Alice staring at him. Thrown off balance, she blushed, and was annoyed with herself for feeling wrong-footed.

"So this is your foreign friend, Ricardo," Enrique said in English, smiling. "Welcome to Argentina."

"Enrique, this is Alice Fitzsimons, from Ireland," said Ricardo.

Alice held out her hand, expecting to shake hands with Ricardo's brother, but Enrique paused, scratched his head and stared at her. "*Madre de dios*, this is very strange. What is your name again?"

"Alice Fitzsimons," said Alice, feeling annoyed at his brusque behaviour. Ricardo's brother was certainly lacking in good manners!

"But this is impossible," said Enrique, now looking extremely perturbed. He leaned forward on his desk, searched briefly among a pile of papers, picked up a document and waved it in front of her. "It says here that you are dead."

"Believe me, brother, my Irish friend is truly alive and kicking," said Ricardo in amusement.

"D-dead? What do you mean?" asked Alice.

Enrique didn't answer her, but scanned the document in his hand. "A woman called Alice Fitzsimons was murdered last week in Santa Katerina. At first, we thought she had fallen down one of the caves by accident, but the post mortem revealed that there had been a struggle prior to the fall." He scanned the document further, then looked up. "Injuries to the face and head made her virtually unrecognisable. The body was released shortly afterwards, and flown home to Ireland. See –" he passed the document to Alice, "– there is no doubt about it."

"Well, there is no doubt that my friend Alice here is alive," said Ricardo, attempting to lighten the atmosphere, "so there has obviously been some mistake."

"Oh my God!" Alice suddenly gasped, as the realisation of what might have happened suddenly dawned on her. Quickly she rummaged in her bag, pulled out the passport inside and opened it. Staring back at her was a picture of Patricia Martin.

"Oh God – our passports must have got mixed up – look, this one is hers, and she's probably got mine!" groaned Alice. "I mean, she did have mine – before she died."

"What are you talking about?" Enrique asked.

"Oh my God," whispered Alice, "I met this Irish woman when I was backpacking, and we travelled together for a few days, and stayed together in the same hostels, even the same room, since the hostels were nearly always full. That must be when –"

"And this other woman's name is – ?"

"Patricia Martin," said Alice, handing over Patricia's passport.

Enrique looked at the passport, then back at Alice. He said nothing, continuing to stare at her, making her feel uncomfortable.

Suddenly, she had another thought. "Y-you said the body had been released?"

Enrique nodded. "Yes, I believe the funeral took place yesterday in Dublin."

Alice gasped again as the implication of what had happened began to dawn on her. "Oh my God – my husband and mother think I'm dead! My friends and work colleagues think I'm dead! They think they've buried me!" Tears of shock filled her eyes, and she looked wildly around for a phone. "Do you mind if I ring home? I'll gladly pay for the call, but I need to let them know that I'm okay —"

Already, Alice was on her feet, and grabbing the phone she'd spotted on Enrique's desk.

"No!"

Alice froze as Enrique towered over her, pulling her arm roughly away from the phone.

"What do you —"

"Please." Enrique, realising how upset Alice was, led her gently back to her chair beside Ricardo who was now looking considerably nonplussed.

Enrique shut the door before he spoke again.

"Don't you see?" he said softly, addressing them both. "We must find out *why* this woman was murdered. We need to discover if it was just a robbery, or if she was killed because of *who* she was." His expression was grim. "Or who the perpetrator *thought* she was."

"What do you mean, Enrique?" Ricardo asked his brother.

Ignoring him, Enrique addressed his next comment to Alice. "Do you have any enemies?"

Alice looked bewildered. "I don't understand what you mean . . ."

Enrique grimaced. "I am sorry to have to say this, but has it crossed your mind that *you* might actually have been the target? Maybe it was *you* that someone wanted to kill."

CHAPTER 33

"Maeve, it's Caroline – Gina's niece."

"Oh, hello, Caroline," Maeve replied, her eyes lighting up as she heard Caroline's voice on the phone. "Have you made any progress with your search?"

Caroline hesitated. "Could I come over and see you, or meet you somewhere? I've some photographs of Gina you might like to see."

"Have you *found* her?" Maeve cried, excitement in her voice.

"No, sorry, I'm afraid not – but I *am* making progress."

Maeve's heartbeat slowed down again, disappointment furrowing her brow. She hadn't stopped thinking about her old friend since Caroline had called to her house before. How wonderful it would be to see Gina again! They'd been so close all those years ago.

"Of course you're welcome to come over here, or I'll meet you in town if you like."

The two women arranged that Caroline would call over to Maeve's house the following evening, while her husband Kevin was out playing bridge.

When Caroline arrived, Maeve already had the kettle on, and soon the two women were sitting down at Maeve's kitchen table with mugs of tea in front of them, and a big plate with slices of home-made fruit cake on it.

Caroline explained about her visit to Larry's house in London, and about being given the old suitcase.

"So Larry is alive and well – I'm glad to hear it," said Maeve sincerely. "How clever of you to find him!"

"It wasn't difficult," said Caroline modestly. "You were the one who told me he lived in either Haringey or Hackney, so I simply looked him up in the phone book."

"I always liked Larry," said Maeve. "He was a lovely man. And he has a new wife, you say?"

"Yes, her name is Clare. I haven't met her, but I gather they've been together since shortly after Gina disappeared."

"I'm glad he found someone to love him," said Maeve softly. "No one deserved happiness more than him. Gina led him a merry dance, you know. And he let her walk all over him." She sighed. "I think I already told you that I was the one who told Gina about Owen's death. I rang her in London, but she refused to believe me, and became hysterical. She slammed down the phone, and even though I rang back, she wouldn't answer it. But I knew she was there, probably crying her eyes out, poor love. I think Owen meant more to her than I ever realised."

Reaching into her bag, Caroline produced the wedding photos she'd found in Gina's suitcase.

"Would you like to see Gina's wedding photos?"

Maeve's eyes lit up. "Oh yes, please! I never did get to see any of them. I didn't own a camera myself at the time, and the ink was hardly dry on Gina's marriage certificate before she'd disappeared."

Time After Time

Caroline handed over the folder of photographs to Maeve, who began looking through them eagerly.

"Oh lord, she looked lovely, didn't she?" said Maeve, looking at a picture of Gina, a faraway look in her eyes. "We were all so young back then! I can't believe that those photos were taken over thirty years ago!" She chuckled as she studied the fashions of yesteryear. "Oh my God – look at the hat Rosemary's wearing! It's like an upturned chamber pot! And Eileen – how could she put those two colours together?" Then she spotted a photograph of herself, and dissolved in a fit of giggles. "Oh no! I look dreadful in that dress! Of course, I was a lot thinner back then, so I suppose I was able to get away with that dreadfully garish pattern."

"I hope you and your husband will come to *my* wedding," Caroline said, the words tumbling out before she realised what she was saying. But it was too late to retract the invitation.

"Thanks, Caroline," said Maeve, smiling, "we'd be delighted to attend. And if Gina was there – well, that really *would* be the icing on your cake, wouldn't it?"

Caroline nodded. For her, having Gina there would be a dream come true, and she was determined to make it happen. On the other hand, was there going to *be* a wedding? Caroline was tempted to tell Maeve about Simon, since she felt sure the older woman would understand. Then she decided against it. How could she invite Maeve to her wedding one minute, then tell her about another man in the next breath? She decided it was time to change the subject.

"Tell me about BWF Pharmaceuticals, Maeve – Dolly, Owen and Gina all worked there, didn't they?"

Maeve nodded. "Dolly was secretary to the managing director, Charles Keane. Later, when Owen Brady joined the company as Medical Director, he and Dolly started seeing each other. Shortly after that, they got married, and Gina finished her training as a laboratory technician and went to work there too. Eventually, she was promoted, and became Owen's assistant –" Her brow darkened. "That's when all the trouble started. Owen and Gina developed feelings for each other – and you know the rest of the story. BWF Pharmaceuticals was regarded as a great place to work, and they paid their staff well, but I knew from Gina that some of their work practices were bordering on the unethical. They cut corners where they shouldn't have. She was working on a new vaccine with Owen, and he wasn't happy with the way the Irish trials were going. Gina said Owen believed that if the vaccine went on sale, it would harm people."

"That must be what was in the research paper I found in Gina's suitcase!"

Maeve nodded. "Gina told me that BWF Pharmaceuticals had been trying to suppress Owen's research, but he intended going to the press with his findings. Then the poor man died in a car accident, and I don't know what happened about the vaccine."

Caroline shrugged her shoulders. "Well, assuming the vaccine never went ahead, I've probably wasted Alice Fitzsimons' valuable time," she said ruefully. "I put the copy of Owen's research in the post to her, since it looked like the kind of thing she usually writes about."

Maeve looked startled. "Is that the young woman who investigates fraud and corruption for the *Daily News*?"

Caroline nodded, grinning wryly. "Oh well, I'm sure it's not the first bit of useless information she's received in the post!"

Maeve suddenly jumped up and began rummaging among a pile of discarded newspapers on the floor beside the sofa. Finding the one she wanted, she began rifling through the pages until she found the story she was looking for, then thrust it at Caroline.

"Is that the young woman you mean? Apparently she was killed in Argentina a few days ago."

"What? Oh my God, no! What happened?"

Maeve waited as Caroline quickly scanned the page.

"The poor woman – it says here that she had an accident and was killed while sightseeing in caves at one of the national parks." Caroline put down the newspaper. "Well, now we'll never know if the stuff I sent her was of any use."

Maeve looked pensive. "It's interesting, isn't it, that she was killed just after you sent her Owen's research paper?"

Caroline looked up, astonished. "You mean *I* could be responsible for her death?"

Maeve was immediately contrite. "Sorry, Caroline – I didn't mean it like that, but every time the name of BWF Pharmaceuticals comes up, strange things seem to happen. It's odd, you must admit."

Now it was Caroline's turn to look pensive. "Hmmm – I see what you mean. Owen died, then Gina disappeared. Now Alice Fitzsimons is dead. The link between them all is Owen's research for BWF Pharmaceuticals." Then she shook her head, as though waking herself up. "No, it's too far-fetched, Maeve. Besides, that research paper was thirty years old – what relevance could it have to anything today?"

"Then why did you send it to Alice Fitzsimons?"

Caroline shrugged her shoulders. "I'm not really sure. Knowing the kind of stuff Alice Fitzsimons writes – I mean, wrote – I thought it might be of interest to her." She grinned sheepishly at Maeve. "To be honest, I also knew that it would annoy Aunt Dolly if I sent it to one of the newspapers! She's always so protective of Charles Keane that it makes me sick." She brightened. "Anyway, assuming I can find Gina, she'll probably be able to tell us all about it."

Maeve nodded. "If anyone can find her, Caroline, it's you."

CHAPTER 34

Arriving back at the presbytery in Villanova that night, an exhausted Alice had immediately gone to her room. Although Ricardo was preparing dinner downstairs, she'd desperately needed to be alone for a while. Her entire world had been turned upside down, and she needed space in which to come to terms with it.

As she lay on her bed, staring at the ceiling, Alice shivered. On paper, she was dead. It was a weird feeling. She had this bizarre sense of wanting to know what people were actually saying about her, now that they thought her life was over. She'd often thought how sad it was that the dead always missed the nice things that were said about them at their funerals. But now she herself would be able to read what had been said about her, by scanning in the newspapers from back home on the Internet! On the other hand, she felt awful that her mother and her husband believed she was dead, yet she couldn't let them know the truth yet. It was ironic – she'd run away from home to make a decision that would give her back control of her life – now her life was even more out of control.

No, no – it was all a mistake. Patricia had simply been a random victim. Enrique had said there was definite evidence of theft. She shivered again. Was it possible that Patricia hadn't been the intended target, that she herself was the person the killer was after? But surely no one could want to murder her? She didn't have a single enemy in the world. None that she knew of, anyway.

Why had Enrique insisted that she mustn't contact anyone back in Ireland, not even her mother or husband? He couldn't possibly suspect that anyone in her family would want to kill her!

Suddenly, Alice was overcome by a horrendous thought. What about all the money that Bill would gain if she was out of the equation? Her recent inheritance from her late father's sister would then be his. And with it, he could rescue his business and pay off all the people he owed money to, then continue with his high-flying lifestyle.

No, she refused to believe that of Bill. While he was callous in his business dealings, he'd never stoop to murder, would he? Yet she still felt a nagging doubt. With the hindsight of distance, Alice realised that she hardly knew her husband, and she found herself wondering why she'd married him in the first place. She didn't like admitting to herself that she might have been seduced by the fact that Bill was handsome and charming – and that lots of other women had been after him. Especially Geraldine McEvoy, who'd always fancied Bill, and who'd been livid when Bill had asked Alice to marry him instead. Could I have been so shallow as to marry a man to prevent someone else having him? Alice shook her head vehemently. No, of course not! But she couldn't deny that there had been a particular thrill in being the one Bill had chosen to marry. People had looked at her differently then, with a certain respect in their eyes that hadn't been there before.

Alice sighed. If she was honest with herself, she had to admit that prior to her marriage, she'd never bothered to find out exactly how Bill made his money. She'd known he was in finance, and worked in a big office in the best part of town. Back then, she'd accepted that he must be very clever with money, since he made lots of it. Later, she realised that people who made lots of money were often making it at someone else's expense.

Mentally, Alice shook herself. At least Bill didn't destroy people's lives, or murder people, did he? Then she was overcome by a horrible sense of déjà vu. What about that takeover Bill had been involved in only a few months earlier, which resulted in the owner of the building – a man called Peter Waldron – throwing himself out the top window just before it was repossessed? Bill hadn't been particularly perturbed. Market forces, was how he'd justified it.

Alice also recalled the time when a rare species of toad, which only bred in Ireland and a few other sites in Europe, had been decimated in order to clear the way for a new exclusive golf club.

"Stop whinging about them, for Christ's sake!" Bill had said, irritated. "What on earth use are bloody toads? As far as I can see, every river and stream is full of the damn things!"

"But the ones you've destroyed were a unique and irreplaceable species!" she'd told him angrily.

"Who gives a fuck?" he'd answered her. "You should be grateful that I'm making so much money out of this deal. Are the bloody toads going to buy you a new car?"

The following week, Bill had bought her a new red sports car, but every time she drove it, Alice felt that its colour represented the blood of all those poor toads. Before long she sold it, much to Bill's annoyance, and anonymously sent a bank draft for that amount to an animal charity. She'd felt more comfortable in her old Peugeot.

Alice's hands now shook as she faced a frightening possibility. Maybe, in fact, Bill *had* been the one who had tried to kill her. Her husband often used the expression "I'd kill for a beer" or "I'd kill for a cup of coffee" – would he also kill for an inheritance?

CHAPTER 35

Later that evening, Alice had recovered sufficiently to join Ricardo for dinner. But while both of them went through the motions of eating the simple fare, neither of them were hungry. Alice had bought tomatoes, lettuce, cucumber, eggs and brown bread at the market near the railway station on their way back, but the salad she'd prepared now tasted bland.

"Your brother is rather brusque, isn't he?" she said at last.

Ricardo smiled sadly. "Yes, I suppose he is. But that is just his way – he does not mean to be rude. He has a very responsible job, and he takes it very seriously." He hesitated, as though unsure whether to say anything more. "His job is all Enrique has left – when Maria died, he became a different man."

"Maria?"

"She was his wife, but she died five years ago. They were expecting their first child, but towards the end of the pregnancy, she developed an illness called, I believe, pre-eclampsia." He sighed deeply. "But of course, they did not know this at the time. Enrique knew that there was something wrong – towards the end of Maria's pregnancy, her ankles and wrists were badly swollen, and he begged her to let him get a doctor, but she would not agree. You see, she was determined to give birth at home, and feared that a doctor would tell her that because of the swelling she would need to give birth in hospital."

Alice could feel the pain in Ricardo's voice.

"So Enrique, knowing how upset Maria would be if he went against her wishes, did nothing." He shrugged his shoulders. "Now, he tortures himself daily, believing that if he had ignored Maria's wishes, she and the baby would still be alive."

Alice suddenly felt deeply sorry for poor Enrique, at last understanding the pain he was enduring. No wonder he was brusque – while he dealt with death on a regular basis as a policeman, what could compare to the loss of his wife and child?

"There's so much sadness in the world, isn't there, Ricardo? It amazes me why people want to start wars – isn't there enough unplanned tragedy in the world already?"

The young priest nodded. "People seek power, and they will do anything to get it." He smiled. "Even my bishop likes to control his priests, and all the churches in his diocese."

Alice grimaced. "Most of the time, I prefer animals to people."

"We are both melancholy tonight," Ricardo said, pouring them each a glass of wine. "But you are right – I prefer the company of our goat friend to my bishop any day. The goat does not talk nonsense like the bishop does."

Alice smiled, but her thoughts were elsewhere. Although she was loath to admit it to herself, she was pleased to discover that Enrique hadn't remarried, and her cheeks flushed as she realised how attractive she found him. Oh dear, I'm pathetic, she thought. Just because he's gorgeous-looking, doesn't mean that anything is ever likely to happen between us. He probably doesn't even find me attractive. And why am I even thinking like this? I'm still a married woman, regardless of what Bill may or may not have done.

As they sipped their wine, Ricardo glanced quickly at Alice, then began studying his wine glass intently.

"My brother – I think he likes you."

Alice's cheeks turned puce. My God, had Ricardo read her thoughts? She felt as though she'd suddenly been stripped naked, and all her defences exposed.

"Does he?"

"Since Maria died, Enrique has never looked at another woman. But today, I saw the way he looked at you."

"He – I –" Alice gulped down a large mouthful of wine, unsure of what to say.

"I know you're still a married woman," Ricardo said gently, "but sometimes, when the heart is involved, a piece of paper is meaningless. Unless, Alice, you intend going back to your husband?"

Alice chewed her lip. She was well aware that she was a married woman, although she didn't exactly feel like one anymore. It was difficult to think about loving and cherishing a husband who might actually have tried to kill her.

"I don't think I could go back to Bill – not now, Ricardo. It's suddenly occurred to me – maybe Bill is the one trying to kill me."

Ricardo looked horrified. "*Madre de Dios*, Alice, why would you think that?"

Briefly, Alice reminded him about her upcoming inheritance and Bill's mounting debts. "Even if he's innocent, I could never feel the same about him as I did before," she added. "Besides, if I really loved him – had ever really loved him – how could I even think he'd be capable of killing someone?"

Ricardo nodded, but said nothing.

As Alice took another gulp of her wine, her thoughts returned to the young priest's brother. Her feelings for Enrique were confused, to say the least. Was it simply the distance between her and her husband that made him seem attractive to her? She recalled the old saying: 'Out of sight, out of mind.' Maybe she was just attracted to Enrique because she missed having the attention of a man . . . yet in her heart, she knew that this wasn't true. There was something about Enrique that drew her to him. It was a combination of his strong masculinity combined with a strange vulnerability. Instantly, Alice knew that it was within her power to hurt him. And that was the last thing on earth she wanted. Oh God, she wondered, could Ricardo be right? Could something really happen between Enrique and me?

Suddenly, Alice recalled the words Senora Delgado had said to her on her deathbed – that she had come back from the dead and that they would kill her too.

At the time, Ricardo had dismissed them as merely the confused words of a dying woman, and as time went by, Alice had begun to doubt their significance. But now, in the light of what she'd learnt today from Enrique, could there be a connection? The old woman had also said "they got the picture from your husband"– but she couldn't possibly have meant Bill, could she? Of course not. And what picture was she talking about? No, clearly the woman thought that Alice was someone else. Alice sighed. Although neither she nor Ricardo had known it at the time, when the old woman had spoken to her, Patricia had already been dead. Surely the old woman couldn't have known anything about Patricia's death? And if so, how?

Alice shook her head. That was a ridiculous idea. How could a dying woman have known about the death of another woman, hundreds of miles away? Or about Alice's husband in Dublin? She sighed. On the other hand, she and Patricia had very similar colouring. Both possessed the standard Irish complexion of freckles, dark brown hair and blue eyes, and were of similar height. It would be easy to mistake one for the other, assuming neither of them had been known to the woman personally.

"Ricardo, I think we should tell Enrique what the old woman, Senora Delgado, said to me before she died," she said abruptly. "I'm wondering if she could have known anything about Patricia's murder?"

"Ah yes – we forgot to mention it today," Ricardo said, annoyed with himself for forgetting something so important. "You are right, Alice – probably there is nothing to it, but it is best that we tell Enrique anything that might have a connection."

"I can't help remembering that Senora Delgado seemed to know me – or think she knew me – so I'm wondering if it was Patricia she knew, or had met, or somehow knew that she'd been murdered."

The young priest nodded. "That makes sense. Then when she saw you, she may have thought that you were the spirit of the dead Patricia, coming to her at the moment of death."

Alice nodded. "We'd better tell your brother as soon as possible."

"I agree. We shall phone him at first light tomorrow morning." He hesitated. "But in the meantime," he looked at Alice earnestly, "I think that tonight we should take a look around the Senora's house."

CHAPTER 36

As the young priest produced torches from one of the kitchen cupboards, Alice expressed her doubts once again.

"Won't somebody spot us, Ricardo, and wonder what we're doing there?"

"As a priest, it would be normal for me to visit the houses of the deceased, and to take care of any business or personal matters, since many of the local people cannot read or write," he pointed out. "It's usually the local priest who notifies the authorities and fills out the necessary documentation relating to a deceased's personal effects, especially in a case like this, when there seems to be no one else to do it."

"Well, surely you'd be doing that in daylight, not creeping around in the middle of the night!" Alice retorted. "It's going to look very suspicious if we get caught."

"Who would be likely to catch us?" Ricardo asked mildly. "Anyone we find there will be just as guilty as us, if not more so. I can at least claim that I'm collecting something I accidentally left in the house when I ministered to poor Senora Delgado."

"What was the Senora like?"

Father Ricardo shrugged his shoulders. "The truth is – I knew little about the late Senora. She had lived in the village for many years – she was here long before I arrived – and she attended Mass every Sunday. We would occasionally exchange a few words, and I always assured her that she was welcome to call at the presbytery any time, or call on me if she needed anything, but she never did. She seemed a nice woman, who lived simply and frugally. She was, by all accounts, a very independent and private person, and I had to respect that." He sighed. "But maybe I should have made more of an effort to involve her in the community, eh?"

"I'm sure your instincts were right, Ricardo," Alice said as she digested this information. She felt sorry that the old woman had led such a solitary existence, and that something had distressed her so much at the very end of her life.

She checked the torch Ricardo gave her, and found that the batteries were working well.

"So what's my reason for being in Senora Delgado's house tonight?" she asked.

Ricardo thought for a second. "If anyone asks, we will say that you are a legal expert whose advice I have sought."

"Anyone in the village will know that's not true," Alice retorted. "Besides –" she grinned, unable to resist a jibe, "isn't that a second lie, Ricardo? Shame on you – and you a priest!"

Father Ricardo smiled. "It is only a little lie, my friend, and I know the good Lord will forgive me under these present circumstances. Besides, I have not told the lie yet!"

"Ah, yes, but you plan to commit it – that's enough in itself to make it a sin, isn't it?"

The young priest grinned. "Alice, I must compliment you on your knowledge of theology. Let us hope your knowledge of breaking-and-entering is just as good."

In silence, the two began walking down the hill from the presbytery towards the village. The evening air was pleasant, and full of the sounds of insects, owls and bats going about their nocturnal business. There were no other sounds except their own footfalls as they walked along the road towards Senora Delgado's house.

In the moonlight, the house had taken on a macabre appearance, and Alice shivered as she followed Ricardo up the driveway. The trees that formed a delightful canopy by day now seemed grotesque. The moonlight made their branches look like tentacles, and Alice was reminded of all the horror movies she'd previously enjoyed from the comfort of her own sofa. Now she felt as though she was stepping into a real-life one!

"Ricardo – do you think it's wise to go in?" she whispered. "I don't mind telling you, I'm scared to bits!"

The priest smiled. "Come, my friend – we need to get answers, do we not?"

"Yes, but what if there's someone waiting in there to kill us? Maybe we'll inadvertently stumble on some international drugs cartel –"

Ricardo grinned. "In Villanova? Unlikely."

"But that's why they'd pick here, Ricardo – because no one would ever expect them to be here! So they'll murder us, and no one will ever know the truth!"

Every sound seemed magnified a thousand times as they walked along. A twig cracked underfoot, and to Alice it sounded like gunfire.

"Why on earth couldn't we have waited until tomorrow morning, Ricardo?" Alice grumbled, her nerves in tatters.

"Already we've lost too much time," was the reply. "Perhaps the information we seek has already been removed – I seem to recall that you mentioned seeing light in this house a few nights ago?"

"So you *do* believe that there's something funny going on!"

"I hope, my friend, that we are merely confirming that Senora Delgado had no connection with your friend's murder. A quick look around her house will hopefully confirm that."

"Well, the quicker the better," said Alice ungraciously.

As they reached the back of the house, the young priest slipped his hand through the broken pane of glass, found the key and opened the back door. Once inside, they both turned on their torches, flickering them about the hallway.

"Where will we start?" whispered Alice. She didn't know why she was whispering, but the occasion seemed to demand it.

As if by unspoken agreement, they entered the kitchen together, which revealed that like many old people, Senora Delgado did the minimum of cooking. There was only a very old cooker, an ancient fridge, a few pots and a kettle, several tins of vegetable soup, a packet of instant coffee and some mouldy fruit and vegetables in a cupboard. The sink held a cup still half-filled with tea, and a plate on the draining board held the congealed remnants of what must have been Senora Delgado's last meal. To Alice, the contents of the kitchen seemed to represent a sad and lonely life, and she was glad that she'd been with the old woman when she died. No one should ever have to die alone.

"Let us now go to Senora Delgado's room," Ricardo suggested.

The tiny room on the half-landing had changed little since their last visit. It still retained the cloying smell of sweat and unwashed bed linen. The sheets, pillows and eiderdown were still in the room, albeit neatly piled on the floor now, having been stripped from the bed when Senora Delgado's body was laid out and transferred to her coffin.

Alice noted the wardrobe in the corner of the room. "Maybe we should check the pockets of her clothing for letters or documents," she said, although it wasn't a task she was personally keen to undertake.

"Yes, you are right," said Ricardo, opening the wardrobe door to reveal a row of out-of-date dresses and coats hanging on a rail, with old-fashioned hatboxes on the floor at the bottom. Gingerly, Alice began checking pockets in the coats and dresses while Ricardo looked through the boxes. It felt really weird and she shuddered. She was searching through a dead woman's clothing for something that might, or might not, link the woman to a murder that had happened hundreds of miles away. The whole thing was preposterous!

Alice shuddered as her hand touched an ancient jacket made of ocelot fur. Even in a hot climate, people found dubious status in a fur coat. Poor creature, she thought sadly, barbarically murdered because it had the misfortune to possess beautifully patterned fur. Thankfully, people were more enlightened now – or were they? She'd heard rumours that fur was again appearing on fashion designers' catwalks. Were people still willing to sacrifice their consciences for vanity?

"There's nothing here, Ricardo," said Alice, relieved.

"Nor here. So let us move on to the other bedrooms."

In the next bedroom, there was a wardrobe against one wall and a bed, desk and chest of drawers against another. There was nothing to indicate that it had been used in years. Alice quickly checked it out while Ricardo went to look at the bathroom.

Alice shivered. "I'll be glad to leave this house," she said as Ricardo returned. "I don't think there's anything useful in here."

"You are right, my friend. I, too, have found nothing. Even the bathroom has been emptied. There is not even toilet paper."

Both of them laughed, thinking exactly the same thing. The house made them feel so jittery that there was the ever-present danger that their bowels might turn to liquid!

But in the third bedroom, at the back of the house, Alice and Ricardo got a shock when they entered. It was clear that the room had recently been lived in. It was filled with the smell of recently smoked cigarettes, and there was an ashtray overflowing with butts on the bedside table between the two single beds. Several empty cigarette packets lay on the ground, and there were empty beer bottles on the floor.

From the condition of the room, it looked as though two people had been camping there. On the floor beside one of the beds was a plastic bag with the logo of a Buenos Aires supermarket on it, and in the bag were the remains of several commercially made sandwiches and apple cores.

"Oh my God," whispered Alice, "it looks as though Senora Delgado had some unwanted visitors. I doubt if those beer bottles belonged to her!"

"This may explain the light you saw the other night," Ricardo murmured. "Please don't touch anything, Alice," he added. "There may be things here that could be useful to the police."

Alice's eyes swept around the room. "Come on, Ricardo – I can't wait to get out of here. There's something horrible and creepy about this house. And what if the occupants of this room come back?"

There was a key in the door of the bedroom, so Ricardo locked it when they left, and pocketed the key. "Let us hope no one can now enter until the police check it out," he said.

The living room and dining room were both fine examples of faded elegance from bygone years – rooms once beautiful, but now totally neglected. In the dining room, they surveyed its grandeur, flashing their torches around and marvelling at the ornate ceilings. Briefly, Alice thought of her own house – her soon-to-be ex-house in Killiney – but quickly suppressed the thought. Touching the curtains, Alice jumped back as some of the ancient material fell apart in her hand.

"Ugh, this is awful, Ricardo. It's as though the whole house is disintegrating along with Senora Delgado. I can't wait to get out of here. Besides, the battery in my torch is flat."

Ricardo nodded. "I agree – I think we are probably finished here."

But as Ricardo shone his torch around the room for a final time, Alice noticed that there was something lying flat on the mantelpiece.

"Shine your torch back here, will you, Ricardo?" she asked.

Under the powerful beam from Ricardo's torch, Alice

took down what looked like a small picture frame. Now standing beside her, Ricardo focussed the beam on the frame in Alice's hand.

"Oh God!" Alice felt it slip from her fingers and crash to the floor. Instantly, the frame broke, fracturing the silence of the night, as the sound of splintering glass reverberated through the dark and empty house. Quickly, Ricardo shone his torch on the floor and retrieved the broken frame from where it had fallen, the glass now in smithereens.

He looked at it, then turned to Alice. "This must be some kind of joke," he said, his voice hoarse with dismay. "How on earth could this get here?"

"It's no joke," said Alice bitterly. "At least I know the truth now."

Both of them looked at it again. In the full beam of Ricardo's torch, there could be no mistake. They were both staring at a photograph of Alice in what had once been a wooden frame. Alice recognised it as the one Bill kept on the desk in his office back in Dublin.

CHAPTER 37

Back at the presbytery, Alice and Ricardo sat in silence, each lost in their own thoughts, surrounded by assorted leftovers found in the presbytery cupboard. They were too overwrought to think of food anyway, other than nibbling for the simple purpose of obtaining nourishment. Neither had wanted to sleep, so they'd stayed up, making numerous cups of tea and going over and over every possible explanation for Bill's framed photo of Alice being in the late Senora Delgado's house.

"This is not your problem, Ricardo," Alice had said. "It's unfair of me to take up all your time. You have your own life, and your own parishioners, to attend to. I'll leave as soon as possible."

Ricardo smiled. "My dear Alice, you are my friend, so of course I'm involved. Besides, my brother, as Inspector of the nearest police precinct, is also involved. So please do not bother to – what is the word? – 'waffle' at me. Am I not your friend?"

"Of course you are."

"Then kindly stop this 'waffling', and let us put our heads together."

"There's no need to put our heads together – it's obvious that Bill's been trying to get rid of me," said Alice angrily. "He must have hired someone to kill me while I was here in Argentina. Maybe the killer or killers got me mixed up with Patricia because we look reasonably alike."

Ricardo nodded sadly. "That does indeed seem the most likely interpretation. That would also explain why Senora Delgado thought she recognised you – she must have found the photo, and thought she was seeing a ghost when you appeared in her house. Maybe the killers of Patricia stayed in her house – with or without the Senora's permission – and she was warning you when she made her comments."

"Oh my God!"

Ricardo looked quizzically at her.

"I've just remembered something else. Just before you and I met for the first time at Senora Delgado's, the receptionist at the hotel said that two men were looking for me."

Ricardo frowned. "What sort of people were they? Were they locals or strangers in town?"

Alice bit her lip. "I never asked. I was in such a hurry to find you that I never gave it another thought. Until now."

Ricardo grimaced. There might well be a direct connection between these men and the temporary residents of Senora Delgado's house. He must make sure that Enrique was informed about it at the earliest opportunity.

"What happens next, Ricardo?" Alice asked plaintively. She was in a state of shock, and unable to think for herself. She was very glad to have a friend like Ricardo on hand, because she felt incapable of making any decisions.

"Tomorrow we will contact Enrique and tell him what we have discovered," said Ricardo firmly. "Then, we will be guided by what he says. He will know what to do."

Alice grimaced. She wished she felt as confident about Enrique's powers as Ricardo did.

Suddenly, Alice remembered the night the joyrider had rammed her car in Dublin, as she'd been driving along by the docks on her way home. The guy had tried to push her into the sea! She shuddered. Maybe it hadn't been a random joyrider after all, but a deliberate attempt on her life!

"Oh my God!" she whispered, slumping back in her chair, all the strength draining out of her.

"What is it, Alice?" Ricardo asked, concerned.

Quickly, Alice told him about the incident, and Ricardo's expression darkened. "Did you see the person driving the car?"

Alice shook her head. "Bill was away in Portugal – or should I say, he *told* me he was in Portugal – maybe it was he who tried to run me off the road!"

Suddenly, it all proved too much for Alice, and she dissolved into tears. Her whole world was falling apart. Could Bill care so little about her, and care so much about getting his hands on her inheritance? She found it almost impossible to believe. But then again, desperate needs required desperate measures . . .

"Please, Alice – do not cry," said Ricardo, unsure of what to do or say that would ease her torment. "Tomorrow, things will not seem so bad. Look – it is daylight already! Please try to get some sleep before we call Enrique."

"Okay but I'm too tired even to undress or go to bed." Instead, she lay down on the tattered couch in the living room, and within seconds she was asleep. Tenderly, Ricardo covered her with a blanket from her bedroom, then wearily headed for bed himself. It had been an eventful evening, and one that had created more questions than answers. Hopefully, Enrique would know what to do.

CHAPTER 38

Alice slept late the following morning. Given the trauma of the previous night, it wasn't surprising that she'd been exhausted. Ricardo arrived back from saying morning Mass to find her just waking up on the couch where she'd slept.

"Good morning, Ricardo," said Alice.

"Good morning Alice, it is indeed a beautiful morning," said Ricardo. "I hear our friend the goat head-butting the back door – he clearly believes that it is long past his breakfast time, and that we are neglecting him."

Alice staggered to her feet, still fully dressed from the previous evening. She'd slept deeply and dreamlessly, and now felt quite refreshed. "I badly need a shower," she said, "but other than that, I feel ready to take on the world!"

Ricardo was relieved to see that her good spirits had been restored. He'd been worried that the impact of finding her own photograph in Senora Delgado's house, which seemed to confirm her husband's involvement in the attempt on her life, might temporarily unhinge her. There was also the question surrounding the temporary occupants of Senora

Delgado's third bedroom. Were they just homeless drifters, or did it mean something more sinister?

Not for the first time, Ricardo was pleased that his brother was so high up in the Argentine police force, since he felt totally out of his depth where Alice was concerned, and unable to offer her anything other than his support and a room in the presbytery for as long as she wanted it.

After the goat was fed, Alice and Ricardo settled down to a kind of brunch, each of them hungrier than they could have believed possible. Between them they quickly demolished everything they could find in the pantry, including the leftovers from their late-night snacking. Everything was recycled and consumed, and as they stacked the empty plates by the sink for washing, they commented to each other that their earlier lack of appetite had been more than made up for by just a few hours' sleep!

Outside, the goat continued to head-butt the back door, and Ricardo grinned at the unrelenting hammering.

"Our friend the goat – we must give him a name," he said, thinking that perhaps naming the goat would briefly distract Alice from her worries. "Have you any suggestions, Alice?"

Alice thought for a moment. "Well, in Ireland, a goat skin is used to make a bodhrán."

"A what?"

Alice smiled. "A bodhrán. It's a kind of traditional hand-held drum, which is played with a two-sided drumstick. It makes a wonderful earthy accompaniment to the spoons or the uilleann pipes."

"You want to turn our goat friend into a drum?" asked Ricardo, horrified.

"No, of course not!" said Alice, grinning. "I just thought that 'Bodhrán' might be a humorous name for him."

Ricardo tried the word, rolling it around on his tongue. "Bow-rawn". . .

Repeating the word, Ricardo went out into the yard and announced to the goat that from henceforth, his name would be 'Bow-rawn'. The goat seemed unimpressed, and much more keen on being fed, in the absence of which he decided to chew the hem of Ricardo's surplice.

After the breakfast dishes had been dried and put away, Ricardo and Alice looked at each other, then at the telephone. It was time to ring Enrique.

"Make some more tea, Alice," Ricardo commanded as he lifted the phone. "I believe we may need it by the time this call is over."

After a rapid discussion with his brother in Spanish, Ricardo put the phone down.

"Enrique and his team of officers and forensic experts are coming to Villanova. They will arrive here this afternoon to examine the room in Senora Delgado's house," Ricardo explained. "His officers will stay at the local hotel but Enrique will stay here at the presbytery with us."

Suddenly, Alice's spirits lifted. Despite all the trauma in her life, she was excited at the thought of seeing Enrique again.

CHAPTER 39

Having spent an inordinate amount of time in front of the bathroom mirror in the presbytery, Alice emerged that afternoon wearing her best pair of jeans and a pretty top. She'd never cared about what she wore when Ricardo was around, but all of a sudden she wanted to look good. I'm pathetic, she told herself, but it didn't stop her from making a last-minute check in the mirror before she went downstairs. If Ricardo noticed anything, he made no reference to it. But Alice was sure he could detect her secret joy at seeing his brother again.

Her heart gave a little somersault as Enrique entered the presbytery that afternoon and hugged his brother warmly. How Alice wished that she, too, could receive a warm hug like that! Briefly, she luxuriated in the joy of being able to observe him without him seeing her, but quickly he spotted her and smiling he headed towards her as she reached the bottom of the stairs.

"Ah, my dear Admiral, I am so happy to see you again," he said.

Alice was puzzled. "Why are you calling me Admiral?"

Enrique grinned. "Surely you know of the great link between Ireland and Argentina?"

Then Alice remembered. "Oh yes – now I understand! An Irishman, Admiral William Brown, is called the father of the Argentine Navy, isn't he?"

Enrique nodded. "He is a national hero to us, and we have 1,200 streets named after him! As you can see, we have a lot to be grateful to the Irish for!"

"And Argentina gave the world a hero too – Che Guevara," Alice added, smiling back.

"Yes, and he had Irish descendents too."

"Really?" said Alice, surprised.

"Yes indeed – his father's name was Ernesto Guevara Lynch." As she smiled in response, he touched her arm, and for a second, she felt something like an electric shock run through her. Quickly, she glanced at him to see if he was aware of what had happened to her, but he had already turned to speak to his brother. It must be sunstroke, Alice thought to herself. Or perhaps I'm allowing myself to fancy Enrique so that I can distance myself from Bill. Maybe I'm building some bizarre form of emotional self-protection against Bill, since it looks increasingly likely that Bill's the one who's tried to kill me . . .

Turning back to Alice, Enrique's expression became serious. "This is indeed a most worrying situation. My officers have checked out the other Irish woman, in as far as it is possible without alerting her family, and there seems no reason for anyone to kill her. They are also checking out the routes you have both travelled, the places you've visited and accommodation where you've stayed. But I fear it still looks as though *you* were the intended victim, Admiral Alice. Ricardo informed me that two men were looking for you at the hotel just after you arrived in Villanova and the receptionist there has said they were strangers, not locals."

Alice nodded, suddenly feeling very vulnerable. "And that's not all, Enrique," she said, quickly explaining about the car that tried to run her off the road in Dublin, and the inheritance that would soon be through probate. Everything that had happened so far seemed to point squarely at Bill.

"Do not worry, my lovely Admiral," Enrique said. "Ricardo and I, and the men from the Buenos Aires police department, will all look after you."

Alice thanked him sincerely, but she longed to tell him that his own personal services would be more to her liking!

Having been given the key to the secured bedroom in Senora Delgado's house, with instructions on how to open the back door through the broken windowpane, Enrique left the presbytery and headed for the small hotel in the village, where his scene-of-crime officers were already installed. From there, they would descend en masse on Senora Delgado's house, examining it from top to bottom, with special emphasis on the secured room where they would take samples for forensic analysis.

When Ricardo departed on church business, Alice found herself alone in the presbytery. At Enrique's insistence, she locked both presbytery doors, feeling overcome by a strange sense of unreality. So many people's lives were being altered because of her, all based on the premise that her husband wanted to kill her. Usually, *she* was the one who followed up on other people's stories. Now, her own life was the subject of a major investigation. Her family and friends thought she was dead, and had actually been to her funeral. Sometimes, she could acutely feel their pain, and she panicked because she longed to relieve their misery, but she had to dismiss those thoughts in order to keep going herself.

After Ricardo departed, Alice washed up and tidied away the lunch dishes, then she unlocked the back door and fed the leftovers to Bodhrán, who was once again eagerly waiting for any food that came his way. But as she fed the goat, then locked herself in again, her thoughts were elsewhere. Before he left, Ricardo had mentioned that he'd be very late back, and that she and Enrique should go ahead and eat without him. There was plenty of food in the pantry, he reminded her, since they had already shopped for Enrique's arrival.

Alice suspected that he was staying away on purpose, to give her and Enrique some time alone together. She was both embarrassed and delighted – embarrassed that Ricardo could see she was attracted to his brother, and delighted at the thought of being alone with Enrique. But it slightly scared her too. What if he wasn't interested in her at all, and Ricardo had simply imagined it? Already, the prospect of being alone with Enrique had set her nerves on edge, and she feared she'd become tongue-tied when he returned from Senora Delgado's house.

As Alice prepared a salad for them to eat that evening, she was conscious of the strangeness of her situation. Everything about her life right now seemed surreal. Here she was, thousands of miles from home, preparing a meal for a man she'd only just met, yet with whom she felt a genuine connection. It was as though she had stepped out of her own body and into someone else's. She felt as though there were now two Alices – one who led a very different existence back in Ireland, and another whose life was now firmly rooted in Argentina.

This other Alice was comfortable preparing simple food in the presbytery in Villanova, and she wondered what it would be like if she and Enrique lived together under one roof. Get a grip, she told herself, and stop these stupid fanciful notions. You've only met the man twice, and already you want to move in with him!

Nevertheless, she found she was enjoying preparing a salad for him, and cutting slices of thick brown bread to go with it. It was so different from her life back in Ireland, where she and Bill had dined out most evenings, or sent out for a take-away. She sighed. Maybe the pleasure she was deriving from these simple domestic chores was just a reaction to the fact that it represented a different world from the one in which her own husband might now be a murderer.

Perhaps this was just a natural response to all that had happened to her. Maybe she was distancing herself from her life in Ireland because nothing there would ever be the same again. For some time, she'd known that her marriage was over, regardless of whether Bill was guilty of trying to kill her or not, and regardless of her attraction to Enrique.

Eventually Enrique arrived back from Senora Delgado's house, clearly tired and looking slightly worried.

"All the samples have been collected," he told her, "and early tomorrow morning the forensic team will return to the capital to carry out tests on the items they've found. Obviously, we don't yet know if the people who stayed in

Senora Delgado's house have any connection to Patricia's death, or to the attempt on your life in Dublin, or to the men who called to the hotel. They might simply have been hobos living rough for a few nights before travelling on. Only time will tell. Now, my lovely one, I am going to shower."

Alice blushed as thoughts of a naked Enrique flitted through her mind. She could imagine his strong hairy body with the water cascading down it, and she had to hurry out to the kitchen so that he wouldn't see her confusion.

"Our meal will be ready when you've finished," she called after him, busying herself by gathering up the leftover salad leaves to keep them for Bodhrán.

Later at the table they smiled shyly at each other, and Alice poured Enrique a glass of wine, and one for herself half of which she quickly downed, to relax her nerves.

"How long will you stay here with Ricardo?" Alice asked, for something to say.

"For as long as *you* are here, Alice," Enrique replied. "This murder of Patricia is now my most important case, and you must be protected."

Alice looked alarmed. "What do you mean 'protected'?"

Enrique focussed his attention on his food, dipping pieces of tomato and avocado into the olive oil in the dish. "Since the person or persons who want to murder you have not succeeded, they will try again," he replied nonchalantly.

"But," Alice was astounded, "I thought Patricia's killers had assumed they'd killed me, especially since you haven't notified the authorities here or in Ireland that they've got the wrong person . . ." Her voice trailed off.

"Since we do not know who they are, or where they

are, it is always wiser to assume the worst," added Enrique, now dipping his bread into his salad dish and mopping up the last of the oil.

Alice was dumbfounded. She'd blithely assumed that she was protected by the fact that the killer that assumed Patricia was *her*.

"But if Bill thinks I'm dead, then surely the killer's job is done?"

"What if the assassin, or assassins – maybe these men who came to the hotel looking for you – realise by now that they've killed the wrong person? They will not want their employer – let us assume this is your husband – to know that they have –" Enrique wrinkled his brow, "how do you say it in English? – 'bungled' the job. So they will try again."

Alice shivered, suddenly realising that Enrique was right.

"Do not worry, Alice," Enrique said, noting her stricken expression, "I promise you that my brother and I will take care of you." He reached out and squeezed her hand, and Alice felt herself grow hot under his gaze. He had a most disconcerting way of looking at her!

Suddenly, Alice realised what she needed to do. "Look, there's only one way we can find out if it's my husband," she said. "I'll have to go back to Ireland."

"No! I will not hear of it!" said Enrique. "Woman, you are talking madness! If your husband tried to kill you in Argentina, how much easier will it be for him to kill you back home in Ireland!"

Alice smiled, gratified to see that she'd managed to get Enrique riled up. Since he'd managed to unnerve her so often, it felt like rough justice to do the same to him.

"Let me finish, Enrique," she said quietly. "I'm proposing

to go incognito. I've used disguise before in my job, in order to get into buildings from which I've been barred, and to attend meetings that I'd otherwise be thrown out of."

Suddenly, she had Enrique's full attention.

"What would you hope to do?"

"With your agreement, I'll go back to Ireland using Patricia's passport. I know it means bending the rules, but I think it might be worth it. Before I leave Argentina, I'll buy a wig, different make-up and clothes in Buenos Aires, so that when I get on that plane, no one I know will recognise me. When I arrive in Dublin I'll stay in a hotel under an assumed name, and I'll contact my friend Isobel, who'll help me."

"No, no! I cannot allow you to take such chances! Besides, my own neck is – how do you say it? – already on the chopping block. By now I should have informed the Irish Embassy and the Irish police that you're alive, and filled them in on the details of the case."

"Look, I'll take the blame if anything goes wrong, but I'm the only one who can do this, Enrique," said Alice firmly. "I'm an investigative journalist, so I should be capable of doing some research on my own husband. I could try to find out about his business dealings, look through his e-mails, correspondence and phone records, to find out if there's anything that links him to Patricia's murder or the attempt on my life. Even if you had the technology to break into Bill's files from here, it would be against the law and could result in an international incident. And if you asked the Irish police for help, they'd have to go to court for the right to seize Bill's computer, and you'd have to tell them I was still alive. Think of all the repercussions *that* might have. And the delay would make it even harder to solve the case."

Enrique continued shaking his head vehemently. "I still cannot allow you to do it, Admiral," he said angrily. "Anyway, you can hardly walk into your husband's office, can you? So how else can you find out what is going on?"

Sensing that he was beginning to see her point of view, Alice pressed ahead. "Well, I can easily get to his e-mails and files," she said, smiling triumphantly. "Bill has a computer in our house, and he often works at home. I can download everything from his computer onto an external memory, then check it later on the computer at Isobel's apartment, or in my mother's house. Then I can let you know if there's anything that looks incriminating."

Enrique still shook his head.

"Let me do it, Enrique," Alice begged. "I know where to look, and what to look for. If I don't succeed, then you can contact the Irish police."

"If you don't succeed, you may be dead. Please Alice, no more talk of this right now. I am confident we will solve this case with help from the forensic team."

Enrique smiled pleadingly at her, and Alice's heart did a flip. He really was heart-meltingly gorgeous . . .

Alice concentrated on her salad, although she hardly tasted what she was eating. She was acutely aware of Enrique's presence, and as she surreptitiously watched him cut a slice of bread, she marvelled at his strong hands and hairy arms that sent a delightful shiver down her spine. What was it about Enrique that affected her so much? Perhaps it was intangible things, like his sudden mischievous smile, his dedication to his job, his belief that he could make a difference, and that no matter how insignificant that difference was, it was still worth doing. Like his brother Ricardo, he was a man of principle, yet a man who was prepared to take a chance if the situation warranted it. At least, she hoped he was. She honestly believed that the best way to find out what Bill was up to was to go back to Ireland in disguise. She sighed. Was Enrique also willing to take a chance on her?

It was odd to think that when she'd left Ireland, she'd regarded herself as a married woman – whether she'd have called herself a *happily* married woman was a moot point. But was she ready yet for a new relationship? People often said that you needed time to get over one relationship before beginning another, but what did 'people' know about the individuals involved? You could wait a lifetime to meet that special someone, or you could find them right under your nose, when you least expected to. What mattered was what you *did* with the opportunity if and when it was presented to you . . .

When Enrique finally spoke, Alice jumped with fright.

"A peso for your thoughts, my lovely Admiral," he asked softly.

Alice smiled, this time meeting his stare head on. "I was about to propose a toast," she improvised, refilling their wine glasses. "To the successful conclusion of this case!"

For a fleeting moment, she thought that Enrique looked disappointed, as though he'd been hoping she'd say something else.

Part 2

1978

CHAPTER 40

Gina felt dizzy with shock. It couldn't be. No, it just wasn't possible – was it?

Oh God. She steadied herself on the bar stool, afraid that she might suddenly fall off.

Up until now, she'd been enjoying a pleasant evening in the pub with her best friend Maeve. O'Grady's pub was close to their flat, and was warm and cosy. The décor was shabby, but it attracted a mixed bunch of people, both young and old, and she and Maeve had fallen into the habit of dropping in several evenings a week.

Since she'd been kicked out of home several weeks earlier, Gina had been sharing a flat in the city centre with Maeve and several other young women. But now, a throwaway remark from her friend, en route to the toilet, had left her reeling.

Maeve had made a casual comment about Gina not using any of the sanitary towels in the bathroom cabinet in the flat. "Let's hope you're not pregnant!" she'd chuckled, and suddenly Gina's world came tumbling down around her.

It couldn't be. No, it would be so unfair, after everything else that had happened to her. But since when did 'fair' have anything to do with getting pregnant?

After her bombshell statement, Maeve had climbed down from her bar stool and headed to the ladies' toilets, blithely unaware that her casual comment had left her friend reeling.

The two were drinking Bacardis and cokes, courtesy of Maeve's generosity, since Gina no longer had any money of her own. Since she'd been evicted from home, she hadn't returned to her job in the laboratory. She'd been too scared to come face-to-face with Owen again after their guilty afternoon of passion, and too terrified of possibly encountering Dolly.

When she'd originally arrived at Maeve's flat, shocked and dishevelled and without any possessions of her own, Maeve had generously offered her the use of all her own possessions.

"Luckily we're the same size, so help yourself to any of the clothes in my wardrobe," she'd told her friend. "And don't worry about food – just use the stuff on my side of the fridge, or the tins of beans on the top shelf of the cupboard." Maeve had been equally generous with her toiletries. "My deodorant, shampoo, soap and toothpaste are on the left-hand side of the cabinet," she'd explained to the newly arrived Gina. "Feel free to use whatever you need." Then she'd gestured to the sanitary towels on the same shelf. "Use as many of these as you need, too," she had added, before the two left the bathroom and headed into the living room, where Gina was introduced to the other residents of the flat.

But Gina had never needed any of the sanitary towels. She hadn't taken any notice during the first few weeks, since she'd been adjusting to living away from home for the very first time. The experience had been both exciting and frightening, and at first she'd attributed the absence of her period to the shock of recent events. But somewhere in the back of her mind, in the shadowy area where she stored her scary thoughts, there was an occasional niggle which she instantly dismissed.

But now, Maeve had articulated Gina's own fears, forcing her to confront the unpalatable truth at last. She was undoubtedly pregnant. And she was expecting Owen's baby. As she took a gulp of her Bacardi and coke, Gina wondered why so many bad things had happened to her in such a short time.

Initially, Gina had assumed that the worst day of her life had been when she was evicted from her family home, having been caught making love to her brother-in-law. Even now, she shuddered as she recalled how she and Owen had been found half-naked on the sofa by her mother and Dolly. Truthfully, neither she nor Owen had meant it to happen, but they'd fancied each other for ages, even though neither of them had fully realised it, and a tentative kiss had led to an explosion of passion between them.

With hindsight, it wasn't difficult to understand how it had happened. Working together in the laboratory on a daily basis, sharing jokes and usually lunching together in the staff canteen, she and Owen had come to depend on and support each other. And Gina had gradually admitted to herself that she'd grown envious of her elder sister, who didn't seem to value her gorgeous husband. Dolly seemed to care more about pleasing her boss, managing director Charles Keane, than making her own husband happy.

A sob now rose in Gina's throat. Dear God, what was she going to do? She was pregnant with her sister's husband's baby! She knew that Maeve would help her if she told her, but right now she wasn't sure if she wanted to tell anyone. That would make it more real. For the moment at least, she could pretend to herself that the pregnancy wasn't happening. And maybe, with luck, she might wake up the following morning to find that her period had arrived. For once she would welcome that normally unwelcome show of blood!

There was no way she could ever tell Owen, much as she longed to. Knowing how hot-headed he was, he might opt to leave

Dolly straight away, and much as she wished that could happen, Gina knew that such a turn of events would only further destroy her family. And she'd caused enough family trauma already.

She shuddered. And if he wasn't prepared to leave Dolly – well, she'd feel even worse. Because that would be the proof that she'd meant nothing to him. No, she was too frightened to put that scenario to the test.

Suddenly, Gina felt all alone, unloved by anyone. Her family didn't seem to care what happened to her. She'd been shocked at her mother's attitude. Imagine evicting your own daughter from her home, and not caring what happened to her! A sob caught in Gina's throat. On the other hand, she fully realised the impact of what she'd done. Having sex with her brother-in-law and getting caught hadn't been a very sensible thing to do, but sense had flown out the window when she and Owen had kissed, and even now, she could still feel the softness of his lips on hers, and she longed to feel his arms around her again.

But it had caused a major family upheaval, and she wondered if the situation could ever be resolved. The idea of never seeing her family again was frightening. If only she could rewind time, and go back to the days before it happened! Although she'd never been close to Dolly, she and her mother and her sister Stella had been close enough. And Paddy, her other brother-in-law – she was very fond of him. Now, she had lost all of them! Would they even speak to her if they saw her in the street? Or would they ignore her, or cross to the other side?

Worst of all was the dawning realisation that she would never see Owen again. She'd never again work by his side in the laboratory. Never feel the touch of his lips on hers again, or the feel of his skin against hers. Her only memory of his touch would be of that fateful afternoon . . .

"Hey, Gina – you're miles away!"

Maeve had returned from the toilet, and was now sitting back on her barstool.

"Oh hi, Maeve. Yes, you're right – I was miles away. I was thinking about getting a job," she lied. "Maybe I could try some of the offices around town?"

Maeve looked concerned. "But you've no experience of office work, have you? Why don't you stick to the work you're trained to do? I know you love laboratory work, and besides, you're fully qualified now that you've got your diploma."

Gina nodded. "You're right – I do love the work. But I can hardly tell any future employer that I left my last job because I shagged my brother-in-law, who also happened to be the Medical Director!"

"I'm sure, if you contacted Owen, he'd give you a good reference."

"I couldn't face him. Not after what happened."

"Well, maybe I could phone him. You're probably due some money as well."

"I doubt it. After all, I was supposed to give notice before I left!"

For a few minutes, the duo sat in silence, enjoying the camaraderie of the pub. And as they sipped their drinks, Gina suddenly realised that she wasn't entirely alone and unloved. There was someone else who cared about her. Someone who had cared about her for years, in fact, since they'd been in fifth grade together. Larry Macken had been her boyfriend, on-and-off, for all that time.

He had bright red hair and acne, and had never been considered good-looking, so she'd never been really serious about him. In fact, she had always been on the lookout for someone better. But for Larry, there had never been anyone else but Gina. As a result, she'd always led him a merry dance, flirting with other guys and *preferring to spend most of her time with Maeve and her other school friends. But Larry had waited patiently in the background, happy to accept the meagre crumbs she threw him. She still went out with him from time to time, when there wasn't anyone better on the horizon. But she'd never slept with him, always claiming that she was preserving her virginity for the man she would marry. In her heart, Gina knew that her treatment of Larry had always been unfair, but his fawning adoration had almost invited her to ill-treat him.*

Now, suddenly, Larry was beginning to assume the role of knight in shining armour in Gina's mind. There was only one thing she could do now.

As she and Maeve climbed down from their bar stools and headed out the door of the pub, Gina laid a hand on Maeve's arm.

"Maeve, I'm just going to call round to visit a friend. I'll see you in a while."

Maeve raised an eyebrow. "I presume you'll be back at the flat later?"

"Eh, I'm not sure. Don't wait up for me."

Maeve gave her friend a strange look. "Well, you're a dark horse, aren't you? Did you chat up some fellow while I was out in the toilet?"

Gina laughed. "I wish!" But she didn't answer Maeve's question.

CHAPTER 41

Owen sighed as he gazed out through his office window on his pristine research unit and numerous white-coated employees. To others, he must seem like a man who had it all. He was Medical Director at BWF Pharmaceuticals, a company that was considered to be 'going places', with established links to a major multinational. He was married to the managing director's personal secretary, and had a monthly salary that would take a worker in the developing world a lifetime to make. Yet he felt empty inside. How on earth had his life ended up in this mess? He was doing a job he'd come to hate, and was married to a woman he'd come to despise. Now, he'd fallen for his young sister-in-law, who'd been working as his assistant in the laboratory. Yet suddenly she'd left without giving notice, and disappeared into thin air.

He grimaced. Okay, he shouldn't have ended up making love to his sister-in-law in his mother-in-law's house. And worse still, getting caught. It was the one and only time it had ever happened, and both he and Gina had been momentarily overwhelmed by the strength of their feelings. But with hindsight he realised that they'd been building up to it for months. Working together on a daily basis had created a close bond between them. They were united in their hatred of BWF Pharmaceuticals' managing director Charles Keane, and apprehensive about the loyalty shown to him by Dolly. And they both suspected that Dolly had been keeping Charles informed about Owen's misgivings regarding the vaccine whose Irish trials he had been supervising.

Somehow, in the laboratory, the situation had gradually crystallised into a 'Charles and Dolly' versus 'Owen and Gina' scenario, and together he and Gina had laughed at the antics of their boss and the woman that Owen went home to each night. In fact, he'd begun to wish that he didn't have to go home at all. He had much more fun in Gina's company.

Owen shuddered. He sometimes wondered if he was suited to pharmaceutical research at all. He deplored the use of animals in preclinical trials, yet the scientific world refused to validate anything that had not been rigorously tested on these poor, inoffensive creatures. Like him, Gina also hated seeing animals used to create what they both considered unnecessary medication for human consumption, products that simply put money into company coffers.

In his opinion, only a few of the vast array of drugs developed by the industry were of genuine benefit. In most cases of illness or anxiety, a change of lifestyle would be a cheaper and healthier alternative for most people. The problems that allowed the pharmaceutical companies to prosper were created by society itself. Governments lined their own pockets and gave concessions to their cronies rather than building a decent society in which people had proper healthcare and education, and proper town planning so that each vast housing estate was built with shops, services, playgrounds and youth centres for the youngsters. It was the ill-treated and forgotten in society who went to their doctors for happy pills, in order to shut out the unremitting awfulness of their daily lives.

Owen clenched his fists. He'd also grown to detest his mean-spirited wife, and often wondered why she'd married him. More to the point, Owen wondered why he had married her. She idolised her boss, and as her husband he always felt himself to be a poor second. Perhaps if Charles hadn't been already married, he and Dolly might have tied the knot?

To his own shame, Owen remembered that Charles Keane had acted as matchmaker between him and Dolly. Keane's evident pleasure at getting his secretary and the company's Medical Director together had been balm to the newly arrived Owen, who'd been keen to win the approval of the company's top man. Charles Keane had told him that strong ties between key figures in an organisation led to greater strength, and Owen had been swept along by Charles's great vision.

If only he'd waited. If only he'd had the chance to know Gina before he married Dolly! But Gina had been studying full-time at the College of Technology while he'd been dating Dolly, so he'd hardly ever spoken to her at all. Then when Gina had joined the company — another part of Charles Keane's vision for a strong family-based company — initially she'd been a junior laboratory technician. Owen had a substantial staff at his disposal, so his and Gina's paths rarely crossed. Then when the vacancy for a personal assistant to the Medical Director was advertised, Gina applied. Owen was impressed by her knowledge of the various projects the company was undertaking, and her enthusiasm was like a breath of fresh air. He promptly appointed her to the position, and before long they'd formed an inseparable team. Gina seemed to understand exactly what Owen was thinking before he did himself, and often her insightful suggestions for projects were brilliant, and ones he promptly acted on.

Gina was also tremendous fun. She possessed a great sense of humour, and often Owen found himself smiling for no reason at all. But once he got home, the smile was invariably wiped off his face. His disgruntled and frigid wife found no joy in anything, except when she was reminding Owen of how wonderful her boss Charles Keane was, and how far below him her husband stood in her estimation.

Where on earth was Gina now? Owen bit his lip savagely. He'd never expected things to turn out so badly. Although Dolly had ended up in hysterics the day he and Gina were caught making love, he'd assumed all would eventually be forgiven when he grovelled sufficiently before his wife. On the other hand, he wondered if he genuinely wanted to preserve his marriage. It gave him no joy, and he now knew it had been a dreadful mistake. But there was no divorce in 1970s Ireland, so at best he and Dolly could live apart, but they would still be married until death did them part.

It never crossed his mind that Gina would be evicted from her own home. If anyone deserved to be evicted, it was him – for crossing the line with his young sister-in-law. And since that day, Gina hadn't turned up for work either. Where had she gone? And how was she surviving financially? Owen was desperately worried about her. Gradually he had come to realise how much his sister-in-law meant to him. But since she hadn't been in touch, it seemed unlikely that she felt the same about him.

Owen surveyed his large laboratory wing with distaste. The job had made him cynical. But Gina had been a tower of strength, supporting him in his misgivings when he realised that a vaccine designed to protect people against TB and an assortment of respiratory illnesses, whose Irish clinical trials they were conducting, might cause permanent neurological damage due to the preservative being used.

The vaccine had barely scraped through the Phase 1 trials, which had been conducted on small groups of healthy people. Or at least, they'd been healthy prior to the Irish trials! Several participants had ended up in hospital, and some children had exhibited signs of neurological damage. The Phase 2 trials had confirmed Owen's initial misgivings, when the testing for safety and efficacy led to several more participants in the randomised trials having adverse reactions to the product, and ending up in hospital. At this point, Owen felt the product should be dropped altogether, but Charles Keane and the board of directors were keen to hush up the results of the randomised trials, and push ahead with Phase 3, which would be the final pre-approval round of testing. But for Owen, his initial misgivings had by now crystallised into downright certainty. If the company persisted in marketing this product, he had no doubt at all that people worldwide were going to suffer unnecessarily.

A few weeks earlier, in a rage, he'd forced his way into the boardroom, where the directors were holding their monthly meeting. He'd thrown copies of a report he'd compiled down on the table in front of them, and begged them to read his findings. But as the security guards had dragged him out, he'd heard Charles Keane refer to him deprecatingly as "one of our more eccentric mad scientists" and there had been a ripple of laughter as the directors had nodded their heads in amused agreement.

He'd expected to be sacked immediately, but nothing had happened. That had given him the hope that the directors were reading his report, and were beginning to understand how harmful this latest drug was. But as a week went by without anyone contacting him, he sadly concluded that the directors were more interested in their salaries and bonuses than in the welfare of the public.

CHAPTER 42

"Hello, Larry."

"Gina!" Larry Macken's face lit up. "How are you? Come on in!" He was overcome with joy at seeing her on the doorstep.

Although they'd been going out together for years, and she was the only woman he'd ever loved, she'd never, in all that time, reciprocated his feelings. He knew she was happy enough in his company, and they went to pubs and movies together on a regular basis, but she'd never once said she loved him. He was blue in the face saying it to her, but never getting the response he longed to hear. Now, just when he'd finally accepted defeat and applied for an apprenticeship in London, she'd actually turned up on his doorstep! All his birthdays had come together at once!

"Would you like a cup of tea?" Larry asked her solicitously, leading her down the corridor to his one-room bedsit. "Sit down and take the weight off your feet." He pointed to the sofa.

He saw Gina looking furtively at the unmade bed in the other corner of the room, so he crossed to it, and quickly pulled up the covers. He certainly didn't want to offend Gina's sensibilities. Although she was a party girl in many respects, he knew she was quite prudish in other ways. In all the years they'd been seeing each other, she'd never let him do more than kiss her. She'd been to his bedsit lots of times before, but she'd never even sat on the bed, as though afraid that he might take advantage of her. Which, of course, he would never do. If Gina ever wanted him that way, she'd have to make it quite clear, since he would never do anything to upset her.

"Have you got any booze?"

Larry was surprised at Gina's request, but tried not to show it. "Not much, I'm afraid, but I think there's a bottle of white wine in the fridge – will that do?"

Gina nodded, kicking off her shoes. Larry was pleased. It looked as though Gina planned on staying for more than her usual few minutes. He thought she looked tired, and not at all her usual cheery self. Normally, when she came back to his bedsit, they'd have a laugh together, even if she didn't want to do more than kiss him.

Opening the wine bottle, Larry took down two glasses from the overhead shelf, and sat down beside her. There was nowhere else to sit, even if he'd wanted to. But he wanted to sit beside her, in fact, he wanted to take her in his arms and comfort her, since she looked so sad. But he'd never dare say that to her, since she'd probably empty the wineglass over him if he did.

"Cheers!" Their glasses touched.

There was a moment of silence, and Gina rushed to fill it.

"I've left home, Larry. I'm now sharing a flat with Maeve and several other people."

"Wow, that was sudden! I thought you were perfectly happy at home?"

"Well, no – I've been thinking about moving out for ages. Then when Maeve said there was a vacancy in her flat, I decided to move out."

"But surely your Mum was annoyed?"

"Oh, yes — she was devastated. In fact, she's so annoyed with me that she's hardly spoken to me since I left!" said Gina, considerably embellishing the truth.

"That's a big step to take, Gina. Why did you want to do it?"

Gina shrugged. *"Oh, I don't know. I suppose I felt that it was time I made my own life. I mean, I couldn't stay there forever, could I? I want to spread my wings, do something different."*

Larry gazed at her in admiration. What a gutsy young woman she was! Once again, he was overwhelmed with love for her. But he kept it in check, since he knew that the slightest declaration on his part would have Gina heading for the door.

Larry hesitated. *"In fact, I'm making some changes myself."*

"Oh. Like what?"

"Well, I've been offered an apprenticeship at a big architects' practice in London. It'll mean training for the next four years, but at the end of it I'll be a fully qualified architect!"

"Oh Larry, that's wonderful!" said Gina breathlessly, *"I'm thrilled for you! But what about us?"*

Larry smiled sadly. *"Gina, let's be honest — there never really was an 'us'. It's only ever been me, wanting you and telling you I loved you. But our relationship — if you'd even call it that — never really mattered to you, did it?"*

Tears filled Gina's eyes. *"Oh Larry, that's totally untrue! I've just been scared —scared of making a commitment to one person for the rest of my life, and scared to make love for the first time . . ."*

Larry squeezed her arm. *"Oh Gina, you know I'd never hurt you! Why have you never trusted me? You must know that I'd do anything for you — haven't I told you that millions of times?"*

Gina took a gulp of wine, then leaned closer, one of her breasts now touching Larry's chest. They were very close — closer than two

*people having a normal conversation. But this was no normal
conversation, and Larry could feel his blood pressure rising. Other
things as well. . .*

"Larry, can I come to London with you?" Gina whispered. "I
don't mind leaving the laboratory, as long as I can be with you. I'll
be able to get a job in London without any problem."

Larry took a gulp of his wine, as Gina's magical words sank
into his brain. For years, he'd been longing to hear these words.
"Oh, my darling Gina, I couldn't ask you to give up your career
for me!" he said, still astonished at her suggestion. "That would be
so unfair – I'd be having my career at the expense of yours!"

"I don't mind – honestly," Gina said, smiling. "But the thought
of losing you is more than I could bear." She snuggled close to him,
and could hear his heart beating really fast.

"Gina – please!" Larry pushed her away gently. "Look, you
know how much I care about you, but you're not being fair to me.
It's not easy to sit here beside you, and not want to touch you –
make love to you."

His breath was laboured, and Gina knew how hard he was
trying to control himself.

"But Larry, I want you to make love to me!"

"What?" Larry held her at arm's length, searching her face for
signs that she was joking. "Why now, Gina? After all this time?
Are you absolutely sure?"

Gina nodded, leaning forward until her lips touched his.

Urgently taking the wineglass from her and placing it on the
floor, Larry pulled her close.

"Are you sure?" he whispered again, his voice hoarse with longing.

"Yes, I'm sure," Gina whispered back. "Take me to bed, Larry
– I don't want to be a virgin any longer. Take me, Larry, and make
me yours!"

Needing no further bidding, Larry took her hand and led her across to the bed, each of them kissing and tugging at the other's clothing. Once on the bed, they began exploring each other's bodies, moaning in pleasure.

Suddenly, with great effort and presence of mind, Larry stopped his ministrations. "What about protection, Gina?" he whispered.

"Oh Larry, it doesn't matter —" said Gina, reaching out to grasp his hand, "— not as long as we're going to be together." She groaned sexily. "If you don't hurry up, I might change my mind —"

Larry needed no further incentive. Already tumescent, he could hardly wait to take her. As he slipped between her legs and entered her, Gina arched her back and cried out as though in pain.

"Oh God, I'm sorry, love," Larry whispered, "Did I hurt you?"

"No, it's okay," Gina whispered back, "I didn't realise that the first time would hurt so much!"

"Oh my love!" Larry buried his head in the curve of her neck and she could feel his tears on her skin.

Later, when Larry was fast asleep, Gina crept into his tiny bathroom. Taking one of Larry's razor blades, she held her breath and drew it across her palm. Blood spurted out, and the pain was excruciating, but she watched with satisfaction as a pool of bright red gathered in her hand.

Tiptoeing back to the bed, she climbed in again, smearing the blood on the bottom sheet. It was difficult to see in the dark, but she was reasonably sure that she'd marked the right place.

* * *

In the early hours of the morning, Gina gently nudged Larry awake. "I must go, my love," she whispered. "Maeve will be wondering where I've got to. I never meant to stay out so late."

Larry was instantly awake, contrite at keeping her away from her flatmates.

"When will I see you again?" he asked her. "I can't believe what's happened between us – you've made me the happiest man in the world!"

"Maybe you won't say that when you see the sheets," said Gina, pointing to the bloodstains. "I'm sorry, Larry – but I bled when you made love to me."

"Oh, don't worry about the sheets," said Larry tenderly. "But are you okay? Are you still sore?"

"A little," said Gina, "but that's only to be expected, I believe, when you lose your virginity."

"God, I love you!" said Larry fervently. "I can't believe that we're going to London together! Are you sure you don't mind giving up your own career? Maybe you can get a job in a laboratory in London. With your qualifications, you should have no problem."

Gina smiled at him. "As long as I'm with you, I'll have everything I need."

She arrived back at Maeve's flat just as the milkman was delivering the milk.

"Someone's had a good night, by the looks of it!" he chuckled.

"You have no idea!" said Gina sadly, touching her stomach. *Her palm, where she'd cut it with the razor, was still smarting. But thankfully, the wound had already started to heal.*

CHAPTER 43

Larry was very excited about moving to London, especially now that Gina was going with him. However Gina kept her plans to herself, saying nothing to Maeve or her other flatmates. She knew they'd all be excited on her behalf, and didn't want them querying her own lack of enthusiasm. Maeve would probably realise that she had an ulterior motive for making this decision and she couldn't face her friend's accusing eyes. She also didn't want her emigration plans getting back to her family – as far as she was concerned, they could all get lost. No doubt Dolly was making Owen's life miserable. Gina didn't want to think too much about Owen – it hurt too much.

Well, she'd made her bed, and now she must lie in it. She hated herself for deceiving poor Larry, but she'd taken the only course of action open to her. Now, at least, her child would have a father. Not the one she wanted, but a father nonetheless. And Larry would be thrilled when she eventually told him she was pregnant. And when the time came to give birth, she'd pretend that her labour had started early. Having witnessed the blood from her apparent virginity, it would never cross his mind to query the child's early arrival.

Gina sighed. She really did care about Larry – just not in the way she cared for Owen. Nevertheless, she would try to be a good wife to him. She didn't doubt that Larry would do the decent thing, and marry her when she told him she was pregnant. And she would give him other children in due course.

During the weeks before their departure, she managed to keep Larry and Maeve apart by spending all her free time at Larry's bedsit. Though in any case it wouldn't have been difficult to keep Larry away from the flat, since he was spending a lot of time with his own family down the country prior to departure, as well as organising his luggage and documentation for the new job.

Eventually, Gina couldn't help but get caught up in Larry's enthusiasm. He was thrilled to have Gina accompanying him to London, and euphoric at being given such a wonderful career opportunity. He talked endlessly about where they would get a flat, and about all the exploring they would do. He'd already bought the London A-Z street guide, and spent most of his time with Gina poring over it, and making enthusiastic plans for the outings they would take.

The only really worrying moment had been when Larry suggested to Gina that he go and speak to her family, so that he could assure them all that he'd take good care of her. Luckily, she managed to dissuade him, assuring him that her family weren't happy about her departure to London, and wouldn't look kindly on his intervention.

"To be honest, Larry, they don't approve of you – never have," Gina told him sadly. "When I went round to tell Mum and the others that I was going to London with you, we had a big row. She said she never wanted to see me again."

Larry was appalled. "Gina, that's awful! Look, let me go round and talk to your mother –"

"No, Larry — please don't," said Gina hastily, "that would only make things worse. Maybe she'll come round later, when she sees that I'm determined to be with you, regardless of what they think."

But Larry was still angry on Gina's behalf. "I can't believe your mother could cut you off like that — and your two sisters and their husbands, surely they'd support you? You were always close to Stella ..." He sighed. "Look, I don't want to cause you any problems, love. Maybe you need to reconsider coming to London right now — I don't mind waiting, if it means that you can sort things out with your family before you come over."

"Don't even think of it, Larry," said Gina. "I'm coming with you, and that's that."

Larry, being gullible and so in love with Gina, accepted everything she told him.

There was also the minor problem for Gina of not having many possessions to pack. That fateful afternoon when she'd been kicked out of home, she'd only had time to collect an old suitcase, shove a few clothes and personal possessions into it, and leave as quickly as possible. Fortunately, before they left for London, Larry gave her some money to buy herself something nice to wear, and she was able to stretch it to buy several cheaper outfits, as well as essentials such as toothpaste and deodorant. When he queried her lone suitcase, she assured him that she liked to travel light, and would get new stuff as soon as they got settled in London.

Unable to face Maeve after all her generosity, Gina opted to leave for London at a time when her friend and the other flatmates were at work. She felt overcome by shame at taking this course of action, but felt she had no other option. Maeve knew that she had never been serious about Larry, so she'd immediately suspect that something was amiss. And Gina didn't want to have to face an interrogation from her friend.

On the morning she and Larry left for London, Gina left Maeve an enigmatic note promising to be in touch, then closed the door of the flat, inserted her keys through the letterbox, and headed for Larry's bedsit. From there, they would travel to the airport.

"Are you excited, love?" Larry asked, after they'd checked in at the airport and headed towards the departure lounge.

Gina nodded. It was true, she did feel excited. Despite all that that happened in the previous few weeks, she had come through it all, and was now heading to a new life in London.

CHAPTER 44

The first few weeks in London went by in a blur. On arrival, they booked into a cheap hotel, and while Larry went to his new job each day, Gina toured estate agents, and took down phone numbers from ads in the local shops. They needed to rent somewhere quickly, since they were both tired of living in one room, having to eat out all the time, and having nowhere to wash their undies.

After visiting about a dozen apartments and flats, Gina finally found a pleasant airy flat she thought might suit. Larry was equally impressed when he saw it, and before the week was out they'd paid their deposit and first month's rent, and moved in.

Larry loved his new job, and before long Gina had found herself a job in a veterinary laboratory. It was a junior position, since she couldn't claim to have worked for BWF Pharmaceuticals without explaining why she'd left in such a hurry. So she said she hadn't been employed since she'd graduated from college, and that this would be her first job. She was relieved to be earning money at last, and their combined salaries made life a lot more comfortable.

By now, Gina's pregnancy was beginning to show a little, but she felt confident that no one at her new job would realise it yet. She was also experiencing severe morning sickness, and had to sneak into the bathroom to throw up while Larry was still asleep. Gina realised she couldn't wait any longer. It was time to tell Larry about the situation.

Preparing a particularly tasty evening meal, Gina decided to tell him over dinner, after he'd been mellowed by good food and a glass of wine.

At the end of the main course, Gina felt that it was time to take the plunge. "Larry, I think I might be pregnant," she said, taking a deep breath. "I haven't had a period since that first time in your bedsit, and I've started to feel sick in the mornings."

Larry's face lit up with joy. "Oh Gina, that's wonderful!" Then his expression softened, and he looked at her closely. "You're not upset about it, are you?"

Gina gave a tired smile. "Well, it might have been better if it hadn't happened so soon. I mean, we're only getting settled in London, and your new job is taking up a lot of your time. You don't need me being a burden as well."

"Burden? My God, Gina — I love you! And I'll love our baby!" Whooping for joy, he jumped up from the table, punched the air, then lifted her up and spun her around. "Whoo-hoo — I'm going to be a father!" Then, realising that he might be making her dizzy, he gently released her back onto the ground. "I was going to pop the question just as soon as I could afford a ring," he told her. "But why wait? Let's get married straight away!"

"Okay," said Gina, as though giving it consideration. "When will we do it?"

"As soon as possible, as far as I'm concerned!" Larry replied. "I can't wait to make you Mrs Macken!"

Eagerly, he hurried to the phone directory, and began looking up registry offices and wedding reception venues.

"Maybe we could have the reception in the local pub?" Larry

suggested, thumbing through the pages. "The owners are very friendly, and it's near the underground station that goes into the city, so hopefully, some of my new colleagues from work will be able to come along."

Gina nodded, trying to look enthusiastic. She felt bad about Larry's obvious enthusiasm. She hated having to tell lies. As soon as Larry's wedding ring was on her finger, she'd feel safe at last.

"That's a great idea, love," she told him, putting on a bright smile. "I'll invite Maeve and the others from the flat."

"What about your mother, sisters and brothers-in-law?"

Gina smiled. "Okay, I'll send them all invitations. But don't be surprised if they don't turn up."

Gina had no intention of inviting her family. But she went though the motions to please Larry. The following day, she bought several dozen wedding invitation cards, and ostentatiously addressed separate ones to her mother, Dolly and Owen, Stella and Paddy in Larry's presence. But as soon as Larry had gone to work, she carefully tore then up and burned every trace of them in the fire grate.

As the next week went by, Gina tried to concentrate on her job and her new life with Larry. Her job was boring and routine, and required little effort. Her relationship with Larry needed little effort either. Having Gina in his life seemed more than enough for Larry. He adored her, and couldn't believe his good luck at their forthcoming marriage. Daily, he showered her with little gifts, ranging from a bunch of flowers to a pretty bracelet, and all Gina needed to do was be there.

As she shopped for a wedding dress during her lunch hour, Gina finally decided on a geometric-patterned green and purple maxi-dress, and a big floppy hat that matched the green in the dress. Grimacing, she walked past the shops displaying long white gowns and billowing veils. Not for her the big white wedding she'd dreamed of as a young girl. And the dream she'd once had – of a tall handsome man waiting for her at the altar – had never been one in which Larry featured.

She tried not to think of Owen, since her future was now with Larry. But she couldn't help wondering how Owen was getting on. His work had highlighted major problems in the trials of BWF Pharmaceuticals' latest product. In fact, she'd brought the copy he gave her in her suitcase to London. She'd read through it one day when Larry was out, and had been deeply impressed with the way in which Owen had explained the vaccine's flaws. It was all down to a preservative that could cause neurological damage when it got into young or undeveloped brains. He'd also kindly given her a credit on it too, since she'd helped with the research and shared his viewpoint. They both firmly believed that the vaccine was released onto the open market, a lot of people would be harmed by it. Hopefully, Owen could make Charles Keane and the board of directors see sense.

Her new job, in a veterinary laboratory, didn't involve research, and only had her doing routine testing of veterinary products. Nevertheless, it helped her to feel close to Owen since she was using similar equipment, and the laboratory chemicals filled her nostrils with the same pungent aroma. Sometimes, she would close her eyes, and imagine that she was back in BWF Pharmaceuticals, working alongside Owen again. How wonderful everything would be if he could know about his baby! Of course, her little pipe dream never included Dolly or Charles Keane. In Gina's mind, the laboratory was a separate cocoon that had nothing to do with the problems generated by Owen's research, or the people who were actively trying to scupper it.

* * *

Two weeks later, Gina and Larry were married at the local Town Hall. It was a bright sunny day, and after the brief ceremony they and their guests repaired to the garden of the local pub, where the landlord and his staff served drinks. Later, there would be a small reception in an upstairs room of the pub, before Gina and Larry returned to their flat. There would be no honeymoon, at least for the present, since they'd agreed that they needed any money they had for the new baby.

Standing in the sunny garden of the pub, Gina surreptitiously glanced at her new husband. Poor Larry. His acne had cleared up somewhat, and he looked well in his new suit, but he'd never be a man who would make her pulse race. She wished more than anything that she could love him, because he was such a good and decent man, and he deserved more than she could ever give him. But she derived consolation from the fact that he believed she loved him, and in a way, it was true. But she would never love him in the way that she loved Owen.

Several of their friends and colleagues had brought cameras, so there were lots of photographs being taken. Gina lost count of the number of times she was posed beside her husband, or some other group of guests, and ordered to say 'cheese'. Looking around her, she was delighted to see that so many friends had made the effort to come from Ireland. Larry's family had turned out in force, and Maeve and the other young women from the flat in Dublin had also arrived. Several of Larry's work colleagues were there too, as were several of her own colleagues from the veterinary laboratory. The only people conspicuous by their absence were her own family.

As she stood alone, waiting for Larry to bring her back a refill of wine, Gina saw Maeve approaching. The two friends hugged, both of them with tears in their eyes.

"I'm so glad you could come," Gina whispered. "This day just wouldn't have been the same without you."

"I couldn't believe it when I got the invitation!" Maeve

whispered back. "You and Larry – after all the scathing things you said about him in the past!"

"Well, the past is just that, Maeve – past. Larry and I are going to make our lives here in London from now on. I hope you'll come and visit us regularly – there's plenty of room in the flat."

"Thanks," said Maeve, "I'd love to. I really miss you, you know. We used to have great fun together, didn't we?"

Gina nodded, remembering the walks home from school together, the nights on the town, the way they'd rated boys' ability to kiss properly, the times they'd planned to go as illegals to America.

"Why did you just disappear, and not let me know where you were going?" Maeve asked, hurt in her eyes. "I was really worried about you, but I was afraid to ask any of your family, knowing what happened with Owen."

"Sorry," said Gina contritely. "I just didn't know what to tell you."

Maeve glanced around at the assembled guests. "I see that none of your family are here today either. Do they know you've just got married?"

"No – and don't you dare tell them!" said Gina, angry at the thought of her absent family. "I pretended to Larry that I'd invited them – he thinks they disapprove of me moving to London with him."

"Oh, what a tangled web we weave!" said Maeve, sadly surveying her friend. "I hope you'll be able to accurately remember all these stories you've concocted."

Gina smiled. "I hope so – my life could depend on it."

"So tell me the truth – why did you really marry Larry?"

"It's a long story."

"Is it? You're pregnant, aren't you?"

"Shhh!" Gina glowered at her friend. "For Christ's sake, keep your voice down!"

"Well, you are, aren't you? And it's not Larry's baby, is it?"

"Please, Maeve, don't say a word to anyone. Larry thinks it's his."

"Of course I won't say anything. You know you can trust me. But it's not fair on poor old Larry, is it?"

Gina nodded, her expression clouding. *"I know, Maeve, and I feel really bad about it. Honestly. But I didn't have any choice. Anyway, I'll be good to Larry — I swear it. I've made him happy by marrying him — you know he's always been mad about me."*

"More's the pity," said Maeve dryly, *"The poor man never had any sense."*

The two women smiled, both recalling Larry's slavish devotion to Gina since their teens.

"I would have helped you," Maeve said, searching Gina's face. *"You could have gone to one of those mothers-and-babies places, then maybe had it adopted. Or I'd have come to England with you, for an abortion."*

"But I didn't want to do that!" Gina whispered fiercely. *"I love this baby, and I love the father of this baby too!"*

"Talking about me, are you?" said Larry, suddenly appearing at her side, and Gina had the grace to blush.

"Gina's just been telling me, discreetly of course, that she's expecting," said Maeve. *"Congratulations!"*

"Thanks, Maeve. It's great to see you," said Larry enthusiastically, topping up both women's wine glasses. *"I'm delighted that you could come today. I wanted all our friends to witness the fact that I finally got Gina to the altar! Well, to the registry office, anyway."*

He grinned happily, leaving the two women to chat while he filled up other guests' glasses.

"He really is such a sweetie," Maeve said sadly. *"If you don't treat him well, you'll have me to answer to!"*

"I will, I promise you," said Gina, smiling.

CHAPTER 45

As soon as Owen saw Charles Keane walk through the courtyard and enter the research unit, he quickly hid his copy of the research document. He'd being reading over the data just to confirm his findings, and he was satisfied that he'd clearly documented the dangers of going ahead with the development of the vaccine. Going to one of his filing cabinets, he quickly selected another file and placed it on his desk, sat down and appeared to be reading it by the time Charles Keane reached his office. He kept his head down until Charles Keane knocked politely on the glass door, then beckoned him to enter.

He wondered why Charles Keane had chosen to visit the research facility rather than summoning him to his own office. Clearly, what Charles had to say was not for the ears of his own secretary. If Charles didn't want Dolly to know, then it had to be bad. Perhaps this was the sack at last, he thought, and he felt almost light-hearted at the thought. If that happened, it meant that the company intended going ahead with the vaccine, so he'd have no option but to go to the press with his research document.

"Good morning, Charles," Owen said looking up, his tone

267

formal. He wanted to let Charles know he was well aware that things weren't exactly rosy between them. Far be it from him to let Charles Keane think that he'd be surprised to be sacked.

Without replying, Charles stepped inside and closed the door. "I'm here because I don't want your wife knowing what I have to say," he said, looking sternly at Owen, who had put down his pen and was lolling back in his chair.

"Oh?" Owen said. Let the bastard think I'm not bothered.

"As you know, your position with the company is rather tenuous at the moment. We can't possibly allow your research on these trials to be released. It would destroy the company."

Owen leaned forward angrily. "What about the lives the vaccine will destroy? If you had a conscience, Charles, you'd cut your losses and abandon it altogether."

Charles studied his own fingernails. "After the millions our overseas partners have put into its research and development? I don't think so. But I thought we could count on your loyalty to the company, Owen."

"Not when this vaccine will put people's lives at risk!"

"Very well then, if that's your attitude, there's little else I can say on the matter. But I suspect you may change your mind when you hear what I have to say." He gave a little smirk. "I'm aware of your little eh, liaison with your sister-in-law."

Owen was shocked. How on earth had Charles Keane discovered that? Surely Dolly would never have told her boss – her pride was far too important to her. On the other hand, she confided in Charles Keane about everything, so why not that?

Charles smiled smugly and Owen wished that he hadn't reacted with obvious shock. Nothing about Charles Keane should surprise him by now. Keane had spies everywhere, so nothing much escaped his notice, especially if he felt that it affected the company in any way.

"So, what business is it of yours?" Owen retorted angrily.

Charles Keane smiled again, a tight smug smile this time, and Owen longed to punch him in the mouth.

"Anything that impinges on the company is my business," Charles replied smoothly. *"Although Dolly mentioned this little eh, matter to me —"* he paused for effect, *"I think she'd be a lot more upset if she knew the rest of this sordid little tale."*

He deliberately paused again, and Owen felt his heart pounding uncomfortably. He hoped Keane couldn't see his discomfort. The man was playing with him as a cat would play with a mouse.

"How do you think she'd feel if she knew about her sister's pregnancy?"

"W-what?"

Charles smiled, pleased at Owen's shocked reaction. *"So you see, my dear Owen, there are always consequences for each course of action we take. Your little, eh, liaison has had unfortunate consequences, but nothing that can't be put right."*

Owen was now on his feet. *"Where is she?"*

"I believe your sister-in-law has gone to London, presumably to visit one of those abortion clinics. Best thing that could have happened, under the circumstances." Charles dusted off his hands, as though finished with a particularly nasty problem. *"But I won't be telling Dolly — assuming you and I understand each other. We can forget all about this unfortunate little incident, as long as you keep your side of the bargain, your little research paper is withdrawn, and we proceed with the Phase 3 trials as planned."* He smiled, warmly this time. *"In fact, I think we might even manage to award you a handsome bonus at the end of the month — for your great work on behalf of the company."*

For a moment, Owen was stunned and unable to speak. Gina was pregnant with his child! Joy suddenly filled his heart, but just *as quickly it turned to sadness — assuming it was true that she was about to have, or had already had, an abortion.*

Seeing Owen's discomfiture, Charles attempted to put a benign expression on his face. "It's all water under the bridge now — you have my word that Dolly will never know about the pregnancy. As long as you keep your end of the bargain, we can all continue as one big happy family."

Pushing back his chair, Owen lumbered to his feet. Momentarily, Charles Keane's benign expression faltered as he saw the anger in Owen's eyes. He quickly took a step backwards as Owen's fist pounded on the desk.

"You've made the mistake of assuming that I give a damn about Dolly, or about staying married to her!" Owen said angrily. "As far as your job is concerned, you can stick it! And if you don't postpone your plans for Phase 3 of the vaccine trials immediately, I intend going to the press with my findings!" With that, he moved towards the door of his office, opened it, and indicated for Charles to leave.

Charles took a step backwards. "Now, Owen, be reasonable —"

"Out!"

Charles had no choice but to leave.

"You'll have my resignation within the hour," Owen told him, immediately closing the door behind him.

A stunned Charles Keane made his way out of the laboratory complex, feeling embarrassed at the knowing glances of the staff who'd been alerted by the raised voices, and who'd witnessed his eviction from Owen's office. Cursing his own stupidity in resorting to blackmail, he realised that he'd just made a cardinal error. He'd assumed that Owen wanted to remain married to Dolly. Only now he realised that Owen wasn't bothered about salvaging an already empty marriage. He'd also seemed genuinely concerned about Dolly's younger sister.

Charles cursed his own stupidity in not reading the signs right. No doubt the fool was writing his letter of resignation at this very minute. Well, he himself had no time to lose either.

* * *

With hindsight, Owen wished he hadn't been quite so forthright with Charles Keane. He'd actually shot himself in the foot by alerting the bastard to his intentions to make his misgivings public. On the other hand, it had been deeply satisfying to watch the man's jaw drop and his eyes bulge with fear when his beloved company was threatened with media exposure.

So that explained why he hadn't been sacked immediately after his recent outburst in the boardroom. Charles Keane had been hunting around for some way of blackmailing him! Owen grimaced as he typed his letter of resignation on his office typewriter. No doubt his marriage to Dolly had also been a consideration. As Keane's most ardent supporter and confidante, Dolly was invaluable to him, and if Keane had been able to keep them both working for the company, so much the better from his point of view.

Owen wished that he'd planned his departure in a more structured and organised way. But then, he hadn't expected to be openly blackmailed, had he? He was unlikely to be allowed to take all his documentation away with him, although he had every intention of trying.

Placing his key documents in a file, Owen removed his letter of resignation from the typewriter, placed it in an envelope, picked up the file and left the room without a backward glance. He felt a remarkable sense of freedom, as though he was shaking off the restrictive overcoat and exposing his body to the warmth and comfort of the sun. It was a heady feeling, and he was humming as he walked into Charles Keane's office and placed the letter on his desk.

271

"I'm afraid you can't be allowed to leave the company with any documents relating to your work," Charles Keane told him frostily. *"You've been paid for your research, so now it belongs to the company."*

Without demur, Owen handed over the folders he was carrying. Let Charles think he was winning. Owen could afford to be magnanimous right now, since he knew he had a copy of his research report hidden safely in his sock drawer at home.

"Goodbye, Charles," he'd said, smiling as he walked out the door.

Once home, Owen had gone straight to his sock drawer. But the research report wasn't there. For a moment, his heart almost stopped beating. Then he began to throw all his socks out onto the floor. It had to be there – he'd put it there himself! But no amount of searching yielded the document. By now the sweat was pouring down Owen's face. If it wasn't in the sock drawer, maybe he'd somehow moved it to one of the other drawers. Maybe he'd got up during the night while sleepwalking, and transferred it to another drawer. Anxiously, he threw all his folded shirts and handkerchiefs onto the floor. But no, it wasn't in that drawer either. By now he was in a total panic. Heaving the contents of all the other drawers out onto the floor, he got down on his hands and knees and began rummaging anxiously through them. But there was sign of his research document.

In some distant part of his brain, he heard the front door open and close, and footsteps coming up the stairs. Suddenly, Dolly appeared at the bedroom door.

"Looking for something, Owen?" she asked sweetly.

"Eh, yes."

Dolly looked smug. "What exactly are you looking for?"

"I – it's a document. I seem to have mislaid it."

"Was it, by any chance, a copy of your research conclusions about the vaccine?"

"Yes!" Relief flooded through him, until he looked directly at Dolly, and saw the venom in her eyes.

"W-where is it, Dolly?" he asked hoarsely, real fear threatening to bring on a heart attack.

"Oh, I returned that to Charles about an hour ago," she told him sweetly. "He asked me to make sure that you'd taken nothing from the company before you left."

She tilted her head to one side. "How does it feel to be unemployed, Owen?" she added, no longer bothering to keep the triumph out of her voice. She was extracting her revenge, and was enjoying it to the full. "Well, I hope you'll be able to get another job," she added, amusement in her eyes. "I really don't think you can rely on Charles to give you a good reference. Although I could ask him, if you like. I'm sure he'd do it for me."

As Dolly left the room, Owen crumpled in a heap on the floor. He was finished. There was no way he could convince anyone of the validity of his claims without his research report, with all the facts and figures. So Dolly had finally got her revenge. At least she doesn't know about Gina's pregnancy, he thought. Heaven knows what extra torture she'd mete out to him if she knew about that!

He drew in a deep breath. Without doubt, his marriage was over, and he was actually relieved. Now he would go and find Gina, tell her how he felt about her, and hopefully convince her to start a new life with him. Maybe he would find her before she had the abortion. If so, he would convince her of his love, she would have the baby, and they would live happily ever after.

Suddenly, Owen sat up, immense relief flooding through his body. He'd just remembered — Gina had a copy of his research! Just after he'd photocopied and numbered all the copies, which included *all his research references and his misgivings, he'd given her a copy, asking her to review it and give him her comments. He'd also given her a credit on it, since she'd compiled many of the statistics and graphs on his behalf.*

Regrettably, there had never been an opportunity to discuss it with her. On that fateful afternoon in his mother-in-law's house, they'd actually started discussing the document, but before long what had started as an affectionate kiss had turned into so much more. Owen wiped his brow. After all the drama, Gina had disappeared, and he'd never got a chance to ask her what she thought of it.

Suddenly, Owen was overcome by a new sense of freedom. It felt good to lift the lid on corruption and greed. He would find Gina, and together they would save lives by letting the public know the truth.

CHAPTER 46

For appearances' sake, Dolly wasn't keen to turf Owen out onto the street – what on earth would the neighbours say? Instead, she preferred to maintain the appearance of a solid marriage, to the outside world at least. Since there was no possibility of divorce in Ireland, Dolly expected that the present situation would carry on indefinitely. After all, she was the one with right on her side, so she wasn't leaving. And if Owen left, where on earth could he go? He had no job any more, and fortunately, any chance of him interfering with the new vaccine Charles was trialling had been well and truly scuppered. Dolly smiled smugly to herself. Charles had been so pleased when she'd returned the document from Owen's sock drawer. Did her fool of a husband think she hadn't known what was hidden there?

Dolly didn't need to worry about money, since Charles had assured her that she'd be well rewarded for her loyalty to the company. She already knew that her boss was an extremely generous man – numerous times he'd given her substantial bonuses, and she was undoubtedly the highest-paid secretary in the country. "Loyal employees are worth their weight in gold, Dolly," Charles had told her, and she'd glowed with pride. "Besides," he'd chuckled, "I couldn't afford to let you go, m'dear. You know too much!"

Immediately after Owen resigned, Charles had called her into his office, and assured her that she'd want for nothing.

"I'm sorry that your husband has chosen to behave in such a hot-headed manner," he'd told her ruefully, "but I'm still grateful to him for the great work he's done for the company in the past." He'd patted her shoulder. "I don't want you to suffer because of his unreasonable and disloyal behaviour, so I'm increasing your salary, back-dated to last month, in the hope that it will make things a little easier for you."

He coughed gently. "And if you have any difficulty with the, eh, mortgage, don't hesitate to let me know. A happy employee is an efficient one, and I couldn't bear to see you unhappy, m'dear."

She expressed her thanks profusely and, when she finally rose to go, her feet hardly touched the ground after Charles's accolade.

"By the way, Dolly —" said Charles then, as though he'd suddenly had an afterthought, "there's just one more numbered copy of your husband's research missing. I hate to ask you this, Dolly, but would you mind making a further search at home, just in case Owen hid another copy somewhere else?"

Dolly smoothed her shirt, looking coquettishly at her boss. "I know where the other copy is, Charles," she told him. "At least, I think I do."

Charles, who'd begun pacing the floor, stopped in mid-stride. "Wonderful! Where is it?"

Dolly gazed reflectively into the distance. "Once, when Owen and I were having an argument, he said that my sister Gina was far more interested in his career and future than I was. He told me he'd given her a copy of the finished report to read —" She smiled at Charles. "I suspect she still has it."

Charles stroked his chin reflectively. "But Gina's walked out of her job here at BWF Pharmaceuticals, hasn't she? And taken off to destinations unknown, I believe. Does anyone know where she is right now?"

Dolly shook her head.

Through his network of spies, Charles was well aware of why the little minx had taken off, and where she'd gone, but he didn't want Dolly knowing about his attempts to blackmail her husband.

"Do you think she might have left the research document at your mother's house, Dolly?" he added.

Dolly shook her head. "After Gina left, I cleared out her room. There was no sign of any research paper there, so I can only assume she took it with her."

Charles gave Dolly the benefit of an absentminded smile, a technique he'd perfected over the years. "Oh, well, I suppose there's not much point in worrying about it, then," he remarked affably.

But inwardly, Charles Keane's mood was anything but affable. He would get that research copy back, come hell or high water. That little bitch Gina wasn't going to scupper his long-term plans for BWF Pharmaceuticals.

* * *

Unlike his wife, Owen wasn't receiving any accolades. Since the episode with Gina, he and Dolly were hardly speaking to each other, she leaving the house each morning for Charles Keane's office, returning home at night with food that she cooked for herself in the kitchen, then took to the dining room to eat. She never offered Owen any, for which he was grateful. Instead, he took his meals at an assortment of city-centre cafés and restaurants, although how long he could afford to continue dining out he didn't know.

Luckily, he still had some money in his personal bank account, but it wasn't going to last indefinitely.

Besides, he had to find Gina. He missed her desperately. He wanted nothing more than to wrap his arms around her and tell her how much she meant to him. Wherever she was, he hoped she didn't think that their lovemaking that afternoon on the sofa had been just a fling for him. That afternoon had made him realise that Gina was the woman for him, and her passionate response had indicated that she might feel the same as he did. But why oh why hadn't she told him she was pregnant?

Owen sighed. Dolly had never shown any interest in his work, and his only value to her had been as a 'good catch'. His bloody wife should have married Charles Keane, he thought savagely, and probably would have, if her boss hadn't been married already. Since he and Dolly had married, he'd had to listen to a nightly litany of 'Charles-this' and Charles-that', and his research had only interested Dolly in so far as it impacted on Charles's little fiefdom.

How could two sisters be so unalike? In contrast, Gina knew how much his work had meant to him. She'd supported him through it all, shared his trials and triumphs, and was keenly aware of the danger that this vaccine presented to the public if released. Hopefully, if he could find her – and if she felt the same about him – they could start a new life together.

He'd soon need to get a job, of course, and explain why he'd resigned from BWF Pharmaceuticals. But assuming Gina still had the copy of his research that he'd given her, they'd have the proof to expose the vaccine as the dangerous product that it was, and after that, the job offers would come flooding in. Without doubt, he'd be offered a university lectureship and research facilities. And while the universities wouldn't have state-of-the-art equipment of the kind that BWF Pharmaceuticals could afford, he'd be able to choose his own work projects where his conscience would be clear — no more fighting with the powers-that-be in order to prevent them riding roughshod over the public.

And, of course, he'd have Gina working alongside him. It would be like the old days, the two of them laughing and cracking jokes, smiling at each other as they worked. And they'd be going home together too — to their little love-nest somewhere in suburbia. Where it would be didn't matter, as long as they were together.

Owen sighed. He couldn't wait to see Gina again. But first, he'd have to find her.

CHAPTER 47

"W-what? I don't believe you!"

"I'm sorry, Owen, but I'm telling you the truth."

Maeve topped up his half-empty cup with freshly made tea, but he was totally oblivious to it. Owen was in a state of shock. Maeve had just told him that Gina had got married. She couldn't have — no, she was his Gina, not anyone else's!

"Are you absolutely sure?"

Maeve nodded sadly. "I'm sure — because I was there. She and Larry got married in London a week ago."

"Larry? You mean she married that fellow she couldn't get rid of? The one who was always hanging around her?"

Maeve nodded again but felt duty-bound to defend Larry's character. "He's a genuinely nice fellow," she told Owen, but he wasn't really listening. His heart was breaking, and he wanted to pick up Maeve's teapot and smash it to the ground in anger. Instead, he buried his head in his hands. It just wasn't possible. It couldn't be possible! Gina hadn't even given him time to sort out his own life before she'd gone and married someone else! Quietly, he began to sob.

Maeve bit her lip, unsure of what to do. She hadn't expected a grown man to react quite so badly. Originally when Gina had told her what had happened with Owen that afternoon at her mother's house, Maeve had felt anger towards Owen, assuming that he'd simply been using her friend. But now it was clear that he genuinely cared about her, and Maeve felt only sadness on his behalf. Clearly he hadn't intended to abandon Gina – he'd just needed time to sort out his own domestic and business situations before trying to contact her again. But Maeve knew that Gina, in her haste to find a father for her baby, had rushed into marriage with Larry.

Briefly, Maeve wondered if she should tell Owen about Gina's baby. But no, she decided, it wasn't any of her business. Gina had made her decision, and mightn't want to jeopardise her fledgling marriage by telling Owen that the baby was his. The decision had to be Gina's. But if Owen asked, she'd give him Gina's telephone number in London. She sighed. Sometimes relationships weren't over till they were over. Maybe Owen and Gina still had things to talk through with each other. Maeve just hoped that Larry wouldn't end up a victim yet again.

Owen wiped his eyes with his handkerchief. He felt foolish crying in Maeve's presence, but he'd been shocked to the core to discover that he'd meant so little to Gina. If she'd genuinely cared about him, she wouldn't have gone off and married that Larry fellow. Maybe she'd just wanted to try sex with an older man before tying the knot. And he, like the fool he was, had believed that she might have cared for him! Maybe what Charles Keane had told him wasn't true – maybe Gina wasn't pregnant at all, or she was pregnant by this Larry fellow. Or maybe she'd gone and had an abortion before the wedding. He longed to ask Maeve if she knew anything about Gina's supposed pregnancy, but since she hadn't volunteered any information, she probably didn't know.

Owen stared at the floor, his world in tatters. When he'd begun his search for Gina, he'd remembered that she and Maeve were close friends, so if anyone would know where she was, Maeve would. Gina had told him months earlier that Maeve Harding shared a flat with several other young women in Dublin's Camden Street, so he decided to check all the names on the bells outside likely rental accommodation, and enquire in the local shops.

He'd worked his way through nearly one side of the street when he struck it lucky. The barman in O'Grady's pub knew Maeve and Gina well, and gave him directions to the flat. He'd been so excited as he'd rung the doorbell! At that point, he'd had high hopes of finding Gina there too, since the barman had implied that they came into the pub regularly. But now, as he'd learnt to his cost, he'd found Gina too late.

"What am I going to do?" he asked plaintively. "I can't believe I meant so little to her."

Maeve said nothing, not knowing what to say.

Owen wiped his eyes again, and tried to smile at Maeve. "I'm sorry for behaving like an idiot," he said, "but it's been a shock to discover that she's got married."

He stood up and prepared to leave. "Thanks for the tea, Maeve," he said, a ghost of a smile flitting across his face.

They were both well aware that she could have served him hemlock and he wouldn't have noticed.

"I'd hoped Gina and I might have a future together, but I guess it wasn't meant to be," he said, a slight tremor in his voice as he walked towards the hall door. "But I'd like to send her a card, wishing her well, anyway. Would you mind giving me her address, Maeve?"

Maeve nodded. The poor man seemed more in control of himself now, and his better instincts were asserting themselves once again.

"Of course," she said. "I also have her phone number – do you want that as well?"

Owen nodded. When he was in better control of his emotions, he would decide whether a card or a phone call was more appropriate.

Suddenly, he remembered the research paper that he hoped Gina still had. With the shock of discovering she was married, he'd forgotten all about it! Hopefully, she hadn't got rid of it. On the other hand, since she'd abandoned him so easily, perhaps she no longer felt any affinity with his work either?

At the door, Maeve gave him a hug. An hour earlier, it might have seemed odd to hug a man she'd never met before, but now she felt a genuine empathy towards him. And not for the first time, she marvelled at the effect Gina clearly had on men. It was a gift if used with care and consideration, but knowing her friend, she feared that Gina would never learn to use it wisely.

CHAPTER 48

Gina was walking on air. Owen had telephoned her! He'd traced her to London, and wanted to see her! It was difficult to hide her excitement, but she did her best to appear normal in front of Larry.

Luckily, she always got home from work before Larry, so she'd been the one who'd answered the phone that day.

"Hello, is that you, Gina?"

Gina's heart almost stopped. Was she imagining it, or was she hearing Owen's voice?

"Yes, this is Gina. Who's that?" she asked, playing for time until she composed herself.

"It's Owen. I got your number from Maeve. She told me you've got married."

Gina's heart was pounding. "Eh, yes."

There was a deep sigh at the other end of the phone. "Oh God, Gina – I wish you'd waited until I was free – I'm sure we could have been happy together."

"But I didn't know," Gina whispered back. "After we – after that afternoon, I wasn't sure if I'd ever see you again. I mean, you're married to my sister –"

"I've left Dolly, and I've left BWF Pharmaceuticals. But things like that don't get sorted out overnight, Gina. I thought you'd at least give me a chance to work things out, before rushing off and getting married."

Gina bit her lip. "I'm sorry, Owen. I didn't know if that afternoon meant anything to you, or if it was just a fling as far as you were concerned. I hoped, but I never really expected to hear from you again."

"My God, Gina – I love you! I tried to find you, but you'd disappeared! Thankfully, I remembered where Maeve lived – she told me that you'd stayed with her for a while, before you –" He sighed. "I just wish I'd known what you were planning to do. I might have convinced you that we could be happy together –"

"How is Maeve?"

"She's fine."

"Eh, did she say anything else?"

"Like what?"

"Oh, it doesn't matter."

Clearly Maeve hadn't said anything about her pregnancy. Gina wasn't sure how she felt about that. While she was pleased that Maeve hadn't broken her trust, it meant that she'd now have to tell Owen herself. Or would she? Oh God, everything was in such a mess.

There was silence for a few moments. "I don't suppose you'd like to meet me?" Owen asked tentatively.

Gina gulped. "Of course I would. More than anything."

In her heart, Gina knew that she should say no. But she couldn't resist the opportunity of seeing Owen again. She knew she was playing with fire, but she felt powerless to resist. Owen made her feel like no man had ever done before.

"Can you meet me on Saturday morning, say about eleven?"

Owen asked, excitement in his voice. "I'll fly over to London on Friday night, and stay in a hotel or B&B near King's Cross. I remember a little café called the Blue Crane in Soho, where you can sit and drink coffee all day if you want to. Would that suit? If not, maybe you know somewhere better . . ."

"No, that sounds wonderful, Owen. I'll see you at eleven."

Already Gina was planning what she'd wear when she saw her beloved Owen again . . . and to think that he loved her too!

Suddenly, Gina heard the front door opening. "I must go – Larry's back from work."

"Okay – until Saturday, then."

"Bye."

"Bye."

The door to the flat opened and Larry stepped into the lounge. "Hello, love. Did you have a good day?"

"Yes, fine thanks," said Gina, smiling happily.

"Who was that on the phone?"

"Oh, just a wrong number."

* * *

Now that Owen had contacted her again, Gina couldn't bear to be intimate with Larry any longer. She used her pregnancy as an excuse, feigning headaches and back pain to keep him from making any demands on her. Larry, deeply concerned for her comfort and happiness, rubbed her back instead. Larry found no problem with this state of affairs – his own happiness seemed to have insulated him from any awareness of a change in Gina's mood. He still couldn't believe his luck – he was training for a career he loved, he had Gina as his wife, and she was expecting their baby.

As the week progressed and Saturday got nearer, Gina became increasingly excited. She told Larry that she was meeting one of *the women from work, and that they were going shopping before having lunch together.*

Larry smiled. "That's great, love. I'm glad to see you making friends." He stuck his hand in his pocket and extracted several tenners. "Here, buy yourself something nice," he told her, and Gina felt consumed with guilt.

But even her guilt was no deterrent to her plans for Saturday. During every waking moment, she was obsessed with thoughts of Owen. Thankfully, due to their busy work schedules, she and Larry didn't spend much time together during the working week. Each morning they rose early for their commute into the city, although Gina didn't need to leave the house until half an hour after Larry. She also made a point of getting off the underground several stops before she needed to, and walking the rest of the way to the laboratory. This suited her perfectly, since all her thoughts were focussed on Owen once again, and during the walk to the laboratory, she could spend her time thinking about him without interruption.

On Saturday morning, Gina woke at dawn. It was far too early to get up, so she lay beside a sleeping Larry and thought about Owen once again. Her heart was pounding with excitement, and she wondered what they'd say to each other when they finally met. They'd both declared their feelings for each other on the phone, so there was no longer any need to hold back. But what was going to happen next? Gina didn't want to think about that.

Showering later in their dingy little bathroom, Gina lathered on every sweet-smelling lotion and potion she could find. She wanted to smell good for Owen. She felt so happy that she longed to sing out loud, but instead she contented herself with smiling to herself as she washed. She needed to be careful in case Larry started to suspect something. He would definitely consider it odd if she was bursting with excitement when only going shopping with a friend!

Fortunately, Larry decided to have a lie-in, and while he dozed, Gina was able to try on several dresses, and change her hairstyle several times, without him noticing anything amiss. At last she was reasonably happy with her appearance, and with one final glance in the mirror, she called to a sleepy Larry that she'd see him later that evening. Then she headed out the door of the flat.

"Have fun!" Larry called after her, sleepily.

Gina smiled to herself. At last she was free, and on her way to meet the man she loved!

Exiting from the underground station, Gina found the Blue Crane café without any difficulty. In the cosy interior, she chose a corner table, which gave her a view of the street yet afforded its occupants privacy. Ordering a coffee, she sat down to await Owen's arrival. Excitement coursed through her veins. What would they say to each other? Would she tell him about the baby? Right now, she wasn't sure. She would play it by ear and see how things developed.

As she waited for Owen, part of her hoped that she mightn't feel anything for him when he arrived. That would make life so much easier! Then she could go back to Larry, and carry on with her marriage with a clear conscience. Well, her conscience wasn't exactly clear where poor Larry was concerned. She'd grossly deceived him – and exploited him – because he'd allowed her to. But she'd make it up to him, and do the best she could to make him happy . . .

But all those thoughts evaporated when Owen opened the door of the café and walked in. Gina's thought her heart would burst with love and desire for him. He looked tired, and he'd lost weight, but he was still the most exciting man she'd ever met. And she realised with heart-stopping certainty that she could never let him go.

"Owen!"

"Gina!"

Rising from the table, she fell into his arms, knowing with every fibre of her being that this was meant to be. They hugged fiercely, eventually sitting down at the table, still holding hands as though afraid to let each other go.

Owen gave her an adoring look. "Oh, my love – you look wonderful! Gina, my precious, you're more beautiful then ever – I don't know what it is, but you've developed a glow. Your skin is soft and dewy . . ."

Gina smiled back. She knew why her skin looked so good, and it had nothing to do the lotions she'd applied earlier. It was because she was pregnant. With Owen's baby.

"It's so good to see you again!" *she told him,* "I can't believe you've come all the way to London to see me!"

"Gina, I'd follow you to the ends of the earth! Please tell me that you'll leave this guy you married, and come to live with me! We can have a wonderful life together – I just know it!"

Tears filled Gina's eyes. These were the words she'd longed to hear.

"Owen, my beloved Owen – there's nothing I want more! I don't care where we live, as long as we're together!" *She gripped his hand.* "There's just one thing I need to tell you – I'm pregnant with your baby."

Owen grinned happily. "Yes, I know – but I was afraid you might have had an abortion by now."

Gina then looked quizzically at him. "Why? And how did you know I was pregnant? Did Maeve tell you?"

Shaking his head, Owen explained how Charles Keane had tried to blackmail him over the pregnancy, and how he'd immediately handed in his resignation.

"That bastard!" said Gina vehemently, "Nothing escapes his notice! How would he have found out?"

"Charles has a network of spies, so I suppose it was one of them who kept him informed. Anyway, it doesn't matter now, since we're going to be together at last."

The joy was now back in his eyes again, and he happily surveyed her slightly expanding waistline. "My God, Gina – you're expecting my baby – this is incredible!"

Gina gazed adoringly at him. "I could never get rid of your baby, Owen. That's why I needed to get married so quickly. I assumed you were staying with Dolly, and I didn't want to be left all alone and pregnant."

Then his expression darkened. "But why didn't you contact me? I would have been there for you – you must know that!"

Gina sighed. "It doesn't matter now, love – but after all the fuss, and the big row at home, I didn't know if I'd ever see you again. I mean, you are still married to Dolly . . ."

"And you're still married to this Larry fellow. But I'll move to London, we'll get a flat together, and all three of us – you, me and our baby – will live happily ever after!" Owen was grinning from ear to ear. "I never expected to have a family – Dolly wasn't exactly the most loving, or maternal, of women. This is fantastic!"

A slight cough made them realise that a waiter was standing by their table, waiting to take their order. Both ordered salads and coffee, even though they were too excited to eat. All they could think of was their future together.

When their salads eventually arrived, they moved them around on their plates, hardly touching any of it, totally absorbed in each other.

Suddenly, Owen looked worried. "Oh God! In all the excitement of arranging to meet you, I forgot to ask you something.

Remember the copy of my research that I gave you — have you still got it?"

Gina nodded.

"Where is it?"

"It's in the flat, here in London."

Owen squeezed her hands in gratitude. "Thank God for that! I have no other copy — Dolly delivered the last one I had back to Charles Keane!"

Gina gazed at him in wonderment. "So you're still intending to go public on it?"

"Of course! Morally, I have no other choice. And I can do it now, since you have the data that I need." Owen grinned. "For a while, I thought Charles Keane had beaten me. But now, I can run off lots more photocopies, and send them out to the press. Once my research gets into the public domain, we're home and dry, Gina. BWF Pharmaceuticals and its overseas partners can deny it all they like, but the facts will speak for themselves." He leaned across and kissed her cheek. "After that, the world will be our oyster. I might be out of a job right now, but when this stuff is published, the job offers will be lining up. Then we can buy our own home, and live happily ever after." He looked into her eyes. "We'll be together at last, Gina my love — you, me and our baby. The sooner you leave Larry, the better. It's not fair to either him or me."

Gina nodded, overwhelmed by it all. She felt guilty about all the ways in which she'd deceived poor Larry, but hopefully he'd get over her before long. When he realised how conniving she'd been, he'd stop loving her pretty quickly.

"How soon can you leave Larry?" Owen asked. "I've a bit of money — enough to tide us over until the document goes public. We can rent a flat somewhere cheaply — it doesn't matter just as long as we're together." He delved into his wallet. "Here — will you find *somewhere for us to live, Gina?"* he said, handing her a wad of notes. *"There's a few hundred pounds there – you should have enough money for the deposit and several months' rent. Put whatever's left into a savings account for us."*

Excited, Gina took the money. *"Wow, that's great! I'll start looking straight away,"* she promised him, her eyes glowing with joy. *"By the time we meet again, my love – I'll have our living accommodation all sorted out!"*

Owen grinned. *"Apart from my own Vauxhall, I've also got the vintage Bentley in Dublin – hopefully I can sell it quickly to a collector, so we'll have enough to survive on until the job offers start rolling in!"*

They gazed at each other in wonderment. Everything was working out so well!

Eventually, Gina squeezed his hand. *"Poor Larry – I'll have to figure out the best time to tell him."* She grimaced. *"Or maybe I'll just leave him a note – I know that's the coward's way out, but how can I tell him he's losing his wife, and the child he thinks is his – all in one go?"*

But even thoughts of Larry's distress couldn't dampen Gina's own happiness. Already she was making plans for her new life with Owen. She would find a basement flat with a garden, so that their baby could play outside in the sunshine. It was always sunny in this new world of Gina's, and rainy days were translated into cosy nights in by the fire. Then, when Owen's research gained him the credit he deserved, they would buy a big house with a tall tree in the back garden, where she would make a swing for their child to play on, and before long, there would be another brother or sister to play on it as well . . .

Owen's voice was husky with desire. *"Gina, I'm staying at a small hotel a few blocks from here – will you come back with me, for the afternoon at least? I want to make love to you so much!"*

There was nothing Gina wanted more than to feel Owen's body against hers, to hear him gasp with desire as she touched him . . .

Resolutely she shook her head. "You know I'd love to, Owen – but I need to get back to Larry. He thinks I've gone shopping with a friend, and I'll need to buy a few things to make it look as though I've genuinely been shopping. I can't let him know the truth just yet. Until we're ready." She leaned across the table and kissed his nose. "Besides, the next time I see you, it'll be for always, won't it?"

"Thank God for that!" said Owen fervently. "I don't think I can wait much longer, my love."

As they stood up to leave the café, Gina threw her arms around him. "I love you so much, Owen," she whispered. "How soon can you move to London?"

"I'll be back next week," Owen promised, returning her kisses. "All I have to do is pack a few things, sell the Bentley, say goodbye to a few friends, and tell Dolly that I'm leaving." He grinned. "I can't wait to see Dolly's face when I tell her I'm moving out! She'll be livid – she expects me to hang around for the rest of my life, being grateful to her for not evicting me from my own house."

Gina nodded. She knew how vindictive Dolly could be.

"I'll be counting the hours until you get back," said Gina fervently. "And I'll look out for a flat for us in the meantime."

They arranged to meet at the same café, at the same time, the following Friday morning. They chose a weekday this time, so that Larry would have left for work, enabling Gina to leave a note for him on the table before she left – ostensibly for work – herself.

"I can't believe it!" Gina whispered, tears in her eyes. "We're going to be together at last!"

"Make sure you pack my research report, won't you, love?"

said Owen, smiling lovingly at her. "I don't think you'll want to go back and ask Larry for it later!"

They both grinned at each other. Already, the future was looking wonderful.

* * *

"Have a good day?"

Larry was cooking dinner, and wearing a silly apron as he stirred the pots on the cooker.

"Yes, we had such fun!" Gina told him, her eyes sparkling, unable to disguise her inner happiness.

Larry was pleased; he hadn't seen Gina look so happy in ages. In fact, he'd never seen her look this happy before. It was good for her to have her own friends, and to spend time with them.

"Well, dinner will be ready in about five minutes — after that, you can show me what you bought."

In the bedroom, Gina tried to compose herself. On the one hand, she was bubbling with excitement about the future, but on the other hand, she felt wretched at what she was about to do to Larry. She really did care for him — but as a friend, not as a life partner. If only he didn't love her so much!

She wondered how she was going to get through the next week. She'd have no difficulty working in the laboratory, but coming home to Larry each evening would be a major problem. How would she look him in the eye, knowing that in a matter of days, she'd be gone from his life?

At least, she was managing to avoid any sexual intimacy. Since she'd first heard from Owen, she couldn't bear the thought of being touched by another man. But that didn't stop Larry from wanting to please her in other ways. And each little kindness was like a dagger in her heart.

Later that evening, as he rubbed her back, she longed to have the courage to tell him she was leaving. But each time she looked at his happy smiling face, her eyes filled with tears at the thought of what she was going to do to him. At one stage, he noticed her tears and held her tightly, thinking she was having a hormonal reaction to pregnancy.

I should leave now, Gina thought, as she lay awake that night beside a sleeping Larry. How can I behave normally, talk to him normally, pretend to love him, when all the time I want to be with another man? It was nearly dawn before Gina managed to sleep.

CHAPTER 49

By the following Friday morning, Gina was over the moon with joy. Today, she was finally leaving Larry, and beginning her new life with Owen! As she prepared the breakfast, she did her best to suppress her exuberance and delight. Hopefully, Larry wouldn't notice anything amiss. She'd been careful not to begin her packing yet — she'd start it just as soon as Larry left for work.

Despite working all week herself, Gina had used her lunch breaks to search for a flat for her and Owen. She'd deliberately chosen to search in different areas of London than where she and Larry rented their flat. Since she and Larry lived north of the Thames, she and Owen would move south. Hopefully, once she and Larry had parted, their paths would be unlikely to cross again.

On the third day of her search, Gina found exactly what she was looking for. It was a pretty basement flat with a side garden, situated on a tree-lined avenue. Without further ado, Gina paid the deposit and the first month's rent, and opened a savings account where she stored the rest of the money that Owen had given her. There was still enough money in the account to pay for several more months' rent.

"Bye, love, see you this evening," said Larry, placing a kiss on her cheek before he left for the office.

"Goodbye, Larry," Gina replied, careful not to say that she would see him that evening. She did not want her last words to her husband to contain a lie. Although, she conceded, her whole life with Larry had been based on a lie anyway.

As soon as Larry left, Gina surveyed the flat with a mixture of sadness and excitement. In an hour's time, she'd be leaving here forever, and soon she'd be in Owen's arms. Tonight, at last, they'd be sleeping together in the same bed, in the new flat she'd found for them. After making love, they'd fall sleep with their arms wrapped around each other, their love confirmed and their future secure. And in a matter of months their child would be born, and it would be the most loved child in the whole world.

In the bedroom, Gina put the all-important research paper in the suitcase, then folded each item of clothing and packed it neatly on top. She was so excited! She didn't have much to pack, and she decided to leave all the clothes that Larry had bought for her. Somehow it didn't seem right to take what he'd given her and use it in her new life with another man.

She wrote Larry a brief enigmatic letter, since she didn't know what else to say. She didn't mention Owen, or the fact that the baby wasn't Larry's. These were things she would tell him later, on the phone. He deserved that much. It was cowardly, she knew, not to tell him face to face. But she couldn't bear to see the sadness in his eyes when she told him she was leaving. He'd be devastated, and she knew they'd both end up crying. Nor could she face his disgust when she told him how she'd deceived him by pretending that another man's child was his.

Closing the front door behind her, Gina began walking quickly up the road towards the underground station. She felt giddy and light-headed, and excited about the future. But guilt wasn't far away either. She was acutely aware that when Larry returned home *that evening, his world would fall apart, whereas hers would be overflowing with happiness. It wasn't fair that poor inoffensive Larry should suffer in this way. She felt bad that her happiest day would also be Larry's saddest.*

As the train hurtled along, taking her nearer and nearer to Owen, Gina couldn't help smiling to herself. Clutching her suitcase on her lap, she surveyed the other passengers, and wondered if any of them were on the brink of a new and exciting life like she was. Most of them looked bored or fed up, and Gina wished that all of them could feel the way she did.

As she walked from the underground station to the Blue Crane café, Gina realised that she was smiling broadly. People must think I'm a nutcase, she thought, but I don't care! I'm so happy I could die!

In the café, she was pleased to see that the table she and Owen had shared the previous weekend was vacant. A good omen, she thought, placing her suitcase beneath the table, and ordering a coffee. She was a little early, but that meant she had more time to experience the delicious joy of anticipation.

Smiling, she checked her pocket — yes, thankfully she hadn't forgotten the keys to the new flat. In a few hours' time, she and Owen would be in their own little love nest! But to her dismay, she discovered that she still had the keys to Larry's flat as well. She'd intended dropping them through the letterbox as she left, but in her excitement she'd forgotten. Oh well, she thought, I'll post them to him. He might need them if he took on a flatmate to share costs.

As the minutes went by, Gina sipped her coffee and watched the door for Owen's arrival. She liked the atmosphere in Blue Crane, and decided that it would become the place where they'd celebrate the milestones of their life together. There was a pleasant low-key buzz about the place, and when their son or daughter was old enough, they'd bring him or her along too.

Gina wondered what her work colleagues were thinking, now that it was clear she wasn't turning up for work that day. She hadn't even bothered to call in sick that day, since she had no intention of ever going back there again. The veterinary laboratory was too close to where Larry worked, and besides, she'd probably get a job working with Owen anyway. Once he went public with his research on the dangers of the new vaccine, the universities would be falling over themselves to have him on their staff. And hopefully, she would be his consort and assistant.

Suddenly, Gina realised that half an hour had gone by, and there was still no sign of Owen. Perhaps he was held up in traffic. No doubt he'd be here before very long. In the meantime, she would have another coffee.

An hour later, Gina began to worry. What on earth could have delayed him? Then she mentally chastised herself. After all, Owen was coming from Dublin — so his plane had probably been delayed. Or there had been a lightning strike by baggage handlers at the airport. Undoubtedly, he'd arrive within the next few minutes, out of breath and very apologetic, although the delay was in no way his fault. Then they'd hug, and he'd tell her how much he'd longed for this moment . . .

Two hours later, Gina was starting to panic. She checked her watch repeatedly to make sure that the delay wasn't in her imagination. She was well aware that time seemed to move more slowly when you were anticipating something, but no, there was no doubt that Owen was very late.

To cheer herself up and keep stress at bay, Gina began to create little scenarios in her mind, her favourite one being of Dolly falling apart when she realised that Owen was really leaving her. For added satisfaction, Gina envisaged Dolly on her knees, begging Owen to stay, while he announced loftily that he was leaving her, to set up home with her younger sister.

But even these pleasant thoughts couldn't keep Gina's fears at bay for long. Maybe, she thought, Dolly has managed to convince Owen to stay with her. Maybe he hasn't got the nerve to tell me. Maybe he's not coming today. Or maybe he's broken his leg and can't come today. He's unable to get in touch with me because I'm sitting here, whereas the only phone number he has for me is back at Larry's place. On the other hand, Gina thought, Owen knows we're meeting in the Blue Crane, so he could have called Directory Enquiries, got the number and phoned the café, then asked the proprietor to give me a message

By now, the sweat was standing out on Gina's forehead. She fought hard to suppress the feelings of panic that threatened to envelope her. It felt as though a huge lump was stuck in her throat. It was preventing her from breathing, and she let out a gasp just as the waiter was passing her table.

"Are you okay?" he asked, and Gina's panic receded.

"Yes, fine thanks," she told him, "but could I have another coffee – and maybe a ham sandwich?"

The waiter nodded and went to place her order. Gina forced herself to calm down – Owen was simply delayed, and before long they'd both be laughing about her silly insecurities.

When the coffee and sandwich arrived, Gina began eating and drinking slowly. She didn't really want either, but she needed a reason to continue occupying the table, and keeping a seat for Owen when he arrived. If he arrived. By now, Gina was beginning to realise the fragility of her situation. Owen was now several hours late. He could hardly expect her to sit here in the Blue Crane until closing time, could he? On the other hand, maybe that's exactly what she would do – she couldn't risk missing him if he did turn up.

But what would she do if he didn't turn up at all? Suddenly, Gina realised that she'd have no choice but to go back to Larry's flat. There was no point in going to the new flat, since Owen didn't *know where it was, and he had no way of contacting her other than by telephoning her at Larry's flat.*

Glancing at her watch again, Gina realised that Larry would be returning from work in less than an hour. And if she didn't get there ahead of him, he'd find the incriminating letter!

Suddenly galvanised into action, she retrieved her suitcase from under the table, paid her bill and rushed out, leaving the bemused waiter wondering why her long and patient vigil had ended so abruptly.

Running now, Gina just made it to the underground station in time to leap onto her local train just before the doors closed. Heaving a sigh of relief, she sank into an empty seat. She was just ahead of the rush hour, and with a bit of luck, she might get back to the house before Larry got home from work. In fact, she had to get there ahead of him! Her life depended on it.

Although it was the last place on earth she wanted to be, Gina needed to stay at Larry's place until Owen contacted her again. When he phoned and explained what had gone wrong, they'd arrange another rendezvous, then she'd take him to their new flat. Whatever had delayed Owen would be forgotten in the joy of being together at last. All she had to do was spend another few days with Larry. It was only a small sacrifice to make, since a lifetime of happiness was just around the corner . . .

As she came out of the station, checking to make sure that Larry wasn't on the same train, she hurried past other commuters, many of whom were ambling along slowly, briefcases and umbrellas in hand, tired after a hard day's work. Skirting around several slow movers, Gina hoped that wherever Larry was, he'd be taking his time too, so that she could get as far ahead of him as possible. While it was perfectly plausible that she was returning from work herself, Larry would wonder why she was carrying her suitcase. Thank goodness she still had the keys to get in! Gina couldn't bear to think what would have happened if she'd put the keys through the letterbox as planned.

Suddenly, Gina's heart skipped a beat. She could see Larry, walking just ahead of her! Glancing furtively around her, and ensuring that no one was watching, she flung her suitcase over a neighbour's wall and into their garden. Hopefully, no one had seen her and she could retrieve it later. But now, she had to get into the flat before Larry did. Her heart was thumping painfully in her chest, yet she now had to give the performance of her life.

"Larry!" she called, smiling as she ran to catch up with him.

Surprised and pleased, Larry turned to greet her, and linked her arm as they crossed the road to the flat. Gina was frantically trying to think of how she could keep Larry out of the flat and prevent him from seeing the note before she could retrieve it. Desperate measures were called for, since it would be visible immediately they stepped into the open-plan living area.

"Larry," said Gina breathlessly, blocking the path to the front door, "I've suddenly got this awful craving for chips — would you be a love and nip round to the chipper for me? It's the pregnancy, you see — when I get these terrible cravings, I need to satisfy them immediately. Otherwise, I'll end up feeling really sick." Gina despised herself more and more with each lie she was telling. Hopefully, it would all be over soon . . .

"Of course," said Larry obligingly, "but I'll just come in and collect my jacket first. It looks like it's going to rain."

"No, you can't!" Gina cried. "Oh Larry, I'm really desperate for those chips. Please, can you get them straight away?"

Larry looked surprised at the vehemence of her outcry, but he leaned forward and kissed her on the nose affectionately. "Okay, don't get yourself upset," he told her kindly. "It's the least I can do, seeing as you're the one having to put up with all the hassle of carrying our baby. Salt and vinegar?"

Gina nodded, sighing with relief as Larry began walking down the road in the direction of the chip shop. Quickly, she hurried inside, grabbed the letter and stuffed it into the pocket of her cardigan. Then, after checking to ensure that Larry had turned the corner leading to the chip shop, she hurried back down the street and retrieved her suitcase from the neighbour's garden. Back in the house, she hurriedly unpacked the case and returned it to its usual place at the bottom of the wardrobe. Then she hid the note.

As the impact of all that had happened that day finally caught up with her, Gina began weeping and found that she couldn't stop. When Larry returned with the chips, she was curled up in a ball on the sofa, sobbing quietly.

"You poor love," he whispered tenderly, "those hormones are certainly playing havoc with your mood. Maybe a cup of tea with your chips would help?"

Gina nodded, despising herself yet again, and hating Larry for being so gullible. Nevertheless, the chips smelled wonderful, and Gina hungrily tucked into them, realising that she'd eaten nothing but a ham sandwich all day.

When Larry returned with the tea, he found Gina asleep on the sofa, her bag of chips already eaten. Tenderly, he covered her with a rug and left her to sleep. To Larry, the mysteries of pregnancy were manifold, but he surmised that poor Gina was finding it harder than most. Not for the first time, he was deeply grateful to her for all that she was going through on his behalf. When their baby was born, he intended showing his gratitude by surprising her with the deposit for a house of their own. He'd been saving since taking up his new job, and he was on course for a salary increase at the end of the year. Smiling happily, he left Gina to sleep.

CHAPTER 50

Several days went by without any word from Owen. Gina was tetchy over the weekend, and on Monday morning she claimed to be too ill to go to work. Larry phoned the laboratory on her behalf, and explained that she wasn't well enough to attend. Fortunately, no one mentioned her absence from work on the previous Friday, so he continued in blissful ignorance of her plans.

Gina was relieved when Larry left for work each morning. It meant that she had the whole day to wait for Owen's call, and to fantasise about Owen and their future life together. She was afraid to leave the house, in case that was the very moment when Owen chose to ring, so she told Larry that her legs were swelling up due to the pregnancy, and that she couldn't walk to the local shops to get the groceries. Patiently, Larry did the shopping during his lunchtime, and prepared their evening meal when he got home from work.

On the third morning of her self-imposed exile from work, Gina heard the phone ringing shortly after Larry had left for the office. Leaping out of bed, she rushed out into the hall, almost tripping over the bedclothes in her anxiety to get to the phone. At last — this was the call she'd been waiting for! Owen was on his way to London at last, and everything was going to be wonderful!

"Hello, Owen — is that you?" Gina asked joyously, pressing the phone to her ear, as though she could hold him closer by this very act.

There was a moment's silence at the other end of the line, then Gina heard a deep intake of breath.

"Owen?" Gina asked again, this time tentatively.

"Sorry, Gina — it's only me," said the voice at the other end, and Gina immediately recognised her friend Maeve.

"Maeve! How are you?" She was glad to hear from her friend, and was anxious that Maeve wouldn't detect any disappointment in her voice.

"Gina, I'm afraid I've got some bad news," Maeve told her, without preamble.

Gina clutched her chest. Something must have happened to her mother, or one of her sisters. Despite having been evicted from home, and feeling particularly ambivalent about Dolly, she nevertheless felt a deep emotional connection to them all.

"Oh my God! Who is it, Maeve?"

There was a silence at the other end, which seemed interminable to Gina.

"C'mon, Maeve, put me out of my misery. Has something happened to Mum?"

Maeve sighed. "No, Gina — I'm afraid it's Owen."

"Owen? What do you mean?" Then she laughed with relief. "Oh, now I understand — he's asked you to ring and explain why he's been delayed!" She knew she was babbling, but she couldn't stop. At last, she was about to find out what had happened to delay him!

"Delayed? Sorry, Gina — I don't know what you mean. Look,

there's no easy way to say this, but –" she hesitated, "– Owen was killed in a car accident last Thursday. His funeral was yesterday. I thought you'd want to know."

Gina felt the world spinning out of control. She grabbed the phone table for support as she slid to the floor.

"Gina – are you all right?" Maeve cried, receiving no reply. "Gina – please answer me!"

At last, Gina pressed the phone to her ear once again. "Please tell me this is a joke, Maeve," she begged, now crying uncontrollably. "It can't be true!"

"Gina – oh, Gina, I wish things could be different," Maeve groaned, "But there's no doubt about it. His car skidded out of control, crashed through a barrier and went into the canal. I was at the funeral myself."

"It's just not true – you're lying!" Gina screamed down the phone. Then she slammed it back onto the receiver, cutting off her friend in mid-sentence. Gina didn't want to hear any more lies. Owen was coming to collect her, just as soon as he could get away.

She had no idea how long she lay there on the floor. Had she slept, or passed out? Stiff and sore, Gina staggered to her feet. Had she imagined that Maeve rang, telling her all sorts of lies about Owen? Then the awful pain of reality swept through her, and she experienced the impact of Maeve's words all over again. It was as though someone had punched her in the stomach, leaving her winded and crushed. But she knew Maeve would never lie to her, so she had to accept the truth, no matter how unpalatable it was. Owen wasn't coming to London . . . Owen was dead, and she would never see him again. Now she realised that as she'd waited joyously in the Blue Café the previous Friday, Owen had already been dead.

When the crying had subsided, leaving her feeling that she'd *no tears left, Gina suddenly realised that she needed to make choices about her future. All she wanted to do was curl up into a ball and hibernate, but she was aware that time wasn't on her side. She was five months pregnant, married to a man she didn't love, and expecting a dead man's baby. All the raw emotions she's managed to sublimate during her brief marriage to Larry came rising to the surface, and she started crying again. Maybe suicide would be best for herself and the baby. She could offer it no real future now.*

Briefly, she thought of staying with Larry. It would be the easiest thing to do, given her circumstances. When she hadn't known that Owen cared for her, she'd been prepared to live a lie to give her baby a father. Why couldn't she continue to do that now?

Gina shook her head. After Maeve's devastating news, she wouldn't be able to hide her sorrow indefinitely. As it was, she'd used her pregnancy, and its supposed effect on her hormones, to fool Larry several times. She'd only managed to do it because she knew it wouldn't be for long – only until she could leave to be with Owen. But now, if she stayed, it would mean taking on a permanent acting role, and she knew she was too distraught to pull it off. Besides, it wasn't fair on Larry either. He had a right to find someone who could truly love him.

So what other options did she have? She needed to make decisions quickly, since Larry would soon detect that her pregnancy wasn't solely responsible for her mood changes. She also feared that his genuine concern might prompt an outpouring of the truth from her, and that would do neither of them any good.

Suddenly, Gina remembered the flat she'd rented for her and Owen to live in. She could move there, at least for the immediate future. Owen had given her enough money to pay the rent for a few months, so she'd be safe there, at least until after the baby was born.

The phone rang again, but Gina ignored it. Undoubtedly it was Maeve, ringing back to see if she was okay, but right now she couldn't bear to speak to anybody. She needed to be alone with her pain, alone to mourn for Owen. Gina stifled a sob. No doubt Dolly was playing the role of grieving widow to perfection. Well, Gina would soon pay her own respects to Owen – but in a very special and unique way. His child would be his living monument, which Dolly would never know about.

Resolutely Gina stood up, went to the bathroom, washed her blotchy face and brushed her hair. She had to be strong if she was to honour Owen's memory and give his child a decent start in life. She also owed Larry the truth, although she didn't feel quite able to deal with that just yet. She would tell him in due course – either by letter or phone – but right now, she would do the decent thing and leave him.

Pulling her suitcase out from the bottom of the wardrobe, she packed it again with the same items. Then she produced the enigmatic letter she'd written previously, and left it once again on the table in the living room. It would be several hours before Larry returned from work, so she wouldn't bump into him on her way to the underground station. She couldn't bear to see his kind and concerned expression even one more time.

Looking at the open suitcase, and the clothes inside it, the same clothes she had packed so joyfully for her new life with Owen, Gina shuddered. These were now part of her past. Part of the life she was meant to have with Owen. She didn't want anything to do with them. When she left here, she would take nothing with her.

She walked determinedly out the front door, closing it firmly behind her. Then she took Larry's keys and dropped them in through the letterbox. This time, there would be no going back.

As she started walking down the street, Gina suddenly

remembered that she'd left Owen's research paper in the bottom of the suitcase. She shrugged. It was too late now – she wasn't going back to ask Larry for it! Besides, Owen was dead, so his fight with BWF Pharmaceuticals was over. And it wasn't her fight any longer. She had neither the money nor the resolve to take on BWF Pharmaceuticals in a battle she was never likely to win.

She patted her stomach. This was her future now. Resolutely, she walked towards the underground station that would take her to her new home.

Part 3

CHAPTER 51

The following morning, after Alice, Enrique and Ricardo had breakfast together and Bodhrán had been given the leftovers, Enrique departed for the hotel to supervise the departure of his officers and the forensic team in their police vans. Ricardo headed off to say Mass, and hear confessions, while Alice – locked in again on Enrique's advice – set about clearing up and washing the dishes.

As she tidied, Alice pondered on the ridiculousness of the locked doors. While she accepted that she could still be in danger, she felt the risk had to be minimal. Surely, since Bill believed she was already dead and buried, there would be no reason for anyone to make another attempt on her life? Although she found it difficult to believe that Bill wanted her dead, there was no other likely culprit that she could think of. As far as she knew, no one else had anything to gain from her death but him. Alice tried to convince herself that the temporary residents at Senora Delgado's house were people simply passing through – maybe backpackers like herself and Patricia – people who had assumed the house was derelict and were just looking for an inexpensive night's accommodation.

313

It was obvious that they'd left the house before she and Ricardo found the signs of their habitation, so there was nothing for her to worry about, was there? But there was still the presence of her photograph in Senora Delgado's house, and nothing but Bill's guilt could logically explain that . . .

At lunchtime, Enrique appeared again, and once more Alice prepared a light snack for the two of them. There was no sign of Ricardo, and smiling to herself, Alice wondered if he was still playing Cupid! Well, that suited her fine, because she welcomed every opportunity to get to know Enrique better. Because soon, he would be returning to Buenos Aires, and at some point, she would be going back to Ireland. Would Enrique ever want to see her again, when all this crazy business was over?

Putting an assortment of cheeses, tomatoes, cucumber and crusty bread on the table, Alice returned to her argument of the night before.

"Enrique, please listen," she said firmly, "I know you're against it, but I think it would make sense if I go back to Dublin, and sooner rather than later. Besides, you've told me yourself that I'm not safe here in Argentina, so the false passport will keep me safe. At least in Dublin I can start looking for evidence that Bill tried to kill me."

For a while Enrique said nothing, the only sound being the ticking of the old clock on the wall. "I feel sure we are missing something," he said at last. "Are you certain there is no one else who might want to kill you?"

"Well, maybe my boss, Dan Daly – for taking so much time off," Alice replied, trying to inject a little humour into the proceedings.

Enrique didn't look amused. Instead he was deep in

314

thought. At this point, he felt that he had little other choice but to accede to Alice's request if the investigation was to move forward. He knew it was risky, both for his own career and for Alice's safety, but more than anything he wanted to keep her safe. And being on a false passport might keep her safe for a little longer, until the case could be solved. He longed to ask her if she'd be coming back to Argentina, since he feared that once she left, he'd never see her again. But he didn't have the nerve.

"Okay, you have two weeks to get the information we need – no longer," he said. "Patricia is due back in Dublin in just over two weeks' time, and her parents, brothers and sisters will be expecting her back. They need to be informed of her death before then."

Alice bit her lip. "I really feel bad about that, Enrique – the fact that her family still don't know that she's dead. It doesn't seem right, somehow, to keep them in the dark."

"The dark will happen for them when they *do* find out," Enrique said gruffly. "Look at it this way, Alice. We are giving them another two weeks of happiness. Because once they know Patricia is dead, their happiness will be over. And their lives will be changed forever."

His words hung in the air like motes in the dazzling sunlight of the window, and despite the sunshine, Alice shivered, recalling Enrique's own loss. Only a man who had lost someone he loved would think in those terms. Alice wondered if every murder and every accidental death that came within his jurisdiction resulted in Enrique reliving Maria's death.

"I'm sorry about your wife, Enrique – Ricardo told me what happened."

Enrique shrugged his shoulders. "Life must go on. When I lost Maria and our baby, I thought I would never be able to smile again. I blamed myself for her death, and that made it worse. So to fill the emptiness, I threw myself into my work. I thought that maybe I could redeem myself by bringing bad people to justice." He sighed. "But as time went by, I came to realise that there are no such things as bad and good, black and white – only many shades of grey. No one is all good, or all bad. Nothing in my job is – what is that expression you use – cut and dried? I now see my job as mainly keeping the peace."

Alice nodded enthusiastically. "Our police force in Ireland is rather like that – they're called Guardians of the Peace, not law enforcement officers. It's a subtle difference, but Irish people like the attitude it represents. Our police force isn't armed either – except one or two special task units."

Enrique smiled. "Maybe some day I will visit your police force, yes? We would have much to talk about."

"I'm sure you'd be very welcome, Enrique," said Alice, smiling. But secretly, she was disappointed. Had she misread the situation entirely? Maybe he *was* genuinely interested in talking shop with members of the Irish police force. But he hadn't even suggested visiting *her* if he came to Ireland!

He looked at her closely. "I'm sure you're aware of Argentina's recent history, and the 'dirty war' waged by our then military rulers between 1976 and 1983?"

Alice nodded.

"It led to the death of thousands of ordinary people who 'disappeared' – to be tortured, electrocuted and thrown alive from planes," Enrique said, his eyes filled with anger. "Today, we are still coming to terms with our past, but there is now some good news. The Supreme Court has finally ruled that there will no longer be amnesty laws protecting former military officers suspected of human rights abuses."

"Yes, I read about that – it's really great news," Alice replied.

There was a moment's silence before Alice spoke again.

"Did you lose any of your own family during the 'dirty war'?"

Enrique nodded. "Few families were untouched. Some day, my lovely Irish Admiral, I will tell you all about it. But right now, no more sadness. We must think positively about the future – yours and mine."

Alice felt a thrill run through her. She was aware that Enrique was just using a figure of speech, but she allowed her mind to run riot. Imagine if Enrique was referring to their combined futures . . . then she mentally gave herself a shake. What silly fantasies she was indulging in! She was like some pathetic woman who couldn't envisage her life without a man in it! Yet even as she berated herself, Alice knew that she had no need of any man to fill a vacuum in her life. Although her life with Bill might be over, it didn't mean she wanted to immediately replace him. Nevertheless, something told her that fate might have brought her to this point . . .

Suddenly Enrique spoke. "It must be painful for you, Alice – to think that your husband may have tried to kill you," he said, his dark eyes staring into hers.

Alice felt her cheeks flush. "Yes, it's not the nicest of feelings."

"It is a little like a death, is it not?" Enrique added, "The death of the future you've hoped and dreamed about."

Alice nodded and the silence between them lengthened, each of them lost in their own reverie, and thinking of how things might have been.

"And now, Enrique?" Alice asked softly. "Do you still think of Maria and your child?"

"Of course. But it feels different now. I will never forget them, but it is also time to move on."

As he held her gaze, Alice's heart was racing. How wonderful it would be if by 'moving on' Enrique meant that it was time to begin a relationship again – maybe with her? But even if he *was* attracted to her, no doubt he'd feel constrained by the fact that she was still legally married. And she herself was scared to show any interest in him, in case he considered her a shallow and fickle woman who'd barely finished with one man before eyeing up another. The thought of experiencing his contempt brought tears to her eyes.

"Are you all right, Alice?" Enrique asked, his dark eyes filled with concern.

"I'm fine thanks, Enrique," Alice lied. "I'm just sad to be leaving Argentina."

"Then maybe you'll come back some day?" Enrique said, although it didn't sound to him as though Alice ever intended to return. If he wasn't such a fool, he'd say something to her now – something that would let her know he liked her. A lot. But his tongue felt like a brick inside his mouth, and suddenly, before he could even galvanise his thoughts any further, Alice had jumped up from the table and left the room.

318

CHAPTER 52

Later that evening, after Alice took a shower, she surveyed herself in the cracked bathroom mirror and concluded that she'd lost weight. She certainly hadn't intended to, but it wasn't surprising really, after all that had happened in the last few weeks. She wasn't particularly pleased about it, since she'd no wish to be stick-thin, and she abhorred the things women were prepared to do to their bodies to be accepted by their peers. But it did cross her mind that looking a little different would certainly help with her disguise when she returned to Dublin.

As she dressed, Alice could smell the delicious aroma of the meal Ricardo was cooking downstairs. She marvelled to think that several weeks earlier she hadn't known either Ricardo or Enrique, yet here she was, perfectly at home in a tiny Argentine village. And dreading leaving it.

Peering out from her bedroom window, Alice could see the top of Enrique's dark head as he sat drinking a cup of maté on the old rusty bench in the yard. The goat was grazing nearby in the yard, and the scene was one of tranquillity.

Alice watched, pleased and amused, as Enrique offered Bodhrán the remains of his biscuit, which was gratefully received and quickly munched. When the goat finished eating, he remained close to Enrique, who began stroking the animal's ears gently.

Then she realised that Enrique was saying something, and Alice strained to hear.

"My good friend, I need your advice," she heard Enrique say to the goat, who appeared to be giving him his full attention. "What would you do if you liked a female, but you didn't know how she felt about you?"

Alice felt her heart beat faster. Was Enrique talking about her? That would be too good to be true. On the other hand, maybe there was someone in his office that he fancied ... Her heart plummeted as she considered such a possibility.

Bodhran ignored Enrique and began chewing the ends of his trousers.

Enrique chuckled. "My friend, that is no answer! I really do need your advice – sometimes, animals know things that we humans miss. Do you think she likes me?"

Alice's heart soared. Surely it had to be her, since the goat wouldn't know any of Enrique's work colleagues. Then she grimaced at her own stupidity – he was talking to a *goat*, for heaven's sake! Which made her heart plummet even more. Maybe Enrique was just having a joke at her expense, realising that she fancied him and was listening upstairs. Oh God, that would be even more embarrassing! No, she decided, he'd never behave like that ...

The goat began to nuzzle Enrique's face, then suddenly decided to nip his nose instead. As Enrique laughed and stood up to avoid the goat's attentions, Alice quickly drew back from the window. If he didn't know already, she certainly didn't want him realising that she'd overheard his conversation!

Perhaps 'conversation' was the wrong word, Alice mused, pulling on clean jeans. The goat hadn't exactly answered Enrique's question! On the other hand, perhaps man and beast had communicated non-verbally. Alice was well aware that animals didn't need to speak in order to communicate with each other. Language wasn't always the best way of communicating. There were lots of times when the human ability with words actually got in the way of real communication . . . weren't she and Enrique the perfect example? Was there something between her and Enrique, or was it just wishful thinking on her part? She felt totally mixed up. They'd talked a lot the previous evening, and if anything her attraction to him had grown. But that's all it had been – talk. Was her marriage the barrier? Or was she just expecting too much too soon? But she didn't have any time to spare! She was due to leave Argentina soon, and was unlikely to be back again unless she had a reason to return . . .

At the dinner table that evening, the conversation was deliberately kept light, although an undercurrent was nevertheless there. Alice had already explained to Ricardo that she was heading back to Dublin in disguise, and like Enrique, he'd expressed serious reservations. Ricardo was deeply worried at the idea of Alice travelling on a false passport, both for her sake, and because of the possible repercussions for his brother if anyone ever found out. Once again, she reassured him that she'd be fine, and would accept full responsibility if the deception ever came to light.

"Please do not worry about me, Alice – I can look after

myself," Enrique growled. "I am more worried about your safety. What you are proposing to do is quite insane, you know. I can't allow it!"

"You can't stop me, Enrique. Besides, you won't complain if I deliver your killer," she told him, as Ricardo nodded supportively. "Your brother has more faith in me than you do."

Enrique said nothing, and silence reigned at the table once again. All three of them were also conscious that tonight might be the last dinner they'd ever have together, so there was an aura of sadness present as well.

Alice wondered yet again if she'd ever be back to Argentina. Unless Enrique took things further, it seemed unlikely at the moment. Unless, of course, she had to return on some police business relating to Patricia's murder?

At last, Alice felt she had to broach the subject of her departure again.

"Look, can either of you tell me where I can locate a computer? I need to book a new flight back to Dublin. And as soon as possible –"

"No, no – I've changed my mind!" said Enrique truculently. "It's a dangerous and preposterous idea! And the more I think about it, the more I reject it out of hand!"

"You can't go back on your word, Enrique – you know you agreed already!"

Enrique looked embarrassed. "Okay, I admit it. I did agree. But now I've changed my mind! It's far too dangerous, Admiral!"

Ricardo looked from one to the other. "If you've agreed to Alice going, what's changed your mind, Enrique?" he asked mildly.

"I'm not convinced that the culprit is Alice's husband," Enrique replied, looking worried. "I feel certain there is something else we are missing."

Alice's heart sank. She'd almost accepted that Bill was the guilty party by now. It would be even more frightening to have to consider another unknown assailant. Also, Enrique's words seemed to confirm that he was happy for her to go back to her marriage, and take up where she left off.

Enrique turned to her. "Maybe there is something in Patricia's life that we still don't know about. Maybe there is more that you can tell us, Alice."

"So now *I'm* a suspect," said Alice, scowling.

Enrique gave her a sarcastic smile. "Yes, Alice, I am regarding you as my number one suspect. Maybe I will lock you in a cell and keep you there, until I discover who the murderer is."

"You and what army?" Alice retorted. There was something about Enrique that always managed to rile her. He seemed to be laughing at her. Was she too obvious about finding him attractive?

"Please!" Ever the peacemaker, Ricardo could see that if the two started sparring, it would take ages to get down to business.

Enrique grinned at his brother, and held up his hands in appeasement.

"It's obvious you're just saying all this to prevent Alice going," said Ricardo. "Like you, I am frightened to see her go, but I think she's right. She is the only one who can get you her husband's e-mails and computer files, and find out about his business dealings. At the moment, he really *is* the only suspect, right?"

Enrique grimaced, saying nothing. But it was clear, as he topped up their wine glasses, that he'd accepted defeat.

* * *

During the early hours of the morning the telephone rang. It jangled across time and space, and registered in three sleepy brains at exactly the same time.

"What on earth is that?" Enrique called out from his bedroom.

"What time is it?" Alice mumbled, turning over in her bed.

"It's the phone, and it's three a.m.," Ricardo answered, as he pulled on his dressing-gown and hurried down the stairs.

"I'm sorry," he said, coming back upstairs again, "please go back to sleep, both of you. I have to go out – someone is dying and wants to receive the last rites."

Enrique yawned, padding out onto the landing in his bare feet. "Is it far?"

"No, just a few miles out the road. The caller gave me directions."

"Is that old jalopy of yours dependable enough?" Enrique asked. "Last time we spoke about it, you told me you were going to update it to something a bit better."

"It's fine," said Ricardo, smiling. "I'm sure God will keep it going, since I'm going out on His business!"

Dressing quickly in his soutane, Ricardo picked up his bag and his keys.

"See you later," he said to Enrique who had lingered on the landing, then he headed down the stairs and out the door, turning off the lights as he went.

Enrique retired to his bedroom once again. There was no sound from Alice's room, so he assumed she'd gone back to sleep.

In the darkness, Enrique lay awake thinking of Alice. She was only in the next room, yet that might as well be a million miles as far as he was concerned. He wished he was one of those swaggeringly confident men, who could come right out and say what he felt. He really liked her. No, if he was honest with himself, it was a lot more than like – it was *much* more than that! He might as well admit that he already cared deeply about her, even if only to himself. How could this have happened so quickly to a hard-bitten cop, who'd built a wall around himself so that he'd never be hurt again? Now Alice was leaving, and he was scared he'd never see her again. For her sake, he hoped her husband wasn't guilty, but then she'd go back to this Bill fellow, and they'd live happily ever after. He should want that for her, of course. But he didn't. He wanted her for himself!

Turning on his side, he pulled up the bedclothes. On the other hand, if Alice's husband wasn't Patricia's murderer, that meant there was still someone out there who wanted her dead. His beloved Admiral would be killed because his stupid brain couldn't work out why anyone wanted to kill her. The helplessness he felt was like experiencing Maria's death all over again.

He was starting to drift off to sleep when something woke him again. It sounded like breaking glass, followed by what sounded like whispering voices.

"Enrique, did you hear that noise downstairs?" Alice whispered, suddenly appearing at his door in her nightdress. It was dark, and he could barely see her, but he motioned to her to enter, all his policeman's instincts now on high alert. Momentarily, he felt relief that he was already wearing pyjamas – contrary to his usual custom of sleeping naked – then he heard another sound downstairs, followed by a creaking noise on the stairs. Enrique was aware that the sounds might be caused by Ricardo returning – perhaps his car hadn't even started.

Putting his finger to his lips, he edged towards the door and peered out onto the landing. There were two forms outlined in the gloom, groping their way down the passageway in the opposite direction. They definitely weren't Ricardo!

Lurking in the doorway of his own room, his service revolver in hand, Enrique waited until both intruders had entered Ricardo's bedroom.

"She's not here," he heard one say to the other.

Just as they turned to move on to the next room, he confronted them.

"Stop right there!" he shouted, pointing his gun at them, "I'm a policeman!" But both intruders launched themselves at him instead, and as Enrique fired Alice saw the blade of a knife being raised by one of the men. There was a scream from Enrique, followed by a thud as he hit the ground, blood pouring from his shoulder.

Grabbing Enrique's gun, the two men advanced on her, and Alice seemed frozen by indecision. One of the men had clearly been wounded by Enrique's shot, but if anything, this had only inflamed their anger.

"Get the bitch!" one said to the other in Spanish, and Alice watched mesmerised as the blade was raised again.

Then Enrique was shouting, "Run, Alice – run!"

"I won't leave you!"

"Go – that's an order!"

Then she was running down the stairs, faster than she'd ever run before. Behind her, she heard a scream as the first of the men fell down the stairs in the dark, cursing as the second wounded man landed on top of him. This gave her vital seconds, and she rushed out the front door, searching desperately for somewhere to hide in the dark. As she ran, she heard something whiz by her ear, and she realised that it was a bullet, probably fired by the man who'd snatched Enrique's gun. Her lungs felt ready to burst, and she could sense that one of the men was gaining on her. Where could she go? Where could she hide?

Having raced out the presbytery gate, she headed up the road towards the open farmland beside the cemetery. When her body could no longer keep up the pace, Alice opted for a clump of bushes nearby. She threw herself into them, not even feeling the thorns that reefed her skin, and crouching down she tried to silence her heavy breathing.

She could hear one of the men searching in the vicinity of the scrub around her, shouting and cursing, and Alice resigned herself to being caught. But she didn't want to die. Dammit, she thought with hysterical humour, I'll never get to win the Pulitzer Prize now . . .

Suddenly, her heart almost stopped beating with fright, as she heard rustling of the branches around her. Then the bushes parted, and as she prepared for the worst she heard a bleating sound. It was Bodhrán the goat! Clearly, he'd escaped from the yard at the presbytery when the intruders had opened the gate, and he'd come further afield in search of tastier titbits. Just then, the man came upon the goat, but didn't notice Alice lurking in the undergrowth directly behind him, and walked right by her. She heard him let out a few disgruntled curses as he made his way through the briars and tall weeds, then he moved away. Thank you, Bodhrán, Alice thought, thank you, thank you, thank you. The goat stared at her, then continued munching the thorny bushes in front of her.

Shaking from head to toe, Alice realised the ghastly dilemma she was in. Should she try to get back to the presbytery or stay where she was? Were the two men likely to continue their search, or had Enrique's presence at the presbytery scared them off? Maybe they'd gone back to the presbytery to finish off Enrique – if he wasn't dead already . . . Her eyes filled with tears as she thought of her beloved Enrique. She had to get back to him! Oh please Enrique, don't die on me, she begged him silently.

What would she say to Ricardo if he came back and found his brother dead? It was all her fault! She should have stayed in Ireland and given Bill the money, then none of this would ever have happened.

Crawling on all fours, she grabbed Bodhrán's long beard to hold him steady and then peered cautiously over his back. Instinctively the goat seemed to know what was required of him, and he allowed her to use him as a shield while she checked the area to see where the hitman had gone. And where was his partner-in-crime? Was he lurking somewhere nearby, ready to grab her when she tried to make her escape? Nevertheless, she wanted nothing more than to get back to the presbytery to find Enrique.

Guiding Bodhrán slowly down the slope of the road and back towards the presbytery, Alice stayed bent double, hiding behind his flank on the side away from the road. She was hoping that if the men were still looking for her, they'd only see the goat in the darkness. Hopefully they wouldn't notice that the goat had six legs, two of them human.

Suddenly Alice realised that the wounded man hadn't played any part in the hunt, and as she neared the presbytery she heard him groaning somewhere nearby.

"Leave the bloody woman!" he howled in Spanish to his partner-in-crime, clearly in pain. "I need a doctor!"

As she and the goat neared the presbytery garden wall, Alice froze as she heard a car start up and drive off at breakneck speed, and as it zoomed past she could make out two figures inside. It was too dark to see the registration number, and anyway, she reckoned, the car was probably stolen.

Abandoning Bodhrán, she raced back into the presbytery, turning on the lights and screaming Enrique's name. He was still at the top of the stairs where she'd last seen him, and her heart almost stopped as she saw him lying there, blood oozing from his shoulder. He was dead! Oh my God, her heart was breaking . . .

"Alice, my beloved Alice . . ."

Joy filled her heart. "Oh my darling Enrique, you're still alive!"

His dark eyes were filled with pain, but there was relief in them too. "Of course I'm alive! You don't think a little cut like this would kill me?" Nevertheless he winced as Alice tried to help him up. "Are *you* all right, my love?" he asked, and neither of them found it strange that the other was using such endearments.

"Yes, I'm fine. The goat saved me from those villains. Now, let me phone for an ambulance –"

Enrique laughed despite his pain. "My dear Admiral, you're deep in the Argentine countryside! There isn't a hospital for two hundred miles! The best you can do for me is get Doctor Sanchez." He grabbed her hand as she stood up to go. "I'm sorry I couldn't protect you from those men, Alice," he said softly, "but I think I wounded one of them, didn't I?"

"Yes, you did," Alice assured him, "and I think that's what saved my life." She smiled. "Well, you and Bodhrán together!"

When Ricardo returned moments later, his annoyance at being sent on a wild goose chase turned to shock, then terror, when he saw Enrique lying on the sofa with blood pouring from his shoulder, and Alice doing her best to staunch the flow. He quickly rushed off to get the local doctor who lived just across the street.

"I thought I'd lost you," Alice said, one hand holding a towel against Enrique's wound, the other tenderly brushing the hair off his forehead, as one might do with a beloved child. Enrique didn't answer, and Alice feared he was losing consciousness. "Oh Enrique, my dear Enrique, hang on!" she whispered, a sob in her voice. "Help will be here soon!"

Suddenly he opened an eye and looked at her wickedly. "I like it when you worry about me!" he whispered, and although she felt herself blushing Alice no longer cared.

"You didn't have to go this far to get my attention, Enrique – I fancied you already!" she replied, relief in her voice.

But by this time Enrique had genuinely passed out, and Alice was relieved to see Ricardo arrive with Doctor Sanchez in tow. The elderly doctor was still wearing his night attire under his coat, having wasted no time in answering Ricardo's urgent summons.

Leaving them both to attend to Enrique, Alice headed for the kitchen where she did what Irish people invariably do in a crisis — she put the kettle on. At that point, the impact of what had happened began to register with her, and she felt faint and nauseous herself. Before long, she was shivering uncontrollably, and when Ricardo and the doctor came to find her, her teeth were chattering and she could hardly hold the cup of tea she'd made.

"Is Enrique all right?" she asked, not caring about anything else.

"He's fine," said Doctor Sanchez. "The knife wound wasn't too deep, and he's a strong young man. He'll make a full recovery. I've immobilised his arm to give his shoulder a chance to heal, and I've given him a sedative to help him get the sleep he needs." He looked sternly at Alice. "Now, young lady, you look as though you need a sedative yourself."

With the doctor's and Ricardo's help, Enrique and Alice were both helped upstairs and put to bed. Within minutes, they were fast asleep.

"I'll call back in the morning," the doctor told Ricardo as he gathered up his bag

Ricardo nodded. For the rest of the night, he would hold vigil over two of the people he most cared about in the world.

CHAPTER 53

The following morning, Enrique insisted that he was fine. Despite Ricardo's entreaties to rest, he insisted on getting up to make calls to his precinct in Buenos Aires, filling them in on what had happened the night before. Descriptions of the two men were logged, and Alice was able to supply a description of the car in which the would-be assassins had driven off. Needless to say, the police felt certain that the car would have been abandoned as soon as possible.

At breakfast, Ricardo announced that he was cancelling church services until further notice, so that he could look after Enrique and Alice. However neither of them would hear of it, and they both protested loudly.

"I'm fine, and I can look after Enrique," Alice told him firmly.

"I agree with the Admiral," Enrique told his brother, winking at Alice. "There are people out there who need you more than we do."

"Like that bogus parishioner's call last night?" groaned Ricardo, still smarting from the vicious trick that had been played on him. "I wish I'd been here to help, instead of on a wild-goose chase up and down country lanes —"

"Thank goodness you weren't here — you'd probably have been shot or knifed," Enrique told him cheerfully. "I didn't even manage to protect Alice — imagine if I'd had you to protect as well!" His brow darkened. "Obviously, with you out of the way, Ricardo, they thought Alice was here alone. I should have been more alert, more ready for what happened." He scowled. "They even got away with my gun!"

"You were wonderful, Enrique," Alice said fervently, and Ricardo smiled to himself as he left for the church, deciding to take them at their word. He could see they didn't need him. All they needed was each other.

After Ricardo's departure, Doctor Sanchez arrived, examined the wound on Enrique's shoulder and applied a new dressing. He grunted his approval at the way the wound was already healing, and ordered Alice to ensure that he didn't engage in any strenuous activity. He also checked Alice, and seeing that she was in good humour, concluded that she, too, was on the road to recovery.

After his departure, Alice and Enrique sat in silence, each of them re-living the terrifying events of the night before. Alice longed to soothe Enrique's brow, but she was afraid to touch him, in case the intimacy and rapport of the previous night had evaporated. She was well aware that sometimes extreme situations created a false intimacy between people, which often didn't last.

"Would you like something to drink, Enrique?" she asked, brightly, since it would give her something to do. "I'm going to make myself a cup of tea."

"Thank you, a cup of maté would be wonderful."

LINDA KAVANAGH

In the kitchen, Alice busied herself by putting on the kettle and getting two mugs from the old cupboard. Then, she realised that Enrique had followed her, and was standing close behind her.

Gently, using his unbandaged arm, he turned her round.

"I do not want you to leave Argentina," he said, his brow furrowed. "But right now, I think Ireland may be the safest place for you."

Alice nodded. She didn't want to go either, especially now that Enrique had been wounded. She wanted to stay and look after him, hold him, love him . . .

"But do not let down your guard for an instant," he cautioned her. "Even though you will be in disguise, you could still be in danger." He groaned softly. "Oh God, what if something happens to you, and I never see you again?"

Alice looked directly into his eyes. "Do you want to see me again, Enrique?"

"Of course I do! You know I do."

"I *don't* know, Enrique. You've never actually told me," Alice replied boldly. This time, there would be no more ambiguity.

Enrique grimaced angrily. "This is not easy to say – I am a proud man who depends on nobody." He smiled. "Except, maybe, my brother. But you, Alice –"

For a moment, Alice thought – and hoped – that he was going to take her into his arms. But he had something else to say first.

Enrique stared intently at her. "This husband of yours – if he is not the one who has tried to kill you – you will go back to him?"

Suddenly, Alice's feet had wings. She shook her head.

"No, Enrique, even if Bill is not guilty, I know that I don't want to be married to him any more."

Enrique digested this information. "So you do not love him any more?"

Alice nodded. "That's true, Enrique, I do not love him any more."

"But you will stay in Ireland?"

"Not if there's a reason for me to come back to Argentina," said Alice, gazing directly at him, her heart beating frantically.

"Am I reason enough for you to come back?" Enrique demanded, his face so close to hers that she could feel the sweetness of his breath on her cheeks.

Throwing caution to the wind, Alice leaned forward and kissed him tenderly, revelling in the touch of his lips and the stubble on his chin. "Yes, Enrique, you're the best reason in the world," she told him.

Suddenly, the kiss that began tenderly turned into a raging passion. As their lips met again, Enrique crushed her to him, his lips and tongue urgently probing hers. For a moment, it seemed as if time had stood still, and Alice could feel their two hearts beating in unison.

"Please come back to me, my beautiful Irish Admiral," Enrique whispered, as he let her go. "I will keep you in my heart until then."

"And when I come back, Enrique?" Alice asked mischievously.

"I like the name Alice Alvarez – I hope you do too, eh?" he said solemnly. "As long as you are willing to stay, I will never let you go."

"That sounds like a good deal to me, Enrique," said Alice, before he kissed her yet again.

LINDA KAVANAGH

That night, Enrique left his bed and crept into Alice's room. In silence, they made love, afraid of disturbing Ricardo, whose room was only just across the landing. For Alice, feeling the strength and warmth of Enrique's body beside her made her feel safe and loved. As he caressed her secret places, she opened herself to him, experiencing the sheer joy of abandonment for the first time in her life. She had to resist crying out as Enrique finally brought her to ecstasy.

As they whispered endearments to each other in the dark, a smile suddenly flitted across Alice's face. "Doctor Sanchez said I was to stop you doing anything too strenuous!" Alice whispered. In answer, Enrique kissed her, and they began to make love once again.

In the early hours of the morning they parted company. As Enrique crept back to his room, Alice moved into the warm area of the bed that Enrique had just vacated, still revelling in the touch and smell of his body. Before long, she was fast asleep.

* * *

Two days later, Alice, Enrique and Ricardo took the train to Buenos Aires. After a shopping expedition to find a wig and assorted new clothes, the new Alice made her first appearance.

"I feel really weird," Alice told the two brothers as they surveyed her in her new attire. "I'd never wear clothes like this myself – I hope all this effort is worth it!"

Enrique hugged her. "You still look wonderful to me," he whispered.

The next stop was the airport, where Alice was booked

on a flight to Madrid, then on to Dublin, under Patricia's name, and using Patricia's passport.

In the taxi from the city centre, Enrique and Alice sat close together, holding hands, and casting glances at each other from time to time. They were both overwhelmed at the thought of parting, especially since they'd only just got together.

At the Departure gate, all three were tense and emotional.

"God bless you, Alice – I'll be praying that everything goes well," Ricardo told her, hugging her tightly.

"Thanks, Ricardo – you've been the best friend anyone could have!" Alice told him, tears in her eyes. "Please look after Enrique for me," she added, then grinned. "Or you'll have me to reckon with!"

"I will," Ricardo promised solemnly. "But even though he's on sick leave, I know I won't be able to stop him running this investigation by phone!"

Alice grinned. Already, Enrique had been on the phone to his office daily, barking out instructions and asking for updates, and ordering his officers to read the latest reports to him over the phone. There had been several sightings of the two villains, and the team at headquarters were hopeful that they'd be picked up soon.

"I want this case solved, because it involves someone very precious to me," said Enrique. "So you have two weeks, Alice – only two weeks. Patricia's family must be notified, and besides, I cannot bear to be without you for any longer." He hugged her silently, unable to find the words to express his fears. Once again, he dreaded losing someone he loved, just as he'd once lost Maria. "Please – take no chances, Alice. Do not confront this Bill of yours."

Then he suddenly hugged her again fiercely, desperation in his voice this time. "Oh Alice, please change your mind and stay, I beg you! Let your husband have the money! It is nothing – *you* are what matters to me."

"You know I must go, Enrique," Alice told him through her tears. "It's the only way we can find out the truth. Patricia is dead, and I, like you, need to know why."

With a final hug each for Ricardo and Enrique, Alice went through the Departure gate without looking back. She didn't want them to see the fresh tears that were threatening to dissolve her new-style make-up. She was also conscious of the auburn wig, and it felt hot on her head. Hopefully, she'd get used to it before long, since there was no way she could chance taking it off in public.

In the wake of Alice's departure, Enrique stood forlornly at the entrance to the Departure gate, unable and unwilling to leave the airport until Alice's plane had actually taken off.

"Come, brother – we can watch it take off from the viewing deck, if you like," Ricardo said kindly. He could see how upset his elder brother was. Even on the viewing deck, Enrique paced back and forth, on edge and worried.

"I should have stopped her!" he said at last, letting out a tortured groan.

"You know that would be wrong, Enrique," said Ricardo gently. "Alice has a mind of her own, you know. I'll miss her too – but I'll ask God to watch over her and bring her back safely."

"Pah! Your God let my Maria die. It is better to stop Alice going in the first place. That is how I could keep her safe!"

"Then that is how you'd lose her," said Ricardo mildly.

Enrique bowed his head. His brother was right, but he was frightened, for the second time in his life, of losing the woman he loved. He was also scared that if Alice's husband was proved innocent, she might opt to return to her married life in Ireland. Maybe she'd decide that Bill had more to offer her than an Argentine policeman who hid his vulnerability behind wisecracks, and who found it almost impossible to admit how he felt. Was there enough history between them to convince her to take the chance and come back to him?

"Alice, I love you!" he called after her as he watched her walk out across the tarmac to the waiting aircraft. But his heart was heavy because he knew she hadn't heard him.

"She knows," said Ricardo, putting his arm around him.

CHAPTER 54

"Hello – Isobel?"

Isobel Dunne pressed the phone to her ear, tears already forming in her eyes. Everything made her cry these days. The voice at the other end sounded remarkably like her dear departed friend, but then everything reminded her of Alice these days. Since her friend's death in Argentina several weeks earlier, Isobel had shed gallons of tears, and wondered if she'd ever be able to stop crying.

"Yes, this is Isobel. Who's that?"

"Izzy – are you alone?"

Isobel's heart missed a beat. It couldn't be! Yet the voice sounded exactly like Alice!

"Yes – who's that?"

"Izzy – please don't overreact, but this is Alice."

"W-what?" Isobel shrieked, doing exactly what she'd been asked not to do.

"Please – calm down, Izzy. You can't tell *anyone* that it's me. If you're alone, I'll call around to your place in five minutes."

"Hang on, is this some kind of joke — because if it is, I don't think it's very funny!"

"It's no joke — put the kettle on, will you? I'll be with you in five minutes. But don't tell *anyone!*"

As the caller rang off, Isobel sat down in a state of shock. No one else called her Izzy except Alice. Her heart was beating uncomfortably, and she was torn between wild elation and fury at the probable hoax. Was she even wise to consider opening her door to some mystery caller? This person was obviously impersonating Alice. Not only was it in extremely bad taste, but what on earth could be the reason for it?

Isobel got up and put the kettle on, not really expecting anyone to call. But she desperately needed a cuppa herself. She felt a fresh bout of weeping coming on, and she let the tears flow freely as she filled the kettle with water. I could fill the kettle with my own tears, she thought bitterly. I miss Alice so much! And now, some spiteful person was playing tricks. How could anyone be so heartless? She tried to think of anyone who could be so cruel, but her mind drew a blank. All her friends and colleagues had been wonderfully supportive since Alice's death. They knew how close the two had been, and how devastated Isobel had been after hearing about Alice's death in Argentina.

Making a solitary cup of tea, Isobel took it back to her armchair in front of the TV. Flicking from one channel to another, she rejected the documentary on endangered species as too depressing, the detective series as too violent, and the news bulletins as invariably filled with bad news. She felt miserable enough without wallowing in the misery of others. Resolutely, she turned the television off, just as the doorbell rang.

Isobel's anger reasserted itself. If this was the hoaxer, well, she'd quickly tell them what she thought of them. How dare they impersonate her dear friend's voice!

Isobel put down her mug of tea and stood up. Maybe she was being ridiculous. The person at the door was probably a friend calling to see if she was okay. Her mood suddenly brightened. Maybe it was Brian Kelly! Although, she had to admit to herself, she didn't really fancy him any more . . .

When Isobel opened the door, there was a strange woman standing outside, with short reddish hair and glasses. Boldly, the woman marched past Isobel and into the apartment, leaving Isobel gaping at her open-mouthed.

"Hey, just a moment! Who the hell are you? You can't just walk into someone's place like that –"

Her jaw dropped even further when the woman took her jacket off, then proceeded to remove her glasses and wig. As a cascade of dark hair appeared from underneath the red wig, Isobel clutched her chest, unsure of whether she was having a heart attack or a stroke. No, it just wasn't possible. The woman looked a bit like Alice, but her colouring was different, and she was thinner than her late friend. Besides which, Alice was dead!

"Sorry, Izzy – I didn't want to give you a shock, but–"

Alice was quickly silenced as Isobel threw her arms around her friend, sobbing loudly. "I can't believe it! Is it really you? I mean, how–"

Gently, Alice disengaged herself from her friend's tight embrace. "Yes, it's really me. But you can't tell anyone else that I'm alive."

"But how – I mean, what happened? I was at your

funeral —" Suddenly, Isobel began laughing hysterically. "In fact, I made a total fool of myself by bawling my head off at the graveside!"

The two women hugged each other again.

"I can't believe it!" said Isobel again, staring incredulously at Alice. "For God's sake, tell me what happened!"

As briefly as possible, Alice explained all had transpired in Argentina. Isobel was shocked to learn that Bill might be guilty of trying to get his own wife killed. She'd already known about Bill's financial difficulties, and the probable loss of the house Alice loved. But the idea that Alice's own husband would try to kill her was too horrific a notion to take on board.

"It's impossible to believe!" Isobel told her friend. "I know that Bill, like lots of other financiers, takes occasional short cuts in his business career, but I can't believe that he'd actually try to kill you!"

Alice agreed, tears in her eyes. She still found the idea utterly repugnant. Within a very short period of time, life as she knew it had altered irrevocably. Only weeks earlier, she'd been a happily married woman, with a husband, a home she adored, and a future that promised to fulfil all her dreams. Now, she was a fugitive from her own husband, on the brink of losing her home, and her life was in danger.

"The next thing I've got to do is tell Mum," said Alice. "It's going to be difficult, because she's had a huge shock already." Alice felt a rush of emotion as she thought of how her poor mother must feel, believing that her beloved daughter was dead. "I don't know how she's going to react when I turn up at her door."

Isobel shuddered. "Well, *I* nearly had a heart attack

when you arrived here, so I'm not sure what it'll do to your poor mother!"

"You'll have to help me prepare her, Izzy. I'm not sure how – but I don't think I can go barging in there, out of the blue. Imagine the irony if I turn up alive, and the shock of it kills her stone dead!"

Isobel nodded. "Your poor mother is devastated. She was a wreck at the funeral, and when I went round to visit her last week she was still finding it impossible to come to terms with your death."

Alice squeezed her friend's arm. "Thanks, Izzy – for keeping in touch with Mum."

Isobel had tears in her eyes again. "Well, you asked me to keep an eye on her when you left for Argentina." She sniffled. "But I never expected that to mean holding up your mother at your funeral!"

Alice smiled.

Isobel started to cry once again, then she brightened, and hugged Alice again. "God, your mother will be thrilled to see you!"

Alice nodded. "It's a really weird feeling – you know, having people think that you're dead." She grinned at her friend. "I hope no one said anything too awful about me?"

"What's it worth?" said Isobel, grinning back. Then her expression brightened. "Hey, I've just realised – if your disguise was good enough to fool me, you could actually use it to talk to people you know, and find out what they thought of you!"

Alice shuddered. "No, thanks – isn't there a saying: 'Eavesdroppers never hear good of themselves'? I'd be afraid to put it to the test!"

Isobel shrugged. "It's a golden opportunity to discover who your enemies are, and who are your friends!"

Alice grimaced. "I don't know how I'm going to manage it, Izzy, but I have to find out if I really was the intended victim. And if so, why. At the moment, it's definitely looking that way, and it isn't a very nice feeling."

Isobel put her arms around her friend supportively. "Well, you know I'll help you in any way I can. Are you planning to pose as a new secretary or personal assistant in Bill's office?"

"Not a chance. I don't know that my disguise would stand up to that much scrutiny! Besides, I don't know enough about business and finance to fool anyone in that area," said Alice. "The main thing I'm here to do is to see if I can find out if it was Bill that tried to kill me, and that's where I'm going to need your help."

"No problem," said Isobel.

Alice smiled gratefully. "So will you give my mum a ring – and tell her you're going to call over? Then I'll go with you –"

Isobel paused. "Are you sure this is the best way to do it? Maybe I should visit her first, and gradually bring her round to the possibility –"

Alice nodded. "You're right. I suppose the shock could genuinely bring on a heart attack. A shock is still a shock, whether the news is good or bad."

"Let's take this slowly. I'll visit her, introduce the possibility that you could still be alive, and see where we go from there."

"I can almost feel *myself* having a heart attack by just thinking about it!" said Alice anxiously. "I hope she'll be able to take the news . . ."

345

"You can wait outside in the car, and only come in if I phone you," said Isobel. "Have I your word on that?"

Alice nodded. "God, I'm dying to see Mum again!"

"Well, we're going to make sure that neither of you will be dying," said Isobel firmly, as she lifted the phone and dialled, holding the phone far enough from her ear to enable Alice to hear.

"Joan? It's Isobel."

"Oh, hello, Isobel. How are you?"

"Fine thanks," Isobel replied, holding the phone out from her ear so that Alice could hear. "Can I call over to see you? Are you alone?"

"You know you're always welcome," said Alice's mother. "Yes, I'm alone – why do you ask?"

"Oh, no particular reason. I just thought we could have a chat. I'll bring some wine with me, if that's okay."

"Sounds great, Isobel," said Joan warmly. "Look, I really do appreciate the amount of time you've been spending with me lately. It can't be much fun for you – sitting here chatting to an old woman – but I know you've been doing it for Alice . . ."

A sob caught in Joan's throat, and Alice longed to snatch the phone and scream to her mother that she was still alive. But she said nothing, tears running down her cheeks as she joyfully anticipated the eventual moment when she'd be able to see her mother's face again.

CHAPTER 55

As Isobel parked her car outside Joan's house in Stillorgan, her heart was pounding. Beside her, Alice was equally tense, and once again she was wearing her short red wig and glasses.

"Now, don't even think of moving from this car until I phone you," said Isobel sharply. "And if I don't think the time is right, I'll have a glass of wine with your mother, then just say goodbye and come back to the car myself."

Alice nodded vigorously. She was both excited and frightened. So much depended on how Joan reacted to Isobel's news. If indeed Isobel felt that the time was right to tell her mother that she was still alive. Alice fervently hoped that Isobel's approach would work, but she was equally terrified in case the news would have an adverse affect on her mother's health.

The minutes seemed like years, and Alice counted the raindrops that were falling onto the car's front windowpane. She'd brought a newspaper with her, but when she'd tried to read it, the words had danced in front of her eyes, and nothing she read made any sense. She was well aware that Isobel needed to take her time in leading up to the news of her survival, but Alice was nevertheless impatient, and longed to be a fly on the wall of her mother's drawing room. How was Isobel getting on? Had her mother collapsed with shock? Alice half expected to see an ambulance roll up and transport her mother to hospital. Or were she and Isobel just drinking wine and talking about the weather?

After what seemed like hours, Alice's mobile phone rang. Quickly she grabbed it, her hands shaking.

"Come to your mother's front door," Isobel instructed her. "I'll let you in myself. I've explained to your mother – very slowly – that you mightn't actually be dead. She's utterly confused, and protesting that she saw you buried. But she's holding up well."

Jumping out of the car, Alice ran through the rain to her mother's front door just as Isobel opened it.

"Please – take it easy," her friend cautioned. "Your mother is in a fragile state, but I think she can deal with the situation. But we'll do this very slowly . . ."

In the drawing room, Alice's mother sat huddled in a chair, and Alice's heart contracted with love for her. Her mother looked much older than when she'd last seen her – which wasn't surprising, since the poor woman believed that she'd recently buried her only daughter.

As Alice stood in the doorway, Joan glanced at her but then turned to Isobel, a quizzical look on her face. "Isobel, before you went out to let your friend in – you said that Alice – " she hesitated, bewildered, then shook her head. "Sorry, Isobel – I clearly misunderstood you." She gave a little hysterical laugh. "D'you know, I almost thought you said that Alice might still be alive – what a silly old fool I am!" She dabbed her eyes with a handkerchief. "But the death of your child makes you think strange things, and to hope against hope . . . it's madness, I know, but I still can't believe she's gone . . ." She turned to Alice, who stood just inside the door in her short red wig, glasses and dark make-up. "I'm sorry, dear, for ignoring you – you're very welcome. I presume you're a friend of Isobel's?"

Alice nodded, feeling as though her heart was about to break. She longed to throw her arms around her mother, but she knew that Joan needed to be introduced gradually to the fact she was still alive. On the other hand, how could she achieve that? There would be a moment when her mother would go from not knowing to knowing. And she herself couldn't predict, or prevent, how her mother might react.

Alice and Isobel made eye contact over Joan's head.

"Joan, how would you feel if Alice walked in the door right now?" Isobel asked softly, as the two younger women pulled up chairs on either side of Joan's chair.

Joan bit her lip. "Please, Isobel, you may think you're helping," she said imploringly "but I don't even want to think about something like that. It hurts too much. Now, can we please change the subject?"

She turned to Alice, putting on a brave smile. "Would you like some wine, dear?" She jumped up out of her chair and started moving towards the kitchen. "Let me get you a glass –"

"Joan – wait," said Isobel, "I wasn't trying to upset you. Please just answer one question for me – do you think my friend here looks in any way like Alice?"

Joan hesitated, not wanting to be rude, but not wanting to discuss the topic any further.

"No," she said at last. "She's too thin, and besides my daughter had dark hair. Now can we *please* drop the subject?"

Isobel stood up and followed Joan to the kitchen, putting her arm around the older woman's shoulder and urging her back into the drawing room. "Joan," said Isobel softly, "there's no easy way to break this to you, but this woman *is* Alice."

On cue, Alice stood up and first removed her glasses, then her red wig. As the hairgrips underneath released her dark hair and it fell loosely around her shoulders, Joan let out a cry, standing rooted to the spot, and gripping Isobel's hand so tightly that she almost drew blood.

"Tell me I'm not dreaming!" she whispered fiercely, as Isobel led her across the room to Alice.

"You're not dreaming," Isobel said happily, as mother and daughter embraced.

"I don't understand!" said Joan. "I'm afraid I'm going to wake up any second! I saw my daughter's coffin go into the ground!" Releasing herself from her daughter's embrace, Joan stepped back and surveyed Alice, hardly believing what she was seeing. "How could this – I mean – oh, I don't know what I mean!" Then she grasped Alice once again, and clung to her as though she'd never let her go.

"Oh Mum, it's so good to be back!" said Alice, tears now running down her cheeks, as she and her mother gazed at each other in wonder.

"I can't believe it!" Joan sobbed happily. "Am I dreaming? How can this be possible? I was at your funeral myself – Bill was there, and all your friends . . ."

"It was all a mistake, Mum – someone else was killed instead."

Joan looked at Alice, wild-eyed. "What does Bill think? He must be thrilled to have you back!"

"No, Mum – he doesn't know. And I won't be telling him."

As Joan's face registered further shock, Alice gradually explained what had happened in Argentina, and how Bill might be implicated in an attempt to murder her.

Joan clung to Alice, as though unable to cope with the barrage of changes impacting on her life. One minute, she'd been experiencing the joy of a lost daughter coming back into her life, now she had reason to fear her son-in-law!

Alice explained about Patricia's death, the mix-up over their identities, and the discovery of her own photograph from Bill's office in Senora Delgado's house.

"That's why I'm back here incognito, Mum – I've got to find out what Bill is up to."

"But you could be in danger!" said Joan, squeezing her daughter's hand. "Now that I've got you back, I don't want to lose you again!"

"Don't worry, Mum – since Bill and everyone else thinks I'm dead, it'll be easy to move among them. Even you didn't recognise me! No one but you and Isobel know the truth, and that's the way it must stay. For the foreseeable future, at any rate."

Joan still looked worried. "This must be a terrible shock for you, love – to find out that Bill might have tried to kill you." She bit her lip. "I mean, I know how much you love him –"

"Actually, I don't, Mum," said Alice, articulating the

351

words to her mother and Isobel for the very first time. Whether or not Bill was guilty of trying to kill her, she'd long ago fallen out of love with him. His double-dealing had destroyed her respect for him, and without respect, there could be no real love. She knew that now. Now, her heart belonged to Enrique Alvarez.

"Oh." Joan was unsure of what to say. Her world was changing by the minute. She'd known all about Bill's financial problems, having been given an edited version of events by Alice before she'd left for Argentina. But while she'd known Alice was taking a break from her marriage, Joan had never expected the couple to actually break up.

"But your beautiful home in Killiney – surely you'll want to go back to it, when all this is over?"

Alice gave a winsome smile. "It's not home for me any more, Mum." She kissed her mother's cheek. "Yes, I know I used to adore the place, but too many things have happened since then. Besides, it'll soon be repossessed anyway."

Joan looked perturbed, but Alice knew in her heart that the house didn't matter any more. In fact, she never wanted to see it again. Perhaps it had simply been a substitute for the things she really wanted out of life, but had never found in her marriage. Like the love of a man whose passion, depth and commitment to bettering his world was worth more than all the wealth that Bill, or anyone else, could give her. As she thought about these things, an image of Enrique came into her mind, and Alice smiled to herself. By now she'd learnt that the love Bill had given her hadn't been enough, and never would be enough. It was as though she'd merely been coasting along through life, waiting for real love to come her way.

CHAPTER 56

"Let's go out tonight, and test your new persona!" Isobel suggested, as she sat with Alice in the kitchen of her mother's house. "I've got invites for a photographic exhibition in town. My friend Deirdre Power is exhibiting some of her stuff, and I know she'd like me to be there. There'll be champagne and some finger food. What do you think?"

Alice looked doubtful. "To tell you the truth, I'm terrified, Izzy. It seemed like a great idea when I was in Argentina, but now, I'm not so sure . . ."

"You can't stay hidden in your mother's house forever, Alice," said Isobel reasonably. "Look, I can assure you that your disguise is brilliant. Even your own mother didn't recognise you! No one's going to know who you are – besides, you're not going to find out what Bill's up to if you're sitting at home. And it'll give you confidence that your disguise passes muster."

"No, I think I'll give it a miss. Maybe next time."

Isobel gave an exasperated sigh as Alice idly picked up the invitation and glanced down the list of exhibitors.

"I've changed my mind – I *will* come with you," Alice told a surprised Isobel, pointing to one of the names on the list. "I see that one of the exhibitors is Maureen Waldron – she's the woman whose husband threw himself out of the top-floor window of a building he was forced to sell, just before Bill's consortium took possession of it."

Isobel looked at the name on the invitation. "Oh yes, I know who you mean. I've met her at a few exhibitions and photographic events myslf. But surely you'd want to avoid her?"

"I'm hoping she might know something about Bill's current business dealings," Alice said. "As you're aware, Izzy, she's never forgiven him for what happened, and she's always taken a – shall we say – unhealthy interest in whatever he's doing."

"Is she still sending the letters?" Isobel asked, concerned.

"Well, not lately – but for months after her husband's death, she bombarded the offices of the consortium members with vitriolic letters. She's never been happy about their explanation of what drove her husband to suicide – and, I suppose, neither have I."

Isobel shrugged her shoulders. "Well, Maureen's husband chose to play with the big boys, and he got his fingers burnt. That's the world of big business – it's not nice, but that's the way it is. Presumably that's how Bill's landed himself in a financial mess too." She turned to Alice and grinned. "I'll make a point of talking to Maureen at the exhibition – let's do a bit of shit-stirring, and see what happens."

"We'd better figure out who I'm going to be," Alice said. "What on earth will I do if we meet people I know, such as work colleagues? They'll surely see through my disguise!"

"They won't. Everyone thinks you're dead, Alice. And

even if they thought you looked vaguely like the late Alice Fitzsimons, they're hardly going to think you've risen from the grave, are they? Well, unless they believe in miracles or reincarnation!" Isobel grinned. "Anyway, isn't everyone supposed to have a doppelganger?"

"So who am I?" Alice asked testily. "I thought a lot about this on the plane coming over, but I still couldn't make up my mind."

"I think you'd better keep your mouth shut," said Isobel, "because voices are so easily recognisable. Why don't we pretend you don't speak English? I could tell people you're Spanish, and since you're pretty fluent in the language anyway, you'll be okay if you *do* meet any Spaniards at the exhibition."

Alice nodded. It made sense for her to keep her mouth shut. That way, she could listen to everything that was going on without having to get involved.

"Now, what about a name?" added Isobel. "Obviously, it has to be something Spanish – how about Maria?"

Alice shuddered. That was the name of Enrique's late wife. "No, anything but that – what about Conchita?"

"Excellent."

But Alice still didn't look happy. "I hope I can do this. Izzy, I'm terrified that I'll make some kind of *faux pas* and end up being publicly unmasked."

"Don't worry," said Isobel, patting her friend on the back. "All you have to do is stand beside me and look exotic in your red wig. I'll do all the talking. It'll be child's play. In fact, it'll be just like playing a kids' game of make-believe, won't it?"

Alice shuddered. "A deadly game, Izzy. If I slip up, it could go horribly wrong – and I could be horribly dead."

* * *

The exhibition hall was full by the time Alice and Isobel arrived.

"Hopefully, it'll be a great night," said Isobel positively. "With a bit of luck we'll know no one, we'll guzzle lots of free champagne, and have a laugh."

Alice nodded. "I hope you're right," she said, grabbing two glasses of bubbly from the tray of a passing waiter, "but I hope my career as a spy will be short-lived. I don't think I'm cut out for all this Mata Hari stuff!"

Suddenly, Alice grabbed Isobel's arm.

"Oh my God – there's Bill over there! What am I going to do?"

"Oh Christ! What a bummer – I seem to have thrown you in at the deep end," said Isobel. "Just relax! You're another person now – he'll never recognise you. Just act natural."

"What will I do if he talks to me?"

"There's no reason why he should," said Isobel, "but if he does, just smile and say nothing. You're Spanish now, and Bill doesn't speak Spanish, right? Then move off as soon as you can."

"Oh, Izzy, I'm terrified!" said Alice out of the corner of her mouth.

"Look!" said Isobel. "There's Maureen Waldron over there. Let's go and talk to her –" She grinned at Alice. "That was just a figure of speech, by the way – you're saying nothing!"

They crossed the room, Isobel leading the way.

"Hello, Maureen," said Isobel, insinuating herself into the group in which the older woman was holding court, "I see you're exhibiting here tonight – great stuff!"

"Thank you, Isobel." Maureen looked inquisitively at Alice.

"Let me introduce my Spanish friend, eh —"

Suddenly, Isobel's mind went blank, and Alice had to come to the rescue.

"— Conchita," she said, pronouncing it with a Spanish accent.

"I'm afraid she doesn't speak English," said Isobel, recovering, "I've been asked by another friend to bring her along this evening."

"I presume you don't speak Spanish yourself, Isobel?" asked Maureen, looking curiously at Alice. "It must be a bloody pain having to drag her around with you. Still, we must all do our duty for our friends."

Alice had to cover her mouth to hide her grin, afraid that Maureen would realise she'd understood all too well what was being said!

"I — well —" Quickly Isobel changed the subject. "So tell me, Maureen, how many pictures have you in the exhibition?"

Maureen was more than happy to talk about her exhibits, and Alice stood patiently by as the two photographers talked shop, discussing lenses and exposures, digital photography and image-editing programmes.

At last, Isobel felt that it was time to move the discussion along to more pertinent matters. "So, how are you *coping*, Maureen?" she asked, knowing that with the introduction of that key word, Maureen could be guaranteed to begin her tirade.

"Can you believe it — that bastard's actually turned up here!" Maureen hissed. "He has some nerve!"

Surreptitiously, Alice looked round to where Maureen was pointing, and sure enough, Bill was there, chatting animatedly to a group of people that included Geraldine McEvoy.

"Well, it's a free country," Isobel reasoned. "I'm sure if you stay well away from him, everything will be fine."

"His wife died recently, you know."

"Yes, I know," said Isobel. "In fact, she was a good friend of mine."

Maureen's hand went to her mouth. "Oh lord, I should have remembered that – sorry – it must be all the champagne I've drunk this evening! Well, the poor woman didn't have much taste in husbands, did she? He's not wasting any time mourning over her – he's already lining up wife number two!" She nodded towards Geraldine McEvoy, who was clinging to Bill's arm proprietarily.

Isobel gave a concerned glance at Alice, hoping that her friend hadn't been upset by what she'd just heard. But Alice was gazing nonchalantly around her as though she hadn't a care in the world. Nevertheless, Isobel knew that Maureen's words must have cut her to the quick.

Maureen lowered her voice conspiratorially. "I also heard on the grapevine that he's in serious financial difficulties – couldn't happen to a nicer guy, as far as I'm concerned!"

"Do you know if he's doing any business in Argentina?" Isobel asked casually, "I heard a rumour that he was investing in some projects there . . ."

Maureen nodded. "Funny you should mention that – I keep in touch with a woman who works in his office – ear to the ground and all that – and only last week, she told me that he'd been continually singing 'Don't cry for me, Argentina' in the office, and driving everyone crazy, since he can't sing for nuts. Sounds as though something about Argentina is making him happy. Bastard!"

Isobel glanced at Alice, worried that her friend might be

bothered at what she'd overheard, but Alice was still wearing the benign expression of someone who hadn't understood a single word of what had been said.

"Well, Maureen, it's been great seeing you again!" Isobel said heartily. "Now I must excuse myself and take my Spanish friend to meet Deirdre Power, who's also exhibiting here tonight."

Taking their leave of Maureen Waldron – with Alice waving a silent goodbye – they headed into the throng of people who were milling around the bar where waiters were replenishing glasses of champagne. Quickly, Alice helped herself to two more glasses.

"Come on over this way, and let me introduce you to Deirdre," Isobel told Alice. "Just remember – not a word out of you! I'll do all the talking." She squeezed Alice's arm supportively. "You're doing great," she whispered.

Soon Isobel was chatting to the irrepressible Deirdre, who was making the most of the occasion.

"This is my fifth glass of champagne," she confided. "I'm so nervous! It's the first time I've been asked to exhibit here – what do you think?"

"Your stuff is fantastic," Isobel assured her warmly. "I've heard nothing but praise for your pictures this evening."

"Oh thanks," said Deirdre, relieved and pleased. Quickly, as a waiter passed by, she helped herself to yet another glass of champagne. She lowered her voice. "Do you see that hunk over there?"

"Where?"

Both Alice and Isobel looked to where Deirdre was pointing.

"The gorgeous fellow in the striped shirt."

Isobel and Alice nearly collapsed – Deirdre was pointing at Alice's husband Bill! Isobel nudged Alice, and the pair of them bit their lips to control the mounting hysterical laughter they felt about to burst forth.

"What do you think?" asked Deirdre. "He's very attractive, isn't he?" Then she lowered her voice. "He's been widowed recently, so I was thinking of going over and chatting him up. Do you think I'd stand a chance?" Then her hand went to her mouth. "Oh God, Isobel – you were a friend of his wife's, weren't you?"

Isobel nodded. "Yes, she was a lovely person," she said, digging Alice in the ribs.

"Excuse us, Deirdre, we've got to talk to someone over here – see you later."

By tacit agreement, both women headed straight for the toilets, each of them afraid that they were about to explode with nervous laughter.

"Oh my God," said Alice, as she surveyed the strange red-haired woman in the mirror, "I don't know how much more of this I can endure. It's weird!"

"You were great!" Isobel called out from her cubicle in the toilet. "It really works when you just let me to do the talking, doesn't it? Now, let's have one more glass of champagne, and we'll leave after that. There's just one other photographer I want to have a quick word with first, okay?"

"No problem," said Alice. "I'll wander round the exhibits while you chat to your friend."

"Will you be okay?"

"Yes, but don't leave me on my own for too long, will you?"

With Isobel's assurances that she'd only talk shop for a few minutes, the two women left the toilets and joined the throng of guests outside. Then Isobel melted away into the crowd, and Alice was left alone to survey the milling guests. It felt strange and surreal to be posing as someone else, and Alice felt as though she was standing behind a screen that separated her from everyone else. She wondered if this was how women wearing burkas felt. They were present, yet in another sense, they weren't, since their identity was entirely hidden beneath the garment they were wearing.

"Oh hello," said a voice beside her, "are you enjoying the exhibition?"

Suddenly, Alice's heart almost stopped. Her own husband was standing beside her!

"My name is Bill," he said, extending his hand.

"Conchita," said Alice, using her best Spanish accent, and feeling decidedly weird to be shaking her own husband's hand so formally!

Wildly, she looked around for Isobel. Why on earth had her friend decided to disappear at this precise time?

Bill looked at her closely, and Alice could feel her heart pounding as he scrutinised her features. She fervently hoped that her very different make-up would conceal the trembling woman within.

"I'm sorry if you thought I was staring," he said at last, "but something about you reminds me of my late wife."

Alice smiled enigmatically, not daring to open her mouth.

Bill looked really sad, and Alice felt a sudden desire to throw herself into his arms and confess that she was really alive and well. Bill didn't seem to be pretending – he seemed to be genuinely missing her. Nevertheless, there was still the little matter of the framed photograph on Senora Delgado's mantelpiece in Argentina.

Alice bit her lip. It felt decidedly odd to be standing beside her own husband while posing as somebody else, and noting how everyone else regarded him as a widower, and knowing that at least two women present had designs on him!

Just then, Geraldine McEvoy materialised out of nowhere, and possessively slipped her arm around Bill's waist. "Come along, Bill darling," she whispered proprietarily, "There are some important people over here who want to meet you."

"Excuse me, Conchita −" Bill said apologetically.

Then he was whisked away, leaving Alice in no doubt that she wasn't regarded by Geraldine McEvoy as one of the important people worthy of Bill's attention. If only for revenge, Alice longed to be able to drop her guard and announce who she was. She'd give anything to watch Geraldine McEvoy's face! But she was also aware that she didn't feel even slightly jealous of Geraldine any more. The woman was welcome to Bill, and the shallow world they both inhabited.

It was a sobering thought, and confirmation to Alice that she no longer loved Bill, if proof was actually needed. Instead, she longed to be back in Argentina, gazing into the eyes of a certain dark-haired, dark-eyed policeman, who'd made her pulse race every time he looked at her.

Alice sighed. It was just as well that she hadn't needed to converse with Bill! She felt weak and shaky after their brief encounter, and unsure of how well she could have carried it off if Geraldine McEvoy hadn't intervened. She smiled grimly to herself. She'd never expected to feel grateful to Geraldine McEvoy for anything!

Almost immediately, Isobel was at her side. "Ready to go, then?"

"Yes," said Alice faintly, "I was never so ready in all my life!"

CHAPTER 57

As Isobel drove out towards Killiney, Alice in the passenger seat, she wondered again about the wisdom of what they were about to do.

"Are you sure this is wise, Alice? I mean –"

"There's no other way," Alice replied determinedly. "I have to start somewhere, and checking his bank statements and home computer makes sense."

They knew that Bill was attending a charity dinner that evening, organised by Geraldine McEvoy, who regarded herself as a major player on the Dublin charity circuit. This meant they had several hours in which to get access to his computer.

"Aren't you scared?" asked Isobel, glancing quickly at her friend. "I know *I* am, and I'm not even going into the house!"

Alice grinned. "You forget, my dear friend, I'm a veteran housebreaker. I got plenty of experience while with Ricardo in Argentina."

Briefly, she thought of Ricardo with nostalgia and affection. The gentle unassuming priest had taught her to value what really mattered. Money and possessions were nothing compared to love, commitment and integrity. As they drove along, Alice recalled her night-time escapade with the gentle priest at Senora Delgado's house. By comparison, this one would be a doddle – it was her own house, she knew every nook and cranny of it, and Bill would be away for several hours – maybe even overnight, if Geraldine McEvoy had her way.

It felt odd to think coldly about her husband in another woman's arms. Part of her still loved Bill – and always would – but Argentina had changed everything. So much had changed. *She'd* changed. She was no longer the Alice Fitzsimons who'd once lived a charmed life in a big house, with a handsome husband and no money worries. Maybe coming so close to death had changed her perspective. She shivered. Tonight she might get the answers she was looking for.

As they drove along in silence, Alice was relieved to see that darkness was falling rapidly. Although the house in Killiney wasn't overlooked, she still didn't want to take the chance of being spotted by a neighbour. Although she was wearing her usual disguise, she didn't want anyone later informing Bill that a woman had been seen prowling around the premises.

"Are you sure you don't want me to come in with you?" Isobel asked, breaking in on her thoughts.

Alice shook her head. "No, Izzy, I'll be fine – honestly. I'll be in and out before you know it."

"What about Murphy's Law?" queried Isobel, grinning, "You know what it says – if anything can go wrong, it will!"

Alice shivered. "Stop making me nervous!"

"Sorry – you're right," Isobel said, as much to convince Alice as herself. "Now let's just run over the plan once more."

Alice grinned in exasperation. They'd gone over it millions of times already! "Okay, I'm going to zap open the electric gates, walk up the drive to the front door, open it, turn off the alarm, then go to the bedroom and pick up my briefcase – assuming Bill hasn't turfed it out already, then –"

"Couldn't you just forget about the bloody briefcase?" Isobel said, looking annoyed. "That'll just delay you longer!"

Alice shook her head. "There's a research document in it that a woman sent to me at the *Daily News*, ages ago – it's about BWF Pharmaceuticals – and I want to start reading it."

Isobel grinned. "Always the journalist – even though you're supposed to be dead!"

"Well, hopefully I'll be able to come back to life some day soon. This document looks interesting, so I want to spend some time reading it. There might even be a story in it."

"Okay," said Isobel. "Tell me what you do next."

"I then go to Bill's study, where I'll download his e-mails and files onto my external memory. Then I'll shut down the computer, go downstairs again and turn the alarm back on, shut the front door and walk down the driveway and back to your car."

"Sounds fine – in theory anyway. But I still think we need a contingency plan."

"Nothing is going to go wrong," said Alice firmly. "Making contingency plans is like tempting fate. I won't be able to go through with it if I have to think about things going wrong!"

"Okay," said Isobel, "but just in case anything *does* go wrong, get as far away from here as possible. Don't bother trying to get back to the car. Get a taxi or a bus home if necessary."

"Stop it!" said Alice angrily. "Everything's going to be fine!"

In silence they drove through Killiney village, and onto the quiet and meandering tree-lined road that would ultimately lead to Ivy Lodge. All along the road, driveways led to magnificent mansions, all of them set in off the road amid beautiful trees and shrubs. Ivy Lodge was situated up a driveway shared by several houses, and at the entrance to the driveway, Isobel disgorged her passenger.

"Best of luck," she whispered. "I'll wait in the recess near the entrance to your neighbour's house."

Alice nodded, then slipped away into the darkness. As she made her way up the driveway to her old home, everything felt surreal and bizarre. She was about to become an intruder in her own home! Well, she conceded, it was only her home – or Bill's for that matter – until the bank finally repossessed it.

Quickly she glanced around her as she reached the front door. It was now almost dark, and as far as she could see there was no one around to witness her entry. Using her key, she opened the door, switched off the alarm and stepped inside.

The old familiar aromas of her home assailed her nostrils, and she breathed in deeply. She could smell the familiar mix of carpets, oriental rugs and Bill's aftershave. It produced a sudden wave of nostalgia, and she had to shake herself mentally from her reverie. There was work to be done – and fast. Every minute she stayed in the house was an extra minute in which something could go wrong.

Upstairs, the landing light had been left on, so she had no difficulty in making her way up the stairs. In the bedroom she'd once shared with Bill, she was relieved to find that her briefcase was still where she'd left it – a lifetime ago – and she grabbed it and headed towards Bill's study.

Deciding that she would start with his computer, Alice turned it on and waited anxiously until the icons appeared on screen. Then she clicked on Bill's e-mails, and quickly scrolled down through them. She then inserted her external memory into the base of the computer and downloaded everything quickly. Later, she would check it all on the computer at her mother's house, and phone Enrique with details of any incriminating e-mails or relevant addresses. He would then know what to do.

At the thought of Enrique, her heart did a little flip. She was longing to speak to him again, to hear his sexy voice and the cute way he pronounced words when he tried them in English . . .

Suddenly, her heart leapt in her chest. Was that the sound of the front door opening? It couldn't be – Bill wasn't due back for hours! Then she heard the door closing, confirming her worst fears.

Quickly, she slipped the external memory into her briefcase, and looked around frantically for somewhere to hide. But the study offered no hiding places. The only safe option was to head for the back stairs that led down to the scullery, and ultimately out to the back garden. Creeping out of the study, she turned off the landing light so that she could make her way under cover of darkness. She took care not to tread on any of the steps that creaked, while listening for sounds that might tell her where Bill was.

Damn – she hadn't turned off the computer! But it was too late now. Anyway, the most important thing was to get away from there as quickly as possible. If Bill managed to corner her, he'd quickly realise who she was, and assuming he'd already tried to arrange her death, he might see fit to finish her off himself . . .

Just as she reached the bottom step, she heard Bill making his way into the kitchen. She froze as he walked by her, so close that he'd have heard her breathing if she hadn't been holding it in. Fortunately, the back stairs were completely in the dark, and he appeared to notice nothing amiss. Now on her hands and knees, briefcase between her teeth, Alice edged her way through the scullery and towards the door into the back garden. Once she got there, she'd feel relatively safe. Then all she had to do was creep down the garden to the gate at the bottom, and let herself out onto the road.

Just as she managed to get the scullery door open, some sixth sense seemed to alert Bill to the fact that he wasn't entirely alone in the house.

"What the hell –"

As Alice disappeared through the door, Bill rushed out into the scullery, and finding the back door now ajar, raced out into the garden hot on her heels. Alice felt like weeping with frustration. Would she reach the back gate in time? Right now, she really did fear for her life . . .

CHAPTER 58

Isobel slumped in the driver's seat and waited anxiously. To take her mind off what Alice was doing, she put a CD in the car player, and listened to its soothing orchestral sounds. Alice was right, she conceded. Everything was going to be fine. Within a few minutes, Alice would be back at the car, and they'd drive back to Stillorgan, mission accomplished. Isobel closed her eyes, swaying gently to the rhythm of the CD. She was beginning to relax at last.

She was so relaxed that she almost didn't hear the sound of the car until it swept past her and the driver zapped open the gates and turned into the driveway of Ivy Lodge. Isobel gulped in shock. That was Bill's car! Oh my God, she'd have to warn Alice somehow! Taking out her mobile phone, she was about to dial Alice's number, but by then Bill had parked his car, got out and reached the front door. Too late! If she phoned Alice now, Bill would hear her phone ringing inside the house. By now, the electric gates had shut themselves again, so Isobel was overcome with panic. Grabbing a torch from the glove compartment, she jumped out of the car and rushed down the roadway, not sure what she was going to do, but knowing she had to do something.

Since Ivy Lodge was at right angles to the road, there was a gate built into the 6-foot wall running alongside it. Quickly Isobel checked, and confirmed that the gate was locked from the inside. What on earth could she do now? She decided that she'd no option but to climb over the wall. The ivy hanging over the top of the wall would give her something to grip onto while she levered herself up. In an adrenalin-fuelled frenzy, she grabbed several strands of ivy, and using gaps in the granite stones as footholds, she pulled herself up onto the top of the wall. Jumping down into the garden on the other side, her hands now scratched and bleeding, she was relieved that the torch had survived the climb and was still in her pocket.

Her plan, insofar as she'd thought of one, was to shine the torch up at the window of Bill's study in the hope of alerting Alice. Too late, Isobel realised that it might have been better if she'd rung the bell at the gates, distracting Bill until Alice escaped via the back garden. But panic had clouded her thought processes, and she'd made a serious error of judgement.

Suddenly, her torch wavered as someone came hurtling through the shrubbery. Isobel was just about to throw herself into the bushes when she realised it was Alice.

"It's Bill!" hissed Alice. "Run!"

"Did he see you?" Isobel whispered as Alice fumbled for the latch on the back gate.

"Not properly – but I wasn't able to turn off the computer!"

As soon as Alice managed to open the gate, she

disappeared through it and melted away into the darkness. Isobel was about to follow her, but she dropped her torch, then fell over it in the dark, and went sprawling onto the flagstone path.

Suddenly, Bill appeared, wielding some kind of weapon.

"Who's there?" he roared. "Come out and show yourself, you rotten thieving bastard!"

Spotting Isobel's outline in the dark, he headed straight for her.

"Gottcha!" he yelled, lashing out with what looked like a poker, barely missing Isobel's head as she struggled to get up off the ground.

"Stop, Bill – for God's sake!"

Bill looked down in astonishment as Isobel materialised at his feet.

"Oh Jesus, Isobel – I almost killed you! What on earth are *you* doing here?"

"Eh, hello, Bill. I – well, I thought I'd call round to see how you were," said Isobel, frantically improvising.

"Well, what on earth were you doing around the back?" he asked, studying her warily. "I thought you were a burglar! I could have sworn there was someone snooping around the house –" He looked closely at her as he helped her up. "You didn't see anyone else out here, did you?"

Isobel shook her head. Hopefully, Alice was far away by now.

Bill scratched his head, looking puzzled. "But if you were calling to see me, Isobel, what on earth were you doing in the back garden?"

"When I rang the bell and got no answer, I thought I'd check round the back," Isobel lied, improvising as best she could. "I – eh, the back gate was open, and I was worried, in case you were sitting all alone in the kitchen, brooding –"

Bill laughed harshly. "Go on, Isobel – tell the truth – you thought I might be committing suicide!"

Isobel nodded, relief flooding through her. It looked as though Bill had accepted her story. "You wouldn't be the first man to feel devastated at the loss of his wife," she said.

Bill gently patted Isobel's arm. "I really appreciate your concern, but I'm okay, honestly. Come on inside and let me make you a cup of coffee."

Meekly, Isobel followed him up the garden path and into the house. Her heart had slowed down a little, since the worst appeared to be over.

In the big stone-flagged kitchen, Bill put the kettle on, and Isobel sat down at the table. The same table where she and Alice had shared many cuppas in the past.

At last, Bill spoke. "If you were worried about me, Isobel, what were you doing at the bottom of the garden? Did you think I was going to hang myself from one of the bushes?"

Isobel blushed at his sarcasm, but was determined not to appear disconcerted. She put a sad expression on her face, while she frantically tried to think of a suitable answer. "I – well – it's a bit embarrassing, Bill," she said, playing for time. Oh God, what am I going to say, she asked herself. My mind's gone blank! I can't think of anything to tell him . . .

"I know," said Bill, smiling slyly, "I know what you were up to."

Isobel stared at him, her heart pounding. Had he seen Alice? He couldn't have! And even if he had, he wouldn't have seen through her disguise, would he?

"You're still mourning for Alice, aren't you?" said Bill

softly. "So you were looking around the garden shed, where she spent so much of her time."

Isobel sighed with relief. "Yes, you're right, Bill. That's exactly it. When I couldn't see any sign of you at the back of the house, I felt drawn to the shed. I miss her so much, Bill, and I wanted to feel close to her again."

Phew! Isobel thought, you've no idea *how* close I was, Bill!

"But I'm positive I heard you talking to someone," said Bill, a query in his voice.

"Yes, you're right, Bill," Isobel replied, warming to her theme. "I was talking to Alice." Even as she said it, Isobel felt like giggling hysterically. Bill had no idea how true that statement was either! "Down at the shed," she continued, "I felt as though her spirit was there, among her beloved plants. So I was trying to communicate with her beyond the grave."

"I miss her too," said Bill ruefully. "When I'm here alone in the house, I still feel her presence. Sometimes I forget that she's gone, and I expect her to suddenly appear and ask if I want a cup of tea."

Isobel nodded sympathetically. Bill seemed genuinely sad. It was difficult for her to see him as a potential murderer. Then Isobel mentally corrected herself. There was no 'potential' about it – whoever wanted to kill Alice had already murdered another Irish woman in Argentina.

Suddenly, Isobel realised that Bill was staring at her. "You weren't actually *in* the house, were you, Isobel?"

Isobel looked startled and her heart began to pound again. "No, of course not!" she said vehemently, glad that she could protest her innocence truthfully. "Why would you think such a thing?"

Bill pursed his lips. He didn't look convinced. "It's just odd, that's all."

"What is?"

"Well, before I went out, I was certain I put the alarm on. Yet when I came in, it was turned off."

"You probably just forgot," said Isobel brightly. "You're under a lot of strain, Bill. It wouldn't be surprising if something like that slipped your mind."

Bill still didn't look convinced. "Then there was the landing light. I always leave it on before I go out – to make the place look lived-in. But it was off when I came back."

"Probably the bulb's blown," said Isobel. "That kind of thing is always happening to me."

Bill shook his head. "But Alice always bought those longlife bulbs – she said they were more energy-efficient, and better for the environment."

"Well, you must have got a dud one," Isobel told him firmly.

"And the back door was open too."

"Oh. Well, I suppose you just forgot to check it before you went out, Bill," said Isobel firmly. "I'm always leaving doors open myself."

"But if the door was left open before I went out, I wouldn't have been able to turn on the alarm," Bill told her, looking directly at her.

Isobel shrugged her shoulders, and tried to appear nonchalant. "But you *didn't* set the alarm, Bill. As we said, you must have forgotten." But she was now becoming extremely worried. Bill would never accept that he'd left his computer turned on as well.

Isobel tried to think logically. What was the worst that

could happen when he discovered it was on? Well, for starters, the finger of suspicion would point directly at her. After all, she was Alice's friend, he'd found her skulking around in his back garden late at night, it was distinctly possible that she could have got her hands on a key to the house, and would know the alarm sequence. Isobel shivered. Assuming he'd already tried to kill Alice, maybe he'd try to kill her as well. Oh God, he'd become so enraged with her that he'd pick up a poker or vase, and crash it down on her head . . .

"Isobel – your tea."

"Oh – thanks, Bill," she said, as he placed a cup in front of her. Her thoughts were running riot, and she needed to calm down and think logically. As she sipped her tea, and made some casual conversation with Bill, she realised she would somehow have to get to Bill's computer and turn it off.

Gulping down the last of her tea, she smiled warmly at him. "Great cuppa – thanks, Bill. Now, may I use your loo before I go?"

"Yes, of course. There's one just outside the kitchen, off the pantry –"

Isobel pretended not to hear him, quickly heading upstairs instead, to the bathroom beside Bill's study.

Loudly closing the bathroom door for effect, she remained outside on the landing, then quickly ducked into the adjacent room. The computer was on screensaver, but as soon as she touched the mouse, Bill's e-mails appeared. Hopefully, Alice had managed to copy everything she needed before she was interrupted.

Quickly, Isobel closed the site down, then started the process of turning the whole computer off. It seemed to take ages, but Isobel was aware that it wasn't really taking any longer than usual – it was just her nerves that made it seem so! At last, the computer clicked off and she sighed with relief.

Just as she turned to leave the room, she froze as she heard a footfall on the landing outside, and Bill suddenly appeared in the doorway.

"Isobel – what on earth are you doing in here?"

Isobel thought rapidly. "Oh! I – well, I thought I heard a sound coming from here, and when I stepped inside the door, I got the most powerful sense of Alice – I think she might be trying to tell us something, Bill. People who suffer violent deaths often come back, you know. They can't rest until their murderer is brought to justice."

Bill looked sceptical. "My knowledge of these matters is limited, Isobel, but I always thought it was the scene of a tragedy that was haunted. In that event, Alice wouldn't be here – she'd be haunting somewhere in Argentina."

Isobel nodded, unsure of whether Bill was playing with her or not. They went downstairs in silence, Isobel now genuinely dying to use the toilet. But she didn't dare go back. Right now, she considered it more prudent to get out of the house as soon as possible. There was no point in tempting fate any further!

Back in the kitchen, Isobel didn't bother to sit down again. She intended leaving at once.

"Will you be okay, Bill?" she asked, her feelings for Alice's husband genuinely confused at this point.

Suddenly, Bill's face crumpled, and he began to cry. "Oh God, Isobel, what have I done? What have I done to poor Alice?"

Isobel froze. Was this the remorse of a killer, or a husband deeply distressed by his wife's death?

"What do you mean – 'what you've done'?"

Bill seemed to regain some of his composure. "I-I meant that –" He wiped his eyes with his handkerchief, then looked closely at Isobel. "I presume you know all about my – eh, financial problems? I guess Alice would have told you."

Isobel nodded.

"Well, if I hadn't got us into this mess, Alice wouldn't have gone to Argentina, then she wouldn't have been killed over there."

Isobel nodded again. She could understand Bill's twisted logic. It was the kind that countless bereaved people put themselves through, as they searched for a reason to explain the death of a loved one. Assuming he hadn't planned her death himself, that is. However, he seemed genuinely remorseful, and Isobel felt her heart warming to him again. If Bill was innocent, then he was undoubtedly in pain and consumed with guilt.

She sighed. On the other hand, if he really was a murderer, and could coldly consign Alice to her death, then he could surely muster up a few tears if they were needed for effect.

"Bill – I'd better be going. Thanks for the tea."

Bill gave her a warm smile. "Thanks for calling around, Isobel. And –" he hesitated, "– thanks for thinking that I might need some support. People always assume that men can cope with these things – stiff upper lip, and all that – but we have feelings too."

Oh God, Isobel thought, if I don't get out of here fast, I'm in danger of spilling my guts and telling him that Alice is still alive. Anything to take away the pain in his eyes.

"Bill —"

"Yes?"

Isobel clamped her mouth shut just in time. She'd been about to ask him why he'd returned from the charity dinner so early! If she'd done that, he'd know she hadn't genuinely called to see him. She needed to get away fast, before she made another *faux pas*.

"Oh, nothing."

Standing on the front steps, Bill gave her a hug.

"Goodnight Isobel."

"Goodnight, Bill."

As she made her way down the steps – to freedom at last – Bill had one final question.

"Do you really believe in ghosts, Isobel?"

"I do, Bill," she lied glibly. "Occasionally I've experienced things that can't be explained rationally."

Bill nodded. "It's funny, but this evening, I got a real sense of Alice in the house, so maybe it *is* true. I even thought I could smell her perfume when I came in."

Isobel gulped. "I'm sure that's bound to happen when you've recently lost a loved one. Goodnight again, Bill."

"Goodnight, Isobel."

As Bill zapped open the gates, Isobel headed quickly down the driveway and back to her car. There was no sign of Alice. Let me get out of here quickly, she told herself, and then phone her. Was Bill genuinely upset, or was he just toying with her?

CHAPTER 59

As soon as she'd driven a reasonable distance from Killiney, Isobel stopped and phoned Alice. "Are you okay?"

"Yeah, I'm back at Mum's place. But what took *you* so long? I thought you were just behind me! When you didn't come back to the car, I headed for the village and flagged down a taxi."

"Well, I decided to stay and have tea with Bill instead."

"You *what*?"

"He almost hit me over the head — accidentally, of course."

Quickly, Isobel explained what had transpired. "I think I deserve an Oscar for my performance," she finished. "Bill was very pleased that I'd driven all the way to Killiney to see if he was okay!"

"You told him that? Well, he won't be so pleased when he discovers that his computer was left on."

"Well, that's where the Second Act of my Oscar-winning performance comes in," said Isobel, feeling very pleased with herself. "I told him I'd felt your presence in his office."

"What?" Alice shrieked again.

"Relax —" Isobel chuckled, "— it was your ghost I was talking about! I managed to turn the computer off, but Bill caught me in his study, so I told him I'd gone in there because I felt your spiritual presence."

Alice laughed heartily. "Surely he didn't fall for that twaddle?"

"I don't know — but it doesn't matter, as long as he thinks *I* believe it! Have you looked at the e-mails yet?"

"No, I'm putting off that particular treat for tomorrow morning."

"Right, well, let me know how you get on. Sleep well."

"You too, Izzy — and thanks for everything."

The following morning, Alice was up bright and early, and seated at her mother's computer immediately after breakfast. Now was the moment of truth — she would soon find out if there were any incriminating e-mails that might link Bill to Patricia's death in Argentina. In fact, any connection with Argentina would probably be evidence enough.

As she inserted her external memory, Alice sincerely hoped that she'd find nothing incriminating. She didn't want Bill to be guilty. She wanted to be able to phone Enrique and tell him that Bill appeared to be in the clear. At the thought of Enrique, Alice's heart gave a little jump for joy. He loved her, and she loved him! She wondered what it would be like being a policemen's wife in Argentina, but she was certainly looking forward to the adventure!

None of the e-mails in Bill's Inbox contained anything incriminating. But when Alice clicked on his Sent Items folder, she suddenly froze. Bill had sent two e-mails to an address in Argentina! Hardly believing her eyes, she read the first one, dated just a few days after she'd left for Argentina herself:

Dear Michael –

Can you confirm progress with our arrangement in Argentina, as discussed in my office last week? I would like to know as soon as possible.

Bill

Alice quickly confirmed that both e-mails had been sent through an Argentine Internet service provider. Oh my God, Alice thought, so Bill *is* the one who's been trying to kill me! He's never had contact with anyone in Argentina before I went there. Her hand was shaking so much that she couldn't use the computer any more. No wonder he'd been singing 'Don't cry for me, Argentina' in the office, she thought – he must have been rejoicing to think he'd got rid of me at last, and all my inheritance money would soon be his!

A second e-mail, a week later, seemed to confirm the contents of the first:

Michael –

Please get in touch. I need confirmation that the Argentina project is still on target.

Bill

The word "target" sent shivers down Alice's spine. She was shocked and horrified. It seemed to confirm that Bill had been keeping tabs on her in Argentina! Quickly, she jotted down the e-mail address to which Bill had forwarded his replies. Hopefully, Enrique would be able to trace it.

Alice laid her head on the desk. Sometimes she wondered why she was bothering to try to solve the mystery of Patricia's killer. She could simply give Bill the money he wanted so badly. She'd happily give it to him, if it meant that she and Enrique could live in peace forever more. If she gave the money to him, presumably the threat to her life would be over?

She pictured herself and Enrique several years down the line, with two plump and healthy babies on their knees, smiling joyously at each other, their family complete. Or maybe Enrique would like more children? She wondered what they'd look like, these half-Irish, half-Argentine babies. She'd make sure that they knew all about their Irish roots . . .

Printing off the e-mails, Alice closed down the computer and removed the external memory. Now she'd phone Enrique and tell him what she'd learnt. She was longing to hear his voice again, although she heartily wished that their conversation could be about happier things . . . like how much they missed each other. More than anything, she longed to be back in his arms.

Alice rang Enrique immediately, and felt comforted by the sound of his voice. She didn't feel quite so alone and frightened when she talked to him. She quickly told him about the Argentine e-mail address, and he promised to have it checked immediately.

"There is good news at this end, Alice," he told her. "The forensic results from Senora Delgado's house are back, and we got two sets of fingerprints from the third bedroom. They belong to two well-known hit-men, one of whom was admitted to a hospital in the town nearest to Villanova, with a bullet in his arm. The doctor in charge let our officers know, and when his partner-in-crime came to collect him, we took them both in for questioning. Of course the fingerprints matched."

Alice knew that Enrique was smiling. "So maybe, that night in Ricardo's house, I was not so useless after all."

"You were even better the following night, my love," she whispered seductively, remembering the night they'd first made love.

She could hear Enrique chuckling at the other end of the phone.

"So what happens next, Enrique?"

"We've been putting pressure on these two men, and they've told us the name of their Argentine contact – another well-known criminal – who gave them their first payment in cash. Of course he has disappeared, so for now the trail has gone cold again."

"Have they told you anything else?"

"Yes – we now know that you were followed from the hostel where you met Patricia. The mix-up on your passports meant the receptionist had you listed as Patricia, and she as you. When the two men called to the hostel, posing as friends of yours, the receptionist told them you'd already left for Santa Katerina, so they went there – and you know the rest."

Alice shivered. It was horrifying to think that someone had been watching her all that time. Watching and waiting for an opportunity to kill her.

"So the two men then followed me to Villanova?"

"Yes," Enrique confirmed. "When they realised they'd killed the wrong woman, they found out where you'd gone, and followed you. Since they wanted to collect their final payment, they had to complete the job."

"But how did they know they'd killed the wrong person?"

Enrique sighed. "When they ransacked Patricia's rucksack for cash and valuables, and discovered that all her documentation – other than the passport – were in her name, they realised their mistake. So they removed anything that identified Patricia, so that the body would be identified as yours, Alice – and they would get paid. In the meantime, they intended to find you and kill you, so that there would be no repercussions for them when the mix-up was discovered. Then they rang the hostel and asked where 'Patricia' had gone.' Then they followed you to Villanova."

"So those two men who called to the hotel were the killers."

"Yes, my love – I'm afraid so. But luckily for you, the receptionist told them you'd left Villanova – since you'd cancelled your booking at the hotel shortly before – and they set off for the next hostel you'd booked, several hundred miles away."

Alice shivered. "So they'd been dossing at the Senora's house, waiting for me to arrive in Villanova, so that they could kill me."

She knew by Enrique's silence that she was right.

"And it's thanks to the receptionist at the hotel that they didn't manage to kill me."

"Yes," said Enrique. "When all this is over, and you are safely back with me, we will send a great big bouquet of flowers to that woman."

"But then the killers came back to Villanova," Alice added.

"Yes — when they realised you'd cancelled your hostel booking in the next town, they went back again to the Senora's house — that obviously explains the light you saw after she'd died."

"So that means that when they camped there the first time, the poor woman was living in the house!" said Alice, appalled. "No wonder she was frightened when I found her. The stress must have brought on the heart attack that killed her."

"The killers have told us that they thought the house was empty — as you did too, Alice, when you first went there. Since the old woman lived frugally, and only in the small attic room of the house, there was little to indicate that anyone was occupying it."

"Senora Delgado spoke to me about being frightened of 'them', and that they would kill her too. I hope they didn't imprison her?"

"I think the Senora remained hidden in her attic room, because the men claim they never saw her," Enrique replied. "They said they sometimes heard noises, and thought the house was haunted. That is why your photograph was on the mantelpiece — one of the men put it down there. They heard a noise and ran, thinking the house was haunted, then forgot to go back for it."

Alice smiled. It seemed amazing that two hard-bitten hit-men would even believe in ghosts!

"The Senora must have discovered the photo," Enrique added, "and when you turned up at her house, she recognised you immediately. Assuming she'd already overheard the men talking about having killed the wrong woman, and going in search of you, that would explain the things she said to you."

"How stressful her last days must have been," said Alice sadly.

"At least you were there to comfort her as she died," said Enrique kindly.

Alice sighed. She wanted to believe that her presence had helped the old woman, but she suspected her arrival had actually caused the Senora to become more agitated.

"So what else do we know, Enrique? The killers then came back to Villanova, made a bogus call to the presbytery to get Ricardo out of the way, not realising that you were staying there, right?"

"Yes, my love."

"And you saved my life."

"Well, the goat and I together," said Enrique, and Alice knew he was smiling.

"But I still don't understand how they found me in the first place!" said Alice, bewildered.

"It was not difficult, Alice," Enrique told her. "When you stayed at each hostel, you booked ahead for the next one, right? All our villains had to do was chat up the receptionist, or maybe offer a little bribe. We now know now they posed as your Argentine cousins, or friends, who were anxious to contact you."

Alice was shocked. How easy it was to track down an unsuspecting quarry!

"You booked ahead for the village hotel in Villanova, too, yes?" said Enrique. "People in small towns and villages gossip, Alice. It is the life-blood of these places, since nothing else ever happens there. So people in the town would have known that you went to stay at the presbytery. Meaning no harm, they would probably have gossiped about it to someone else – maybe even to the two men, if they called to any of the local shops, or to the hotel itself."

"But the photo of me from Bill's office – how did that end up in Senora Delgado's house?"

"The killers have admitted they were given the photo by their Argentine contact, so that they could identify you. But we still do not know if your husband gave it willingly, or if it was stolen from his office. Hopefully, this e-mail address you have given me will provide us with more information."

"So it's still possible that Bill is the murderer?"

"I'm sorry, Alice – but yes, it is still possible."

"But it won't be long before we know for certain."

"True. Cheer up, Alice," said Enrique when she didn't reply. "Soon, like a stack of dominoes, they will all begin to fall, one by one . . ."

* * *

Within half an hour, Enrique was back with information on the Argentine e-mail address.

"My lovely Alice, the news is not good. It was bought from a domain registration company in Buenos Aires, but when we checked with them, we discovered that it had been paid for in cash, by someone who gave a false address." He sighed. "So no such person or address exists."

"So what does that mean?"

"I am not sure, but whatever deal your husband was trying to do, it has not happened. I suspect it was just a con-man who contacted him, promising your husband some kind of deal that a man in financial difficulties would be very happy with."

"So does that mean Bill is or isn't guilty?"

"We still don't know for sure. But it looks as though someone may have used your husband to get information about you."

Alice shivered. If it wasn't Bill, then who was using him to get information about her? She also wished Enrique would stop referring to Bill as her husband. As far as she was concerned, he wasn't her husband any more. Maybe Enrique was doing it to provoke a reaction from her – perhaps he needed confirmation that Bill wouldn't be her husband for much longer.

As though he read her mind, Enrique suddenly said: "And you, Alice? Are you glad to be back in Ireland?"

Even though he was several thousand miles away, Alice could detect the anxiety in his voice. She smiled to herself, knowing that he needed reassurance. "It's great to see my mother and Isobel," she told him. "I've told them about you, and they're looking forward to meeting you. But I can't wait to get back to you, Enrique."

She could hear his relieved sigh across the miles.

CHAPTER 60

The doorbell rang at Alice's mother's house, and by arrangement Alice quickly tiptoed upstairs before Joan opened the front door. Of necessity, Alice had been posing as a distant cousin in front of the neighbours, but there was no need for any other callers to see her at all.

From the safety of her bedroom, Alice peeped out the window, and realised that the car parked outside was Bill's! She was shocked, although she shouldn't really be surprised. There was no reason why he shouldn't call to see the bereaved mother of his late wife. It was a thoughtful gesture that she wouldn't have expected of Bill, but then, she hadn't been thinking kindly of him for quite some time.

Tiptoeing onto the landing, Alice listened to the conversation taking place in the hall below. She hoped that her mother would be able to hold her nerve and deal with this unexpected visit without becoming too flustered. She also hoped that Joan would take Bill into the kitchen rather than the drawing room, since from her vantage point on the stairs, she could overhear things a lot easier from there.

Good, her mother was taking Bill into the kitchen. Alice craned to hear as much as possible, and she heard her mother putting on the kettle to make tea.

Bill cleared his throat. "Eh, the probate on Alice's inheritance has just been completed, Joan – the solicitor contacted me yesterday."

"So you're a rich man," said Joan tartly.

"Well, that's what I want to talk to you about," said Bill. "It's a lot of money, and it was rightly Alice's. So I have a proposal to make – with your help, I think we should set up an animal charity in her memory. Alice was very upset when I made money from a golf course that killed off some rare toads. I feel it would be the right thing to do."

"That's very thoughtful of you, Bill," said Joan, still shocked at his arrival, and unsure of how to handle the situation. She hesitated before she spoke again. "I assumed you'd be using the money to get yourself out of debt. Alice told me that your business was in trouble."

"I'd never touch Alice's money," Bill replied, looking sad. "Even though I know it's now technically mine, since we each willed everything to the other. But it would feel wrong to use it, especially since Alice made it clear that she didn't want me to have it." He tried to smile. "Anyway, things are a lot better now. I've restructured the loans, and I had a bit of luck with another smaller project that's paid off handsomely."

Joan said nothing, then Alice heard the clinking of cups and surmised that the tea had been poured out.

"Here's the probate cheque," said Bill. "I'd like you to mind it, Joan, until we decide what to do with it."

"Oh – thank you, Bill."

He bit his lip. "In some peculiar way, I wanted to prove

to Alice that I could sort things out without using her money – even though she's not around any more. After all, if I hadn't got myself into a financial mess, she might never have gone to Argentina and been killed. I'll never forgive myself for that."

Joan and Bill hugged each other in a gesture of support and comfort, and Alice's mother was still in a state of shock as Bill indicated his intention to leave.

"Are you managing all right, Joan?" he asked kindly, "I'm sure, like me, you miss her terribly."

Joan nodded, not trusting herself to speak.

"I'll be in touch," said Bill, and Alice heard the front door being opened.

Then, after the door closed, she heard Bill start his car and drive away.

Alice sat rigidly in a state of shock. The main reason for her trip to Dublin, the main reason for her disguise had just disintegrated. It was now patently obvious that Bill wasn't the killer – he hadn't wanted her money after all!

Alice left the bedroom and walked down the stairs like an automaton. No doubt Joan was as shocked as she was, and equally relieved that Bill was no longer a suspect. It was time to put the kettle on again! Then she would ring Enrique ...

Then, just as suddenly, Alice's relief was replaced by a feeling of nausea. If it wasn't Bill who wanted to kill her, then who was it?

* * *

Alice wasted no time in getting on the phone to Enrique, almost hysterical as she related what had happened. She was relieved that Bill was innocent, and felt guilty that she'd thought so badly of him for so long. She could tell that Enrique was stunned too, since much of the case so far had been built on an assumption of Bill's guilt.

"So what do we do now, Enrique? Can I stop posing as Conchita, and start being Alice again?"

"No – definitely not!" Enrique warned her. "Not until we know who the killer is. You could still be in danger, my love, and don't forget that you have travelled to Ireland on Patricia's passport. But now we must widen the net – can you think of anyone else to whom you might be a threat? What about your work as a journalist – were you working on any stories that might have upset anyone?"

Suddenly, Alice felt weak at the knees. Oh my God – the research document she'd been sent in the post – the one she hadn't yet got round to studying, but which looked decidedly interesting. Could it be valuable enough to kill for? Could someone at BWF Pharmaceuticals know that she'd received it?

"I – yes, it's very possible, Enrique."

Briefly, she told him about the letter and document she'd received in the post shortly before leaving for Argentina.

"I need to contact the woman who sent it to me," she told Enrique. "Maybe she can tell me where she got it, and why she's only sending it to me now – thirty years after it was written."

"A thirty-year-old document doesn't sound like something worth killing for," said Enrique dubiously. "Anyway, how would anyone at the company know that you'd received it?"

"I don't know," said Alice, "but that's what I aim to find

out. There's also something else I can do, Enrique — now that we know Bill is innocent, and the trail in Argentina has gone cold, I can talk to Bill and ask him if someone with some connection to Argentina did visit his office and could have taken the photo of me. After I've told him who I am, that is."

"Good idea, my lovely Alice," said Enrique approvingly, "but can you depend on him to keep the secret of your identity?"

"Yes," said Alice. "I may not love him any more, Enrique, but I do trust him."

Then she remembered that, only hours earlier, she hadn't trusted him at all.

"If your husband can provide any useful information about such a contact, let me know immediately. I will speak to the Irish police and explain the situation. Then it will be up to them to find the contact, assuming he is still in Ireland. Then the next step will be to get this man-in-the-middle to divulge the name of the person who actually ordered the hit."

Hearing about the likely involvement of the Gardaí, Alice was worried.

But Enrique had heard her sharp intake of breath. "Don't worry, my lovely Admiral," he told her. "There is no need for them to know about your incognito trip to Ireland. That little piece of information we will keep to ourselves." He paused. "The sooner this case is closed, the sooner you will come back to me."

Alice smiled happily. She, too, needed to know that Enrique was missing her.

CHAPTER 61

"Caroline!"

Rushing towards her through the evening rush-hour commuters in Euston Station, Simon scooped her up in his arms and swung her around. All around them, people hurried by, but they were both oblivious to anyone else.

"Simon – oh, it's wonderful to see you again!"

"Did you have a pleasant journey?" Simon enquired, as he steered her and her luggage deftly though the crowds and over to the escalator leading down to the underground trains.

"Yes, fine thanks," Caroline replied, remembering how she'd spent the last hour on the train in one of the tiny toilet cubicles, perfecting her hair and make-up so that she'd look casual but glamorous when she arrived. With typical insecurity, she'd changed her hairstyle several times, first tying it up in a ponytail, then deciding it might look better down. Then she'd decided that no, it looked better up, and she'd keep the loose hairstyle for later that evening, since it might make her look more sexy . . .

Yet when she'd arrived in Euston, Simon had bounded

up to her like a puppy, neither noticing what she was wearing nor what hairstyle she was sporting, so she needn't have bothered. He was just thrilled to see her, and she to see him. They were like two school kids, kissing and hugging as they stood beside each other on the escalator, much to the annoyance of commuters trying to get past them.

On the underground train that took them to Caroline's hotel, they sat holding hands, unable to talk much because of the noise of the speeding train, but both longing to throw their arms around each other. Caroline grinned to herself. She couldn't wait to get into her hotel room, because she knew exactly what would happen as soon as she and Simon closed the door . . .

Once inside her hotel room, she and Simon looked at each other, then melted into each other's arms. Within seconds, all their clothes had been discarded on the floor, and they were frantically making love on the large double bed.

"Oh Caroline, my beautiful Caroline, I've been counting the days!" Simon groaned, as he planted kisses all over her body.

"Oh God, Simon – no man has ever made me feel like this!" Caroline whispered, arching her back as her body thrilled to his touch.

At first they made love frantically, then later with tenderness. They just couldn't get enough of each other. Finally, they lay sated, their arms still wrapped around each other, as though unable to let go, even for a minute.

"Do we have to go out?" Caroline asked sleepily, when they eventually woke up some hours later.

Simon smiled languidly at her as he checked his watch. "Well, if we don't, we'll miss a reservation at one of London's best restaurants! I had to fight for this booking, so I won't ever dare show my face there again!"

"Oh well, all right," said Caroline in mock annoyance, as she threw a pillow at him. But nothing could alter her happy mood. No doubt they'd be back in the room after their meal, and they'd be making love once again . . .

After a leisurely shower together, they dressed for their evening out. This time, Caroline was wearing a pretty dress she'd bought in a sale in Dublin during the week. It was frothy and elegant, and she felt great in it. In the bathroom, she giggled to herself as she applied fresh make-up. She'd only be in the dress for an hour or two, then hopefully Simon would be removing it again!

Of necessity, Simon was wearing the same clothes as before. "I wish I'd hung up these trousers before I jumped into bed," he chuckled. "They're rather creased now."

"Well, if you hadn't been so hot under the collar, you could have," Caroline reasoned, smiling slyly at him.

"It wasn't just under my collar that was hot," he grumbled amiably, "what chance did I have with a she-devil like you around?" He pulled her close to him again. "In fact, you can rumple my clothes any time you like, my dear Caroline –"

As she felt his manhood prepare for more lovemaking, Caroline pointed to her watch. "You stand to lose your reputation as a *bon viveur* if we don't get moving," she told him, smiling.

"Oh all right then, I'll go – on condition that I can make love to you again later . . ."

"I'd be very annoyed if you didn't," said Caroline coquettishly. "Now let's get out of here before I change my mind and ravage you myself instead!"

"Oh yes, please!" murmured Simon, but he followed her meekly out of the room.

The restaurant was as delightful as Simon had claimed it would be, and Caroline wondered joyfully if life with Simon would always be this much fun. She truly believed so. They shared a similar sense of humour, and their bodies made beautiful music together. He was an educated, generous man, and he loved animals too.

"By the way, how are Anne and Derek?" she asked.

Simon looked momentarily shocked, then his brow cleared. "Oh, you mean the two cats! They're fine, thanks."

Pleasant background music was being played by a trio in the corner, giving the place real continental appeal. Every table was full, and waiters bustled about cheerfully. Service was quick and efficient, the wine list offered superb value for money, and before long Simon and Caroline were tucking into their delicious main courses.

"Hmmm – this place is great!" Caroline told him, in between mouthfuls.

Throughout the meal, they traded information on their families, their interests and hobbies, their hopes and aspirations. They found more and more in common as they talked, and as the evening progressed, Caroline was even more convinced – if such convincing was needed – that she and Simon had a viable future together. Which would mean eventually moving to London, she conceded, but that would simply mean she'd end up back where her life had started! She knew that she was counting her chickens before they were hatched, but all her instincts were telling her that Simon could be the man for her. And judging by his ardour, he felt pretty much the same as she did.

But with the eventual introduction of the topic of Gina, Simon's mood seemed to change.

Perhaps, Caroline reasoned, I'm boring him with all this talk about my aunt. Ken wasn't happy about my search either, so maybe it's not the best time to discuss finding her. Simon had already been extremely helpful, and maybe he felt that he'd already done enough.

Quickly, she changed the subject, and began telling him about Liz's husband's recent mountaineering trip to Kerry. But Simon seemed to be only half-listening, and Caroline's voice trailed off when she noticed him staring vacantly into space.

"Is there something the matter, Simon?" she asked at last.

Simon grimaced, and put down his fork. "Look, I've got a confession to make. I should have told you ages ago, but I just didn't have the courage. I loved seeing you so happy – I didn't want to tell you anything that might spoil it."

Caroline's heart almost stopped beating.

"I'm sorry, but I can't keep this from you any longer," he added, looking contrite. "I just wish it didn't have to end like this."

A lump stuck in Caroline's throat, and momentarily she couldn't speak as her world began to disintegrate. Suddenly, with blinding clarity, she realised why Simon hadn't taken her to his apartment. He couldn't, because he lived there with another woman! The beautiful wife and perfect baby loomed on the horizon once again. So he'd been toying with her all along, making love to her, making her fall in love with him . . .

Simon couldn't even look at her. "I know you were hoping for something more, and I'm sorry that I can't give it to you. I don't quite know how to say this, but –"

Caroline jumped up, nearly spilling her glass of wine. "It's all right, Simon – please don't say anything more."

"Look, I know you're bound to be upset –"

"I think 'upset' is an understatement, Simon," she said coldly. "But please don't say another word. Now I'm leaving, and going back to the hotel."

"Caroline! Please let me explain – there's no point in taking this attitude – I just thought you should know the truth –"

"Goodnight, Simon, and goodbye."

"What? Oh, for God's sake, Caroline, don't be so childish about it! You must have known there was always the possibility that things wouldn't work out . . ."

But Caroline no longer heard his words. She was already out the door of the restaurant, nearly colliding with a waiter on her way out, and hailing a passing taxi. She was in the taxi and on her way back to the hotel by the time Simon had paid the bill and hurried out of the restaurant onto the street.

In the back of the taxi, Caroline seethed. Getting his apartment painted, indeed! How could she have been so gullible? What a fool she'd been – a silly, stupid, romantic fool! Why hadn't she read the signs right? Once again, she'd allowed her heart to rule her head. She'd met an attractive man, and immediately read more into his flirting than had really been there. In retrospect, she realised with toe-curling embarrassment that she'd almost thrown herself at him on their first date – what opportunist male could be blamed for taking advantage of what was so freely on offer?

Then she remembered how easily he'd taken her in with his supposed love of animals. Two cats indeed! Anne and Derek were probably the names of his wife and son. He'd probably slipped up and said something he'd regretted, so he'd quickly covered up by pretending to have two cats, and she'd fallen for it.

Then, she realised guiltily, she'd been just as duplicitous as Simon! She hadn't told him about Ken, and she was still stringing Ken along unfairly. Suddenly she remembered guiltily the times when Ken had phoned her mother's house in Blackrock, and she'd got her mother to tell him she wasn't there. And when he'd phoned her mobile and his name had appeared, she'd cut the connection. She knew she was being totally unfair to him, but she didn't feel able to see him while she was seeing Simon. She'd wanted to see if her relationship with Simon was going to develop further before she told Ken they were finished.

Well, now that Simon had let her down, she wasn't sure what she was going to do. She felt totally confused, and shocked that she could have read Simon so wrongly. She'd been sure he cared about her! That just showed how unreliable her own judgement was. Maybe, because she and Ken had been together for so long, she'd never needed to develop that sixth sense that warned of approaching predatory males. Well, it proved one thing to her – she wasn't ready for marriage to *anyone*. Just as soon as she got back to Dublin, she'd tell Ken that the wedding was off.

Back at the hotel, Caroline quickly collected her key from the reception desk and headed upstairs to her room. To think that she'd expected to be bringing Simon back here tonight! No doubt by now, he was on his way home to his wife, where he'd explain to her that his 'business trip' had been cancelled, or he'd amend the yarn he'd already concocted to explain his absence.

Once inside her room, Caroline was able to let her guard down at last, and she burst into tears. Everything in her life was a mess! Quickly, she stripped off her clothes and got ready for bed. Although it was still quite early, she felt exhausted from the emotional upheaval of parting from Simon. Angrily, she threw her fancy undies into the bin in the bathroom. She'd never need *those* again!

Determinedly, Caroline wiped away her tears. Maybe the answer was to marry someone ordinary and boring like Liz's husband Ronnie. Caroline had never understood what her glamorous cousin saw in such a weedy little man, but maybe it was better to avoid the highs and lows of emotion, and settle for someone who'd never cause you heartache, because you'd never care enough. But, a little voice whispered, you'd never experience the highs either.

The phone rang, but Caroline ignored it, turning up the television even louder. She was going to have a cosy night in, sitting up in bed in her pyjamas, and maybe she'd even raid the mini-bar in her room.

After several double vodkas, Caroline fell into a deep sleep.

CHAPTER 62

Immediately after her talk with Enrique, Alice went straight to her briefcase, retrieving the document she'd received in the post at the *Daily News* before she'd left for Argentina. She remembered thinking it looked promising at the time, but she hadn't given it more than a cursory glance. With so many other things going on in her life – like Bill's debts and her subsequent escape to Argentina – she just hadn't got around to reading it. Now she was beginning to think that it might hold the key to everything that had happened so far.

Quickly she reread the covering letter that accompanied it. It was just a handwritten note from someone called Caroline Leyden, who claimed that she'd recently found the document in an old suitcase belonging to her aunt. The writer apologised for taking up Alice's time should the document prove of no use, but concluded that since Alice was an investigative journalist, it was more likely to be of benefit to her than anyone else. Alice was pleased to note that there was an address and phone number on the letter as well.

Now she turned her attention to the document itself. It

was old, dated thirty years earlier, and had been written by a research scientist, Dr Owen Brady, assisted by laboratory technician Gina Kiernan. Since it had been written in the days before computers, it had been typed on a typewriter, and its subject matter was the clinical trials being carried out on a vaccine against TB and a variety of respiratory illnesses. The Irish trials were being conducted by BWF Pharmaceuticals, then a small Irish company, on behalf a multinational drug company.

Wading through the report, Alice realised that what she was reading was explosive. The proposed vaccine had, according to Medical Director Dr Brady, failed in its first and second Irish trials, resulting in adverse effects and the hospitalisation of several patients taking part. Dr Brady believed that the problem lay in the use of a preservative, a known neurotoxin, which could easily be replaced by a safer, but more expensive, preservative, or by none at all. Dr Brady's document proposed the immediate cessation of the trials, the withdrawal of the present preservative from the vaccine, and its substitution by a safer preservative, prior to new trials being conducted.

Alice sat back and rubbed her eyes. Presumably this document had never made it into the public domain. On the other hand, maybe the product had been withdrawn, in which case there was no story, and no case to answer. Therefore her next job was to find out if the vaccine had ever been licensed, and if so, where it was on sale and whether or not there had been any casualties. And where was Dr Brady today? And what about the woman also named on the document, Gina Kiernan?

But before she did anything else, Alice decided that she

needed to talk to the woman who had sent her the document in the first place. Isobel would have to arrange it, and they would have to hope that this Caroline Leyden could be trusted to preserve Alice's anonymity. In fact, Alice's anonymity was ideal for covering a story like this, where money and lives were clearly at stake. She could dig away in peace without fearing for her life.

Alice stood up and stretched. It was time for a cuppa. It had just dawned on her that none of the attempts on her life had happened until after she'd received the document. Could someone else apart from the sender know that she'd received it, and want to silence her before she could write up the story? There undoubtedly was a story – one that seemed to have all the ingredients of criminal negligence, dangerous cost cutting and endangerment of life. Not to mention Patricia's murder, if someone from the company was genuinely out to silence her.

But if the product was defective, thousands of people could have been harmed over the previous thirty years. So why hadn't there been an outcry? How had BWF Pharmaceuticals and its multinational partner got away with it?

Alice sighed. She felt sure she already knew the answer. Since the product was listed for distribution mainly in the developing world, it wouldn't be subject to the same scrutiny that it would face in Europe or the US. There would be few controls, no monitoring, and corrupt governments would pocket backhanders for turning a blind eye to any problems that might occur. On the other hand, there had occasionally been scandals in the industry involving first world countries too. It seemed that greed and arrogance were major factors in big business everywhere.

Flicking through her personal phone book, Alice found the number of an elderly journalist at the *Irish Journal*, who used to write science and medical features, and might have known about the drug trials at the time. Of course she'd have to pretend she was someone else!

"Hi, Tim, my name is Margaret O'Brien she lied, altering the pitch of her voice slightly. "I'm a journalist with the *Regional News*. I'm wondering if you might remember a research scientist, Owen Brady, who worked for BWF Pharmaceuticals thirty years ago . . ."

The journalist thought for a minute. "Hmmm – let me think – he died in 1978, in a car accident, didn't he? Car went into the river, if I remember correctly – there was a rumour going round at the time that his death wasn't entirely straightforward – apparently the brake fluid reservoir in the car was empty when they hauled it out of the water, but it was never proved conclusively. I heard that from one of the cops working on the case."

Alice felt her heart beating rapidly. She was definitely on the scent of a big story.

"He was conducting trials on a new vaccine against TB and respiratory illnesses at the time," Alice prompted. "Have you any idea if it was ever licensed?"

"I'd have to look that up. Give me your number and I'll call you back."

"I'll give you my mobile number," Alice improvised quickly. "I'm not working from the office at the moment."

She gave Tim her number, and he promised to call back within the next day or so. Alice hoped Tim wouldn't check back with the *Regional News*, but hopefully her story had been convincing enough.

LINDA KAVANAGH

The following day, true to his word, the elderly journalist rang back.

"Hello, Margaret. I rang a colleague at another newspaper, who used to be a medical correspondent in the 70s," he told her. "He's always kept extensive files, and he tells me that vaccine you asked about was licensed for worldwide use shortly after Dr Brady's death." He paused, and Alice could hear him rifling through his notes. "Apparently my colleague heard on the grapevine at the time that Dr Brady wasn't happy with the product, and he was insisting on the vaccine being scrapped. But after his death and the appointment of a new head honcho of research, the product passed its Irish trials with flying colours. Since then, it's been licensed for use worldwide, but is mostly sold in Africa, and is still being manufactured."

Alice nodded to herself. She wasn't surprised at what she was hearing.

"Do you know if anyone's ever had a problem with the vaccine? Have any doctors in Africa complained?"

"As a matter of fact, there have been rumblings over the years from doctors who are unhappy with its effects. Some have claimed it causes deaths, others have said it causes neurological disorders, particularly in children, but the African governments have always backed the pharmaceutical company – probably got large back-handers to keep them sweet. Of course, the spread of AIDS has been a handy illness to blame for lots of things, including unexplained deaths."

"Wow," said Alice. At last she was getting somewhere.

"Do I detect a hint of a story?" Tim asked hopefully.

Alice laughed. "Not at the moment," she told him, "but I promise to let you in on it if it happens. After we've got the exclusive, of course."

406

Tim chuckled.

Thanking him for his help, Alice rang off.

Lifting the phone again, she rang Isobel. "Izzy, would you mind trying to contact this woman, Caroline Leyden? I need to find out what she knows about this document and how she got it."

"No problem. When do you want to meet her?"

"As soon as possible."

CHAPTER 63

Caroline awoke with a hangover, and the sound of the telephone ringing in her ears. For a moment, she couldn't remember where she was. Then she realised she was alone in a London hotel, Simon having more or less admitted that he was married, and only having a fling with her. She groaned and turned over, trying to ignore the telephone, but it kept on ringing insistently. Then she heard knocking on the door outside and, fearing it was Simon, she snuggled deeper down in the bed and tried to ignore the knocking and the ringing.

However, it was the maid and when she got no reply she obviously assumed the room was empty, so she and her cleaning trolley trundled in the door of Caroline's room. Seeing Caroline still in bed, she was profuse in her apologies, but an annoyed Caroline reluctantly conceded that it was pointless to try and sleep. She might as well get up, and get on with her Simon-less life.

Today, she decided, she needed to keep herself occupied, so that she could forget all about Simon. But it wasn't easy. He was constantly in her thoughts, try as she might to banish him. Briefly, she recalled the night before – how dare he think she'd go out with a married man!

After taking a quick shower, she felt that it would be sensible to get out of the hotel as quickly as possible, just in case Simon decided to call round in the hopes of persuading her to reconsider. Caroline fumed. Reconsider what? That she'd accept being his bit-on-the-side? She'd never willingly go out with a married man! Did he really think that she'd accept the crumbs from his table, rather than have the whole cake? She sighed. On the other hand, maybe he was happy to settle for a night or two with his conquests, before moving on to the next one. Yet it was still difficult to forget his infectious chuckle, the lock of dark hair that kept falling over his left eye, and the look of genuine happiness on his face as he'd bounded up to her in Euston station.

Grabbing her bag, Caroline left the hotel, relieved to see that Simon wasn't waiting in the foyer. But she also felt a dart of disappointment – had she meant so little to him that he wasn't even making any attempt to see her again?

Determinedly she walked towards the underground station. Maybe she'd go shopping first, and buy some clothes for her new life. The new life she was going to have without any men in it. She'd devote herself to her career from now on, and she'd work hard for promotion. And she'd spend more time with her women friends. And maybe take up hockey again, or even golf.

Suddenly her mobile phone rang. Suspiciously she looked at the caller ID – it wasn't a number she recognised. But could it be Simon, using someone else's phone in order to get her to answer? She wasn't going to bother answering, then she reconsidered. In this new life of hers, she'd decided to seize every opportunity that presented itself. Who knows what opportunity she could be missing if she didn't answer this call?

"Hello?"

"Oh, hi. Is that Caroline Leyden?" asked a woman's voice.

Caroline froze. It could be Simon's wife, about to chew her ear off for daring to seduce her husband. Then common sense asserted itself again, and Caroline realised that the accent was Irish. Of course, there was no reason why Simon couldn't have an Irish wife. It was obvious that he had a thing for Irishwomen . . .

"Yes, this is Caroline."

The voice at the other end hesitated. "My name is Isobel Dunne. I'm a photographer with the *Daily News*. Do you think we could arrange to meet?"

Caroline was amazed. "What for? You want to take a photograph of me for the newspaper?"

Isobel laughed. "No, I'm afraid not. Although I'm sure you're well worth photographing. But on this occasion, I need to talk to you about something else."

Then Caroline remembered the research paper she'd sent to poor Alice Fitzsimons, the reporter who'd been killed in Argentina.

"Is it about the research paper I posted to your late colleague?" Caroline asked.

"Eh, yes."

Caroline was intrigued. She'd assumed that since the journalist was now dead, any post that came for her would have been thrown away. Then it occurred to her that any stories Alice Fitzsimons had been working on might be passed to other colleagues.

"I'm in London at the moment, but I'll be back in Dublin on Sunday night," she said. "When do you want to meet?"

"The sooner the better, if you don't mind. Would Sunday night be okay?"

"Yes, that's fine. Where do you want to meet?"

The two women arranged to meet in a city-centre pub, and after describing each other's hair colour and height, Caroline rang off, still intrigued. What on earth could this Isobel Dunne want? Clearly, she wasn't the one writing up the story – if there was any story to be written – since she was a photographer, not a writer. Still, meeting her would be a bit of a diversion. It would occupy her evening and take her mind off Simon for a while.

Caroline was also dreading her confrontation with Ken. And the inevitable fall-out that would result from the end of her engagement. She and Ken had been an item for so long that her relationships with everyone else she knew would change as well.

Suddenly, she was actually frightened of what lay ahead. She dreaded hurting Ken, and she hated disappointing all the people who had been destined to play roles at her wedding. Hazel and Liz had been lined up as bridesmaids, and her mother had already chosen her mother-of-the-bride hat and dress. Even Aunt Dolly and Charles Keane had indicated that they'd be attending, and her mother had informed her that Dolly was going to buy a new outfit this very week.

Caroline sighed. The sooner she got back to Dublin and faced the music, the better. Initially, the cancellation of the wedding would be a nine-day wonder, but hopefully something else would soon replace it, and she could get on with her new life.

However, she had one more night to spend in London, since she was booked into the hotel for two nights, and her train and boat trip back to Dublin was only valid for travel on Sunday.

Well, she intended making the most of her day. Originally, she'd intended spending it with Simon, but since he was probably spending it with his wife and child now, she'd go shopping. Then she'd have her evening meal in the hotel restaurant, and have an early night, in preparation for her train and boat journey the following day.

Yet when she reached her favourite shopping area around Oxford Street, Caroline found that she just didn't have the heart to buy anything. Instead, she wandered around aimlessly, looking in shop windows and occasionally venturing inside, but by the afternoon, she conceded defeat and went into a café for a cup of coffee and a bun before heading back to the hotel. What a waste of a weekend, she thought. To think that I was prepared to uproot myself, leave my job in Dublin and settle over here – all because of some lying, cheating man!

No doubt Liz and Hazel would be wearing their smug I-told-you-so expressions when she told them what happened with Simon. *If* she told them. Maybe she wouldn't bother. She'd invent some story in which she was the brave heroine who'd ended the relationship. She'd tell them that Simon had turned out to be a total bore, or he snored too loudly. Of course, both women would be scrutinising her closely as she told them, so she'd have to tell her story with conviction. If she went over it often enough in her own head, she might even convince herself that it was true.

Back at the hotel, Caroline opted for room service

rather than sit alone in the restaurant, where she'd probably be surrounded by loving couples, making her feel even more lonely than she was. As she chewed a club sandwich without tasting it, she was overwhelmed by sadness. This should have been her second night with Simon, but instead she was spending it alone in her room, then going back to Dublin with her tail between her legs. Well, she'd learnt a lot about herself this weekend, and maybe they were lessons she needed to learn. She now knew that she wasn't going to marry anyone in October. As soon as she got home, she'd inform Ken of her decision first, then her family and friends. The sooner everyone knew, the better. Maybe, at some future date, she and Ken might have a future together, but it certainly wasn't now.

Having packed her travel bag in readiness for the morning, Caroline climbed into bed and set the alarm on her watch. It was ridiculously early to be going to bed, but she was at a loss for anything more interesting to do. No doubt the bar downstairs was heaving, and the restaurant packed with happy couples dining. Never had she felt so alone. She needed to get a life – and fast!

Snuggling down in her bed, Caroline turned out the light. At least she had the intriguing meeting with Isobel Dunne to look forward to.

CHAPTER 64

Caroline had just settled down at the bar and ordered a vodka when she was approached by a small sandy-haired woman.

"Hello, are you Caroline? I'm Isobel."

As the two woman shook hands, Caroline signalled to the barman, who quickly added Isobel's tipple of choice – a whiskey – to her order. Then the two women took their drinks to a more isolated area of the pub.

"I must admit, I'm intrigued," said Caroline, as they sat down. "I have absolutely no idea why you'd want to meet me. By the way, I'm sorry about the death of your colleague – what bad luck to be killed on holiday!"

"Well, yes," said Isobel, clearly uncomfortable.

"So why are we meeting?"

"Well, you sent Alice a document – a research paper about a vaccine that was being tested thirty years ago – can you tell me how you came by it?"

Briefly, Caroline explained how she had uncovered the document during her search for her missing aunt. "I wasn't really sure what to do with it," she confirmed, "but since Alice Fitzsimons sometimes investigated companies, I thought it might be of interest to her. I only glanced at it myself, but even though it was old, it seemed to have some hard-hitting things to say."

"Yes," said Isobel. She seemed on the verge of saying something, but then stayed silent.

"So – is the paper of interest to some other journalist?" Caroline prompted. So far, there seemed no reason why she needed to be here.

"Yes, it could be," Isobel replied.

Caroline felt uncomfortable under Isobel's obvious scrutiny. "Look, I get the impression that you're trying to size me up," she said, at last. "Am I on trial for something?"

Isobel grinned, and the tense atmosphere was dispelled. "Can you keep a secret?" she asked, her expression now serious again. "This is no idle question, Caroline – if you're one of those people who just *has* to tell her friends or family everything, please tell me now."

Caroline was surprised at Isobel's tone, and at the unusual question, so she gave it the deliberation it deserved. "Well," she said at last, "I wouldn't guarantee not to tell the police if someone tried to involve me in something illegal. But if I've been trusted with a confidence, nothing would drag it out of me." Then she grinned. "Unless, of course, someone started pulling out my fingernails. I *might* give in then!"

Isobel grinned back. "That seems fair enough to me. Because I'm going to ask you to trust me. I know you don't know me –" she reached into her jacket pocket and produced her Press Card, "but take a look at this, and verify that I'm really who I say I am."

Caroline took the Press Card and studied it before handing it back. "Why would I need to be certain that you're who you say you are?"

"Because I'm going to ask you to come with me – now, if you don't mind – to Stillorgan. There's someone there who'd like to meet you."

All sorts of strange thoughts flitted through Caroline's brain. Had Ken – or even Simon – arranged to have her transported to some secret location where they'd have her undivided attention?

"You're not going to kidnap me, are you?" she asked jovially, a little worried nonetheless. "I don't have any money, and my rich aunt would let me rot before she'd pay the ransom."

Isobel shook her head. "If you're in the slightest bit worried, please don't come. But believe me, if you're the kind of woman I think you are, you'll be glad you did."

"Just answer me one thing," said Caroline. "Am I meeting a man or a woman?"

"A woman."

On the drive to Stillorgan, the two women chatted about generalities. Caroline told Isobel about her job, and about her forthcoming marriage that probably wouldn't now happen. In turn, Isobel regaled Caroline with interesting stories of her life as a photographer, and of the funny, tragic and downright boring aspects of her job.

"Alice and I have covered loads of stories together over the years," Isobel added. "There isn't a corner of this country we haven't visited, and we've travelled abroad a lot too."

"I notice that you talk about her as though she was still

alive – it must be difficult to accept that she's gone," said Caroline sympathetically. "Were you very close?"

"Best friends," said Isobel, careful not to use either the past or present tense.

At last they reached a small red-brick housing development off the Kilmacud Road. As Isobel parked her car, Caroline glanced around her. She'd never been to this part of Stillorgan before, but she liked the tree-lined avenue and the large open green space in front of the houses.

As Isobel and Caroline walked up to a house with a welcoming light over its door, Caroline wondered briefly if she should have been more cautious. She'd travelled here with a stranger, and she was now about to meet another woman she didn't know either. It was all very mysterious, and neither her family nor friends knew where she was. On the other hand, Isobel seemed like a perfectly nice woman, so hopefully everything would be okay . . .

Just then, the door opened, and Caroline was hustled inside. In the drawing room, a table was laid out with mugs, plates, a selection of sandwiches. The sight of such familiar things reassured Caroline. At least they were going to give her refreshments either before or after the interrogation!

A tall slender dark-haired woman crossed the room and grasped Caroline's hand. "Thank you so much for coming," she said. Turning to Isobel, she gave her a quick hug before the three woman sat down in the large armchairs and sofa that almost filled the room.

"And who are you?" asked Caroline, mystified.

The woman smiled. "I hope this won't come as too much of a shock, but I'm Alice Fitzsimons."

For a moment, Caroline was stunned. "But I thought — wasn't it in the newspaper? It definitely said you were —" Her voice trailed off. This was most bizarre. Surely this couldn't be true?

"Yes, I'm supposed to be dead," agreed Alice.

Quickly, she brought Caroline up to date on what had happened in Argentina, her initial fears that Bill might have tried to kill her for her inheritance, the photo that turned up in Senora Delgado's house, Patricia's tragic murder and her own return to Ireland in disguise. Caroline could hardly believe what she was hearing. She felt as though she was on the set of some cloak-and-dagger movie!

"I've already been though my husband's e-mails, and found nothing incriminating," Alice told her. "There *was* mention of a deal in Argentina, but it appears it was just a ruse to get information from Bill about my whereabouts. Enrique says —"

Caroline noticed how Alice blushed when she mentioned the name. "Who's Enrique?"

"He's the police officer who's investigating Patricia's death, and all the other things that have happened so far. He says that I have to stay incognito until we know who took out the original contract on me."

"So they haven't got anyone for Patricia's murder yet?"

Alice smiled. "Some of Enrique's officers have just picked up the two hit-men at a hospital. They tried to kill me in Villanova, but Enrique shot one of them . . ." She blushed again, although there was pride in her voice this time. "It's a long story."

Caroline smiled to herself. It looked as though she

wasn't the only woman present who had a complicated love life!

"Anyway, the two hit-men have been prepared to barter information about the person who contracted them to do the job, in return for a shorter sentence. But that doesn't give us the name of the person who ordered the hit in the first place. It seems that I was always the target – but not for the reason I thought." Alice looked from Caroline to Isobel. "Around the same time as we discovered Bill was innocent, I started studying the research report you sent me. I immediately realised it was a time bomb that had been ticking away over the last thirty years. Over the years, I've gathered various snippets of information on BWF Pharmaceuticals and their dubious practices, but none of it was ever strong enough to do more than marginally challenge them. This document changes everything. When I read it, I realised that someone at BWF Pharmaceuticals was probably responsible for the attempts on my life."

"I don't understand," said Caroline. "Why would you suddenly assume it was BWF Pharmaceuticals?"

"None of the attacks started until after I got the research paper, so I began to wonder if someone was trying to stop me reading it and realising what was going on," Alice explained. "The next thing I had to ask myself was – how would they know that I'd got this document? That's why I asked Isobel to contact you. I was hoping you might be able to throw some light on that, Caroline. I mean, did you mention to anyone else that you were sending this to me?"

Caroline racked her brains. Since it hadn't seemed particularly top-secret to her, she remembered mentioning it to her mother. And possibly to Ken. Maybe also to Liz and Hazel. Had she mentioned it to Simon? She couldn't quite remember. She didn't *want* to remember anything about Simon . . .

Then she remembered that her mother had been having lunch with Dolly the day after she'd mentioned it to her. She particularly remembered because they'd argued that day. Caroline had been angry with her mother for continuing to collect Dolly and ferry her to and from their destination, when Dolly could well afford to take taxis. But that meant that if her mother told her older sister that day, then Aunt Dolly could have told Charles Keane at one of their regular lunch dates . . .

"Your aunt knows Charles Keane?" asked Alice in alarm when Caroline told her.

Caroline explained that Dolly had been his secretary and was still a lifelong friend, and that Dolly's late husband Owen had been the author of the research paper, and Gina Kiernan, her younger sister, had been his assistant.

"Owen died back in 1978," Caroline told her. "He was killed in a car accident."

Alice looked apprehensive. "I wonder if it really *was* an accident. I spoke to another journalist the other day, who said there was something fishy about his death."

Caroline nodded. "Funny you should say that – Maeve, an old friend of Gina's whom I met recently, said exactly the same thing. She pointed out that Own had been killed, Gina had disappeared, and we thought you'd been killed too. Each of you had some connection, however tenuous, to BWF Pharmaceuticals."

"There's a lot at stake for BWF Pharmaceuticals," Alice confirmed. "This research paper highlights the dangers of a vaccine which failed to make it through the first and second-stage Irish trials. Yet amazingly, after Owen Brady died, it sailed through the amended trials, and the product was awarded a licence the following year."

"But if it's dangerous, why hasn't there been a public outcry about it?" Caroline asked, a puzzled expression on her face.

"Because it's largely been sold in the developing world – where standards of care aren't quite so high. It *has* been the subject of several local investigations, but any injuries or neurological damage it may have caused have been conveniently attributed to other illnesses, including AIDS. But I do believe – and I doubt if I'm the only one – that this product is harming people. But there's never been any proof – up until now."

Alice looked from Caroline to Isobel. "Obviously, Owen Brady realised that it was dangerous thirty years ago, and he wrote this paper, summing up all the reasons why it should be withdrawn, but then he conveniently died in a so-called accident, and before long, the product was released onto the market. No doubt all the copies of this document were rounded up and destroyed, but somehow – mercifully – this one copy escaped. With this, I can try to prove that BWF Pharmaceuticals have known all along about the dangers."

"Wow!" said Caroline. "I hope you've made copies of that document. I didn't realise its significance when I sent it to you."

"I've made several copies," Alice confirmed. "Isobel has

one, and there are copies lodged with my mother's bank and her solicitor. So even if something happens to me, this information isn't going to go away."

In the silence that followed, the three women looked at each other. Then Alice looked in the direction of the table. "Oh dear, I meant to make some coffee, but I forgot all about it!"

"I think, in view of what you've just told me, we should be having something stronger," said Caroline.

Alice grinned back. "When it's all over, and lives have been saved, hopefully we'll all be drinking champagne!"

CHAPTER 65

When the phone in her mother's house rang the following evening, Caroline picked it up.

"Caroline," said an English accent, "you're going to have to face the truth some time."

It was Simon!

"How dare you phone me, you – you –" For once, Caroline was at a loss for words. "You cheat and liar!" she managed to say at last.

There was a moment's silence at the other end of the phone. "Caroline – what on earth are you talking about?"

"You led me on, Simon – but I don't go out with married men. I hope you, Anne and Derek will be very happy together, but please don't pretend that your wife and kid are two cats! Now go to hell!"

Caroline slammed down the phone, but it rang again almost immediately. Her first instinct was to ignore it, but she lifted the phone anyway, a little calmer this time.

"Simon, please don't bother ringing again," she said wearily.

There was a brief silence. "Caroline, it's me – Ken."

"Oh."

"Who's this Simon guy?"

"Oh, he's someone I met in London." She paused. "He's been helping me to trace my Aunt Gina."

"Then why would you be telling him not to ring again?"

Caroline hesitated, unsure of how to reply. This wasn't how she planned to end her relationship with Ken. She'd never intended hurting him by mentioning Simon at all. And since she'd never be seeing Simon again anyway, there was no point in telling Ken about him.

"Ken, it really doesn't matter," she replied, improvising quickly. "He was from one of those agencies that trace missing people, and I felt he'd overcharged me."

"Oh. Have you found your aunt yet?"

"No, but I intend to keep trying."

"Do you want me to help you? I hadn't realised how much it meant to you."

"Ken, I think you're a little too late with your offer of help," said Caroline angrily.

"Well, can I see you? I mean, we've got to discuss the wedding."

Caroline laughed harshly. "Ken, is there a brain between your two ears? Hasn't it crossed your mind that a wedding is the last thing I want to think about right now? We haven't even spoken to each other in ages – surely it must have crossed your mind that things weren't exactly great between us?"

"Look Caro, I know you're upset – and you've every right to be annoyed with me because I didn't fully appreciate how much you wanted to find your aunt. But I'll change, you know I'll do anything for you –"

"Please Ken, don't demean yourself," said Caroline sadly.

"I don't want you to change – I've no right to ask that of you. I just don't think that you and I have a future together any more."

"Oh God, Caro –"

Caroline could hear the desperation in his voice, and she longed to be able to tell him everything would be all right, but it just wasn't going to happen. Too much had changed already.

"Look, Ken – I'm sorry, but there's nothing more to be said. I'll return your ring as soon as I can, and at a later date we can decide what to do about the house."

"Please, Caro – don't do this to me! I love you so much –"

"Bye, Ken."

Gently, Caroline put the phone down. Then the enormity of what she'd done seemed to finally register with her, and she sat down on the stairs and wept.

* * *

Stella was sitting at the table in the large cosy kitchen, finishing the crossword in the daily newspaper. She looked up and smiled as Caroline entered, then her expression turned to one of concern when she saw her daughter's blotchy face.

"Caroline – what's the matter?"

Caroline took a deep breath. "Mum, I suppose I'd better tell you – Ken and I won't be getting married in October. We're finished."

Stella looked at her daughter, aghast. "But why? I mean, you and Ken have always been . . ." Her voice trailed off.

"That's the problem," said Caroline grimly. "Everyone expects Ken and me to get married, but we've been together so long that the magic isn't there any more."

"Oh my goodness – what am I going to do with my new hat?" said Stella inappropriately. "And what will Dolly say? Oh Caroline, are you absolutely sure, dear? Sometimes, when a wedding is getting near, people get the jitters."

Caroline smiled sadly. "No, Mum, it's not the jitters. The truth is, I met someone else. But that's over too, so you don't need to worry about it."

Stella said nothing for a few seconds as she processed this new information. It was, after all, something she'd never expected to happen.

"Oh Caroline!" her mother sighed at last, as though she was dealing with a recalcitrant child who'd just thrown all her toys out of the playpen. "How on earth did this happen?"

"I met a man called Simon when I was in London," Caroline explained. "He helped me when someone tried to snatch my handbag. But it was just a fling, and I won't be seeing him any more."

"I might have guessed!" Stella said, annoyed. "I always knew your search for Gina would cause nothing but problems!"

Caroline sighed, exasperated. "Mum, you should be glad I'm not going to make a mistake by marrying the wrong man."

"Oh dear," said her mother once again, fiddling with her reading glasses, "you've let this Simon fellow turn your head, and you've dumped a perfectly good man because of it!" Looking forlornly at her daughter, she struggled for the words. "Oh, Caroline, what on earth's going to become of you? Are you always going to put romance before something solid and lasting?"

"I don't know, Mum," said Caroline, "but I *do* know that 'something solid and lasting', as you call it, isn't enough for me."

* * *

Upstairs in her bedroom, Caroline could hear the phone in the hall ringing as she undressed, but there was no way she was going to answer it. The phone wasn't her friend right now – confrontational calls from both Simon and Ken had seen to that!

"Caroline!"

Caroline could hear her mother calling, but she ignored her. Instead, she turned on the shower in her ensuite. She could always plead inability to hear over the noise of the water if her mother queried her lack of response.

"Caroline!" Suddenly, her mother was at her bedroom door. "There's a man with an English accent on the phone who says his name is Simon – and he says he's going to keep phoning until you speak to him. He's threatening to come over here and sit outside your front door until you stop ignoring him."

Angrily, Caroline grabbed a towel, stormed out of her bedroom and down the stairs to the phone. Simon was being really petty by drawing her mother into the situation! She'd soon give him a piece of her mind, and tell him where to go!

"I thought you said it was just a fling?" Stella said archly from the landing, as she headed off to bed. "That man is evidently steamed up about something."

"What do you want?" Caroline barked rudely into the phone as soon as she heard her mother close her bedroom door behind her. "I told you to take a hike, Simon, and I meant it!"

"Caroline – what on earth do you mean by saying I'm a cheat and a liar? Please – you at least owe me an explanation!"

Caroline was feeling very angry and truculent. "Well, last time we met, you started telling me, in a roundabout way, that you didn't want to see me again – because you were married! Well, Simon, I'm not going to be anyone's plaything! I don't think –"

Caroline was suddenly speechless. Simon was laughing at the other end of the phone!

"Stop it, you bastard! I hate you!" she screamed, and was just about to slam the phone down again, when Simon spoke.

"Caroline, please – what did I say that made you think that I was married? I'm not – honestly!"

"You said – and I quote – that you had a confession to make . . ."

"Oh *that*! God, Caroline, you can add one-and-one and get three! Just listen to me without hanging up – please?"

Caroline gave an exaggerated sigh. "Okay. You've got two seconds."

"Well, since you won't give me time to explain things gradually, I'll have to jump in at the deep end. The body of a female was recently found here in London, when an apartment block near the docks was demolished."

Despite her anger towards Simon, Caroline's interest was piqued. "What do you mean 'found'?"

"The apartment block was built with high-alumina cement, a fast-setting product that was once hailed as a miracle in the building trade, but which is now regarded as not being strong enough. After flooding in the area a few weeks ago, the building became unstable and had to be demolished." He hesitated, playing for time, not wanting to throw everything at her at once. She needed time to get used to the idea. "They found the remains of a woman in the foundations of the building, which was built in 1978 – the year your aunt disappeared."

Caroline's hand went to her mouth. "Oh God – but why would you think that it might be Gina? I mean, why on earth would she end up buried in the foundations of a building?"

"I don't know," Simon replied sadly, "but the police do have a certain amount of information on her. This woman was aged between twenty and thirty, five feet three inches tall, and she'd recently had a baby." He sighed. "Look, I'm sorry to have to tell you this. I know how much finding your aunt means to you, and how disappointed you'd be if this body proved to be hers. *That's* what I meant when I said I'd a confession to make – I'd held off telling you this because I didn't want to upset you. You know what they say about shooting the messenger – I was afraid you'd blow me out for even considering it. And you did. You *are* rather impulsive, you know."

Caroline grinned, feeling contrite and embarrassed. "Sorry, Simon, I didn't even give you a *chance* to deliver the message!"

"It's just as much *my* fault," Simon replied. "I obviously faffed around so much that I gave you the wrong impression."

But amid the joy of realising that she'd come to the

wrong conclusion about Simon, was the fear that this new information was true. Caroline shuddered. Surely this couldn't be the end of all her hopes of finding her aunt? But she did remember trying on her aunt's wedding dress, which had only reached mid-calf length, but which had covered her aunts' feet in her wedding photographs. The difference in their heights would therefore have been about four inches, and Caroline was five feet seven inches tall . . .

"No, Simon," she said stubbornly, "it couldn't possibly be my aunt. You must be mistaken. I'm positive my aunt is out there somewhere, living happily with her child, maybe with a new husband and more children –"

Then she suddenly remembered her meeting with Alice Fitzsimons, their discussion about Owen's mysterious death, and the threat to Alice's own life. She gulped. Oh God, maybe Simon was right . . .

"I know that's what you *want* to believe," Simon said gently, "but you must admit, it would explain a lot. I've checked your aunt's documentation, and discovered that her national insurance card hasn't been used since early 1978, and she's paid no income tax since then either. Nor has there been any movement on her almost-empty savings account, which has also been dormant since 1978."

"Then she's probably in America or Australia," Caroline said stubbornly, still unwilling to let go of her dream, despite the mounting evidence.

Simon hesitated. "I'm afraid not," he said at last. "I've checked with the Passport Office in Dublin and the Irish embassy in London, and Gina never owned a passport. So she couldn't have gone abroad. I'm sorry, Caroline."

Caroline felt sick inside. If this body was Gina's, could

BWF Pharmaceuticals have some connection to her death?

"Did they find a baby with her?"

"No."

Caroline sighed with relief. "So the baby may have survived. Assuming that's the case, wouldn't there be a record of the birth at one of the maternity hospitals? Or a birth certificate for the child?"

"We can certainly try to check it out."

"So how can we find out if this woman is Gina?" asked Caroline, finally accepting that she needed to know the truth.

"The easiest way we can find out for certain is through a DNA sample. I suppose your mother, as Gina's next-of-kin, would be the ideal person to give it."

Caroline shook her head vehemently. "There's no way I'm going to tell Mum. I mean, there's no point in upsetting her if it isn't necessary."

She still didn't believe that her aunt could have met with such a violent death. Things like that happened to other people, not to *her* family.

"Well then, I suppose *you* could give a sample," said Simon. "You know, a few cells from inside your mouth. That, at least, would establish if you're related to her."

Caroline agreed reluctantly. "Okay," she said at last.

"One more thing –" said Simon, and Caroline could hear the laughter in his voice, "– my cats really *are* called Anne and Derek. You can meet them just as soon as you like. And now that my flat's been painted, you'll be staying with me in Belsize Park when you come back to London. I'm not letting you out of my sight again!"

CHAPTER 66

Caroline still found it impossible to accept that the dead woman found in London could be her aunt. And while she longed for the following weekend, when she could head back to London, she also dreaded going for the DNA test on the Monday morning before returning to Dublin.

All week, she alternated between delight and despair. Delight that she'd be seeing Simon yet again, and staying in his flat in Belsize Park this time, coupled with despair that the DNA might not produce the results she wanted. Her work colleagues commented on her erratic behaviour, and got their noses bitten off for their pains.

By mid-week, Caroline was itching to do something positive to further the search for Gina. If she did nothing, it felt like acceptance that the body was Gina's. There had to be something she could do to further the search! So on Wednesday evening, as soon as she got home from work, she dialled Larry Macken in London. Hopefully, he'd be home from work himself.

Relief flooded through her as he answered the phone. "Larry, it's Caroline. I'm sorry to bother you again – I hope you don't mind – but there's something else I need to ask you."

At the other end of the phone, Caroline could hear Larry's intake of breath.

"Go on," he said.

"I presume Gina was working somewhere before she disappeared –"

"Yes, she was working for a veterinary laboratory. She didn't particularly like it – she found the work boring and repetitious after working in research at BWF Pharmaceuticals in Dublin. But she claimed she didn't mind giving up that job so that she could come to London with me." He laughed harshly. "Then, after all the effort of moving, she disappeared on me! Doesn't make sense, does it?"

"Do you happen to remember the name of the company?"

Larry racked his brains for a minute. "Yes, I think it was called Equine & General Farm Products Ltd. It was only a few tube stations from where we had our flat – so it was somewhere around Finsbury Park."

"Did you ever contact them after Gina left?"

"Good God, no. Gina left of her own free will, and her letter made it clear that she didn't want to be with me any more. Why would I contact them?"

"No reason, I guess. I'm just wondering if they could tell me anything more about her – like, did she stay working there after she left you? Did she give them a change of address, for example?"

Larry laughed. "You're determined to find her, aren't you? Well, I wish you the best of luck. I'm curious myself

433

– you'll let me know, won't you, if you find out anything?"

"Of course."

"So – how are the wedding plans coming along?"

There was a brief silence. "I – well, to be honest, I don't think there *is* going to be a wedding, Larry."

Larry chuckled. "Oh dear – pre-wedding nerves, is it?"

Caroline grimaced. "No, it's not that. I've met someone else – and he's made me wonder if I ever knew what love was before."

Although he didn't say so, Larry suddenly thought how impulsive Caroline was – exactly like her Aunt Gina.

"Don't throw away something good for something that might just be a flash-in-the-pan," he said kindly.

Yet even as he said it, he realised that Caroline's situation was almost a mirror image – albeit thirty years later – of his own relationship with Gina. If you didn't both feel the magic, you didn't have anything. Maybe he was wrong to offer any advice – Caroline's own heart would hopefully lead her to the right answer.

"Tell me about this new guy," he asked her gently, noting the upbeat tone in her voice the moment she spoke Simon's name.

* * *

"Honestly, Caroline, I don't know what to make of your on-off-on relationship with this Simon fellow," Stella muttered, obviously dismayed at the latest turn of events.

"Everything's fine, Mum – don't worry," Caroline told her breezily. "Simon and I are now back together, and I'm going to London on Friday, and staying with him for a week."

She didn't tell her mother that she'd be giving a DNA

sample at a London police station, as well as making love every night to the gorgeous Simon . . .

"Don't you think you should take a break before you get involved with someone else?" Stella said pointedly. "You've only just finished with Ken. Oh Caroline, I really wish you'd reconsider – poor Ken is devastated."

"Mum, please stop hounding me!" said Caroline crossly. "Ken and I are finished, and that's that."

"If you're so happy about this Simon fellow, then why are you so edgy?" said Stella tartly.

Caroline took a deep breath. Her mother was right – but for the wrong reason. Caroline had to admit that she *was* edgy – but it had nothing to do with Simon. She was really worried that the body found in the London building might turn out to be her aunt. She'd pinned so many hopes on finding Gina that it would be devastating to find that her aunt had been murdered.

"I'm not edgy, Mum – just pissed off at the way you keep going on about Ken!" she said angrily. "I *do* feel bad about hurting him, but there's nothing I can do about that. Anyway, I'm sure he'll find somebody else before long."

"But you know nothing about this Simon fellow," Stella said plaintively, trying yet again to build a case for Ken. "Maybe he's a bigamist, or a child molester –"

"Mum, when you meet him, you'll realise how nice he is," Caroline said.

And it was true, Caroline suddenly thought. Simon *was* genuinely nice. As well as being gorgeous, sexy and a wonderful lover . . .

"I hope you know what you're sacrificing," Stella said darkly.

Caroline nodded. She was abandoning a safe and secure life with a man whom she could be sure would always adore her, in order to experience the heights of love and passion that might nevertheless fizzle out at some time in the future. One man represented living safely, with the future all mapped out and no surprises. The other represented the heady excitement of an intense and passionate love affair that might – or might not – last a lifetime.

As far as Caroline was concerned, there was no contest. She would go where her heart led her. Life had offered her an unexpected choice, and she was going to grasp it with both hands.

Part 4

CHAPTER 67

"Dolly, I'm pregnant," said Stella, smiling at her older sister, willing her to be pleased for her.

Dolly sniffed. "Well, I never expected to hear those words from you, Stella. How far are you gone?"

"Five months," Stella replied, aware that her sister hadn't even bothered to offer congratulations. "I haven't been feeling well for ages, but it never occurred to me that I might be expecting. It's a wonderful surprise, and Paddy and I are thrilled."

Dolly surveyed her sister's midriff. "Hrrmph! So that explains the extra weight you've been putting on."

Nasty old cow, Stella thought to herself, she can't even bring herself to say something nice to me. I suppose she's actually jealous – since Owen's now dead, she's not likely to have any children herself.

Looking at Dolly's pursed lips and disapproving expression, Stella was suddenly overwhelmed with pity for her elder sister, who seemed to derive little joy from her life.

She has money to burn, yet she hoards it like it's going out of fashion, Stella thought. On the other hand, while Paddy and I have little money, this latest news of ours has made us richer *beyond measure, and the happiest people in the world. I wouldn't swap places with Dolly for anything.*

"There's something else, Dolly," added Stella, as Dolly turned quizzically towards her.

"Oh?"

"Yes – Paddy and I are moving to London. As I'm sure you're well aware, McCarthy Brothers have recently been letting a lot of staff go. But there's plenty of work available in the building trade in London." Stella eyed her older sister. "We've no money, Dolly – so we have to go. Hopefully, we'll be able to come back in a few years, when we've saved enough to buy a place of our own."

Stella waited, hoping that her wealthy sister might offer them a lifeline. Dolly had so much money she could instantly offer to support them if she wished. But Dolly said nothing.

Angrily, Stella left the room, fearful that if she stayed, she might say something she'd regret. Although she knew that neither she nor Paddy would have accepted any help from Dolly, it would have meant a lot if the offer had been made.

* * *

Back in their rented flat, Stella was still nursing her secret joy. Her anger at Dolly's earlier meanness had dissipated by now. Besides, she'd only been testing Dolly, to see if her older sister could be goaded into making a generous gesture, perhaps for the first time in her life. But no, Dolly was holding tight to her wealthy purse strings!

Stella and Paddy sat together on the sofa that evening, holding hands while they watched TV and darting occasional joyful glances at each other. Dolly and her wealth were far from their thoughts. They still couldn't believe their good fortune – they were going to have a baby! After years of trying, they'd finally given up hope of ever having a child of their own. But now, a miracle had happened, *and now they would hold their very own baby in four months' time!*

Stella patted her stomach in amusement. Trust Dolly to turn a happy occasion into an opportunity to imply her sister was putting on weight! If only Dolly knew how very inaccurate her observations were . . .

Stella gave up any pretence of watching the television, lay back and closed her eyes. She'd told Dolly a white lie – Paddy hadn't lost his job at McCarthy Brothers – he'd handed in his notice. She'd only said that to make Dolly feel guilty, but of course her older sister hadn't responded with any concern for their welfare.

Nevertheless, it was unfortunate that she'd had to tell Dolly about the baby almost immediately after Owen died. It would probably seem like a double blow to her older sister, who might have longed for a family herself, but was now unlikely to ever have one. Though Stella wondered if children had ever been part of Dolly's hopes for the future. But she and Dolly had never been close enough to talk about things like that. Maybe she'd talked to her mother about it, but certainly her two younger sisters had never been considered worthy of Dolly's confidences!

The opportunity of having their own child had come. as a complete surprise to them. After years of trying, Stella and Paddy had reluctantly concluded that they were unlikely ever to be parents. They'd followed charts and visited numerous doctors. They'd been told that everything seemed perfectly normal – there was no obvious reason why they shouldn't be able to have a child – yet every month the result was the same. As the time of her monthly period approached, Stella invariably became depressed, anticipating the inevitable let-down that its arrival would bring. Although she and Paddy were still young, the fact that they'd been trying to have a baby right from the time they'd got married didn't augur well for a pregnancy later in life either.

But everything had changed when Stella received that fateful telephone call. The call had come late one night. Paddy had already gone upstairs to bed, and Stella wasn't going to answer it, since it was rather late for social calls. But then it crossed her mind that it might be an emergency. Quickly she picked up the phone. Maybe her mother or Dolly was ill . . .

"Hello?"

"Stella – it's Gina."

"Oh my God, I don't believe it! After all these months! Are you all right?"

"Yes, but please don't tell anyone I've phoned. Promise?"

"Yes, of course – where are you?"

"I'm in London. Look, I've a proposition for you. But time is of the essence. I need to talk to you in person, and it needs to be soon."

Stella hesitated. "Gina – do you know that Owen died recently? It was a car accident –"

"Yes, I heard."

"Dolly is devastated. I'm sure she'd love to hear from you, now that –"

"No," said Gina firmly.

There was a palpable silence. "Well – " Stella was about to argue, then changed her mind. "You said you wanted to meet me. Are you coming back to Dublin?"

"No, I'm not," Gina replied, "but I'm hoping that you'll come to London. It might sound like a lot to ask, but when you get here, I think you'll agree that the effort's been worth it."

"Okay – but I can't get there before next week."

"That's fine. Bring Paddy too – I need to talk to both of you."

"Oh, okay."

"Make a long weekend of it," Gina suggested. "You can both

*stay with me – I have a spare bedroom here. Just don't tell anyone
else that you're coming to see me."*

Stella gulped. "What's this all about, Gina – are you really
okay? You're not ill, are you?"

Gina laughed. "No, I'm not. Well, there's nothing wrong with
me that won't be cured by the passage of time."

"Oh God, you haven't got cancer, have you?"

"No, I'm fine – I promise you." Gina's voice softened. "And
I'm really looking forward to seeing you."

"Me too. But I wish you'd tell me what all this is about,
Gina," Stella said peevishly. "I'm sure Dolly and Mother would
want to know that you're all right –"

"Stella, if you mention me to either of them, you'll be the
loser."

There was a silence, and Stella knew there was no point in
pushing Gina any further. "Oh, all right," she said resignedly, "you
have my word."

Gina gave her sister her address and phone number in London.
"Come by boat and train from Dun Laoghaire. I'll meet you off
the train at Euston Station around six next Friday."

As she wrote down Gina's details, Stella couldn't resist a last-
ditch attempt at getting Gina to talk to her mother and her older
sister.

"Are you sure you wouldn't like to offer your condolences to
Dolly? I mean –"

There was silence at the other end of the line, and Stella
suddenly feared that Gina had already hung up.

"Gina – are you there?"

"Yes, I'm here. Just forget it, Stella. Now, are you coming to
London or not?"

CHAPTER 68

When Stella and Paddy had arrived in London, much to their relief, they'd found a robustly healthy and enlarged Gina. And she'd put a wonderful proposition to them. Knowing how much they longed for a child of their own, she offered them the option of adopting her own child, when it was due in four months' time.

But this wouldn't be any ordinary adoption. No one, outside the three of them, would ever know that the baby wasn't Stella's and Paddy's own flesh and blood. Gina would sign in at the hospital under Stella's name, and the child's birth certificate would say that it had been born to Stella and Paddy Leyden.

"Since I'm five months' pregnant, there's still time for you to announce your pregnancy back home," Gina told her older sister. "Of course, the two of you would have to leave Dublin and live over here – at least until the baby's born – so that your 'pregnancy' could progress well away from prying eyes back home."

Stella's eyes filled with tears of joy. "Oh my God, Paddy – it's a dream come true!"

Paddy looked gratefully at his sister-in-law, his voice now

hoarse with emotion. "That would be wonderful – oh Gina, you've made us the happiest couple in the world!"

Then they were both silent, realising that their dream-come-true was only possible because of Gina's own tragedy.

"You'll be able to see the baby any time you want," Stella assured her. "We'd want you to be a part of its life."

Gina smiled, trying to hide her sadness. "I think it would probably be better if I wasn't. Besides, I'll be moving on anyway – new life, new places to see."

In reality, she could feel the pain of parting already. This baby was all she had left of Owen, and parting with it would be like losing Owen all over again. Already she loved this baby inside her, but her child's future was all that mattered now.

Stella and Paddy were more than willing to do anything that would make this miracle possible for them. Since Paddy could work as a site manager just as easily in London as in Dublin, they quickly arranged to move abroad for the immediate future.

They'd gone back to Dublin after their weekend visit, and told their families and friends about Stella's 'surprise' pregnancy, and that Paddy was also starting a new job in London. Stella's mother had been thrilled at the thought of being a grandmother at last, but Dolly had been her usual begrudging self. But thankfully, no one considered anything amiss, and the move had gone according to plan.

For Gina, it was an added joy to have her sister living in London. For the first few weeks, Stella and Paddy shared her flat and helped her with the rent, but they all agreed that it was better if they found their own place. They realised that it wouldn't be fair on Gina to have the baby – the baby she was giving up – living under the same roof.

"Besides, Paddy and I need to find somewhere for the long

term," Stella told her younger sister. "We'll probably stay in London for a few years. At least until we make enough money to buy a house back in Dublin."

Nevertheless, Gina was relieved to have a family member living close by, and the support of Stella and Paddy to help her through the remainder of her pregnancy.

At least she'd had Stella and Paddy to call on when her contractions started, and they'd quickly whisked her off to the hospital by taxi. Stella had stayed with her throughout her entire labour, reading to her and chatting as the hours dragged on. In a sense, the time together had given them a chance to bond again as sisters, and to lament on Dolly's pomposity and their mother's ostracisation of Gina from the family.

Once in the hospital, Gina became Stella Leyden, whose younger sister 'Gina' was there to hold her hand and urge her on, mopping her brow as the contractions became increasingly painful.

There had been a few difficult moments when, during a particularly painful contraction, Gina had called Stella by her real name. Luckily, neither the nurses nor midwife seemed to notice, but it reminded both women of the constant need for vigilance, and of how easily their house of cards could come tumbling down around them.

After hours of exhausting labour, Gina had given birth to an eight-pound baby girl, and she felt a strange mixture of joy and sorrow as the baby was handed to her, and she held her little daughter close. She was overcome by the strength of her love for this tiny scrap of humanity, who bawled lustily to be fed. As the midwife showed her how to put the baby to her breast, Gina couldn't stop the tears that fell on the baby's downy head. If only Owen had lived to see his beautiful daughter!

Sitting up in her hospital bed after the birth, Gina found it

*increasingly difficult to remember that her name was meant to be
'Stella'. More than once she hadn't responded when a nurse or
doctor had asked her a question. It also made it difficult to converse
with the other women in the ward, but in truth, she didn't feel
much like talking to them, since the circumstance of their babies'
births and hers were so different.*

*Gina sighed. She hadn't realised how hard it would be to hand
over her child when the time came. Surrounded by other mothers
who'd just given birth, Gina had been filled with envy. They'd all
be taking their babies home when they left. Gina would be the
only one handing hers over to other people to rear.*

*But she acknowledged that she was luckier than most of the
women who had to give their babies away. The majority were never
likely to see theirs again, whereas she'd be able to watch her child
grow and mature, albeit from a distance.*

*How different everything would have been if Owen had lived!
They'd now be a family, living in a pretty house with a big garden
full of fruit trees where the sun would always shine, Owen would
have blown the whistle on BWF Pharmaceuticals, and he'd have
a top job at one of the universities. Their beautiful daughter would
be the most loved child in the world, and she would bask in the
reflected joy of her parents' love for each other. Gina stifled a sob.
She'd done the next best thing for her child. She knew the child
would always be the centre of Stella's and Paddy's universe.*

*Unable to contain his own joy, Paddy had rung both their
families in Dublin immediately after the birth, and told them the
good news – that Stella had given birth to a beautiful eight-pound
daughter in London. Stella's mother had been ecstatic at becoming
a grandmother, but Dolly's response had been less than lukewarm.*

*"Congratulations," she'd eventually managed to say, in a
strangled voice that sounded as though the word was choking her.*

But Dolly's indifference couldn't dampen Paddy's and Stella's happiness. As they sat at Gina's hospital bedside, she laughed along with them while Paddy relayed details of Dolly's less than enthusiastic response to their news. But inside, Gina's heart was breaking, and she could only guess at her widowed sister's feelings.

As a gesture of gratitude to Gina, Stella and Paddy had offered to let her pick a name for the baby. But she'd declined. The baby was now theirs, and she felt that its name should rightly be chosen by them. In any event, she actually liked the name they eventually selected – Caroline had a nice ring to it, and she had visions of a little girl with blond pigtails and a sprinkling of freckles across her nose.

During the days she spent in hospital, Gina breastfed her baby daughter, alternately experiencing the joy of loving her, and the sorrow of parting with her. Soon, she would hand over the baby to Paddy and Stella, who would then begin bottle-feeding her. While Gina longed to prolong her time with her little daughter by offering to continue breastfeeding her at their new flat, she knew that emotionally she needed to make the break.

When Gina and Caroline were discharged from the hospital three days later, they stood with Paddy and Stella on the hospital steps.

"How can we ever thank you?" said Stella, tears of joy streaming down her face as Gina handed over the baby to her, having cuddled her for the very last time.

"By being the best parents in the world," said Gina, wiping away her own tears.

"Gina, we'll do everything in our power to honour the trust you've placed in us," Paddy assured her, his voice hoarse with emotion.

Although they'd invited her to come back to their flat with them, Gina had firmly refused. The sooner she got used to being alone again, the better it would be for all of them. Besides, it was vital that Stella, Paddy and the baby quickly bonded together as a family. She was now an outsider again, and she would start as she meant to go on.

After a quick hug, Gina turned away from Stella, Paddy and Caroline and walked down the street towards the nearest underground station. As the tears streamed down her own face, she didn't look back.

CHAPTER 69

Once Stella and Paddy had taken the baby home, Gina was determined to put the past behind her and get on with her life. She was still young, and needed to look positively towards the future. But she wasn't finding it easy – some days, it was even an effort to get out of bed.

Her beloved Owen was dead, and her baby was now living with its new parents. At least she'd managed to secure her child's future, and she was relieved to know that it had adoring parents, and would grow up surrounded by love. It was the only thing she could do for her child, since she had no way of rearing it herself. All the money Owen had given her was now gone, and she'd soon have to give up the flat and move into a bedsit. And once she'd recovered sufficiently from the birth, she'd have to find a job again.

Often, when she thought of Owen, Gina couldn't help wondering where he had been going to, or coming from, on that fateful night of the accident. She'd go through the possibilities over and over in her mind – had he been on his way to say goodbye to a friend, before joining her in London? Had he had one too many in the pub before going home? Was he thinking about her and their future when the accident happened? She hoped his death had been mercifully quick. She couldn't bear to think of her dear Owen suffering . . .

Already, several weeks had passed since she'd handed over her baby to Stella and Paddy, but she still felt too lethargic to start looking for a job. But now, at last, things were beginning to look up. Out of the blue, an employment agency had contacted her to say they had just the job for her – there was a vacancy for a research assistant at a state-of-the-art university research laboratory just outside London. She didn't remember having contacted the agency, but they'd obviously got her name and details somewhere. The job offered a substantial salary and lots of perks, so she intended making every effort to impress.

The caller had also been very specific in requesting that she bring with her any research papers or reports she might ever have worked on. It didn't matter whether they'd been published or not, the caller assured her, they just wanted to see what she was capable of. And she wasn't to worry about a lack of references from any previous jobs – they'd heard about her work, they assured her, and were keen to have someone of her calibre in the research department. Gina was flattered, although she couldn't for the life of her think how they might know about her.

Their request to see any research papers she'd worked was the only blip on the horizon, as far as Gina was concerned. If only she'd kept Owen's research paper, she could have brought it with her! Since Owen had generously credited her contribution to his work, the university department would undoubtedly have been impressed. Unfortunately, that paper had been left in her suitcase at Larry's flat.

Gina was also flattered when an official at the laboratory phoned her directly at the pay-phone in the house, and offered to send a company car to take her to the interview venue. Excitement bubbled up inside her for the first time since she'd handed over her baby to Stella and Paddy. Things were really looking up – if she got the job at this laboratory, she might be able to afford something better than the bedsit she'd intended moving into at the end of the month. Stella and Paddy had been helping her financially over the last few months, but they didn't have much money either, and now they needed everything they had for their new baby.

Gina grimaced. It sounded odd referring to little Caroline as 'their' baby. But she had to get used to calling her that, since a slip of the tongue could cause problems for all three of them. She was now beginning life again as a single woman, and no one must know that she'd ever given birth.

Gina surveyed her reflection in her mirror in her bedsit. She was wearing a crisp white blouse and a flecked tweed suit, since she wanted to look both sleek and professional. She was actually excited at the idea of going back to work, of having colleagues to chat to again, and hopefully of developing a new social life. This in itself was a revelation to her – after Owen died, she'd wondered if she'd ever want to socialise again, or be capable of experiencing happiness ever again.

She looked approvingly at her hair in the mirror. She'd tied it up in a chignon, and it looked neat and sophisticated. All in all, she looked the epitome of professionalism. Only the absence of Owen's research paper annoyed her. In fact, she might even mention it to the interviewers, and if the job offer depended on it, she'd just have to contact Larry.

She wondered briefly how he was getting on. Very soon, she'd have to contact him anyway, and explain her reasons for leaving him. Obviously, she wouldn't tell him that she'd given the baby to Stella and Paddy, but she'd need to explain that the baby wasn't *his, and that it had been adopted. Hopefully, he'd managed to get over her. Gina still felt guilty about the way she'd treated poor Larry. Without doubt, she'd exploited his good nature, but what other option had she had at the time?*

At exactly the agreed time, the doorbell rang, and Gina surveyed herself for a last time in the mirror before she hurried out. She felt good about how she looked – she'd quickly got her figure back after childbirth – and confident that her qualifications matched the job specification perfectly. In fact, it was amazing that the job almost seemed tailored to her qualifications and experience. That was probably another good omen.

Outside, a driver and car was waiting for her. As she closed the door to her flat, the man stepped out of the driver's seat and silently opened the back door for her. Smiling at him, Gina climbed inside. She felt like royalty as they drove along. I could get used to this, she thought happily. I hope I get this job – the company obviously treats its employees well. Maybe the future will be better than I ever expected . . .

In the back seat, Gina checked in her handbag for her documentation. She'd brought along her school and college certificates, and she'd belatedly asked for – and got – a reference from the veterinary laboratory where she'd briefly worked while living with Larry. What a pity that she hadn't got a reference from Owen – that would have counted for a lot! But today, she mustn't think of Owen. Or her baby. She couldn't afford to feel sad. Right now, she needed to be at her best for the interview.

At first, Gina hadn't been paying much attention to where the car was taking her. Most of London was unfamiliar to her, so one suburb looked much like the next, and she assumed the driver knew where he was going. Now, she began to wonder if he was lost, since it looked as though they were heading down towards the docks. The sea appeared to be straight ahead, while on either side there were lots of dingy and deserted warehouses. A few attempts were being made at gentrification of the area, and Gina could see that several apartment blocks had already been built. What an odd place to be interviewed, she thought, still curious rather than concerned.

"Excuse me, where exactly are we going?" she asked the driver. But there was no reply. Instead, he now seemed to be speeding even faster, and Gina shrugged her shoulders. Mr Personality he certainly wasn't!

Eventually, he pulled up outside a building site, where the concrete foundations of a large building were being laid. Gina looked out in surprise. Several men appeared to be tamping in the cement as it descended from an overhead chute. There was no sign of anywhere that looked suitable for holding interviews. She'd expected to be interviewed in plush offices, so the location was rather a disappointment to her. Then she brightened. Perhaps they were just collecting another interviewee before heading back to the main thoroughfare?

Gina leaned forward for a better look. On the other hand, maybe this building was going to be the company's new laboratory – perhaps they wanted her to take a look at the place where she'd eventually be working, or ask for her comments on it, so she'd better pay attention!

As the driver got out of the car and opened the back door for her, Gina eagerly stepped out. This was certainly an unconventional interview, but she intended to give it her best shot! Smiling at the driver, she was just about to speak when she noticed that he was holding what looked like an iron bar in his right hand. The incongruity was just registering with her when he raised his arm.

The first blow came as a complete surprise. It struck her so hard that she blacked out momentarily. Even still, her brain couldn't quite comprehend what was happening. The second blow caught her on the side of the head, splitting her skull before she hit the ground. The surprise was still on her face as she died.

Quickly, two other men appeared as though out of nowhere, collected Gina's body in silence, and dragged it across to where the foundations of the building were being laid. Her light frame, now heavier in death, was dropped into the foundations, and the signal given for another load of concrete to descend from the chute above and cover it. The entire sequence of events had been perfectly choreographed. Within seconds, all trace of Gina's body was gone.

Nodding briefly to the men on the site, the driver picked up Gina's handbag from where she had dropped it, stepped into the car again and drove off.

Within minutes, the car was back in the city, and Gina's handbag was silently handed over to another man, who quickly rifled through it.

"It's not there," he said angrily. "You should have checked before you killed her. Now we'll have to turn over her bloody apartment."

The driver shrugged. He'd done the job he'd been asked to do. No one had asked him to use his initiative. That would have cost them extra.

Back at the docklands building site, work continued unabated. The men continued laying the foundations, as though nothing untoward had ever happened there. Before the year was out, a brand new apartment block was standing on the site. No trace of Gina existed any more.

CHAPTER 70

Stella and Paddy were puzzled and worried. They'd called around to Gina's flat several days in succession, but there was never any answer to their insistent ringing of the doorbell.

"Perhaps she never intended to keep in touch once she'd given us the baby," said Paddy thoughtfully. "Don't you remember her saying that she intended moving on? I even remember the words she used – 'new life, new places to see,' she said."

Stella shook her head. "I can't believe that, Paddy! She and I had become close again – like the way it used to be, before Mum threw her out. She wouldn't just disappear again – I'm sure something must have happened to her. I think we should go to the police."

Paddy looked doubtful. "But what if she's just chosen to disappear? We might be making things awkward for her." He put his arms around his wife. "Look, she's probably just chosen to do a runner again. I remember her telling us that when she walked out on Larry, she just left everything behind her. I guess it's just something that Gina does. I think we should respect her right to disappear, if that's what she chooses to do."

Stella didn't look convinced. "Her landlady, who lives upstairs, saw her leaving the flat in a big flashy car."

"Well, there's your answer!" said Paddy triumphantly. "She was probably taking a taxi to the airport. Maybe she's gone to America, like she always said she would." He hugged his wife. "I'll bet you we'll get a card from New York or Los Angeles in the next few weeks, telling us that she's having a great time."

"But she had no money, Paddy."

"Oh." Paddy's face dropped. "Unless she's managed to borrow it from someone . . ."

But they both knew that was highly unlikely. Gina didn't have many friends in London, and she was unlikely to have approached Larry. If she'd needed or wanted money, Stella and Paddy would have been the ones she'd turn to.

Eventually, they persuaded Gina's landlady to open up the flat and let them in. A shock awaited them all. Inside, the contents of drawers had been thrown out onto the floor. Every cupboard had been opened, and all the contents rummaged through.

"Surely Gina wouldn't have left the place like this?" Paddy whispered, appalled.

"I hope not," Stella replied. "She was always very tidy when she lived at home. But maybe she was in a hurry when she left."

"Well, that's the last time I'll ever let this place to an Irish person," sniffed the landlady. "You lot are nothing but trouble. Thank goodness her lease was up next week anyway."

Feeling miserable and depressed, Stella and Paddy tidied up the flat, taking away the rubbish, and anything that they knew belonged to Gina.

At the local police station, the duty sergeant wasn't particularly helpful either. "Have you any idea how many people disappear in *this city each year?" he asked rhetorically. "Are you sure she hasn't just gone back to Ireland?"*

Stella shook her head. "Definitely not," she told him, "you see, there was a family quarrel —"

"Aah," said the sergeant knowingly, "that's one of the main reasons why people disappear. She'll probably turn up when she's ready."

"But she hasn't quarrelled with us," said Stella imploringly.

"Maybe she's joined the IRA," said the sergeant, making it clear that Irish people didn't rate very highly in his scheme of things. The bombings in London throughout the mid-70s had created a lot of anti-Irish feeling, which was still running high.

"Please — we'd be very grateful if you'd try to find her," said Stella, biting her tongue. She longed to tell the sergeant that while she didn't condone blowing up anyone, Irish people were the original victims — of English oppression over a period of nearly eight hundred years. But ideological confrontation was unlikely to further the search for Gina, so Stella kept her mouth shut.

Grudgingly, the sergeant took down the details, but Stella and Paddy were well aware that Gina's details would probably be filed away somewhere and forgotten about. In 1978, a missing Irish woman wasn't a high priority in a city where Irish people were regarded with suspicion and derision.

Back in their flat, they talked into the early hours of the morning, while Caroline slept in her cot.

"I don't suppose we'll ever know where Gina's gone, unless she gets in touch with us," said Stella sadly. "I miss her already, you know, and I'll always be eternally grateful to her for Caroline."

Paddy nodded. "Me too. She's made our dreams come true — I wish there was something we could do for her in return."

"I thought she'd want to keep in touch this time — you know,

because of Caroline. I always assumed she'd want to be around, to watch her grow up."

"Maybe it's just too painful for her," said Paddy thoughtfully. "It's obvious that she still misses Owen desperately, and keeps thinking about how things might have been if he'd lived. She might also think it's for the best to leave us alone to rear Caroline."

"I still can't help feeling that something's wrong," said Stella, a worried frown on her face. "I don't think that sergeant took our concerns very seriously."

Paddy nodded in agreement. "But I doubt if anything's amiss, love," he assured his wife. "I'm sure Gina will be in touch when she's ready."

"Do you really think so?"

Paddy hugged his wife. "Of course I do. The ball is now back in Gina's court. There's nothing we can really do until she decides to make contact again. In the meantime, the best thing we can do for her is make a good job of rearing Caroline."

Part 5

Chapter 71

The following Friday afternoon, Caroline finished work early and went straight to Dublin airport for a week-long stay in London. Having flown into Stanstead, she took the train into Liverpool Street station, where Simon was already waiting for her. As the train pulled in to the platform, she could make out his curly mop of dark brown hair, and that lock that always hung enticingly over his left eye. Her heart soared at the thought of eight whole days in his company!

This time, Caroline was even more excited than before. She was going to stay at Simon's flat, and meet the redoubtable Anne and Derek! In anticipation of this meeting, she'd even bought some cat treats. Hopefully she could get them to like her. However, she was well aware that most felines regarded humans as pathetic specimens, and she knew she might have to wait some time before gaining their approval.

As Simon hugged her, he took her bag in one hand and put his other arm around her shoulders. Caroline snuggled in. It felt wonderful to be here, and to be with the most gorgeous man on the planet! She was also keen to see where he lived, and learn more about the man. She felt embarrassed as she remembered accusing him of having a wife and child – how could she have jumped to such ludicrous conclusions?

On the tube, they sat close, and Caroline suddenly thought of Ken. It brought a lump to her throat when she thought about all the years they'd spent together as a couple, yet they'd never once shared a train ride together, been to the theatre together, or visited a gallery together. It seemed an odd thing to think of, but in retrospect, Caroline had found herself increasingly examining their relationship, perhaps to ensure that she didn't make the same mistakes this time . . .

Caroline hoped that Simon liked art galleries and museums, and would enjoy showing her the city where he lived. She particularly wanted to visit the British Museum, the Victoria & Albert Museum, the Tate and National Galleries. She'd also enjoyed her night at the theatre with Liz and Hazel so much, that she'd like a repeat performance.

"This is our stop, my little treasure," Simon whispered in her ear.

Jolted back to reality, Caroline was pleased to hear Simon refer to her by such a term of endearment. He called her an assortment of such names, all of which she liked very much. Ken had never used any name for her other than Caro. Oh God, Caroline thought, I'll have to stop making these comparisons with Ken!

At Simon's one-bedroom garden flat, which consisted of the lower ground floor of a Victorian house, Caroline was impressed by the high ceilings and amount of space. Anne

and Derek soon made their appearance, and decided fairly
quickly that if Simon liked Caroline, then they would too.
However Caroline had a sneaking suspicion that the treats
she'd brought had played some part in their decision!

In turn, Simon seemed pleased that Caroline and the
cats had taken to each other.

"When I visited the animal refuge, and saw Anne, I
decided to take her," Simon told Caroline, explaining how
he'd acquired the twosome. "Then when the staff told me
she had a son, I decided to take the two of them. It
wouldn't have been fair to separate them."

As if to show his gratitude, Derek rubbed himself against
Simon's trousers.

"By the way, we're having dinner *in* this evening," Simon
told her, smiling. "I've never had a chance to cook for you,
so I've marinaded some lamb chops, which will be served
with garlic potatoes *au gratin*. Hope that's to your liking, my
precious."

"Wow! A man who enjoys cooking!" said Caroline,
smiling. "How lucky can one woman get?" She was thrilled
to know that he'd been thinking about her, and planning
their meal, far in advance of her actual arrival.

By tacit agreement, neither of them made any mention
of Gina. Nevertheless, the spectre of Caroline's aunt hung
over the evening, and later, when they'd finished eating and
Simon had made coffee, Caroline told him about phoning
Larry and learning that Gina had been working in a
veterinary laboratory at the time she left him.

Simon smiled gently. "Certainly we can look into it.
Maybe someone at the company can tell us what Gina's
new address was. But it's thirty years ago, Caroline – I doubt

if any of the people working there now would know anything about it."

"But it's worth a chance, isn't it?" said Caroline, pleadingly.

Simon took her hand and began stroking it, and Caroline felt all sorts of wonderful sensations running through her. Hopefully, he would soon extend his ministrations to other areas of her body . . .

"You're just avoiding facing the inevitable, aren't you?" Simon said, looking closely at her. "I hope you intend giving a DNA sample, Caroline –" he grinned malevolently, "otherwise, I'm going to forcibly carry you to the police station myself!"

"Yes, of course I'm going," said Caroline, annoyed that he could read her so easily. But she willingly admitted to herself that she still wanted to believe Gina was out there, living happily somewhere, waiting to welcome her new-found niece with open arms.

"We'll go there on Monday morning," Simon told her, as he began to caress her ears, neck and shoulders, "because the sooner you give the sample, the sooner they can start processing it."

But Caroline didn't reply. Her mind – and body – were already elsewhere, transported to some land of earthly delights caused by Simon's increasingly passionate caresses. Caroline gasped. Simon was starting to do amazing things to her with his tongue . . .

* * *

The following Monday morning, Caroline rang the veterinary laboratory where Gina used to work, and enquired about her aunt's employment record with the company.

Initially, no one was able to tell her anything, but a particularly helpful young clerk agreed to look through the company's employee records and see if she could find out anything about Gina's time with the company. She promised to call back that afternoon if she found anything in the files.

That afternoon, Simon, who had taken time off work, took Caroline to the police station where she filled out the necessary forms and gave a DNA sample.

"How long will it take?" Caroline asked the desk sergeant as he bagged up her sample for departure to the state laboratories, for testing and comparison against samples taken from Gina's body.

"It should be back in a week or two," he told her cheerfully, not realising how devastating she regarded such a delay.

"I really don't know if I can wait that long," said Caroline imploringly. "Is there any way to hurry it up?"

The police sergeant laughed. "I'll see what I can do. It all depends on how many samples are in the queue before yours. But I'll make it a priority at this end."

"Oh thank you!" said Caroline fervently. "I'd hug you if you weren't on the far side of the counter! I feel that my whole life is on hold until I find out if this is my aunt or not!"

"Well, I hope you get the answer you want," said the sergeant, sealing up the sample, and placing it in an envelope marked *Urgent*.

Caroline crossed her fingers. Now, all she could do was wait.

As she and Simon waited for the tube back to Belsize Park, Caroline's mobile phone rang. It was the young clerk from the veterinary laboratory, who had some news to impart. It was clear to Caroline from the information the clerk gave her that Gina had left the company before her baby was born.

"There's a note in the files saying she wasn't well as her pregnancy advanced, then she didn't turn up for ages and her employment was automatically terminated."

"Oh."

"But there was another note in the files, dated a few months later, saying that she'd applied to the company for a job reference."

"And that's it?"

"Yes, I'm afraid so."

"I don't suppose there's a mention of the company she wanted the reference for?"

"No, sorry. They're usually made out with 'To Whom It May Concern' on them."

"Well, thanks very much – you've been very kind," Caroline assured the clerk, ringing off.

"Well?" asked Simon.

Caroline explained. "So Gina must have been going for a job interview!" she concluded.

Simon smiled, always pleased to see Caroline happy. But he feared that this was yet another dead-end. He'd already used the search facilities in his office to check records of births during 1978, but found nothing under the name of Gina Kiernan. He'd even checked under Larry's surname – Macken – and finally under Owen's surname – Brady – just in case Gina had decided to register the child with its father's name, as a gesture towards its future identity. But none of his searches yielded any results.

"Let's go to the British Museum tomorrow," Simon suggested. "There's an exhibition of 19th century ceramics which I'd like to see. What do you think?"

"Wonderful," Caroline told him, smiling. Simon was determined that she'd see and experience lots of cultural events this week, and she was looking forward to it. He was also taking her to see *The Mousetrap* by Agatha Christie, the longest running play in the world, which had been on in London's West End for more than fifty years.

Caroline smiled to herself. And in the evenings, having been sated with culture, she'd go back to Belsize Park to be further sated by endless lovemaking with Simon . . . Could life get any better? Yes, a little voice told her, you could finally find your Aunt Gina . . .

As the week flew by, Simon ensured that she saw every landmark, statue, building and exhibition worth seeing. They dined in little bistros and cafés, visited art galleries and fed the pigeons in Trafalgar Square. And in the evenings, they snuggled up together in Simon's flat, with Anne and Derek curled up beside them in the bed. Caroline was blissfully happy, but she wondered, somewhere in the deep recesses of her mind, if such happiness could last.

The bubble burst on Thursday, when Simon was phoned by a colleague in Scotland Yard who'd been doing some searching for him in the Missing Persons files.

"There's something you should know," Simon told her as he put the phone down. "When your mother and father were living in London, they filed a missing person's report, dated 1978. So they were obviously worried about Gina at that time."

Caroline was puzzled. Her mother had told her that the

last time she'd seen Gina was when she'd been kicked out of home in disgrace. But that couldn't be true if both her parents had been searching for Gina in London nearly a year later! The report gave Gina's last known address, which her parents wouldn't have known unless they'd been in contact with Gina in London. It was all very confusing. But one thing was certain. Her mother had some explaining to do..

Since Gina's last known address was listed on the Missing Persons report, Simon took Caroline to the house in South London. However, the house had been bought and sold several times in the interim, and no one knew – or cared – about someone who'd rented a flat there thirty years earlier. Despondent, Caroline accepted that another avenue had effectively been closed.

On Friday morning, there was a telephone call from the city's divisional police headquarters, and Simon listened gravely as the duty sergeant informed him that the results of Caroline's DNA test was back. The sergeant informed him that he'd personally pulled strings to get the results as early as possible for the 'lovely young lady', and if they'd like to call to the station, he'd be glad to furnish them with the results.

"I'm terrified," Caroline confided, when Simon told her the news. "Although I want to know what happened to my aunt, I hope this isn't her."

"I'm edgy myself," Simon admitted, "because I know you'll be disappointed whatever the results. C'mon, let's get it over with, my little treasure – there's no time like the present."

Dragging a reluctant Caroline, Simon headed to the tube and the divisional police headquarters. But when they arrived outside, Caroline froze.

"I don't think I can go in," she told Simon.

"Come on – you need to know, one way or another."

"But what'll I do if it *is* Gina?"

"Then we'll face it together."

Inside the police station, Caroline sat on the waiting-room bench while Simon went to the desk. She was more frightened than she'd ever been. She didn't want her poor aunt to have been a victim. In Caroline's mind, Gina was lively, full of fun, a woman who lived life to the full. She wasn't meant to be a dead body buried under a building. If this unknown person *was* her aunt, then her own life would be changed forever.

Suddenly, Simon was standing beside her, an envelope in his hand.

"Caroline – come on, let's get out of here and go for a cup of coffee."

"Simon, what's the matter? You look as though you've seen a ghost!"

"Yes, I think I just have. Now, let's go to the café next door – *I* need a cup of coffee, whatever about you." He looked at her. "I think you *will* need a cup when I tell you what I've just discovered."

Following Simon out of the police station and into the adjacent café, Caroline found a seat and sat tensely waiting while Simon paid for two cups of coffee and brought them back to their table.

"Okay, this had better be good!" she said, smiling, trying to lighten the atmosphere.

But the tense expression still remained on Simon's face. "I'm afraid it's bad news," he said gently, reaching for her hand. "There's no doubt about it any more – the dead woman is Gina."

Caroline said nothing, gazing into space as though she could postpone accepting the truth of what Simon was saying. No, it couldn't be true! All these months, she'd built up her hopes of finally finding her aunt, and inviting her to the wedding. But there would be no wedding anyway, and no aunt either.

At last the tears came. They cascaded silently down her cheeks, although she was totally unaware of their presence. Her mind was far away, in the world she and Gina had once inhabited, the magical world she had conjured up, in which she and Gina went shopping, dined out together, laughed and joked together. Now, she'd never know her aunt. In one fell swoop, a part of her own personal history had been wiped out.

Simon leaned forward and silently wiped her tears away with his handkerchief.

"Caroline, there's something else."

He waited until he had her full attention before continuing.

"The results of the test show that you share fifty percent of your genes with the dead woman –"

Caroline looked at him uncomprehendingly. "So? I *am* related to her!"

"More than that. We get fifty percent of our genes from each parent," said Simon, grasping her hand.

Caroline stared back at him, unable to take in the enormity of what he was telling her. "So that means?"

"It means that this woman – Gina – is, I mean was, your mother."

Caroline looked aghast, then shook her head vehemently. "That's just not possible! There must be some mistake in the test results."

"Why couldn't it be possible? You've got to ask your mother – I mean Stella."

"But my birth certificate shows that Stella Kiernan is my mother, and Paddy Leyden is my father. How could that be, if Gina was my mother?"

"I don't know, Caroline," said Simon, looking worried. "But there's only one way to find out. You'll just have to ask Stella."

Back at Simon's flat, Caroline put the kettle on, always the answer when she was under stress. Then she fed Anne and Derek, who didn't believe that a mere human was entitled to be upset when they were in need of their food.

Caroline felt as though she was living in a dream. How on earth could Gina be her mother? That would mean that Owen Brady was her father! No, it wasn't possible. Her birth certificate listed Stella and Paddy as her parents. She was happy with her parents and didn't need any others. The test must be wrong. While she sadly accepted that this dead woman had been her Aunt Gina, she couldn't accept that her aunt had also been her mother! There had to be some other explanation.

The rest of the weekend passed in a daze for Caroline, and on Sunday afternoon at Stanstead Airport Simon kissed her tenderly before she went through to the departure lounge. He couldn't help grinning to himself – he'd be seeing Caroline a lot sooner than she expected! Of course, he wasn't going to tell her that he'd taken several extra days off work and was travelling to Dublin the following Wednesday afternoon. It was Caroline's thirtieth birthday that day, and he intended surprising her! He'd nonchalantly enquired if she was doing anything special for her birthday, and having been assured that her family and friends had planned a celebratory meal for later in the week, he'd booked a meal for two at one of Dublin's top restaurants, and booked himself into a small luxurious hotel in the centre of the city. Hopefully, Caroline would be spending her nights there with him . . .

He'd never been to Dublin before, but he assumed he'd have no problems taking a taxi from the airport to Caroline's mother's house. It was time he met Caroline's family. As he hugged her and kissed her goodbye, he wished he could go to Dublin straight away, so that he could be there to support her when she spoke to Stella. But it just wasn't possible. He'd needed to give notice before taking time off from his job.

"Bye, Simon – I'm missing you already!" whispered Caroline as she walked through to the departure lounge.

"Bye, my precious Caroline – let me know what happens when you talk to your mother."

Simon and Caroline waved until they could no longer see each other.

I should feel sad, Simon thought, as he left the station and headed for the underground, but he didn't, because he was going to Dublin in just a few days. Everything had been perfectly planned. Caroline would be thrilled to see him, and after being introduced to Stella, he intended whisking Caroline away for an evening of pampering, and later on, he had an even bigger surprise in store for her . . .

CHAPTER 72

Immediately Caroline arrived back from her trip to London, Stella could see that something was amiss.

"Are you all right, dear?" she asked. "Maybe all this travelling is taking its toll on you?"

"No, Mum – I'm upset because I've found out that Gina is dead. She died nearly thirty years ago."

"W-what? Oh my God! What happened to her?"

Briefly, Caroline explained about the body under the building, and about the DNA test she'd taken.

A tearful Stella was immediately defensive. "Oh dear! I knew that no good would come of you searching for Gina!"

"But is it true, Mum?" Caroline implored her. "That I'm Gina's child? And if it is – how could my birth certificate have both your name and Dad's on it?"

Reluctantly nodding, Stella sat down at the big kitchen table. Her hands were shaking. "Put the kettle on, will you, dear?" she said quietly. "It's a long story."

Obediently, Caroline put on the kettle, then brought

two mugs of tea to the table, where her mother was now weeping quietly.

"It was all meant for the best," Stella said at last, turning her tear-stained face towards Caroline. "Your father and I couldn't have a child, and Gina ended up pregnant with Owen's baby. Since she couldn't possibly keep you after Owen's death, she offered you to us – and, obviously, we were thrilled." Stella warmed her hands around the mug of tea. "There was a lot of stigma attached to single parenthood back then, you know. People are more enlightened today, and there are services and support available nowadays." Stella bit her lip to stop herself from crying again. "We never told Mother or Dolly about our arrangement, and Gina signed in at the hospital under my name. Later, your father and I registered your birth in our names."

"So that's why we couldn't find any record of a baby born to Gina," said Caroline. Then she took Stella's hand. "Look, Mum – you'll always be my mother. If it wasn't for you and Dad, who knows where I might have ended up? In fact, I *did* spend my life with my own family –" She threw her arms around Stella. "What are a few genes between people who love each other?"

The two women hugged each other tightly, each of them now crying unashamedly.

"I'm sorry, Caroline – but your father and I did the best we could for you," said Stella at last. "We never meant for you to find out – when everything was arranged, there was no such thing as DNA. But I can tell you honestly – we never knew what happened to Gina. More than anything, I wanted her to be around – to watch you grow up, and to know that we'd honoured the faith she'd placed in us."

"I know, Mum – Simon discovered that you and Dad had filed a Missing Persons report back in 1978."

Stella wiped away a tear. "And to think that she was probably dead already when we filed that report! Poor Gina – she was so full of life, so sure that everything was going to work out." She looked at Caroline. "You know, you're very like her. I've often worried that Gina's impulsive streak would get you into trouble too. And when you told me that you and Ken were breaking up – well, I needn't tell you, I was worried sick."

"Well, you needn't worry on my account," said Caroline lightly.

"By the way, Ken has called here several times," Stella told her. "I really think you need to talk to him – are you so sure there's no future for you together?"

"No, Mum," said Caroline resolutely.

Stella sighed. She was too old for change, yet so many things were changing. Still, as long as Caroline was happy, she would have to accept whoever was part of her life. Even this Simon fellow, if necessary.

"Look, Mum," said Caroline, "as far as I'm concerned, the fact that Gina is my biological mother changes nothing, and there's no need for anyone else to know. You're still my mum, and always will be."

"Thank you, Caroline," said Stella, weeping again. "I couldn't bear to lose you as my daughter. I've always been so proud of you, as was your dad. I wish he'd lived to see you grow into the fine young woman you are today."

Caroline brushed away her own tears. For a while, the two women sat silently, holding each other's hands.

Then Stella suddenly spoke. "Will we ever know who killed Gina?"

Caroline grimaced. "At the moment, it's not known for sure. But there's reason to believe that it was done by someone hired by BWF Pharmaceuticals."

Stella looked bewildered. "But why? Gina only worked there! Was it because of Owen?"

Caroline nodded. "Owen may have been killed too. It all seems to be connected with research Owen did thirty years ago, which Gina helped him with, and which BWF Pharmaceuticals wanted suppressed."

"Didn't Dolly have something to do with that? I seem to remember her saying that Owen was trying to destabilise the company, whereas Charles Keane was trying to save it."

"Aunt Dolly tends to get things the wrong way round," said Caroline grimly. "I think she's done a lot of harm with her hardline attitudes."

"Can anything be done about BWF Pharmaceuticals after all this time?"

"I don't know, Mum. There's no statute of limitations on murder, and I have a friend who's already talking to the police about it. Only time will tell. BWF Pharmaceuticals is now part of a multinational company, and even more powerful than before."

"I'd like justice for my poor dead sister," said Stella. "Are you saying that Dolly had something to do with Gina's and Owen's deaths?"

"If she did, it was unintentional – she just got caught up in something she didn't understand because of her devotion to Charles Keane," said Caroline. "Unfortunately, sometimes women let their hearts rule their heads."

"I seem to recall something similar happening to

someone not a million miles away from here," said Stella dryly. "Maybe it *is* nature rather than nurture after all."

* * *

The phone rang in Alice's mother's house in Stillorgan.

"Alice – it's Caroline."

"Oh, hi, Caroline, how are you?"

"Fine, thanks – well, a little upset, to tell you the truth. I thought you ought to know – we've discovered that my Aunt Gina was murdered in London. Back in 1978."

"Oh my God, I'm so sorry! How did it happen?"

Briefly, Caroline filled Alice in on the discovery of Gina's body in the foundations of the flooded apartment building, and how she had done a DNA test and proved their relationship. Caroline didn't tell her that Gina was actually her mother – there was no need for Alice to know that.

Alice sighed. "Yet another possible link to BWF Pharmaceuticals. The two key employees who worked on this report died in suspicious circumstances."

"I know," said Caroline. "By the way, how's Enrique?" She just couldn't resist making a mischievous comment.

"He's fine – you've guessed, haven't you?"

Caroline laughed. "I thought there was something going on there. The day I met you, you blushed every time you mentioned his name."

Alice laughed. "And I'm blushing now, even though you can't see me! I couldn't go back to Bill. I'll always be fond of him, but I've never felt about him the way I do for Enrique. When all this is over, I'm going back to Argentina."

"I presume Enrique feels the same?" asked Caroline, alarmed. "You're not just going back there on spec, hoping that something will happen?"

Alice laughed again. "No, we've committed to each other already. I love him, and he loves me. It happened very quickly – some people mightn't understand that. They think you have to go out with someone for years –"

"I understand – totally," Caroline replied.

CHAPTER 73

As Simon stepped out of the taxi in Blackrock, he noticed another man heading towards the same house as he was. The man was carrying a large bouquet of flowers, and Simon kicked himself for not thinking of doing the same. In his anxiety to get to Caroline, he'd completely forgotten the importance of flowers for birthdays and special occasions. No doubt this delivery man was dropping off a floral arrangement for Caroline, and Simon was angry at his own stupidity. He should have arranged to have a bouquet sent in advance of his arrival.

As the two men reached the door of Stella's house at the same time, they nodded warily at each other. As they stood there, the minutes dragged by without anyone answering the doorbell.

"Dammit, she's refusing to answer," said the man with the bouquet. "I might have guessed she wouldn't want to accept these bloody flowers."

Simon thought it odd for a delivery man to speak so familiarly and rudely about a customer's order, but he said nothing.

"She can be very stubborn, you know," added the man with the bouquet. "It wouldn't surprise me if she's watching from an upstairs window, and hoping that I'll eventually go away."

"Do you *know* Caroline?" Simon asked at last.

"Of course I do. I'm Ken – her fiancé, or at least I *was* until she decided to dump me last week. Who the fuck are you?"

"My name is Simon Ford."

"Oh. So you're the guy who's been helping her with the search for her aunt?"

"Er, yes."

Suddenly, before he realised what was happening, Simon found himself lying on the ground with a bloody nose and a splitting headache.

"How dare you overcharge her!" roared Ken, towering over him, the bouquet now discarded on the ground. "Stand up and let me thump you again, you coward! Imagine taking advantage of a woman like that!"

"What? What the hell are you talking about?" asked Simon, staggering to his feet. "*I'm* the one who should feel pissed off – I never heard about *you*, you violent oaf!"

The two men squared up to each other.

"How long have you been engaged to Caroline?" asked Simon, staunching the flow of blood with his handkerchief.

"Five years, although it's none of your bloody business!" roared Ken, making another swipe at Simon, and missing this time as Simon quickly ducked.

Just then, Caroline appeared, and stared aghast from one to the other. "Oh God – so you two have met . . ."

"What is *he* doing here?" roared Ken. "If he's come to put

pressure on you to pay him more money, so help me, I'll swing for him again!"

"More money – for what?" croaked Simon, as Ken hit him again.

"Stop it, Ken, for God's sake!" shouted Caroline. "You've got it all wrong, and it's all my fault!"

"Then tell him to get the hell out of here!" shouted Ken. "If anyone's going to help you find your aunt, it's going to be me – not some half-baked investigator who's been ripping you off!"

"You're all mental!" muttered Simon. "I'm getting out of here – and fast! Caroline, you're welcome to that big ape! He says you and he were engaged for the last five years!"

"Simon, please – I can explain!"

"No, thank you, Caroline," said Simon, nursing his bloodied nose, "you needn't bother. Apparently it's okay for *you* to have a self-righteous tantrum because you thought I was married, but you never once mentioned that *you* had a fiancé!"

"Oh God, I'm sorry, Simon – once I met you, I knew it was over with Ken. I just didn't see any point in telling you, until I knew if our relationship was going anywhere or not!"

"I think 'not' is the operative word here!"

"What? You can't mean that!"

"Oh yes, I bloody well can! I value my nose and my health, so I'm getting out of here fast, before that lunatic does me any more damage! Goodbye, Caroline – it was fun while it lasted."

"Well, we're quits now," Caroline wheedled. "Why don't we start again with a clean slate?"

"Quits? I never *was* married! But you *did* happen to have a fiancé!"

"Simon – please!"

But Simon was already striding down the road angrily.

"You know we're meant to be together, Caro," said Ken, taking her in his arms. "I can't believe that guy would take advantage of you like that! If only you'd let me help you, you wouldn't have needed to engage a professional to help you." Ken's expression darkened. "A professional scoundrel, that is!"

Caroline smiled sweetly. "Just in case you don't remember, Ken – you were totally against me finding my aunt."

Ken had the grace to look chastened. "You're right, I was. Well, I was wrong, Caro – and I admit it. I hadn't realised how much finding her mattered to you."

"Anyway, it doesn't matter now – as it happens, my aunt is actually dead."

"What? Oh my God, Caro – I'm so sorry!"

Suddenly, they were hugging each other tightly. "Oh Caro, this is terrible news! You must be so disappointed. What happened? Look, I've a better idea – let's go to the pub and you can tell me how you found out. Then, if you want to, we can go to a restaurant for something to eat." He grinned. "It shouldn't be difficult to get a booking on a weekday night. And it *is* your birthday, after all."

Caroline nodded. "Okay," she told him.

Although Simon was devastated at Caroline's duplicity, part of him hoped that she'd come after him as he hurried down the road. He'd really believed that they had a future together, but finding out that she'd omitted to mention her engagement to that violent lunatic had been the last straw. No wonder she hadn't invited him to Dublin before now! She'd already had a fiancé, and now he realised she'd simply been using him to help find her aunt. She must have thought that all her birthdays had come together at once when she discovered that he was a probate detective, with all the search resources at his fingertips! Well, she was welcome to her family revelations, and to that idiot of a fiancé, whom she was obviously going back to.

Yet even in his anger, Simon still felt that there might be a teeny-weeny bit of hope that he and Caroline could work things out. But that hope was finally dashed when he eventually looked back, and saw that Caroline was already back in Ken's arms.

* * *

Late that evening, when Caroline returned to the house, she was smiling. Stella was pleased, since Caroline had left with Ken and had been absent for several hours. Hopefully they'd sorted things out and their relationship was now back on track. They were meant for each other – of that Stella had no doubt. Maybe they'd both had a wake-up call, and that couldn't be a bad thing.

"Did you have a nice birthday, dear?"

"Fine thanks," said Caroline casually, and Stella knew better than to push for any further information. But she did notice that the engagement ring was back on Caroline's finger.

"I'm glad you and Ken have got things sorted. He really is a lovely guy."

"You're right, Mum. Ken is one in a million."

Taking a deep breath, Stella decided to risk asking. She had to know what was happening! "So is everything sorted out between you?"

"Yes, it is," said Caroline, pirouetting round the kitchen table. "So hang onto your new hat, Mum – there's going to be a wedding after all."

CHAPTER 74

Alice knew that it was now time to let Bill know she was still alive.

She considered asking her mother to phone him, and asking him to call to the house again. But somehow, after all she and Bill had been through together – and all they'd once meant to each other – she felt she owed him more than that. It would be more respectful to tell him the truth without her mother or Isobel being involved. She knew she could ask her mother to vacate the house for a while, but decided against it. Instead, she would go to see him at Ivy Lodge. Alice smiled to herself. Bill had no idea how recently she'd actually been there!

She knew the time he left his office each evening, so she decided she'd wait outside and follow him back to the house in Killiney. Unless, of course, he was meeting Geraldine McEvoy, or going back to her place, in which case she'd just have to try again the following day. She was nervous, and hoped poor Bill wouldn't have a heart attack when he found out she was still alive.

Much to Alice's relief, Bill left the office at the usual time that evening, collected his car from the underground car park, and headed south in the direction of Killiney. Following in her mother's car, Alice drove the same route, arriving at Ivy Lodge just minutes after Bill, and she pulled into the driveway just as he was opening the front door.

Still wearing her red wig and dark make-up, she jumped out of her car and confronted him. If she didn't do it quickly, she was afraid that she might lose her nerve

"Bill – hello."

Bill looked mystified, then suddenly he remembered. "Oh, hello. I met you at that photographic exhibition last week, didn't I? I'm sorry, but I've forgotten your name . . ."

"Conchita. Or at least that's my pretend name."

Bill eyes narrowed. "Your voice – you sound exactly like my late wife . . ."

Mystified, he stood aside as Alice swept past him, and headed straight down the back stairs towards the kitchen.

"Hey, you seem to know your way around!" Bill said, astonished. "Have you been here before?"

Without replying, Alice went to the kettle, filled it and turned it on. "We might both need a cuppa by the time I've finished," she told him, smiling nervously.

"You know, you really do speak exactly like my late wife," said Bill for the second time, a wary look now on his face.

Alice took a deep breath. "That's because I *am* your late wife. Except I'm not 'late' any more."

"Is this some kind of joke?"

"No, Bill – I really am Alice."

"You're winding me up!" said Bill, his voice getting

louder. "Is this some kind of sick joke? How dare you barge in here like that! I'm going to call the police!"

He began to cross the room towards the landline phone.

"No – wait!" Alice urged. It would be disastrous if Bill got the Gardaí involved at this stage. So much for her attempts to broach the subject gently! If he continued in this vein, Bill was likely to have the heart attack she was trying to avoid!

"Bill, if you'd just calm down, I'll prove to you that I'm Alice. Someone else was killed instead of me."

Bill put the phone down, his eyes narrowing suspiciously.

"Then prove it to me! Let me see – what colour are the walls in our bedroom?"

"Blue."

Bill still wasn't satisfied. "What's at the bottom of the garden?"

"The shed, where I do all my repotting."

"Jesus Christ! No, it's not possible. Anyone could have told you that – hah!" He leered at her triumphantly. "You were with Isobel Dunne at the exhibition – *she* told you!"

"No –"

"What sort of sick game are you playing? Why you're impersonating my wife I don't know –"

"Bill, it's not impersonating if it's true," said Alice, "Oh dammit – I'd intended doing this gradually, but you're not leaving me much option!" Quickly, Alice whipped off her wig. "Now, are you convinced?"

Bill's jaw dropped, and suddenly his eyes were filled with tears. "I don't believe this. How can it be? Is this some kind of cruel joke?" Then he leaned forward. "Did Alice have a long-lost *twin*?"

"Look, I'm sorry, Bill, but this is no joke. It really is me," said Alice. "Someone else was murdered instead of me – it was a case of mistaken identity. But I could still be at risk – that's why I'm in disguise." She looked into his eyes. "And I need your word that you'll say nothing to anyone else. In Ireland, only my mother and Isobel know."

Bill was silent for ages, and Alice could see that his jaw was trembling. "Is it really you, Alice?" he said at last.

"Yes, Bill – it's me."

Slowly, he crossed the kitchen floor and took her hand in his, staring at it as though it was some kind of alien object. "Yes, I can see it *is* you," he said at last. "You've got that tiny scar on your thumb – where you caught it in a swing when you were a kid." His eyes filled with tears again. "This is like something out of a surrealist movie!" he whispered.

"I know, Bill, I know –"

Suddenly, they were in each other's arms, and Bill was crushing her tightly to him.

"Oh my God, I can't get my head around this! You're really alive!" he whispered. "But I stood at your graveside – well, obviously I didn't, but – " He held her at arm's length while gazing at her in wonderment, then he hugged her tightly again. "This is amazing – Jesus, I need a double brandy, not a cup of tea!"

Bill went to the cupboard in the kitchen where they'd always kept their supply of alcohol, returning to Alice with two glasses and a bottle of brandy.

"None for me thanks, Bill," Alice said hastily. "I'm driving."

Bill looked aghast. "But this is your home – surely you're staying here – with me?"

Alice hesitated. She needed to tell Bill about her new life in Argentina, but she didn't want to hurt him either. Yet she also needed to make it clear that their life as they'd lived it previously was definitely over.

Alice suspected that he must be wondering why she'd confided in her mother and Isobel, and not him. Hopefully, she could invent a story about needing to keep him in the dark so that they could track down the killer. She'd hate Bill to know that he'd been a suspect. And she was now overwhelmed with guilt to think she'd ever believed he'd try to kill her.

"I think for the moment I'll stay at Mum's house," said Alice quickly. "We need time to talk properly."

"What about *us*, Alice?" Bill asked bleakly. "I mean, I still love you – I think we could make a go of it again, now that the money's been sorted out, do you agree?"

"No, I don't think so, Bill," said Alice gently. Since Bill was pushing for answers, she owed him honesty at least. "You'll always be special to me, but –" she hesitated, allowing herself a small smile, "I think Geraldine McEvoy is more your type of woman. You both want the same things out of life."

Bill suddenly looked guilty.

Alice grimaced. "Look, I know that she's been throwing herself at you already, Bill – and I'm sure you haven't been slow to respond to her charms."

Bill looked down at the ground. "I thought you were dead, Alice."

Alice nodded. "I've no problem with that, Bill – you were entitled to have other relationships since you never expected to see me again."

Bill eyed her longingly. "It was just a fling, and it meant

nothing. But now that you're back – it's you I want, always have."

Alice shook her head. "No, Bill," she said gently, "I think you and I have gone past the point of no return. Besides, I'm going back to Argentina."

Bill's mouth dropped open. "Argentina?"

Alice nodded. "Yes, Argentina. I've met someone special there." She reached out and touched his hand. "I'm sorry, Bill, but so much has happened in such a short time."

Bill grimaced. "You can say that again!"

There were a few uncomfortable seconds of silence before Bill spoke again. "You'll be glad to know that I've managed to sort out our financial situation, and I think we'll be out of the woods before long. I've restructured the loans, by negotiating a longer term at a lower rate of interest. The remaining apartments in Portugal sold much quicker than I expected, which brought in some much-needed cash."

Alice nodded. She knew already, but didn't want Bill to know that she'd overheard his conversation with her mother two days earlier.

He smiled happily at her. "And the news *you'll* want to hear is that I've managed to save Ivy Lodge. We won't have to sell it after all."

Alice smiled back, but she felt only sadness. Maybe Bill thought he could convince her to stay with him by dangling the house in front of her as bait. But the house meant nothing to her any more. It was odd to think that not so long ago it had meant the world to her.

When she didn't reply, Bill opted to change the subject yet again. "D'you know, Alice, I nearly did some business with Argentina myself!" he said brightly. "It was an amazing coincidence – just after you flew to Buenos Aires, this guy comes into my office and offers to cut me in on a deal to build holiday apartments in one of the big holiday resorts. The idea was that I'd sell them off-plans here in Ireland. At a big profit. He offered me a wonderful deal – but then he never got back to me."

"I suppose he was amazed to hear that I was over there already," said Alice dryly.

"Yes, as a matter of fact, he was!" said Bill, his face lighting up. "He wanted to know where you were staying –" Bill made a face, "– but of course I wasn't able to tell him, since you hadn't bothered to tell me, had you?"

"No," admitted Alice. "Did he by any chance admire the photo of me on your desk?"

"Yes, he did – he asked me if it was a picture of my wife – but how did you know that?"

"And that photo is now missing?"

"Yes! How – ?"

"I have my sources," Alice smiled. Everything was falling into place.

Just then, the kettle boiled and Alice made herself tea in her favourite mug. It felt an unbelievably strange thing to do, in view of all that had happened since she'd last made a mug of tea there.

"I need to stay in disguise for a little longer, so I need your word that you'll tell no one else, Bill."

"Of course not."

"And I mean no one – not even Geraldine McEvoy," she added, an impish grin on her face.

Bill's cheeks turned red.

"And in view of what you've told me about the guy

who offered you the deal in Argentina," Alice added, "I'm going to ask Enrique to liaise with the Gardaí, and arrange for you to look at some mug shots."

"Who's Enrique?"

"He's the police officer in charge of the case in Argentina," she said quickly. Which was perfectly true. But there was no point in hitting Bill with any further details for a while yet. He'd had enough to cope with for one day.

"Will you take a look? For me?"

"Of course. Who am I looking for?"

"Let's see if you recognise anybody."

* * *

With lightning speed, Enrique arranged with the Gardaí to have all their files of the relevant suspects made available, and Alice accompanied Bill to the Garda station the following day.

It wasn't long before Bill reacted. "Hey, that's the guy who came into the office, and wanted me to sell apartments in Argentina!"

Bill was pointing to a photograph of a heavy-set dark-haired man in his fifties.

The sergeant smiled. "We'd like to nail this one – he's a slippery customer who's involved in prostitution and a range of other unsavoury activities. All of them criminal, I might add."

Bill looked astonished. "So why was he offering me a deal on apartments in Argentina?"

"I doubt if there was any deal," Alice told him. "The guy was after a photograph of me, and information on where I was in Argentina."

Suddenly, it all fell into place for Bill. "So that's where the photo of you got to! It disappeared off my desk a few weeks ago." He frowned. "So what happens now?"

"We'll bring him in for questioning," the sergeant informed him. "Then we'll see what he can tell us about the person who contracted him to organise the hit in Argentina. These guys have no loyalty to each other, and when a few home truths are pointed out to this fellow, he'll probably decide that cooperation would be his best course of action." The sergeant smiled. "Sometimes the threat of a long prison sentence can do wonders to focus someone's mind. I don't think it'll be long before we have the name we want."

As Alice and Bill stood on the steps outside the Garda station, each of them felt unsure of how to say goodbye yet again.

"Are you sure you won't come back to Killiney this evening?" Bill said at last. "We could get a take-away, and it would be like old times. I've really missed you, Alice."

"Thanks, Bill – but no," said Alice, a note of regret in her voice. Partings were always difficult, and even more so when the people had once meant so much to each other.

"Okay." Bill sighed in resignation. It felt odd having Alice back from the dead, yet no longer belonging to him. He felt overwhelmed by a terrible sadness.

Just as she was about to take her leave of him, Alice turned back to face him once more. "Just one more thing, Bill. I don't think I could bear to know that Geraldine McEvoy was living in the home that you and I once shared. Would you mind selling the house?"

Bill nodded. He, too, accepted that Ivy Lodge had been

theirs alone, and the memories of their time there should never be shared by anyone else.

"Consider it done. And I'll see to it that your half of the money is lodged in your account."

"Thanks, Bill."

"We had some good times together, didn't we, Alice?"

Alice smiled. "We did, Bill – we had great times that I'll never forget."

Bill seemed satisfied with her response. Awkwardly, he stepped forward and bent to kiss her cheek. "Good luck, Alice. Send me a postcard from Argentina, won't you?"

Alice smiled back at him with genuine affection. "I will, Bill – of course I will." Suddenly, tears filled her eyes and she couldn't see him any more.

"Come here!" he said, wrapping his arms around her, and they hugged each other again.

Guiltily, Alice buried her face in his jacket. Luckily, Bill didn't know that she was crying from remorse for once thinking so badly of him. Fortunately, he need never know that not so long ago she'd believed he was her enemy.

CHAPTER 75

"Enrique, I've booked my flight back to Argentina."

"My beloved Alice, that is wonderful news! I can't wait to hold you in my arms again!" He sighed. "Patricia's family have now been informed of her death."

"Oh. Those poor people," said Alice sadly. "I'll go and see them before I fly back."

"Yes, I think they would appreciate that very much. Now tell me, my dearest Admiral, have the Irish police arranged everything for tomorrow morning?"

Alice chuckled. "Yes, I think someone is going to get a very great shock at 6 a.m."

"After that, your work is done and you can come back to me."

"Yes, I can't wait, my love. But first, I have a world exclusive to write up."

* * *

Alice walked slowly through the offices of the *Daily News*, as pre-arranged with Isobel, and sauntered in the direction of Dan Daly's office. One or two colleagues gave her a cursory glance, then did a double take as they realised who it was – but couldn't possibly be either!

"Hi, Alice," said Isobel casually, as she walked by. "Had a nice holiday?"

Suddenly, the office started buzzing, no one quite believing their eyes. Most of them had been at Alice's funeral! They looked from one to the other, uncertain what to do next. It couldn't possibly be her!

By then, Alice had reached Dan Daly's office and, tapping on the door, she walked in.

"For fuck's sake, piss off!" Dan muttered. "Can't you see I'm busy?" He was peering over some galleys and muttering to himself. Then he looked up, and the snarl froze on his face. For a split second he stared at her, bereft of words for perhaps the first time in his life.

Alice gave him a broad smile. "Hello, Dan – I'm back."

"Jesus Christ, do you want to give me a heart attack? It *can't* be you! You're supposed to be dead! Or are you the evil twin?"

"Oh, news of my death has been greatly exaggerated," she said, quoting Mark Twain.

After the initial shock, Dan was quickly back to his old self. "Christ, Fitzsimons, I thought I'd got rid of you! I hope you're not expecting your old job back – being dead does tend to limit your career options, you know. Besides, I've got a quality journalist doing your job now."

Alice laughed. "No, Dan – I won't be coming back. But I do have an exclusive for you. You might call it a parting gift." She pulled an exaggerated face. "Although you're such a nasty old bollocks, I might just sell it elsewhere. I'm sure the *Indo* or the *Times* would love it!"

Dan Daly looked at her sourly. "The headline that immediately springs to mind is: *Irish Journo in Lazarus-type Miracle.*" He peered at her closely. "Is it really you, Fitzsimons?"

Alice nodded, enjoying his discomfiture.

Outside Dan's office, everyone had stopped working, and they were all peering in at the window, the whispers building up from a murmur to a torrent of excited conversation.

"Get back to work, you shower of good-for-nothings!" Dan roared, waving his fist at them. "We go to press in half an hour!"

Outside, Isobel was being quizzed about Alice's apparent return from the dead.

Eagerly, colleagues crowded around her, some even with notebooks in hand, seeing a story like true journalists. "Dan would be proud of you all!" Isobel said laughing, "but I'll leave Alice to tell you her story herself."

Inside Dan's office, there was silence as he continued to stare at Alice with a mixture of awe and his customary contempt for all journalists.

"So what's this so-called exclusive you're hawking around, Fitzsimons?" he asked at last, sitting back in his chair.

Quickly, Alice gave him a brief outline of her story, while holding back enough facts to ensure he couldn't run the story without her input and cooperation. She'd also timed her arrival in the office to ensure that the story couldn't appear until after the police raid, which was scheduled for the following morning. But if written up now, it could be the lead story and world exclusive for tomorrow's edition.

"And I want Isobel Dunne with me as the photographer," she added.

When she'd finished, Dan sat silently, mulling over what she'd just told him. "Hmm," he said at last, "*Journalist Returns From Dead and Files World Exclusive.* Good heading – I like it."

Alice smiled to herself. Finally, she'd got him where she wanted him. Dan Daly was interested. *Very* interested.

Without saying another word, he stood up and walked outside into the main office. And for the first time ever, the astonished assembly of staff watched as the corners of his mouth actually turned up.

"I've always wanted to say this –" he said, smiling as he looked around at them all. "Hold the front page!"

CHAPTER 76

"Well, Aunt Dolly, I see your friend Charles Keane's been arrested," said Caroline, as she and her cousin Liz stood on their aunt's doorstep in Ballsbridge.

"W-what?" Dolly took a step backward. She was surprised to see her niece, accompanied by Teresa's daughter, since neither of them ever called to the house.

"Come in," she said grudgingly, standing aside to let them enter. "I've never heard such nonsense in all my life! You're very nasty, Caroline, to be slandering a wonderful man like Charles."

Inside in the drawing room, Caroline placed a copy of the *Daily News* in front of her aunt. The headlines proclaimed Charles Keane's early morning arrest, written up in an exclusive feature by Alice Fitzsimons. There was also a picture of Charles being led away by Gardaí, photographed by Isobel Dunne.

Dolly clutched the paper and stared at the front page. The colour drained from her face, and a strange groan came from deep in her chest.

"Sit down, Aunt Dolly," said Liz, looking concerned. "I think you've had a bit of a shock. I'll go and put the kettle on."

With that, she scurried out to the large kitchen.

"What are they saying Charles has done?" Dolly asked, her voice barely audible. "There must be some mistake – Charles is a gentleman, not a criminal!"

"He's been arrested for murder and attempted murder – and that's only the beginning," said Caroline triumphantly.

Dolly's mouth opened, then closed. "I've never heard anything so preposterous!" she shouted.

"Well, my dear aunt, you're not entirely blameless yourself either!" Caroline retorted. "Think back, Aunt Dolly, to your days at BWF Pharmaceuticals – you supported Charles Keane against your own husband and sister. Mum told me you were proud of your efforts to help him suppress a research document your husband had written. Then, you even told him that Gina had a copy of the research!" Now Caroline was angry. "Do you realise, Aunt Dolly, that by telling that to Charles Keane, you signed your own sister's death warrant?"

Dolly looked old and confused, her skin thin as crumpled paper, the veins standing out in stark relief. "I don't understand," she kept repeating, "Charles would never do anything like that!"

"Charles Keane is a murderer," Caroline told her. "Nothing's ever mattered to him but his precious BWF Pharmaceuticals, and anyone who got in the way was promptly disposed of."

"I don't believe it!" Dolly shouted, her voice reed-thin, her hands shaking. "Charles would never do anything to hurt me or my family – Charles is a gentleman!"

"Well, he arranged to have your husband killed," Caroline informed her, eyes blazing. "And when he discovered that your sister had the missing copy of Owen's research, he arranged to have her killed as well. Unfortunately for them, Gina left her copy of the research at Larry's place, where it remained hidden in her suitcase for another thirty years. But the information it contains is still explosive. So when Larry gave the suitcase to me, I found the research paper and realised that it might still have implications for people's health today."

She looked down at her aunt, who was cowering in her chair. "Don't worry, Aunt Dolly, you're not the only one who's endangered others' lives by your actions. I nearly got poor Alice Fitzsimons killed, by sending the research report to her and letting you know about it. When you told Charles Keane, 'the dear man' as you call him, tried to have her run her off the road, and when that didn't work, he hired hit-men to kill her in Argentina! He's also responsible for the death of a woman called Patricia Martin whom the killers mistakenly thought was Alice!"

"No, no – I won't listen to you!" Dolly cried, covering her ears with her knarled hands.

Caroline laughed harshly. "Have you any idea how much harm that man Charles Keane has caused? Alice even thought her own husband was the one who wanted to murder her!"

Caroline left her aunt cowering in her armchair, and stormed off to the kitchen to help Liz make the tea.

* * *

As Dolly sat in her armchair, she allowed her mind to drift

off into the past. It was the only way that she could cope with what was happening in the present. How could Caroline say those awful things about her beloved Charles? He would never do such things! Charles was a gentleman, always had been.

He wasn't as dapper these days as he'd once been, but then, neither was she. They'd both grown older, but nevertheless, she'd been looking forward to them spending their golden years together. She'd been certain that it was only a matter of time before Charles proposed . . . now it would never happen, would it? Not if young Caroline was telling the truth.

No, it couldn't be true! Dolly shook her head vehemently. Caroline was just being nasty, because she was jealous of her aunt's wealth. Dolly sighed. Perhaps she could have taken greater care of her niece, but there was always the spectre of her own child in the background . . . how could she care for her sister's child, when she'd aborted her own?

Dolly wept silently, the tears running into the grooves that time had etched on her face. Even after a lifetime, she'd never forgotten the child whose life she'd ended all those years ago. People had always assumed she was barren, but she'd held this precious secret close to her heart. Owen never knew about it, since it had happened before they met. Neither did Stella or her mother. It had been her secret – hers and Charles's.

She'd met the love of her life the day she joined BWF Pharmaceuticals. Charles Keane had been everything she'd ever wanted in a man, except for one small problem – he was married already. But she and Charles hadn't let that get in the way of their mutual attraction. Before long, they'd become lovers. Charles had always been responsible and used condoms, which he usually brought back from business trips abroad. But one day something went wrong, and Dolly eventually realised that she was pregnant.

Charles had urged her to have an abortion, all expenses paid of course. He could write it off as company expenses, he explained, and she could even take a holiday abroad afterwards, if she felt like it.

The abortion clinic had been clean and efficient, but Dolly left there with an emptiness inside her that would never again be filled. The following week, she returned to the office.

"How did it go, m'dear?" Charles asked cheerfully, as though she'd simply been having a tooth out at the dentist. "I'm sure you're relieved to have that little problem out of the way."

Outwardly, Dolly smiled, but inwardly, her heart was breaking. It was obvious that Charles had no real understanding of the trauma she'd been through. "Charles, I'm extremely tired," she told him. "In fact, I'm feeling far from well. It was quite an ordeal, you know."

"You poor dear," Charles said kindly. "But it's all for the best, isn't it? Now why don't you go home and take the next few days off?"

When Dolly burst into tears, she saw the look of panic on Charles's face. It was clear that he didn't want her getting all emotional on him, or blurting out something to another member of staff – or even worse, to her family or his wife.

"My dear! I didn't realise it had affected you so badly!" he said soothingly. "Of course you must take a break – how totally thoughtless of me to expect you back at work so soon." He smiled. "You're so efficient, Dolly, that I've come to expect you to bounce back quickly from any adversity. Unfair of me, I know."

"I'm sorry, Charles, but this really affected me much more than even *I* realised," said Dolly, mopping her eyes. "I think I might avail of that holiday offer you made me."

"A splendid idea!" Charles said, quickly recovering and beaming at her. "Of course, you'll be on full salary, and I'll also arrange an extra bonus, so that you can treat yourself to a nice hair-do, and some nice new dresses." He smiled gently. "Just let me know when you're ready to come back to work." He patted her on the shoulder. "Don't stay away too long, m'dear – no one else on the secretarial staff is as efficient or dependable as you."

Dolly was pleased with the compliment. "Thank you, Charles," she said, feeling pleased. Charles always made her feel important.

Dolly recalled how thrilled her own mother had been at the prospect of her eldest daughter going 'to the continent' for two weeks, at the company's expense. Back then, only wealthy people could afford luxuries like a two-week package holiday in Spain, which Dolly eventually selected.

"Mr Keane obviously thinks very highly of you," her mother had told her proudly. "I hope you'll behave yourself while you're away, and respect the trust Mr Keane has placed in you. You're being offered a wonderful opportunity."

Stella, too, had warmly congratulated her, and for a moment, Dolly had longed to tell her sister what had really happened, and why she was feeling so poorly. But as the elder sister, she had a role to play in the family hierarchy, and she couldn't bear to be seen as fallible. Nor could she cope with the pity she might see in Stella's eyes.

Returning to BWF Pharmaceuticals after her holiday, she'd resumed her job as Charles's secretary. But they'd never again rekindled their physical relationship – perhaps Charles was too scared to risk another unwanted pregnancy. Instead, he quickly found a husband for Dolly in Owen, his newly appointed Medical Director, who was in charge of clinical trials.

Dolly now wiped away a tear that had run down her cheek. If only Charles hadn't been married, they could have had a wonderful life together. They and their child – the child who had been lost to them forever.

From the day of Dolly's return to BWF Pharmaceuticals, as if by tacit agreement there had been no reference to the child they'd conceived together. It was a taboo subject, never to be mentioned again.

But the ache never left her. It festered inside her, tainting every other facet of her life. She'd never been able to give Owen the love he deserved, and Gina's fling with him had only highlighted Dolly's own inability to be a proper wife to him. It had poisoned her relationship with Stella, because of her jealousy over Stella's ability to have – and keep – her child.

It had broken her heart over and over again as she'd watched Caroline blossom and mature, since it only emphasised the loss of her own child. She was aware of her guilt in not helping Stella and young Caroline financially, but to do so would have felt like a betrayal of her own dead infant. So she'd distanced herself from Stella's child, whose very existence brought her pain. And she'd kept her money tightly to herself, wearing it like a protective cloak, because it was all she had left.

Feeling old and tired, Dolly rose unsteadily to her feet. She would go to her room, away from Caroline's accusing eyes. She didn't believe for an instant what Caroline had said about Charles. It was preposterous to think that he would kill people, especially members of her own family. Charles wouldn't hurt a fly!

Making her way unsteadily up the stairs, Dolly tried to recall exactly what Caroline had said. Something about Charles going on trial? That vindictive little hussy only wanted to frighten her!

Dolly felt utterly confused. Cover-ups and corruption had been mentioned, as well as murder. How dare anyone say things like that about Charles! Men like Charles were the backbone of society! Hadn't he created jobs and healed the sick with the wonderful range of drugs and vaccines that BWF Pharmaceutical did work on? It was the thugs and bank robbers that should be in prison, not men like Charles!

And what had Caroline said about Charles causing people's deaths by suppressing Owen's research? Dolly was well aware that Owen's research had been suppressed – hadn't she helped Charles to do it? At the time, he'd fully explained to her how Owen's scaremongering would damage the company. Owen was unhappy about the preservative being used in the vaccines, which he believed would result in neurological damage.

But Charles had explained to her how Owen was mistaken. The preservative in the vaccine was essential, he told her. Developing nations couldn't afford the single-dose vials that didn't contain the preservative. Large-scale dosing of people, for use during epidemics or pandemics, needed multiple-dose vials.

"Besides, if the preservative isn't used, BWF Pharmaceuticals could go under," Charles had told her confidentially. "None of the trials done abroad have reported any ill-effects, so we can't be seen as the ones to start causing problems. Getting this product onto the market is essential if we're to survive." She'd been flattered that he'd used the term 'we'– it may her feel as though she and Charles were in it together.

Charles had even suggested – discreetly, of course – that Owen might need to spend some time at a rest home, since he was clearly delusional, and under a great deal of stress. He'd been gently hinting that Dolly might need to section him when Owen's car went off the road into the river one night, and he'd been killed.

Poor Owen, Dolly thought suddenly, I never gave you what you needed, nor did I support you, even though you were my husband. I always supported Charles, no matter what the issue was. Could I have been wrong all these years?

Suddenly, for the very first time, Dolly examined the possibility that Charles might have killed her husband. Owen's death would certainly have been to Charles's advantage.

And Gina's death. That, perhaps, hurt most of all. Caroline had accused her of being responsible for Gina's death, claiming that there was proof of Charles's guilt, which would feature in his trial.

With remarkable clarity, Dolly now recalled the day Charles had casually asked about the missing copy of Owen's research paper, and Dolly had told him that Gina had it. She'd been pleased and flattered that Charles relied on her so much, and she'd been eager to help him save the company. But had she saved the company at the expense of her sister's life? Had that been the moment when Gina's life became expendable?

It was all too much for her. If only she didn't feel so old and tired . . . I can't cope any more, Dolly thought, as she reached the top of the stairs and entered her bedroom. I no longer seem capable of distinguishing truth from lies. I want to sleep, so that I don't have to think about it all any more. I want to retreat to a world where Charles is the man I've always believed him to be, where there's no doubt about what's right and what's wrong. Otherwise, my whole life's been a lie . . .

* * *

When Caroline marched into the kitchen after her tirade at Aunt Dolly, Liz was lurking behind the door, a concerned look on her face.

"Don't you think you've been a bit tough on her?" she whispered. "I mean, she's always adored Charles Keane, so this must be an awful shock to her."

"It's about time she faced the unpalatable truth," Caroline said harshly. "All my life, she's been lording it over our family, living in her ivory tower, and looking down on the rest of us. She's led a mean and solitary life. She never offered us anything, despite *her* wealth and *our* poverty."

"She was probably always jealous, you know," said Liz philosophically. "She never had a child, whereas your parents were lucky enough to have you. And even when both sisters were left widows, your mother had you to give her life meaning. What did Dolly have, except money?"

Caroline looked at her cousin sarcastically. "You'll have

me weeping into my boots any minute!" she retorted. "Aunt Dolly was left with a fine house and a great pension after her husband died, whereas my mother was left with nothing. As you know, my dad was in the building trade, which made little provision for a pension. After my dad got cancer and died, Mum had hardly enough money to survive on. We lived on cheap food and hand-me-downs for years, while Aunt Dolly sat comfortably in her mansion and looked down on us!"

Liz patted her cousin's arm. "You're very angry, Caro – and I fully understand. But look at it this way – you've made something of your life, whereas what has Aunt Dolly to show for hers? She's spent a lifetime being duped by the man she loved –how must she feel now, having discovered that he killed her own husband and sister? I doubt if she'll sleep too well tonight."

"What do you mean – 'the man she loved'?"

Liz smiled sadly. "Surely you knew? Anyone can see that Dolly's always been in love with Charles Keane."

In the silence that followed, the two young women made the tea, took down the mugs from the dresser, and prepared a tray to bring into the drawing room. Not wanting to confront her Aunt Dolly again so soon, Caroline took some brack from the cupboard and began buttering it slowly. She conceded that preparing it was probably a pointless exercise, since they were all far too overwrought to feel hungry.

"Do you know, Liz," Caroline said as she finished buttering, "I'm so angry this minute, I could put strychnine in Aunt Dolly's tea!"

Liz grinned. "Feeling the way she must right now, I'm sure she'd be glad if you did it for her!"

Suddenly, they both stopped laughing, as the same thought occurred to them simultaneously.

"She wouldn't – would she?" Caroline whispered, looking distraught.

"It wouldn't surprise me if she did," said Liz. "After all, her whole world has collapsed around her. Can you imagine her sitting in on Charles Keane's trial? I certainly can't."

Hurrying out the kitchen door and into the drawing room, both women stared in consternation at the empty chair.

"Oh no –" groaned Caroline, already heading for the stairs, with Liz in rapid pursuit. All Caroline could think of was the sad and pathetic shape of her aunt cowering in the armchair, and of how much she'd enjoyed telling her about Charles Keane.

When they reached Dolly's bedroom door, Caroline tapped gently at first, then harder when there was no answer. Then they started calling out Dolly's name, louder and louder.

"Maybe she's just gone to sleep," Liz suggested, although neither of them believed it for a minute.

"Hardly, after the racket we've just made," Caroline replied.

Turning the handle, the two women realised that the door was locked, confirming their worst fears.

"What do we do now?" Caroline whispered.

"I don't know – hang on, have you got a credit card?"

Caroline nodded.

"Apparently you can open certain types of locks by slipping a credit card in at the side of the door," said Liz, by way of explanation.

"That only happens in the movies!" Caroline retorted.

"Well, have you got any brighter ideas?"

Shaking her head, Caroline rushed downstairs, returning a minute later with her credit card, which she passed to Liz.

"Well, here goes."

Liz began sliding the credit card in between the door and its frame. Suddenly, it swung open, and the two women almost fell into the room. They gazed in silence at the body of their aunt lying in the middle of her bed, a half-empty bottle of brandy and a glass on the bedside table, and an empty pill bottle beside her.

"Oh my God, what have I done?" Caroline whispered.

Wildly, she turned to her cousin. "What should we do, Liz? Can you do CPR? Shouldn't we call for an ambulance?"

"Leave her be," said Liz, gently resting her hand on Caroline's arm. "What would be the point in trying to bring her back? It would be too cruel. Poor old Dolly couldn't cope with the shame."

Caroline nodded, tears now filling her eyes. "You're right – it's for the best, isn't it? I just wish I hadn't wanted to hurt her so much for being unkind to Mum and me over the years. This is all my fault and I'll never be able to forgive myself."

"Don't beat yourself up, Caro," said Liz, putting her arms around her cousin. "It's not your fault that Charles Keane is a murderer." She hugged Caroline. "Okay, so you were direct in the way you told her, but at the end of the day, you only told her the truth."

Linking Caroline's arm in hers, Liz led her cousin down the stairs. "Let's leave her in peace for a while before we call the emergency services."

Back in the kitchen, the two women surveyed the tray,

with its cloth, mugs and plate of brack. A sea change had taken place since the brack had been buttered and the tea poured. Looking at these ordinary things, Caroline was overwhelmed with grief. While she'd been buttering brack, her aunt had been swallowing pills to end her life. And she had been the catalyst. Suddenly, Caroline broke down and wept.

CHAPTER 77

"Hello, Larry."

Larry Macken looked surprised, then apprehensive. "Oh hello, Caroline. Come in, come in. Did you have any luck finding Gina?"

Caroline nodded as Larry ushered her into the cosy sitting room in North London, and once again they sat facing each other.

"So – is it good news?"

"Yes and no," Caroline told him. "First of all, I'm sorry to have to tell you this, but Gina is dead."

She paused, allowing Larry time to absorb the information she'd just given him. Briefly, his eyes filled with tears, and Caroline could see that he was struggling with his emotions.

"She died thirty years ago – shortly after she left you."

"Oh, poor Gina," Larry said, his eyes filling with tears again. "What happened to her?"

"She was murdered."

"Oh my God – how? Why?"

Briefly, Caroline explained what had happened all those

years ago, and the part Charles Keane and BWF Pharmaceuticals played in Gina's death.

Larry's eyes were red as he looked at her. "Poor Gina! All those years, I thought –"

Then a hungry look came into his eyes. "The child she was expecting – our child – I suppose it died too?"

"Well, that's the next thing I have to tell you," Caroline said slowly, "and it's not easy."

"Why? What do you mean?"

"Well, the child was born shortly before Gina was killed – and that child was me."

Larry looked puzzled, then a strangled cry came from his throat. "You're the baby? So that means you're my –"

Caroline shook her head sadly. "No, Larry, I'm afraid not."

She looked at the floor. She was finding it hard to witness Larry's confused emotions, ranging from shock to hope within the space of a few seconds. Now, she was dashing the remaining small glimmer of hope that something good had come out of the tragedy, and that his child had survived.

"I hate to have to tell you this, but Gina was expecting another man's child when she married you."

"What man?"

"Owen, my Aunt Dolly's husband."

Larry grimaced. "Who was Gina's boss when she worked for BWF Pharmaceuticals."

Biting his lip, Larry looked out the window and into the distance. He suddenly looked old and tired, and Caroline wished that she hadn't had to deal him this final blow. But he deserved to know the truth.

At last, he turned to face her. "So I was a patsy," he

remarked grimly. "I suppose I should have realised it at the time. I mean, Gina never wanted to commit to me, even though we'd been seeing each other for years. Then suddenly, out of the blue, she wanted to marry me. I should have guessed something was amiss, but I just wanted to believe that she'd grown to love me."

Caroline said nothing, as Larry retreated into thoughts of the past.

"You know, her mood kept changing during those last few weeks," he said at last. "One minute, she'd be up in the air, the next minute down in the dumps. I assumed it was hormonal changes due to the pregnancy, but with hindsight, I was obviously very naive." He gave a sudden harsh laugh. "After Gina left, I analysed everything she ever said, and every mood she ever had, in an effort to understand what happened. Now it's obvious that she was leaving me for Owen."

"I'm sorry, Larry," said Caroline, reaching across to touch his clenched hands.

"So you're Owen's child, not mine."

Caroline nodded.

Larry had tears in his eyes as he suddenly grasped Caroline's hands in his. "I wish you were mine – I always wanted to have a child, especially a daughter."

Caroline smiled back at him through her own tears. "There's something I'd like to ask you, Larry – I don't have my father to walk me down the aisle when I get married. Would you do me the honour?"

As he wiped away his tears, the joy in Larry's eyes was obvious. "Of course I will! I'd be like your honorary dad, wouldn't I?"

Caroline nodded happily. "That's settled, then."

"So you *are* getting married," added Larry, smiling. "Last time we spoke, you weren't sure if there would be a wedding or not."

"That's all sorted now," said Caroline, smiling back.

Larry sighed. He hoped life would be good to Caroline, and that her impulsive nature would always produce the results she wanted. Like Gina, Caroline possessed a unique and magical quality that made people love her, and he felt sorry for whichever man she'd discarded. He knew what being dumped felt like.

"I'm looking forward to meeting Clare, too," added Caroline. "I can see that she's made you happy."

Larry nodded. Clare had loved him enough to stick around until he'd eventually felt able to return her love, and she'd accepted that Gina's shadow would always be there between them. In time, as Larry's pain had eased and the spectre of Gina had gradually faded, his love for Clare had blossomed. Today, he counted himself a very lucky man.

Chapter 78

"Are you ready, Caro?"

Caroline nodded as Hazel made a last-minute adjustment to her headdress and veil.

Today, she was finally getting married! She'd expected to feel nervous on her wedding day, but instead, she felt calm and serene. Now she understood what people meant when they said it was the happiest day of your life.

"You look gorgeous – you were right to choose that dress from the pattern book," said Liz approvingly. "It suits you perfectly. I always said it would, didn't I?"

Caroline nodded again. To please Liz, she'd have said black was white – today, of all days, she wanted everyone to be happy. In actual fact, she didn't care about the dress, the veil or the wedding cake. She was about to marry the man she loved, and she'd never been more certain of anything in her life. And while she wanted to look her best for him, she knew he wouldn't care if she turned up in a sack.

Looking back on the last few months, she conceded that her life, as she'd known it, had been turned on its head. Today, she was wearing Gina's half-slip underneath her dress as her 'something old', because today, of all days, she wanted to feel close to the woman who had changed her life irrevocably.

Outside Stella's house, the cars were already waiting to drive Caroline and her entourage the short distance to the church. After a last look in the mirror, she descended the stairs, to gasps of delight from the neighbours who had assembled outside the open front door to see the bride and wish her well as she left for the church.

The weather had obliged too – even though the wedding was later in the year than originally planned – it was a mild, sunny day, with no wind to ruffle Caroline's veil or toss the guests' hats into the air. It was further proof for Caroline – if proof indeed was needed – that everything about this day was going to be perfect. But even if it had been pouring rain, nothing would have deterred Caroline from getting to the altar – today, come hell or high water, she was going to marry the man she loved.

The church was beautifully decorated with flowers, and Caroline breathed in their heady scent as she and Larry Macken stood in the porch, preparing to make their entrance. Bridesmaids Liz and Hazel were fussing around, one of them straightening the hem of Caroline's dress, the other making last-minute adjustments to her veil.

"Time to go," Larry whispered, as the organist started playing 'The Wedding March'.

Caroline was suddenly nervous, and looked to him for reassurance. Larry patted her arm and gave her the thumbs-up signal, and she marvelled that she hadn't known this man until very recently. Now he was playing a major role in her life.

"You look beautiful," he told her, and she knew that it was true. Love made her beautiful, on this, her very own special day-of-days.

As she walked up the aisle on Larry's arm, a sea of faces greeted her, all turning round for a glimpse of the approaching bride, all smiling and wishing her luck as she made her way to the altar.

In the blur of faces, she spotted Alice, Isobel and Joan, Liz's husband Ronnie, Aunt Teresa, Larry's wife Clare, Maeve and her husband Kevin. She also spotted her mother's friends Rosemary and Eileen, and in the front row, her mother Stella, looking radiant in a cerise dress, matching jacket and big hat.

As Caroline reached the altar, the man she loved was waiting for her, and he grinned nervously at her as the priest began the ceremony. Soon, she would take her vows to love and honour this man for the rest of her life. She looked into his gorgeous brown eyes, and saw his love for her shining in them. This moment she would cherish forever.

How could I have doubted for a second that it was him? Caroline thought. With hindsight, I think I always knew he was the man for me. I'm gradually learning to trust my instincts, and not allow anyone else to try to sway my opinion. The heart instinctively knows what's right. He'd been worth fighting for.

* * *

And yet it could all have turned out so differently. That day, when Simon and Ken had confronted each other on her mother's doorstep, she'd acutely felt her own ineptness and thoughtlessness. In trying to avoid unpleasantness, she'd hurt Ken far more than if she'd been straight with him right from the beginning. In trying to have her cake and eat it, she'd mismanaged her life, and caused grief to two men who didn't deserve such treatment.

After Simon stormed off, she'd gone with Ken to the local pub. They'd talked for ages, probably for the first time in years. Instead of making assumptions about each other, they'd calmly shared their hopes and dreams, accepting sadly that there was no future for them together. Caroline had returned his ring, and let him know that while she cared about him, he was no longer the man she wanted to spend her life with. After a few feeble attempts at protest, Ken finally and reluctantly accepted the inevitable. He wished her well, and they agreed that at some point in the future, they'd deal with the sale of the house. Ken suggested that he might buy out Caroline's half, which would suit them both perfectly.

Outside the pub, they hugged, and there were tears of sadness in Caroline's eyes as she watched Ken walk away. She was genuinely and deeply fond of him, and she knew he'd make some woman a wonderful husband. He just wasn't the one *she* wanted.

But was it too late for her and Simon? He'd made his feelings very clear. She'd deceived him, and been hypocritical enough to object when she'd thought he'd deceived *her*! Well, even if he continued to reject her, she still knew that finishing with Ken had been the right thing to do. The magic had long ago left their relationship, and meeting Simon had simply confirmed that. Even if he never wanted to see her again, she'd always be grateful to him for showing her how marvellous a relationship could be.

Dialling his mobile number, she now waited anxiously while it rang and rang. Oh God, she thought, has he seen that the call was from her, and decided to ignore it? She couldn't exactly blame him. He was undoubtedly hurting deeply. He'd come all the way from London to surprise her on her birthday, only to be confronted by the revelation that she already had a fiancé, who then proceeded to give him a bloody nose! She grimaced. What a birthday this was turning out to be!

What would she do if he didn't answer? Presumably he was staying at a hotel somewhere in Dublin, since he wouldn't have come just for the day. No doubt he'd intended taking her out for a birthday meal that evening, and her heart was breaking as she thought of how excited he would have been when planning it.

Suddenly her blood ran cold. Maybe he wouldn't remain in Dublin now that he'd found out about Ken! Maybe he'd been so disillusioned that he'd already gone to the airport to wait for a stand-by flight back to London! If so, she'd missed her opportunity.

Caroline wanted to cry with frustration. She'd needed to talk to Ken and finish their relationship before she could offer herself to Simon. But the time that had taken might mean that Simon had already left.

Caroline was so worked up that she almost didn't realise that the phone had been answered. "Simon – please!" she told him when she heard his voice. "Don't hang up, please let me explain things!"

"There's nothing to explain, Caroline – you just forgot to mention you were engaged to another man!"

"I'm sorry, Simon! I wish you'd give me a chance to talk to you! I've just given Ken back his ring."

There was silence at the other end of the line as Simon digested this information. "So you're finished with him for good?"

"Yes, Simon – definitely! But in reality, it's been over for ages! I just didn't realise it, until I met you!"

Simon said nothing, and Caroline was terrified he might disconnect the call.

"Please, Simon – can we at least meet? I'll come to your hotel, or the airport, or the boat terminal – wherever – I just want to see you again – even if it's for the last time!"

There was a deep sigh at the other end of the phone. "Okay," he said grudgingly.

Caroline almost whooped with relief. At least if she could see him face-to-face, she might convince him that he was the man she truly loved. And even if Simon was determined to end their relationship, at least he would do it knowing how she felt about him. Caroline knew she'd messed up badly, but she was prepared to give it everything she'd got.

"Where are you? I'll be there in fifteen minutes."

Simon told her the name of the small hotel where he was staying. Hailing a passing taxi, Caroline gave the address of the hotel. Hopefully she wasn't too late to convince Simon that they could have a future together.

At the hotel, Caroline gave Simon's name to the receptionist, who telephoned his room. After what seemed like an eternity, the receptionist informed her that she was to go up, and Caroline bounded up the stairs, not even waiting for the lift.

As he opened the door, Caroline was once again over-come with love and desire for him.

"Simon," she said without preamble, "I don't want you

to say anything – just listen. Since I met you, I haven't slept with Ken. I couldn't. I was just waiting for the right moment to tell Ken it was over. But your arrival at Mum's house made my careful planning superfluous!"

Simon couldn't prevent a small smile in spite of himself.

"I just got used to being with Ken, having more or less grown up with him," she explained. "Everyone expected us to get married, and it just seemed the easiest thing to do. But then I met you, and I realised that this is *my* life, and that I don't need to fulfil anyone else's expectations!"

"Well since *we're* finished, you can go back to Ken again!" Simon said angrily. "I'm sure he'll take you back – the guy looked pretty lovesick as far as I could see!"

"You just don't get it, Simon, do you?" Caroline shouted. "I love *you!* I've never felt this way about anyone before. Even if you don't want me, Ken still isn't the man I want." She chanced a little smile. "I guess I'll just grow old alone – maybe I'll get a few cats for companionship!"

"You just said you loved me. Is that true?"

"Of course it's true! I think of you night and day, I want to make love to you every moment, I want to spend the rest of my life with you – I absolutely adore you!"

By now, the tears were streaming down Caroline's face. She knew she probably looked a fright, but she just didn't care. The man she loved was about to walk out of her life forever . . .

"Maybe we could grow old together," he said, "and share the cats. Derek and Anne seem to like you."

At first, Caroline wondered if she'd heard correctly.

"Of course, I feel more strongly about you than they do," Simon added. "I *love* you."

Suddenly, they were in each other's arms, both of them crying.

"My precious Caroline, you mean everything to me!"

"Oh Simon, Simon – I thought I'd lost you!"

Eventually, Simon stopped kissing her long enough to speak. "I'd planned that we'd do a tour of Dublin this afternoon. Then I'd take you out for a meal tonight for your birthday. Are we still on track?"

Caroline nodded, too full of emotion to speak.

"But I'm going to make a slight change to the schedule, if you don't mind –" Simon went to his suitcase and opened it. "I intended to give you your present tonight, but I can't wait a moment longer. I want to make you mine as soon as possible!"

With that, Simon produced a tiny box, and watched joyfully as Caroline opened it and gazed at the diamond engagement ring inside.

"It's an ethical diamond," he assured her, "and I can get the size altered if you need to –"

"It's beautiful, Simon – oh, I love you so much!"

Simon slid the ring onto Caroline's finger, and it fitted perfectly, with no need for any alteration.

"See, it was meant to be!" said Simon happily. "I knew the day I met you that you were special. If I could find that mugger again, I'd shake his hand and buy him a drink!"

"And while you're doing that, he'd be making off with your wallet!" Caroline replied, grinning.

Then she was in his arms again, and they were clinging tightly to each other.

Gradually their kisses grew more passionate, and Simon groaned as Caroline pulled him down on the bed.

"What about this tour of Dublin?"

"Later," Caroline had said firmly, "much later . . ."

*   *   *

Suddenly, Caroline realised that the priest was looking expectantly at her. It was time to take their wedding vows!

"Do you, Simon, take Caroline to be your lawfully wedded wife?"

Looking adoringly at her, Simon nodded his head. "I do."

"Do you, Caroline, take Simon as your lawfully wedded husband?"

Caroline returned Simon's joyful smile. "I do."

"I now pronounce you husband and wife."

As they kissed – for the first time as a married couple – Caroline felt joy like she'd never known before. And she thanked her lucky stars that she'd realised in time that familiarity and companionship were poor substitutes for that gut-wrenching passion that had long been missing in her relationship with Ken, and which she'd only discovered with Simon.

Her husband. She rolled the word around on her tongue, and it sounded wonderful.

She was looking forward to a long and happy married life together.

Later, after the photographs had been taken and the wedding party had made their way to the hotel, Caroline took the opportunity of having a few words with her mother. Stella was looking wonderful, if a little sad, and Caroline knew why. She was still mourning the recent death of her sister. Although she and Dolly had never been close, they'd been sisters nonetheless.

It was wonderful to be surrounded by people she cared about, and to share her special day with them. As the guests assembled for the wedding meal, Caroline surveyed her friends, family and work colleagues all in their finery. She was delighted to see that Simon's family had blended in well with hers, and everyone seemed to be having a good time.

She and Simon were moving back to London immediately after the wedding, having postponed their honeymoon – to be spent in Argentina – until later in the year after Alice had her baby. Caroline was also looking forward to meeting Enrique and Ricardo – she'd heard so much about them both that she felt she already knew them well! Caroline had already left her job in Dublin and found another one in London. It was time for major changes, and she was looking forward to the challenge. What's more, she already had friends in London – Larry and Clare were hoping to see her and Simon regularly.

After a delicious meal had been served and the mercifully short speeches were over, Caroline had one more duty to perform. Standing up, she raised her glass before the assembled guests.

"I'd like to propose a toast to absent friends – two people I never met, but without them, today would never have happened. To Owen and Gina!"

The assembled guests raised their glasses, only a few of them knowing to whom Caroline was referring, and why.

But she wasn't finished yet. "And finally, a toast to my

mother, Stella – the best mother in the world – without whom I wouldn't be here. To Stella!"

With tears in her eyes, Stella acknowledged the toast, gripping Caroline's hand tightly as all the guests rose to salute her.

* * *

When the time came for Caroline to mingle with the guests, there was one particular person she was longing to see. Alice had flown from Argentina to Dublin for the wedding, but they hadn't yet found a chance to catch up on all their news.

"Hey, dreamer – a penny for your thoughts!"

Alice started as Caroline appeared beside her, smiling happily.

"You look gorgeous, Caroline."

"Thanks, Alice – I feel great. And you look wonderful too – is your pregnancy going well?"

"Terrific. I never felt better in my life."

"You didn't waste any time!" grinned Caroline, surveying Alice's swelling torso.

"Well, I wasn't prepared to wait for four years until my divorce is through," she told Caroline. "I'm already in my thirties, and if I want to produce the ten children Enrique and I want –"

Seeing Caroline's shocked face, Alice laughed, giving her friend a reassuring pat.

"Only joking!"

"So you're settled in Buenos Aires now?"

"Yes, I've moved into Enrique's house, but we're looking for somewhere bigger to live – preferably a house with a bit of land attached, because I have a very special resident arriving soon from Villanova."

"Ricardo?"

"No, Bodhrán – he's our goat."

"An Argentinian goat with an Irish name!"

Alice nodded, smiling. "Besides, I'll need more space to fit in all the guests who are coming out to visit us!"

Caroline nodded. "Yes, I'm looking forward to seeing Argentina next year."

Nor was she the only one who was planning to visit Alice and Enrique. Liz and her husband Ronnie were going later in the year. Ronnie was planning to do some mountain-climbing, but Liz intended to shop! Stella and Alice's mother Joan had become close, and were planning to visit together.

"Are you happy there?"

Alice nodded. "It's a beautiful country, although not without its problems. But home is where the heart is, isn't it? I'd be happy anywhere that Enrique was."

Both women smiled at each other, knowing that the power of love could move mountains, and they were both lucky to have found it.

"You'll be back for Charles Keane's trial?"

Alice nodded. "I'm a witness for the prosecution. But it won't be for ages yet."

Caroline's brow furrowed. "Do you think BWF Pharmaceuticals and Charles Keane will ever pay for what they've done?"

Alice shrugged her shoulders. "I doubt it. But at least the vaccine has been completely withdrawn. If future lives are saved, at least we'll have achieved something."

As Caroline floated away to talk to other guests, Alice recalled once more the events that had led up to Charles Keane being charged with murder, and attempted murder, and hopefully BWF Pharmaceutical would be charged with corporate irresponsibility and heavily fined.

Cooperating with the Gardaí, Alice had been the only journalist present, and Isobel the only photographer, when Charles Keane's house was raided at six in the morning, and the managing director of BWF Pharmaceuticals taken into custody. Immediately afterwards, she'd phoned Tim at the *Irish Journal* and informed him about what had happened, giving him insider details and a head start that would enable him to write up a lead story for his own paper. Of course, she'd had to explain to him that her name wasn't really Margaret! Alice smiled to herself. It had been a relief to be Alice Fitzsimons once more.

And would it all be worth it? Months – maybe years – down the road, there would be a lengthy and protracted trial, focussing on murder, attempted murder and corporate responsibility. Would anything useful come out of it? It was unlikely, Alice conceded. Everyone in the company would shift the blame onto someone else. Besides, how did you prove the suppression of a thirty-year-old report? There was only one copy, its author was dead, and everyone would claim they'd never seen it. At best, the company's international reputation would be permanently tarnished. Already, the story she'd written for the *Daily News* had been syndicated around the world, resulting in BWF Pharmaceuticals' share price plummeting, and lives in the developing world were being saved by the vaccine's speedy withdrawal.

A small victory, perhaps. But before long, these Third

World victims would be exploited by someone else – their own government's greed, mineral exploration rights sold off for a bribe, indifference in the First World to the needs of the poor elsewhere. At times, Alice didn't like other human beings very much. Animals were a lot more moral.

She smiled as she thought again of dear old Bodhrán. That goat had saved her life. When she'd last spoken to her future brother-in-law on the phone, he'd informed her that the goat would soon be going to live with her and Enrique. "It's my advance wedding gift to you both," he told her, chuckling. "Priests don't have much money, so it is the best I can do."

Alice smiled to herself. Certainly, buying a larger property – to accommodate Bodhrán and their kids – would be no problem, since money was no object. In Argentinian terms, she was a millionaire. She had money from the sale of the Killiney house – after the large mortgage had been repaid, of course – then there was the inheritance from her late father's sister, which was still in the bank. She'd been deeply moved by Bill's suggestion of an animal sanctuary in her memory, and she'd decided that was exactly what she'd do with the money. She intended to donate half the money to a sanctuary in Ireland, and half to one in Argentina.

Of course, she'd already had to deal with Enrique's macho stance about men providing for their wives. He didn't want to use her money, and already they'd had several arguments about it. No doubt there would be many more, but they were arguments she fully intended to win! Of course, the making-up afterwards was always wonderful . . .

Despite all her money, Alice hadn't been able to sit around doing nothing. She'd got a job on an Argentine newspaper, since her fluency in Spanish had improved remarkably. And she'd quickly got her teeth into the scandals and corruption that were as rife in Argentina as anywhere else in the world. She patted her stomach. And before long, there would be another little person joining the Alvarez household...

She wondered how Patricia's family were coping with their loss. When the mistake over the women's identity had been revealed, and Patricia's family informed of her death, Alice had visited the family in Castleknock. It had been a harrowing meeting, and Alice could well understand that while no one held her responsible for Patricia's death, they wished with all their hearts that the two women had never met. Because if they hadn't met, Patricia might still be alive today. And I might be dead, Alice thought. It was still a strange sensation.

Alice was suddenly awoken from her reverie. Caroline was preparing to throw her bouquet! All the unmarried women in the wedding party were making jokes about it, and good-naturedly jostling for the best position in which to catch it.

Suddenly, the bouquet was in the air, and women were jumping to catch it. But it sailed over their heads and headed in Alice's direction. Without thinking, she stretched out her arms – just as the bouquet landed in her lap! Alice turned pink as a round of applause filled the room, and everyone turned to look at her.

"Well, if that's not an omen, I don't know what is!" said Caroline, crossing the room to hug her.

"You deliberately threw it in my direction!" said Alice, now puce with embarrassment.

"No, I didn't," said Caroline. "It just seemed to know where it was going." Her eyes twinkled. "Anyway, you *are* getting married as soon as your divorce is through. This is just the confirmation!"

Alice nodded, clutching the bouquet, her arm around Caroline. She couldn't wait to marry Enrique.

The two women hugged each other. Strange circumstances had brought them together, but a growing friendship would ensure they'd never lose contact. They'd been instrumental in changing each other's lives in so many ways, and between them, they'd toppled Charles Keane's empire once and for all. Now, each was embarking on a voyage of discovery in a new country.

"I was just thinking – our e-mails to each other will never be dull!" said Caroline.

"We'll always have things to talk about!"

"Just don't send me any more thirty-year-old reports!" said Alice, smiling.

Linking arms, the two women joined the throng heading into the ballroom, where the band was beginning to play.

THE END

If you enjoyed *Time After Time*
try *Hush Hush* also published by Poolbeg

Here's a sneak preview of Chapter one

HUSH HUSH
LINDA KAVANAGH

CHAPTER 1

"You lucky cow!"

"God – some people have all the luck!"

Olivia Doyle grinned, her freckled face wreathed in a big smile. "It's probably a wreck, but I still can't believe it myself. My own house!"

"It's not just a house – it's a country estate, by the sounds of it!" said Maggie, grinning back at Olivia. She was thrilled for her friend, and excited at the prospect of seeing the new house. Correction, she thought, *old* house. It sounded the perfect project for Olivia. Although a chartered accountant by profession, Olivia had a particular flair for renovation and decoration. She'd made a great job of her mother's home, and had helped Barbara with the colour scheme for her apartment.

"Is there a roof on it?" asked Barbara, dark-haired and serious, looking worried in case Olivia was taking on the project-from-hell.

"Yes – and apparently it's okay. But just about everything else needs sorting out."

Olivia was the luckiest young woman in the world, and she knew it. While other people of her age were struggling to save for a deposit to buy a house the size of a matchbox, she'd just been given an old country house on three acres of land by her grandmother and great-uncle.

"I wish I had a generous grandmother like yours," said Maggie forlornly. "I'll be saving up for a country estate until I'm a grandmother myself!"

Olivia linked arms with her two friends. "C'mon – I'll buy you each a drink to celebrate."

Not for the first time, she silently marvelled at how different the two girls were from each other. Barbara, the serious one, was now a junior doctor at the new state-of-the-art South City Hospital, where she loved her job, feeling particularly privileged to get a position there, since it offered fantastic training and had a superb Accident & Emergency unit. So different from Maggie, her short blonde hair forever standing on end, who never missed an opportunity to call a spade a shovel. But her direct manner was an invaluable asset in her job as a psychologist with the Health Board.

The three women had been friends since their schooldays, remaining close throughout their university years, even though each of them had chosen different courses. But if anything, they were even closer now, having seen each other grow from childhood to womanhood, sharing their hopes and dreams along the way.

"Maybe there'll be three gorgeous hunks in the pub," Olivia said.

"Huh, chance would be a fine thing!" Maggie raised her eyes to heaven, and turned to Barbara. "Quickly, check that woman's temperature! She must have a fever! If there are three fantastic guys in the pub, you can be sure there'll be three wives or partners lurking in the background!"

Olivia grinned. "Think positive, my dear friends – there's got to be three half-decent fellows out there somewhere!"

Of course, no one mentioned Richard Devlin, who had been Barbara's first serious boyfriend, and the love of her life. But after years together and plans for a happy-ever-after, he'd unceremoniously dumped her and married someone else. And she was still smarting from the pain.

* * *

As the trio headed towards the pub, Olivia recalled the day her grandmother and Great-uncle Eddie had told her that they were giving her Bay Tree House. Had it really only been a week ago? The day had started out like any other, until her grandmother had phoned and asked her to call around as soon as she could.

Detecting an unusual note in her grandmother's voice, she began to worry about their health, and made a point of getting there as soon as possible. But there had been nothing sinister to worry about – both her beloved grandmother and her brother Eddie were in good spirits when she arrived.

Since the death of Olivia's grandfather several years earlier, her gran and Great-uncle Eddie, who'd never married, had shared her gran's old home, the home where Olivia's mother had grown up. Olivia loved both of them dearly, and she dreaded to think that inevitably, some day, she'd lose them. But for now, they were both in good health – and they had something very unusual, and wonderful, to tell her.

"Eddie and I have been left a house," said her grandmother, "and since neither of us intends moving from here, we thought it might give you a start on the property ladder."

Olivia looked from Great-uncle Eddie to her grandmother, and back again. "I don't understand . . . a house? For me?"

"Well, if I were you, I wouldn't get too excited," said her grandmother briskly. "It's probably in need of quite a lot of updating. We haven't seen it ourselves, but that's how the solicitor describes it. So that probably means it's a total wreck. But you needn't worry about the gift tax and stamp duty – Eddie and I are paying that for you. All you'll need to worry about is getting any repairs done."

Olivia could feel the excitement rising in her chest. They couldn't mean it – she was dreaming, wasn't she? They'd said a house – for her! No, she must have misheard. She looked over at Great-uncle Eddie, who sat in a rocking chair, puffing his pipe and smiling expectantly at her.

"You can't be serious – a house – for me?"

"Stop repeating yourself, dear," said her grandmother affectionately, "and shut your mouth, Liv, unless you're trying to catch flies."

Uncle Eddie was grinning happily at her as he sucked

on his pipe and, as she looked from one of them to the other, Olivia longed to freeze that moment, so that she could remember for the rest of her life that look of love for her that Gran and Uncle Eddie had in their eyes. A lump rose in her throat, and she feared that she was about to cry.

"Who left you the house?" she managed to say at last. "And where is it?"

Like a well-rehearsed duet, her grandmother and Uncle Eddie took turns interjecting into each other's sentences, until the story was complete, and Olivia learned that the house was fifty miles outside Dublin – a mere commuter's distance these days – and had been left to them by a woman they'd never heard of.

"It's odd, isn't it?" said Olivia. "I mean, being left a house by someone you don't know – but who obviously knows you, or at least, must know about you."

There was an awkward silence as brother and sister looked at each other. It looked as though they were making up their minds about something, and looking to each other for confirmation as to how to proceed.

At last, Olivia's grandmother spoke. "When we were told by the solicitor that we'd been left this house . . . well, Eddie and I immediately assumed that it must have something to do with –"

"There's something we've never told you, Liv," interrupted Great-uncle Eddie. "Even your mother only knows a few sketchy details."

Her grandmother nodded. "It's been too painful a subject, so we've always avoided talking about it."

"Look, you don't have to tell me anything you don't want to —"

"I think it's time we did talk about it — in fact, it may actually help," said her grandmother. "You do agree, Eddie, don't you?"

Uncle Eddie nodded his head.

"There were actually three children in our family," her grandmother said. "Apart from Eddie and me, there was also our older sister Ada."

"My God, where is she? What happened to her?"

"We don't know. She disappeared," said her grandmother. "That's why we wondered if the woman who left us the house in her will — Mrs Laura Morton — might have been Ada under a different name."

Olivia's mouth was open. She had a great-aunt she'd never known about! And why would her grandmother and great-uncle think that their sister would be living under an assumed name? It was all very mysterious!

"But the solicitor says no," added Eddie, chewing on his pipe.

"It seems there's clear proof that this woman has always been who the will says she is," said her grand-mother. "Her name was definitely Mrs Laura Morton, and she'd been Miss Laura Donaghy before she married, so it's quite clear from the documentation that she isn't Ada."

Uncle Eddie arose, with difficulty, from the rocking chair. "I think a cup of tea is called for," he said, heading out to the kitchen to put on the kettle. Obviously, he found the subject difficult to deal with. The two women could hear him opening the caddy where the tea bags were kept, and taking down the mugs from the shelf on the dresser.

"So what actually happened to Great-aunt Ada?" asked Olivia. "And how come you don't you know where she is?"

Her grandmother gestured towards the kitchen. "Let's wait for the full story until Eddie comes back with the tea. I'll need a strong cuppa to get me through it."

"So you're wondering if there could be some connection between Ada and this woman?" said Olivia.

Her grandmother nodded. "I mean, why else would a woman that neither Eddie nor I know leave us a house? It doesn't make sense."

Olivia grinned mischievously. "Could it be some woman from Uncle Eddie's past – maybe a case of unrequited love, someone who never forgot him?"

Her grandmother smiled, then her expression turned to one of sadness. "I wish that was true – that Eddie had had someone special who'd loved him. But the truth is, Liv – Ada's disappearance put his life, and mine, on hold. It was like we became empty inside after Ada left. There were lots of girls who fancied Eddie, but it was as though he couldn't take that next step – and have a family of his own – until Ada's situation had been resolved."

"Well, *you* got married, Gran – and had my mother."

Her grandmother's face took on a soft, distant look as she stared out the window. "I might never have married either," she said softly. "Eddie wasn't the only one who had difficulty moving on until the whole business of Ada's disappearance was resolved. But then, George Doyle came courting me, and he wouldn't take no for an answer."

Suddenly, it was as though the years had suddenly

fallen away as her grandmother spoke. The old woman blushed, and for a brief moment Olivia could see the girl her grandmother had once been. Following her grandmother's gaze out the window, Olivia could almost feel that her late grandfather was coming up the driveway in his old black Ford.

Olivia remembered her grandfather as a great big bear of a man, and she'd loved his fuzzy beard, and the way it tickled when he'd swing her up in the air, then catch her, and hug her on the way down. But now, for the very first time, she saw her grandmother as a woman who'd loved her husband dearly, and whose life had been blighted for a second time through his premature death.

Her grandmother turned away from the window, and began to clear a space on the table as she heard Eddie approaching with the tea. "I often think that we might have been different people if Ada hadn't disappeared. Not knowing was the worst part – if we'd been told that our sister had died, we'd eventually have come to terms with it. But always wondering what happened to her, well – " her grandmother wiped away a tear, " – it still hurts."

Eddie put down the tray and handed them each a cup and saucer. "We're sure she's long dead now, Liv," he added, "but we'd still like to know what happened to her. Helen and I often wondered if she'd developed TB, and been sent away to hospital . . . it was called consumption back then, and it was rampant throughout the country. Maybe she died in a sanatorium long ago."

Her grandmother bit her lip. "It must seem strange now, but back then, people were ashamed to tell others that there was consumption in their families. They knew they'd be ostracised if they did. So maybe that's what happened to poor Ada. I actually remember her coughing and getting sick as we walked along the road to school."

"We also wondered –" Eddie hesitated for a second "– if she might have had a baby. It was a disgrace in those days, you know, Liv, to have a child without being married."

Olivia nodded. She'd heard that women back then were punished and ostracised for becoming pregnant without a wedding ring, and she'd been astonished that both Church and community had been united in demonising these unfortunate women. Yet the men who got them pregnant didn't suffer at all! Olivia sighed. Not for the first time, she was glad to have been born in more enlightened times.

"Couldn't you have asked your parents about her, later, when you grew up?" asked Olivia, looking from one to the other. "Surely you had a right to know by then? To see her again, if she was still alive?"

Her grandmother answered, shaking her head sadly. "It wasn't that easy, Liv – it's not like today, where people are more frank and open about problems. Back then, secrecy was part and parcel of life. And you'd never challenge your parents, or the clergy, or question their point of view." Her grandmother's voice shook a little. "In later years, both Eddie and I tried to bring the conversation around to Ada, but our parents refused to say anything at all on the subject. There are only so many times you can try to introduce a topic like that." She sighed. "Over the years, Eddie and I checked several times for a death certificate for Ada, but never found one. That gave us hope that she might still be alive somewhere, but as the years went by, we gave up any hope of ever finding her."

"Don't worry, Gran," said Olivia, throwing her arms around her grandmother. "If there's any connection between Ada and this Laura woman, I'll do my best to find out." She then hugged her Great-uncle Eddie. "Oh Great-uncle Eddie, I can't believe that you and Gran have been so good to me! My own house!"

"Look, it could be a pig in a poke," her great-uncle warned her. "Neither Helen nor I have seen it, and I never believe anything that solicitors or estate agents say." He grinned. "It's bound to be falling apart. So don't get your hopes up, Liv. Now, let's all have a cup of tea."

Direct to your home!

If you enjoyed this book why not
visit our website:

www.poolbeg.com

and get another book delivered straight
to your home or to a friend's home!

www.poolbeg.com

All orders are despatched within 24 hours.